GIMME SHELTER

Books by Libby Klein

Poppy McAllister Mysteries

CLASS REUNIONS ARE MURDER

MIDNIGHT SNACKS ARE MURDER

RESTAURANT WEEKS ARE MURDER

THEATER WEEKS ARE MURDER

WINE TASTINGS ARE MURDER

BEAUTY EXPOS ARE MURDER

ANTIQUES AUCTIONS ARE MURDER

MISCHIEF NIGHTS ARE MURDER

SILENT NIGHTS ARE MURDER

Layla Virtue Mysteries

VICE AND VIRTUE

GIMME SHELTER

Published by Kensington Publishing Corp.

GIMME SHELTER

LIBBY KLEIN

kensingtonbooks.com

This book is a work of fiction. Names, characters, businesses, organizations, places, events, and incidents either are the product of the author's imagination or are used fictitiously. Any resemblance to actual persons, living or dead, events, or locales is entirely coincidental.

To the extent that the image or images on the cover of this book depict a person or persons, such person or persons are merely models, and are not intended to portray any character or characters featured in the book.

KENSINGTON BOOKS are published by

Kensington Publishing Corp.
900 Third Avenue
New York, NY 10022

All Kensington titles, imprints and distributed lines are available at special quantity discounts for bulk purchases for sales promotion, premiums, fund-raising, educational or institutional use. Special book excerpts or customized printings can also be created to fit specific needs. For details, write or phone the office of the Kensington Special Sales Manager: Kensington Publishing Corp., 900 Third Avenue, New York, NY, 10022. Attn. Special Sales Department. Phone: 1-800-221-2647.

Library of Congress Control Number: On file

ISBN: 978-1-4967-4858-4

First Kensington Hardcover Edition: May 2026

ISBN: 978-1-4967-4860-7 (ebook)

10 9 8 7 6 5 4 3 2 1

Printed in the United States of America

The authorized representative in the EU for product safety and compliance is eucomply OU, Parnu mnt 139b-14, Apt 123 Tallinn, Berlin 11317, hello@eucompliancepartner.com

For Vader, my emotional support puppy. And Tony, my emotional support human. I'd thank the cat but she's really just in it for herself.

Chapter 1

NOT EVEN AN ELECTRIC GUITAR CAN MAKE YOU LOOK COOL WHEN you're playing square dance music dressed like a giant turkey. The Mighty Thumpers Thanksgiving luncheon gig was definitely not going on my résumé. I'd thought signing with a business manager would be just the thing to finally rocket my career as a musician to stardom. I was very wrong.

I glanced over at the grumpy pilgrim playing the fiddle and knew two things. I had clearly drawn the short straw in the costume department. And my manager, Paula, still hadn't forgiven me for accusing her of murdering the birthday party clown a couple of months ago. She was obviously padding her fifteen percent with my humiliation by sending me to low-budget gigs that involved dressing like holiday poultry.

I couldn't afford to say no to any gig since I desperately needed the money, and I'd rather be stuffed with breadcrumbs up the whoo-hah than let my dad bankroll me and launch my career with a record label. I did not want to be the next nepo baby on the Where Are They Now? circuit. It was bad enough Dad bought me a house behind my back.

No, strike that. Rich dads buy houses. Filthy rich dads buy entire developments. In this case, a mobile home park on a small lake in Northern Virginia where the land alone was worth as much as a platinum hit. As far as I was concerned, the tail feathers currently festooned over my derrière evened things out in the entitlement arena.

The banjo player, a plaid-wearing, gap-toothed man older than mud and obviously a charter member of the Mighty Thumpers and not a sub like I was, said I could pick a song about thankfulness to play for the luncheon. I chose Alanis Morissette's "Thank U." That, apparently, was *not* what he had in mind, and after bringing the festivity to a screeching halt, I was forbidden from leading a song for the rest of the gig.

He gave me a wink and called out "Turkey in the Straw" for the third time this afternoon. The fiddle player sighed, and we launched again into the crowd favorite as they took another promenade around the dance floor.

I blocked out the yellow Styrofoam claws pulled over my Keds, the scent of sage stuffing in the air, and focused on the clock hanging on the back wall of the Preston Woods Clubhouse. Fifteen minutes left in this nightmare. I tried to move the hands forward using mind powers fueled by desperation and heat stroke from my polyester wattle. I had to wrap up this ring-a-ding dingy of a luncheon and get home to meet the movers from LA. All the items Dad couldn't live without from his mansion in Malibu were arriving this afternoon. If I left it up to him, they'd still be lying on the front lawn like at a head banger's estate sale come nightfall.

Dad had to cancel the European leg of his world tour with eighties hair metal band Society's Castoffs due to his recent diagnosis. TMZ reported that Don Virtue had *moved in with his daughter, Layla Virtue, the product of a union from a very brief but explosive marriage to former groupie Barbara Collins to deal with fatigue. Sources say he's getting extensive treatment from some of the nation's best medical experts in New York City. Don will be recovering in his daughter's sprawling penthouse overlooking Central Park.*

We had a good laugh over egg rolls and moo shu pork from my sprawling single wide in the Lake Pinecrest Mobile Home Park overlooking the recycling bins that my neighbor Marguerite's pet rooster, Steppenwolf, was bent on sparring with.

Dad's manager, Jimmy, leaked the penthouse story to TMZ's producer to buy us some privacy while we transitioned Dad into my world.

My sad little world.

That's how I found myself at the bottom of a music career that I'd waited way too long to launch dressed in a costume that made Lady Gaga look normal.

It was a source of frustration for Dad that I refused his help to dig out of the crater I'd landed in when life blew up in my face. If it were not for his poor health, he would have returned to his plush life of extravagance two months ago instead of moving in with me. I was his only child and there was no one else to take care of him. God knows none of his ex-wives could do it. And as unstable as Dad and I were, we looked like the Waltons compared to my mother who, for most of my life, had been alternating between her tour of America's finer rehab facilities and blaming me for her addiction issues. Apparently my birth got in the way of her short-lived tambourine career.

The banjo player strummed the final notes on his third encore and the square dancers gave a group bow to enthusiastic applause and boot stomping before do-si-do-ing back to their tables to fight over the tricolor corn centerpieces.

Strapping my guitar to my back and tucking my amp under my arm, I ripped off my wattle, crossed the dance floor, grabbed a whole pumpkin pie, and pushed through the double doors to the parking lot. *Paula had better be Johnny-on-the-spot with this paycheck. I think I sweated out ten pounds roasting in that turkey suit. If she thinks I'm paying for the dry cleaning out of my cut, she has another thing coming.*

I hit the remote start—my favorite feature on my new used Wrangler, stashed the pie on the back seat, placed my guitar in the case, and nestled it next to the amp in the back. I got a great deal on the Jeep because of an unfortunate custom paint job that left it the color of American cheese. I tossed the wattle in the back seat next to the pie and shoved myself, drumsticks and all, behind the wheel.

My anticipated rise to rock star status had been interrupted by an almost twenty-year career with the Potomac County Police Force. One that ended in an ambush killing my entire team, including my partner, Jacob—the man I'd thought I'd be spending the rest of my life with. Losing Jacob left a gaping wound in my soul that time had not even begun to heal. I'd only recently been able to accept that the disaster was not entirely my fault. Jacob had made some critical errors in judgment by not following protocol. Losing so many people who were important to me due to my own negligence was more pain than I could face.

After the Internal Affairs investigation, I left the force in shame with no plans to ever return. Something I'd been trying to get through to Detective Dayton Castinetto all week as he kept texting me that we needed to talk. A sentiment I did not agree with. I wanted nothing more to do with a badge or a uniform. I'd been off the force for months. I could barely sleep at night as it was.

When Dad bought me the trailer park we lived in—for what he said was my future financial security—he also got the original owner's cottage in the deal. I hadn't seen the inside of the abandoned little lake house since the day the deed was delivered, but I remembered that the large house had lain fallow for a long time and needed some small repairs, a little paint, and possibly a possum eviction, which Dad said he could handle. Hmm, doubtful.

And by *handle*, he meant that he'd call his interior decorator, Fawn, and she'd do a complete overhaul to make the home ready for us by move-in day. This would be my first time seeing what he'd commissioned. I hadn't even been allowed to drive around the back side of the lake because he wanted everything to be a surprise. Dad was known for many things, some of them I'd been trying to live down for thirty years, but being understated was not one of them.

However, his last surprise was that he'd been diagnosed with dementia and that about ripped my heart out. So, at the very least, this had to be a step up from that.

Chapter 2

I TURNED OFF THE HIGHWAY AT THE HIDDEN ENTRANCE BY THE paper birch trees. Their explosion of golden leaves had grown over the welcome sign into the park. Lake Pinecrest was originally a summer camp retreat, so the driveway cut through the woods like a squirrel high on crack planned the route. That meant it took twice as long to get down here as it needed to.

I cruised along the serpentine lane to the north side of the lake through the fallen leaves and roadside decay. Someone needed to clean this up. *I guess that's me now, isn't it? Ugh.* The pressure of responsibility smothered me like a sauna. Low maintenance was one of the reasons I'd moved into a trailer in the first place.

The owner's cottage sat at the top of the lake. A boat ramp that I would probably never use on account that I didn't have a boat, or money to buy a boat, or the desire to own a boat, jutted from the end of a flagstone walkway.

Slung in a graceful arc around the north shore sat the high-rent district—a row of double-wide mobile homes, including the park model and clubhouse. The occupants of the double wides considered themselves the dons of Lake Pinecrest—in charge of reigning in the disorderly and delinquent. Myrtle Jean Maud, Agnes Harcourt, and Clifford Bagstrodt. They were currently dotted around our yard, micromanaging the moving crew as they fought to take a king-sized mattress through the queen-sized door.

Two moving trucks blocked the entire street in front of our butter-colored-stucco cottage. Even from the road I could see that Dad had contracted a lot of custom work in two months' time. The steeply pitched, cross-gabled roof was covered in hand-cut teakwood shingles set in a wave pattern, making the house look like it belonged in the Cotswolds. On the right, a higgledy-piggledy stone chimney looked like beavers had built it themselves. A pale green rounded arch door with long black medieval-looking scrollwork hinges had been propped open with a stone hedgehog next to a blue Adirondack chair. Two moving men were carrying a long skinny crate inside marked VENKMAN.

I pulled onto the cobblestone driveway and parked in front of a weathered garden gate covered in a twist of thorny vines, like the opening to a haunted forest.

I stood on tiptoe to see what awaited me in the backyard. Other than the lake and boat dock that were shrouded in mist, I could see a green-and-gold flagstone patio and a savage garden that I suspected hid a variety of destructive wildlife.

Barren vines climbed up the side of the house around diamond-patterned Gothic windows. I couldn't tell if the house was cursed by a witch or built by the Seven Dwarfs.

A cacophony of barks greeted me, and Ringo, my black Lab, barreled through the open door with reckless abandon. His ears flapping in the afternoon breeze of freedom, his tongue lolling to the side. Pure joy that I had finally come home.

"Silly boy. I was only gone a few hours. How do you like your new house?" He wiggled back and forth on his back in the grass as I rubbed his belly, then he jumped and gave me a lick on the cheek as if to say he approved. I gave him a kiss and stepped inside what could easily have been a movie set.

Dad was just going to spruce up the simple lake house, maybe give it a lick of paint. Not gut and rebuild it for Disney to use as Tinker Bell's fairy cottage.

The kitchen and breakfast nook were painted pale sage with deep turquoise cabinets. Dark teal glass tiles had been installed as a backsplash over a copper farmhouse sink and natural-edge wooden countertops. With a two-story vaulted ceiling of exposed wooden beams—omigod, the one over the window was an actual tree branch—the room had been plucked straight out of a *Grimms' Fairy Tale.* Even the dining table looked like it was made by forest elves from a giant walnut tree. I ran my hand down the polished uneven edge. "Dad really knows how to lean into a theme."

Ringo wagged his tail in response.

I blew my breath out and glanced over at a six-burner lavender range with two ovens that I had no idea how to use, and expected to see a white-haired granny in a checkered apron baking cookies for Hansel and Gretel. "Ringo, if some old lady tries to fatten you up with cookies you just say no."

Ringo gave me a low "ruff."

I walked through to the living room imagining singing bluebirds leading the way. The walls had been painted dark forest green to set off the pale wood floors and stone fireplace. The sliding door at the back had been replaced with French doors and floor-to-ceiling stained-glass arched windows in a pattern of roses and vines. Ringo flopped on a fluffy bear-shaped fur rug that lay in front of a roaring fire and gave me a smile.

Where is my couch? And why did Dad pick all this gingham? I tried to wrap my head around the riotous field of roses, and pillows, and chenille throws before me. Everything was poofy. Even the hardbound books on the built-in bookcases seemed poofy. This room was as far away from rock and roll as you could get. I felt my musician street cred shriveling with every step.

Myrtle Jean Maud, Lake Pinecrest's resident busybody in support hose and sensible shoes, sailed in with a vase of peach cabbage roses and placed them on a wooden side table. "Layla, you're home already." She patted her silver cinnamon-bun hair and giggled. "Ringo, you were supposed to warn me. Well, what do you think? Wait until you see the loft upstairs. Your dad fixed it up for guests. But this room is my favorite. So cozy. Not too girly, not too masculine. I think it's just right."

"Is that why there are three bear statues on the coffee table?"

Ringo gave me a look I interpreted as *Be nice.*

She looked around with a satisfied grin. "Your dad wanted everything to be perfect for his baby girl."

"Does he know I'm not seven anymore?"

Myrtle Jean put her hand on a gnome statue and tried to slide it behind her.

I nodded toward the French doors. "What's out there?"

Myrtle Jean's face pinked with excitement. "Wait till you see it. Don had a gorgeous greenhouse patio with an outdoor kitchen built. And you have a private porch with a swing of your very own just off of your bedroom. It's darling." She wrapped her blue cardigan tighter around her. "Come on. I'll show you."

Ringo and I followed her to an enclosed stone patio with two-story windows and a glass greenhouse ceiling. One side had a pink couch and matching rose-print comfy chairs, a stone coffee table, and way too many green viney plants that I hoped came with a gardener because I sure didn't know how to take care of them. I had more than I could handle with just me and Ringo. "Is that tree growing inside the room?"

Myrtle Jean giggled and spoke in reverent, hushed tones. "It is, yes. That's a miniature weeping cherry tree in a Chinese ornamental pot. I think it was expensive."

Ringo's lack of shock told me he'd already seen the inside tree. "Don't pee on that, okay?"

Ringo's mouth snapped shut and he looked at the tree like he hadn't considered that before now.

I pointed to the brick opening on the far wall. "What's that?"

Myrtle Jean clapped her hands. "An outdoor pizza oven. Don't you love it?"

I was normally so good at locking down my expression from years of being a cop, but my contorted smile may have given her the idea that I thought she was crazy. Also, I was thinking that she was crazy.

Her smile faltered for a brief moment, and she pointed to the pecan wood cabinets that ran along the back of the house.

"There's plenty of storage for your takeout menus in the drawers by the sink there."

"Thank God for that or we'd starve."

I got the feeling that the room had been designed with elaborate parties in mind. Parties that I did not want to throw or attend. A rustic branch chandelier with amber glass globes hung over another long table surrounded by tan leather chairs. The emerald-and-cream marble counter hosted a full bar, and for a moment it caused my heart to stop until I realized that all those fancy bottles were flavored syrups and alcohol-free mixers. No matter what Dad got confused about, at least he remembered that we were both alcoholics in recovery.

Ringo felt left out and shoved his snout into my hand for attention.

"I know, buddy. It's like the Magic Kingdom in here."

Myrtle Jean ran her hand across the dining table. "Isn't it beautiful? I helped Don pick it out. It's called claro walnut."

I was about to ask where Dad was, when Agnes Harcourt, self-appointed homeowner association gestapo, hollered from the other room, "Don't put that there! C-3PO goes in Don's room."

As much as Myrtle Jean was soft and fluffy, Agnes was pointy and prickly. She stood next to a spiral staircase leading to the loft with a cigarette hanging off her bottom lip. Thanks to Miss Clairol, her chocolate-brown hair was caught up in a Rosy the Riveter bandanna that matched her red leather pants. She threw her arm in the direction of the double doors next to a French rococo armoire straight out of *Beauty and the Beast* like she was posing for a rebellious fifties housewife magazine shoot. "Through there, honey."

Agnes had figured out that my father was Don Virtue of Society's Castoffs long before anyone else had. Apparently, they had been at Woodstock at the same time. Dad was the guitar shredder tripping out on stage and Agnes was the rabid fan flinging her bikini top in circles around her head while tripping out in the mud.

Agnes spotted me and sent her gravelly voice purring in my

direction. "Layla, you finally come home to help? Your father has been directing traffic for hours."

I seriously doubted that. One, my father didn't lift a finger to do anything as long as he could pay someone else to do it. And two, Agnes loved bossing people around and she'd be lost if someone took the reins from her. "How long have you been here?"

"Since about noon. Clifford posted as lookout to let us know when the van arrived. It's a good thing too since they were early."

"What'd you need a lookout for? You live next door."

Myrtle Jean giggled. "*The Cleaner* was on. We just love that Greg Davies. He's like a giant Winnie the Pooh."

Agnes shrugged. "Clifford needs to keep busy anyway. A person has to have more hobbies than bird-watching and complaining about water usage."

Dad called from beyond the double doors, "Is that you, baby girl? Come see my room and help me decide where to put my flux capacitor."

Ringo's tail started to wag as soon as he heard Dad's voice. He led the way to the rock and roll inner sanctum that apparently had erupted from the bowels of middle-earth. In the center of the room, Dad had a king-sized four-poster bed made from hand-cut birch trees. His walls were white-and-tan brick, and crossing his ceiling were branches dripping with green leaves and ivy. Dad sat on a brown leather club chair with his feet on the matching ottoman, a walkie-talkie in one hand and a Coke in the other. A workman in overalls hustled around the room doing his bidding. Replace the Coke with a beer and this was a scene straight from my childhood.

He was still a looker at his age—so I'm told. His gray hair flowed in waves past his shoulders, and his blue eyes were bright and sparkled with a bit of mischief. Several tattoos, including one of a naked woman surfing a Gibson Flying V, peeked out from the sleeves of his white silk shirt.

"So, what do you think, baby girl?"

"The walls are beautiful. Is that real stone on the floor?"

"Yeah, I think so."

"And a bamboo mat?"

Dad shrugged. "I dunno. I told Fawn to run with the storybook theme."

I looked around, nodding. "Uh-huh. Sure. Sure. And how exactly does Venkman's *Ghostbusters* uniform fit into that?"

Dad snorted. "I mean, I gotta have my stuff."

Agnes led in two men carrying Indiana Jones's Ark of the Covenant. "Where you want this, Don?"

Dad looked left then right. "How about next to the Droid? I can use it for my socks."

I ran my hands over Ringo's soft ears and chuckled to myself. That movie prop probably cost more at auction than most of the trailers in this park, and he was making it a sock cabinet. I squatted down to face him after Agnes led the men back out for another run. "So, this is the stuff you couldn't live without?"

Dad gave me a wry smile. "This is the stuff I remembered I had."

"Did you at least have Jimmy pack your winter clothes?"

Dad scanned the recesses of his brain for a moment. "I don't think I have winter clothes. Wait. Do I have a house in Canada?"

I nodded. "You have a little farmhouse on an island near Vancouver."

His eyebrows shot up. "I bet I have winter clothes there."

Ringo gave Dad's arm a snoot and I patted his knee. "I'll put a call in to your manager to have someone send things down for you." I watched the workman hanging one of Dad's custom guitars next to three gold records over the gas fireplace. "And I think we need to have Ronnie install a better security system since that wall is worth more than this entire campground."

"Who's Ronnie?"

"Ronnie Voa. Your new head of security? The guy responsible for saving your butt when you forget that crowds of people will trample you to get an autograph."

Dad gave me a one-shoulder shrug and mumbled, "Okay."

His walkie-talkie beeped. "Mr. Virtue, where do you want us to hang the tulle?"

Dad made a face and answered back, "What kind of tools?"

Marguerite's voice came through in her lilting South American accent. "Gimmie. Is like wedding veil, Don. Where you want it?"

I had a growing unease unfurling around my stomach as I remembered a disastrous stint in elementary ballet. "Why would we need tulle, Dad?"

Dad's eyes lit as recognition dawned and he clicked on his walkie. "I think that goes around the girl's bed, doll."

"Sure thing, Don."

The walkie let out a squeeze of static and Dad dropped it to his lap. He grinned, and the hairs on the back of my arm stood to attention. Ringo nosed his way between us and rolled his eyes to mine.

"Dad, I hope you didn't do anything crazy in my room. I'm just a simple girl. An ex-cop trying to be a musician twenty years too late."

Dad waved his hand and shooed my concerns away. He took a sip of his Coke. "You're gonna love it, honey. I told my gal all about you and she designed the perfect house."

I sighed. "Did you tell her I was almost forty?"

Dad grinned. "Wait till you see your bathroom."

I had to prepare myself emotionally, much the same as I had to do for a visit to the gynecologist. "Just remember that we have a neurologist appointment tomorrow, so you shouldn't overdo it today." Judging from his current level of exertion I'd say the danger level was very low.

Dad closed one eye and squinted at me through the other. "Speaking of the crazy doctor. Are you dressed like a turkey or am I hallucinating?"

I looked down at the bulbous brown suit I'd completely forgotten that I was wearing. What does it say about me that not one person seemed shocked enough to mention it before now? I ripped off the foam claws, pulled the zipper down my wishbone, and climbed out. "I'm going over to the trailer to pack up whatever decor we left behind."

Dad grimaced. "If it's gray, leave it there."

"Everything is gray, Dad."

I'd moved into my trailer at rock bottom and did very little to decorate it. And by *very little* I mean nothing. Dad had turned up unannounced for a surprise visit, so he had no right to judge, but he still said it was like staying in a concentration camp, which I thought was rather dramatic.

"I'm taking Ringo with me so don't panic when he's not here."

Ringo started to thump his tail against the leather chair like the beat of a drum, which is exactly how he got his name in the first place.

Dad lifted his hand and clicked on his walkie-talkie to sing me offstage. "Good-bye, Lay-la, it's been nice, hope you love your par-a-di-se . . ."

"Okay then."

He was still wrecking Supertramp when Ringo and I left Rumpelstiltskin Manor. You know you're in trouble when a spinning wheel and a troll tie all the elements of a room together.

I opened the door of the Jeep for Ringo to hop in and threw the turkey suit in the back. Ringo took an immediate fascination to the pie, and I handed it to one of the moving men. "Please put this in Snow White's kitchen for me."

He was whistling "Heigh-Ho" as he headed into the house.

I cranked the Jeep to life and backed out. I was really hoping to run into Nick while I was across the lake. It wasn't that far away, I could walk it in an hour, but I had things to do and a leisurely walk around half the lake wasn't one of them.

Nick had moved to the trailer next door to me a couple of months ago and quickly became one of the most important people in my life. We had an instant attraction to each other that would have resulted in an amazing fling, but I was still mourning the loss of Jacob, and Nick was battling his own demons.

Neither of us were ready for a long-term relationship so we'd chosen to develop a meaningful friendship instead. A friendship that was complicated by the fact that Nick could see right through me. Nick was the first one to recognize that I was struggling. As a Marine Corps vet with three tours in Afghanistan, Nick was very familiar with PTSD.

I hadn't seen him for several days. I knew he was some kind of government computer whiz because he had a tech setup that would fill Mark Zuckerberg with glee, but even hackers come up for air once in a while. I thought maybe he was sick, or out of town. His car was still there this morning when I left for the square dance gig, but he could have Ubered to the airport.

Many of the park trailers were decorated for fall. It wasn't just festive it was a requirement. Agnes and her park beautification henchmen put pressure on everyone. Colorful mums, polyester scarecrows, pumpkins, hay bales. You'd think this was Kansas and not just some place Temu delivered cheap crap to. Donna, my former neighbor and one-time almost-friend across the street, had even strung orange lights around her patio to appease the dons. Frankly, I didn't see the point. Aren't the dead leaves on the ground fall decoration enough? They're the embodiment of autumn.

Donna glared at me through the blinds of her front door. That relationship smoked out just like most of my attempts to have a gal-pal usually did. There was a definite pattern. Invitation to hang out, followed by the discovery of my father's stardom and accompanied wealth, then the expectation for me to donate some manner of goods and services that almost always included Dad under a spotlight in leopard-print leather pants. When I couldn't or wouldn't accommodate those requests, the relationship would end in accusations of my entitlement. Donna did not fail to disappoint me.

Ringo got excited when we pulled into the driveway. He'd only ever known life on this side of the park. His tail started to thump against the seat, and I noticed he was looking at Nick's trailer next door. Still dark.

Nick had not given in to the festivity protocol. He hadn't even taken his trash cans back from the curb, and that infraction would get you one of Clifford's homemade tickets to clean the grills down by the lake. A peach-colored reminder about the mandatory meeting tomorrow night was taped to his door along with the fall spirit flyer that had been delivered two days ago.

I put my hand on Ringo's back. "Let's go see if he's home."

Ringo jumped out of the Jeep, and we crossed the yard. He sat patiently on the front step while I knocked.

Silence.

Ringo whimpered and scratched at the door, so I knocked again.

"Go away!"

A trickle of dread inched across my shoulders. Something wasn't right with Nick. I hadn't known him for long, but he was the kindest, most patient man I'd ever met. This wasn't like him.

"Well, at least we know he's home. Nick! Open up. It's Layla and Ringo."

"It's not a good time. Come back later."

Ringo dropped to his belly and grumbled. He rolled sad eyes to mine.

I squatted next to him and ran my hand down his back. "I'm sorry, buddy." My chest tightened as the thought occurred to me that Ringo might rather live with Nick. Did he miss him? It's not like he understood that Nick was training him to be a support dog, and he was supposed to move on.

He didn't move very far once he honed in on my emotions, but maybe our move across the lake was too stressful. "Let's go next door and get the treats I left. And I happen to know there are some peanut butter bones in the kitchen."

Ringo's ears lifted and he gave me a look that said, *Are you freakin' kidding me!*

"Really. Let's go!"

He jumped to his feet and gave one more look at Nick's door before following me through the yard.

I opened the door to the little beige trailer decorated in the theme of gloom and Ringo crossed the threshold ahead of me. He stopped at a white envelope that had been shoved under the door and gave it a sniff.

I picked it up and turned it over. No address. If this was some threat about my lack of pumpkin spirit from Agnes, why didn't she just leave it at the new house? I skimmed my finger under the seal and popped it open. My chest constricted the moment I pulled out a photograph of a ghost.

Jacob. What sick monster sent this to me?

My hands started to shake. His eyes were narrowed in concern. He wasn't posing for the picture, but he suspected someone was watching him.

His short, sable hair was tinged with gold and reflected the sunlight. Wearing a long-sleeved T-shirt emblazoned with the blue devil of Duke University, he was walking past a nondescript gray building with an edge of red on a brick sidewalk. In front of the gray building was an election sign. The only other thing of note in the photo was a pair of blue-and-purple Uggs boots off to the side.

I wiped a tear from my cheek and tried to breathe. Jacob had a close beard—that was different. When was this? I don't remember seeing him with facial hair. He looked good with it. Nausea traveled up my throat as a wave of grief hit me, and I was overwhelmed with sadness at what we had lost. Jacob died in the explosion at Stratton Park during my failed maneuver.

Two hundred and seventy-nine days ago.

My eyes clouded over as they fixed on the election sign. Harris/Walz? My heart pounded in my chest as I read it again and everything else in the world fell away. Kamala wasn't even running for office when Jacob died. And she chose Walz as her running mate sometime in August.

Three months ago? That isn't possible. He's been . . . gone. What is this?

My ears started to ring, and my hands went hot. The last thing I noticed before the room went black was the hand-scrawled note on the back of the photo.

Jacob Is Alive.

Chapter 3

A WET TONGUE STROKED MY CHEEK AS I CAME TO. RINGO WAS ON his belly in front of me, his nose to mine. I placed my hand on top of his head and his tail began to wag. "Okay, buddy. That's enough kisses."

Ringo was trained to be a companion for returning vets trying to acclimate to civilian life after experiencing the horrors of war. He could sense pain and grief and gave unconditional love and support in return. My fragile emotional state and proximity to Nick had hijacked his training. Ringo kept seeking me out and decided that I was the broken human he was meant to bond with. He probably saved my life, so you'll never hear me complain about a few slobbery licks that made me feel like a Milk Bone. Especially right now.

I pulled myself up with my back against the couch trying to slow my breathing with Ringo's head in my lap. I pulled out my phone with shaking hands and called Dayton Castinetto, a cop from my former precinct familiar with my checkered past on the force and the harassment I'd been receiving from vengeful officers.

Dayton Castinetto and I were not what you would call friends. We'd known each other since high school, and on the force, we'd had an antagonistic relationship at best. Mostly because he always had a stick up his butt. We didn't work closely together because he remained a beat cop after I was promoted to special assignment with the narcotics unit, something that I suspected gave him a rash when he thought about it.

"What!" he barked into the phone.

"I need to report some harassment." There was a crackle of radios and a siren behind him. "Don't worry about it though. I can hear that you're busy. I'll just call dispatch and have them send someone."

"I'll be there in ten minutes." I didn't have time to argue because he'd already hung up.

I ran my hands over Ringo's soft, velvet ears, and made myself do the breathing exercises that I thought were absolutely ridiculous, but for some reason I kept trying them like they would magically work the next time.

Someone had been attacking me over Stratton Park after the operation ended shockingly, brutally wrong. I was in charge, I was the only survivor, and I looked plenty suspicious—so on some level I got it. Their vitriolic accusations were nothing compared to how I felt about myself.

My team had worked for months on a plan to infiltrate Ricky Hurtado's drug ring as they were preparing bricks of heroin for distribution, but on the day of the takedown I wasn't where I was supposed to be.

Images of smoke and ash flooded my mind as I picked up the photograph from where it had fallen. *Why the heck was I at the Gibson getting drunk? And why did you go in without me, Jacob? You broke protocol. Didn't you trust me? Or were you still mad that I didn't want to move in together?*

A ragged breath rattled through my chest.

Even as an alcoholic, it was unlike me to be so unreliable. My team had breached the perimeter without waiting for my command or backup and ran into an ambush.

Why couldn't I remember anything from that day? I had to have been drugged. Surely. The only other explanation was that I'd gotten blackout drunk on the most important day of my career. That was a line I'd never crossed before or since.

All I knew for sure was that every member of my team died, including the face looking back from the photo before me.

I whispered, "I'm sorry."

Ringo snooted my free hand, alerting me that I had stopped the petting. He rolled chocolate-brown eyes to mine and gave me a dog smile. His tail picked up speed.

"How could he be alive, Ringo? The warehouse exploded. His body was burnt beyond recognition. They had to match his dental records. It was definitely Jacob. Right?" I had been living under the crushing guilt and shame that I was responsible for four deaths—and it had taken me to some dark places—but if Jacob was really alive, that opened a Pandora's box of dark possibilities.

"If he's alive, why hasn't he tried to contact me? I've been going through hell, and he just moved on? Living his life without a care? And how did he survive? And whose body did they find in the warehouse?" My stomach bottomed out as the scenarios flew at me like poison darts.

"Did he betray us? Was he working for Hurtado the whole time? Oh no, Ringo. Did he set me up? The last words we'd had were an argument about taking our relationship to the next level, maybe even signing the HR forms, declaring what we'd been keeping secret. Was it all a lie?"

If he's alive, I might just kill him.

Tires crunched the gravel outside my trailer, followed by the catch of a car door. Ringo lifted his head and gave a half-hearted bark then looked back at me. He knew I wasn't ready for him to leave my side. "Ringo, stay."

In a moment, Castinetto banged on the door. I called, "It's open," and he flung the door forward. Ringo hopped up in a flash, standing between me and my potential assailant, also known as Ringo's new best friend because he was sure Castinetto was there to play with him.

Dayton snapped his fingers. "Sit. Good boy."

Dayton had recently been promoted to homicide and our paths crossed a couple of months ago at a humiliating birthday party where I was performing. Then he came here when someone defaced my trailer so I knew I wouldn't have to rehash my entire history to bring him up to speed before showing him what had been shoved under my door.

Dayton paused in the doorway with his hand on the butt of his gun in his shoulder holster and looked around. "Where's the perpetrator?"

I pointed to the photograph on the coffee table.

Dayton quirked an eyebrow like he didn't fully believe me. Then he pulled on a latex glove from a pouch on his belt and plucked the photo off the table. "This is Jacob."

"Yeah, I'm aware. Look at the campaign sign."

Castinetto's eyebrows shot up. "Where'd you get this?"

"It was waiting for me in the trailer. Someone shoved it under the door sometime after I left this morning."

His eyes narrowed and his lip curled in that way that made me want to get arrested for assaulting a police officer. "So, you touched it?"

"Of course I did! It looked like mail. It was in my house."

He chewed the side of his lip, looking around my trailer.

"I'm telling you, somebody shoved it under my door probably to freak me out." Ringo edged over and gave my elbow a lick, telling me to calm down.

I put my hand on his back. "Thank you."

Castinetto blew out his breath. "Are you sure you didn't Photoshop this?"

I pulled myself up with the help of the coffee table, regretting that I'd made the call. "Dude, I don't know how to Photoshop."

He sneered. "You don't have to know how to Photoshop. You just need to know someone who does. Like maybe one of your new lady friends from AA." He raised one black eyebrow again and I wanted to smack it off his chiseled face.

Maybe he did tower over my five-foot-eight frame. But I knew eighteen ways to kill a man with my bare hands. Plus, I was a woman tired of not being taken seriously and could do some serious damage if I snapped. He made me want to snap. "I'm acutely aware of the penalty for filing a fake police report. Do you really think I would report the harassment if I'd made this myself?"

He *tsk*'d and cocked his head to one side. "Maybe you thought this would be a good way to get out from under department scrutiny. Get back in the captain's good graces. Get your job back."

That's what today is gonna be? Just a crap show? If I had known the turkey suit would be the highlight, I would've appreciated it more when it was happening. "Good God, Castinetto. Who do you think I am? I would rather disappear from the captain's radar entirely than ever remind him of Jacob or Stratton Park again." I flicked the photo in his hand. "Don't you think I live with the shame of *this* every day?"

The creases in his forehead softened. "Then what do you want me to do with this, Virtue?"

"I was hoping you could take it to Rami and ask her to do the tech magic she does to see if it's been altered."

Castinetto looked from me to the photo and considered my request. "If Jacob is alive, then who helped him fake his death? How did he get his dental records changed?"

Ringo leaned into my leg and made a quiet snuffle.

I gave Dayton a look that told him he'd finally started asking the right questions and his sneer snapped back into place. "Look, I could take this into tech forensics, but if you made this to somehow make yourself look less guilty, it's going to backfire on you. And you're starting to go in the right direction. I don't want to see you screw it up now with a stunt."

"Dayton."

His eyes widened and his head jerked a little when I said his name like someone had stuck him with a pin. He stared at me.

"You don't have to fully believe me. You just have to give me a small window of doubt."

His long sigh gave away the battle waging in his mind. "Fine. I'll keep it off the books and ask Rami to put a rush on it—but this is a one-time favor."

"Thank you." I wrote my new address down on a Chinese menu and handed it to him. "I'll be here when you get an answer."

He stared at me for a moment too long like he was trying to

choose his words carefully. Then the moment evaporated, and he walked through the door. "Do yourself a favor and get one of those doorbell cameras already." With a nod, he shut the door behind him.

Ringo gave me a smile and thumped his tail against the chair. I ruffled his ears and let my heart fall into rhythm. "What would I do without you, buddy?"

He sat and gave me his paw.

"Yes, you're very smart."

He looked toward the kitchen and the snack cabinet.

I snickered. "I didn't forget." We went around the counter, and I opened the cabinet and took out a bone then handed it to him.

He clamped on it gently and went to the living room to enjoy his treat.

My mind went right back to Jacob. If he was dead, then someone was going out of their way to hurt me. But if Jacob was alive . . .

Anger seared through me. *It has to be a lie. He loved me. He would never endanger his team or betray me like that. Would he? Did I even know him at all?*

I pulled out my phone and sent a group text to my new friends.

I desperately need a drink so I'm coming to the meeting. Everything I thought was real may have been a lie.

Chapter 4

I TOOK RINGO BACK TO THE DISNEY PALACE AND GAVE HIM HUGS and kisses and said I'd be home soon. I could put his orange vest on and take him to the AA meeting with me, but the emotions in the room could be overwhelming for him. Plus, Scarlett had been known to carry Beggin' Strips in a ziplock bag to coerce him to lay on her feet so she could kick off her Chanel stilettos without being seen.

I didn't tell Dad about the photo. No sense in worrying him before we knew if it was a deep fake or not. And he didn't exactly know who Jacob was. Partly because I'd never told him I was in a relationship in the first place, and partly because if I had, he would have forgotten almost immediately since he had the memory of a lightning bug flicker. Dad had enough on his plate with the neurologist appointment tomorrow and deciding whether to place Thor's hammer on his moss-covered mantel or in the Death Star.

I told Dad I was going to a meeting and left him to his elderly ladies fan club and their casseroles and drove over to the John Adams Hotel in McLean. The two best features the hotel had over our old meeting place were a better quality of cookies and a lack of smelling like tuna casserole.

Scarlett was waiting for me in the first-floor event room. The meeting was packed, and I found her swatting people away from the four gold chairs she was trying to save by laying down flat across them like they were a futon. "Thank God you're here! Quick, grab me a cookie and come sit on one of these seats before that snooty woman in the plaid forces her way in. Don't look at me like that, Helen. I'm a five-foot-tall, hundred-pound Asian, but I will still take you down if provoked."

I grabbed two scarecrow cookies and slid into the seat under Scarlett's feet, avoiding Helen's eyes.

Scarlett took the frosted cookie and nibbled it, still lying across the other chairs. "How's the move going?"

"The process is going smoothly. The view is a bit of a shock."

She gave a warning scowl to a man hovering close by. "Why? Your dad paint the house orange or something? You know you can't trust someone with a color palette who's done that much LSD."

I snorted. "It's worse than that. He's recreated an entire Hans Christian Andersen village."

She raised up on her elbows and arched a perfect eyebrow behind designer glasses. "Get out."

I nodded through another bite of my scarecrow. "I've never seen so many hedgehogs in my entire life. I haven't even gone into my bedroom yet. I can't bring myself to face it."

Scarlett whistled. "I cannot wait to see that."

Charisse flew into the room in a tailored winter-white suit, straight from her job at a high-powered investment brokerage where she worked as some muckety-muck. She grabbed a cookie and a coffee and slid into the seat under Scarlett's head. "Where's Bree?"

Scarlett sat up and stuck her designer handbag loudly on the remaining empty chair when a squatter attempted to approach. "Not here yet. And she needs to hurry. That one in the green T-shirt has been circling for ten minutes, and I know she isn't after the coffee."

We'd been coming to this meeting for the past two months and attendance had doubled this week alone. "Why are there so many people here?"

Charisse pulled out her Fenty hot chocolate pressed powder and checked her reflection before dabbing her nose and forehead. “It’s gotta be Thanksgiving. Nothing makes you want to drink like the threat of facing time with your extended family.”

Scarlett chuckled. “Heck, it’s why some of us started drinking in the first place.” She checked the screen on her phone again. “Where is Bree? It’s not like her to be so late.”

I brushed crumbs off my chest. “Does she maybe have a final today or something? I know she’s trying to finish her online classes before the break.”

Scarlett dropped her phone into her bag. “Sometimes I forget how young she is.”

Charisse sipped her coffee and sighed. “I don’t. I’m reminded every time I see that flawless complexion without a hint of crow’s-feet. It’s easy to disguise youth behind all that group therapy wisdom.”

That was certainly true. A gorgeous honey-blonde in her mid-twenties, Bree could be much kinder than the rest of us. She’d had a rough life from bullying and addiction, and still she was the first one of us to reach out to someone and offer comfort and compassion. After being a cop for nearly twenty years, I was the last.

Scarlett was the feisty one. She packed more sass in her tiny frame than anyone I’d ever met. She was also the reason I was here with these women today. From our first meeting she got a tenacious grip on me and refused to let go until the four of us were friends. It was still a learning curve for me to trust women in general, but there was no doubt that I would take a bullet for every one of them.

I glanced at Charisse, the oldest and most successful of us careerwise. Bree hadn’t started her career yet and Scarlett and I had torched ours. Charisse was quieter than usual. She was often bubbly and relaxed, relieved to be away from the office and let her braids down. Tonight, there was a shadow darkening her eyes. “You okay? You seem like something is bothering you.”

She sighed and her eyes took on a glassy sheen. “This will be my first Thanksgiving alone in an empty house. The kids are being weird about where they’re going for the holiday. They say they don't want to take sides, so they'll do their own thing, but I know they're going to Michael and Dollie's in Vermont."

My heart broke for her. "I'm so sorry, Charisse. I'm sure the divorce has been hard on them. Grown kids out on their own probably don't expect their parents to split up after thirty years of marriage."

She patted at the corner of her eye and gave me a tiny nod. "You're right."

Scarlett reached over and squeezed our friend's hand. "You're welcome to come to my house, but just know in advance that it's going to be a hot mess. I have no idea what I'm doing. My husband, Graham, wants a flippin' reenactment of the Pilgrims' first meal with the Native Americans, even though he's British and his whole connection to Thanksgiving is the historical subjugation of an indigenous people."

"Ouch." I laughed under my breath.

Charisse laughed. "You should tell him that."

Scarlett chuckled through her words. "Don't think I haven't. At least I'm an American. I'm used to celebrating Thanksgiving, albeit in a Chinese home where my mom made duck and dumplings instead of turkey and stuffing. I'm just saying—you don't see the Native Americans pissed off at my people."

The meeting organizer, a man we'd finally stopped calling "mustache" about a week ago and started calling by his name—Jonathan—called the meeting to order. Our hoverer in the green T-shirt turned on Scarlett and said, "I called dibs on that seat."

Scarlett chuckled through a breath. "Three weeks ago! You can't call perpetual dibs because you're triggered by the back of people's heads, Judith."

Bree charged into the room and slid onto the seat just as the hoverer reached to remove Scarlett's Kate Spade. "Thanks for holding my purse while I was in the bathroom. You'd better get your seat, Judith. We're starting."

The woman growled softly at the whole row of us and moved to sit in the back of the room.

Charisse patted Bree's knee. "Don't worry, come January we'll probably not see half these people for months."

Scarlett nudged our young friend. "What took you so long?"

Bree gave us a little shake of her head and pulled at the cuffs of her long-sleeved pink Henley. "Nothing. Just . . . distracted I guess."

The three of us passed looks of concern, but there was no time to ask Bree for more information. And she didn't offer any insight during the meeting. We would have to corner her afterward for a cross-examination.

We sat through a litany of shares, all involving the temptation to sip, snort, shoot, or smoke something because of holiday expectations and disappointment. November through New Year's was prime season for addiction meetings. No matter how airbrushed the advertisement, holiday meals and family gatherings didn't usually fulfill their promise of bringing one peace and joy. And if they did, the feeling was fleeting and followed by a dangerous post-holiday letdown as soon as the day was over.

Varish, an older man from Pakistan, shared that he'd be eating a frozen turkey dinner and going to bed at three P.M. to avoid having his mother provoke him for not calling home more.

Throughout the meeting, Bree remained silent, refusing to make eye contact with anyone and closely examining the pattern in the carpet. I caught a couple of glances at her and could see that she wasn't really focused on the shares. Even when I talked about moving into the fairy-tale land of Duloc with Shrek. I know that Charisse and Scarlett noticed too, because the minute we adjourned they were on her with questions.

Charisse put her hand on Bree's back in a motherly way. "What's the matter, darlin'? Why are you so withdrawn tonight?"

Bree shrugged. "Nothing's wrong. I guess I'm just tired."

Scarlett narrowed her eyes as she faced the young woman. "Mmm. No. Something is up with you. You haven't been yourself for a few days now. We agreed to total honesty with each other. Remember?"

Bree wouldn't look her in the eye.

"Did you relapse?" I asked.

She shook her head. "No. It's just. You know. Holidays."

Judging from the others' narrowed eyes, none of us were appeased with the half-truth.

Bree tried to change the subject by patting my arm. "Hey, what did you mean by your text that everything you believed might be a lie?"

I didn't want to turn the focus onto me and my issues, but Bree was clearly looking for a pass from the hot seat, and maybe it would do her good. "Someone sent me a picture of Jacob that said he's alive."

Scarlett punched me on the arm. "Get out! Are you serious? Is it true? Would that be amazing? Wait. Would that be devastating? How do we feel about this?"

Bree's jaw had dropped to her chest and her deep green eyes grew twice their size. "How? Where? Has he like, been in a coma or something? Like, why didn't he call you?"

Even Charisse flew into a tizzy. Her head snapped like a rubber band. "Girl, are you kidding me with that? How is that boy still alive? Didn't he die in the warehouse? Do you think he faked his death? And why would he let you take the blame for everything if he had?"

I pulled them away from the staring eyes of those who didn't leave the meeting fast enough and described the photo and the letter. "I had to call Castinetto and report the harassment. He thinks I Photoshopped it to get out from under department suspicion over Stratton Park."

"That's ridiculous," Scarlett said. "You shouldn't even be under suspicion. Any idiot can see you were set up."

Bree squeezed my arm and gave me a sympathetic murmur. "That's right. And after you helped them catch the clown's killer, too."

Charisse paced for a minute, her lips moving with the conversation in her head. "You need to tell Castinetto to get a grip. That day was so obviously an ambush. The fact that you don't have any memory of the events before the warehouse tells me that you were roofied. Don't the cops know you were roofied? It should be standard operating procedure to run a tox screen when officers show up at the hospital unconscious."

In addition to being a great friend who always had my back, Charisse was also a big fan of true crime podcasts with a frightening amount of information on police procedures and serial killers.

Three sets of eyes watched me, waiting for an explanation.

"Rohypnol and GHB are not part of a routine tox screen. I had to request them hours after I was admitted."

Bree grabbed my arm, her eyes intense. "And?"

"My tox screen was lost by the lab."

The ladies' lips flattened in unison. Charisse rolled her eyes. "Uh-huh. Riiiiight."

Scarlett cursed under her breath. "And that didn't scream conspiracy to you?"

"The forensics lab said it was human error. By the time I found out, it was too late to get retested. Any drug I'd been on was out of my system. Because Rohypnol and GHB mimic intoxication, and my blood alcohol was very high, Internal Affairs attributed my memory issues to a combination of the concussion and alcohol consumption, consistent with trauma.

"I was so ashamed that I'd been drunk on duty and my team died on my watch that I figured I deserved the outcome."

Charisse reached for my hand. "Girl, you gotta let go of that shame. It won't do you any good and keeps you from moving forward with your life."

Scarlett gathered her things, preparing to leave. "I agree. Besides, you know what this means?"

I was afraid I did know. They'd been pestering me to go back to the Gibson, the bar where I'd been while the rest of my narcotics task force was waiting for me at Hurtado's warehouse, sure that I'd recover my memories if I just returned to the scene of the crime. I had been telling them that I wasn't ready, afraid of what I'd see if I had to face my demons. Judging from the look of determination on Scarlett's face, and the shine of hope in Bree's eyes, I had just run out of grace.

"You need to quit putting this off." Scarlett gave me a single nod. "We can go right now."

Bree clapped her hands in mild excitement, then took my hand in hers. "We'll be with you every step. We're your backup, remember?"

Charisse gave me a wry smile. "Besides, lady. Don't you want to find out what really happened? Especially now? This whole thing reeks of a setup. And either someone is yanking your chain or the man you thought was the love of your life is really alive. I'd want to know."

"You're right. I do want to know. Because if Jacob is alive, he's got a lot to answer for."

Chapter 5

THE FOUR OF US WERE STANDING OUTSIDE OF THE GIBSON, AN UPscale craft cocktail bar, tucked away on a side street in historic Old Town Alexandria. It was unseasonably cold for November, and our breath came out in frosty wisps. A sandwich board advertised an apple pie martini Instagram special.

This was the kind of place where your wallet dictated your sobriety. Something that should have worked in my favor with Internal Affairs. No cop on a civil servant salary could afford to binge drink at these prices—something Jacob had complained about many times. If you wanted a sports bar or Coyote Ugly, you'd best be moving on, because this place was swank and swagger, known for having luxury liquor and a VIP room.

I told my heart to slow down to a rational pace. I wasn't in any danger—I was only here to reclaim my memories. *It's now or never.*

Never is starting to sound pretty good though.

One look at my friends and I was reminded that they needed a win as much as I did. None of us were floating on cloud nine.

Scarlett linked her arm in mine and led me inside the dark wood-paneled lounge with deep chocolate padded seats. The room smelled of leather and woodsmoke and expense accounts. "So, what do you remember?"

I thought for a minute. "A Viking and some angels."

Bree breathed out an excited response more to herself than to us. "Oooh, a Viking."

The room was full of suits entertaining wealthy clients. A group of stylishly dressed young women occupied the booth in the back corner. From the looks of the caramel-colored drinks in front of them, they were taking advantage of those fancy Instagram specials. One of the ladies laughed too loudly and all heads turned her way. She was holding her cell phone at arm's length for a group shot of her table.

The Gibson had become one of those trendy night spots mentioned in *Northern Virginia Magazine* that made it impossible to get into and flooded the establishment with wannabe influencers. Something the suits didn't look pleased about at the moment.

Two waitresses in sexy green cocktail dresses worked the full room taking orders. One of them looked to be somewhere around Bree's age. Maybe working her way through college. The other I'd guess to be just a little younger than Scarlett and myself. She carried herself with the disappointed edge of a single mom who wanted to be home with her feet up instead of working the night shift.

An older waitress in a green dress matching the others came out of a back room carrying a takeout bag and took it to a businessman at the bar. Her bottled brass hair was piled up in a messy bun and she appeared to be near retirement age. At least what used to be retirement age before inflation meant you had to work into the grave to keep your house. I didn't recognize anyone, but it had been nine months since I'd been here. "Why don't you guys talk to the servers and ask about security footage? I'll talk to the bartender."

Scarlett licked her lips. "If anyone needs an emergency extraction, the code word is *nacho.*"

Charisse muttered, "Great. Now I want nachos."

We split up, each to our own marks. I examined the polished mahogany bar and the scrollwork shelves of high-end liquor. Temptation surfed in on a wave of shame and a voice in my head taunted that I had no business ever darkening this doorstep again. My face felt hot, and a bell started ringing in the back of my head. I clenched my fist and drove my nails into the palm of my hand to stop myself from blacking out. *You're fine. Everything is fine. Just breathe.*

A memory flashed through my mind like a video trying to buffer. I was talking to a large man behind the bar. He was broad as a billboard with ruddy skin. Peppery hair and a salty beard, pointy like a Viking. His black T-shirt said *Gibson* across the front. It was struggling to hold in his chest and biceps and barely covering the angel tattoos on both arms. "I'm here to see the Scorpion."

The image disappeared. *I was meeting the Scorpion?* I thought the elusive drug lord was a myth made up by gangs to shift suspicion away from their suppliers. The Potomac County Narcotics Unit had been trying to find out who supplied Hurtado for months. That one name was all my informants could ever come up with. We never got a stronger lead or a description.

The bartender tonight was not the Viking. Instead, a small Latin man with a hoop earring and a name tag that said JORGE rinsed a martini shaker as I took one of the leather high-back stools at the counter. He gave me a nod.

"Can I get a ginger ale?"

When he brought my drink, I'd worked up the nerve to ask him a couple of questions. "I was here a few months ago and met someone. They may have gone by the name of the Scorpion?"

He shook his head. "No idea who that is."

"I was in an accident when I left here and I'm still dealing with amnesia from it. I know it's a long shot, but I was wondering if you had any receipts or security footage from that afternoon that I might be able to review to help me put the pieces together."

Jorge stared at me, a mixture of curiosity and concern playing across his face. "I'll do what I can. What was the date?"

"February the twelfth."

His expression fell like wax melting off a candle. "The twelfth?"

I nodded.

He groaned. "We don't have anything that goes back that far. We only keep ninety days of security footage. But we've been under new management since February the thirteenth. The whole system is new. Computers, cameras, everything."

The hairs on my neck tingled up to the top of my scalp. "Since February the thirteenth?"

"Yeah." The look on his face said he couldn't believe it either. "I was hired on the thirteenth as part of a complete staff change."

"You're kidding?"

His lips rolled in, and he shook his head. "My first shift was Valentine's Day when we had our soft re-opening. It did not go well. We were packed all day. Service was a train wreck. Everyone was a new hire."

"That timing is unbelievably suspicious."

He let out a low breath and shook his head like I was the last trial he could take today. "I understand why you would think that."

"Do you know the reason behind the staff change?"

He gave me a weak shrug. "I always assumed the old manager screwed up big-time and everyone walked out. Most of us were hired from an agency that staffs temps for emergency fill-ins and corporate parties."

And just like that, in twenty-four hours, everything from the night I was here—erased. "I'm having trouble believing this is a coincidence."

He threw the rag on the polished bar top. "Look, if I were in your shoes, I'd feel exactly the same way. But I genuinely don't know anything. I can leave a message for the day manager to call you. I'm sorry I couldn't be more help." He reached for a bottle on the shelf behind him, poured a shot of tequila that I had never been able to afford, and placed it before me. "On the house."

My eyes were riveted to the glass and my mouth went dry. *This is insane. A complete staff change screams. Leave no evidence. It's either coincidence or conspiracy—and I don't believe in coincidence.*

I tried to ignore the golden liquid by looking at a crack in the wood at the edge of the bar. "Who's the current owner?"

"An investor. I've never talked with him in person. We communicate through email." He wrote an email address on the back of a cocktail napkin and passed it to me. Astoria Holdings.

I nodded and pulled the napkin past the shot glass with a tremor in my hand. I shoved it down in my front pocket. If Jacob was alive, could he be part of a conspiracy? *Against me?* My blood thundered in my ears like horses galloping down a dirt road toward me. I tried a breathing exercise, but my inhale was shallow and shaky. My eyes went back to the tequila. *No one could blame me for drinking this after the day I've had.*

I reached for my ginger ale with a shaky hand and took a long swig, my eyes never leaving the gold liquid in the square shot glass. I reached into my wallet and took out a ten, slapping it on the counter with more anger than I had a right to feel. My face flamed with shame and regret, and I hauled myself off the barstool. Calling out, "Nacho," I ran through the heavy wooden door into the shivering darkness outside.

Scarlett came through a moment later. "You okay? What the heck happened? Whoa, you're white. Like extra white."

"It was on the house."

"What was?"

"Don Julio."

Her eyes flicked with understanding. "Did you drink it?"

"No."

"Then what's the matter?"

"I really, really wanted to."

She took my arm and led me away from the building. "My friend, that is just called Wednesday for me."

The door opened and Charisse and Bree came out looking around. Charisse pointed in our direction and they joined us.

Charisse's breath came out in tiny white clouds. "What happened?"

Scarlett answered, "Layla was tempted."

The older woman nodded sagely. "What set you off?"

My heart was still pounding, but the horses were slowing their approach. I was beginning to feel foolish. "It was sitting there. It was free. I was angry. You name it."

Charisse nodded. "I understand. I get tempted when I'm sad. Or happy. Or want to drown my feelings, or celebrate. Or in a restaurant. Or at home. Or at work. Or I've had a bad day. Or a good one."

I gave her the hint of a smile. She got me. "I'm sorry to let you all down. I didn't expect to feel so weird coming here."

Scarlett pulled me into a hug. "Don't be ridiculous. You didn't let us down. We're a team."

I patted her back as a way of returning the hug. I still wasn't used to having girlfriends, let alone ones who gave out affection like free samples at Costco. Most of my life had been dominated by what people could get from me—the famous rock star's daughter with unlimited funds. "Thank you. I got an email for the owner. Did you all get anything?"

All three of them shook their heads, but Bree had been swiping on her cell phone since Scarlett's hug.

Charisse gently tugged at one of her braids. "Everyone is new. The older waitress said everyone started on Valentine's Day."

I blew on my hands and rubbed them together. "The bartender said the same thing. Total staff change."

Scarlett threw her hand to her hip. "Which is totally sus, and I don't believe it at all. No way that just happened."

I nodded. "I agree."

Bree didn't look up from her phone. "Did you remember anything?"

"I only had a brief flash and it's not enough to go on. With no receipts, no security footage, and no one here who could possibly offer any insight, I think getting a hold of the owner is our only lead."

"Gotcha." Bree grinned behind the glow of her iPhone.

Scarlett nudged her. "What'd you find?"

Bree smiled broadly and turned the screen. "A group of women tagged the Gibson in a reel the day you were here."

She hit play on a video where one of the women was talking

into the phone. "We're here at the Gibson for my bachelorette party. Hey, girls! We're on a pub crawl and the cocktails here are as delicious as the bartender. Five stars!" She panned her phone, and the video captured the Viking behind the bar. She also caught a shot of the back of my head as I was talking to him. There was no mistaking it was me unless another woman of my size and build had blue streaks in her black hair and came in wearing riot gear. The video went on. "And let me tell you, this Cupid Cocktail is an aphrodisiac. I might not make it to the wedding night—so, Brian, get ready!" The other women squealed in the background and the video ended.

Bree watched us in silent expectation, her face lit with excitement.

I looked at her in wonder. "I can't believe you found that. I'm so impressed."

She shrugged but she was clearly pleased. "It was nothing. The Gibson made it easy. They offer a half-price drink if you tag them in a five-star review on social media. That's where the Instagram specials come from."

Scarlett took the phone from Bree's hand and replayed the video. Her face broke into a grin. "I know one of those bridesmaids. That's Abigail Keller. She babysat for us one summer. Left the house traumatized." She handed Bree's phone back and pulled her own out of her bag. "I'm going to text her and set up a coffee date."

Charisse squeezed my shoulder. "That's two victories tonight. We're making progress."

A smidgen of relief brushed over me even though I still had more questions than answers. Like what were the odds that the Gibson would have an entire staff change just hours after I'd been here? What were they hiding? And was it linked to me? All this time I'd been so ashamed that I'd been too drunk to back up my team, I hadn't wanted to face my memories.

That changes now.

Chapter 6

BREE SEEMED IN MUCH BETTER SPIRITS BY THE TIME WE ALL SAID good night. I, however, felt totally freaked out. Someone may have set me up to take the fall for Stratton Park, and the man I loved and had presumed to be dead for the past nine months could possibly be alive. Could those two things be connected? I mean . . . Jacob didn't set me up. He wouldn't. He obviously has amnesia and was fighting to get back his memories just like me. Right?

I shrugged out from under the weight of that thought, not ready to deal with it so close to a bar.

A bright moon hung in an inky sky when I pulled into my driveway an hour later. The moving trucks were gone, and I had a better view of the front garden. A stone pathway wound through a variety of fall flowers and shrubs that I would have dead in no time. Unless Dad wanted to take up gardening as his new hobby over hot-tubbing with Brazilian models, those rose bushes didn't have a chance. A mushroom-capped amber-glass lantern shone brightly by the front door. It flickered like the fairy trapped inside was trying to escape.

Ringo barked a greeting from the other side of the door and his whimper told me he'd waited long enough for my arrival. A Labrador with a stuffed hippo in his mouth pushed against me and tried to shove his toy into my hand. "Hey, buddy. I missed you too."

The house was quiet. Dad must be watching TV in his room. A note on the counter said that a casserole of macaroni and cheese was waiting for me in the microwave. I warmed it up and ate over the sink, afraid to mark up the new table after the elves had gone to so much trouble to carve it for us. I cleaned my dishes and quietly made my way through the kitchen and breakfast nook into the living room. The fire had been banked and only glowing embers remained.

I glanced at the spiral staircase to the loft, for a moment tempted to explore it to delay the inevitable, but the double doors leading into my bedroom whispered, *Stop stalling and rip off the Band-Aid.* It was time to face the frills and accept that my father still saw me as a little girl, and this was my dollhouse.

I looked at Ringo who gave me a smile. "Well, let's do this." I put my hand on the door. *Please don't be pink.* I threw it open and stood silently trying to take in the scene before me. The ceiling and walls were dark moss green, and the floor looked like solid birch. In the center of the back wall stood a queen-sized canopy bed made of slender branches. White flowers cascaded from vines running across the canopy where ivory tulle draped and twisted end to end over the headboard. The bed was covered in a plush silvery green comforter with a champagne chenille fur throw draped gracefully across the bottom half, and there was a ridiculous mountain of throw pillows in every conceivable fluffy, flowery, feathery material that I would have to hide in the closet because no way was I putting them back on the bed every day.

A foofy black fur graced the floor in front of a French gas fireplace that curved into the room, like the one Dad had. A row of different-sized white flowerpots were lined across the mantel. They were empty—I checked. *Are they decorative or am I supposed to plant something in them?*

I counted three vases of roses, two on the carved nightstands, one on the French provincial four-drawer dresser, probably Myrtle Jean's doing at Dad's behest.

On the far side of the room, double doors led out to a private patio with a swing facing the lake.

Something winked at me behind the headboard, so I found a light switch and flicked on a pendant light made from a gilded birdcage. "Whoa." The back wall behind the bed had a soft hand-painted mural of an enchanted woodland. Metallic golden fairies and fireflies twinkled in the glow of the birdcage light. "How am I supposed to sleep in here, Ringo? It's like an eleven-year-old's Pinterest board threw up."

A statue of a fat frog wearing a crown sat next to a large painted box on the nightstand. It was about the size of a small evidence box and depicted woodland creatures surrounding a gingerbread cottage. I took off the lid to see what was inside. Empty. *Well, what the heck is that even for?* Everything in here was absurd.

Ringo pranced over to a king-sized dog bed that appeared to be carved out of a fallen log. He hopped in and curled himself into a tight ball with a deep sigh of contentment. *I'm glad one of us is happy.*

Someone had moved my guitar into the bedroom. That was a nice touch. It sat next to a table made from a ring of mushrooms circling a log—*that* I could do without.

My eyes went to the hand-carved door leading into the bathroom. What could possibly be waiting for me on the other side of that door? I imagined rainbows and unicorns, which made me swallow so hard that I coughed. I crossed the wide room and pulled open a door, peeking around it. I had to blink twice.

The bathroom was navy blue with Norwegian-inspired embroidery around the ceiling. Shelves of fluffy yellow spa towels were interspersed with pots of greenery. Centered over a navy claw-foot bathtub was a round stained-glass window with two swans gliding across a lake trimmed in red roses. A matching swan had been painted on the front of the tub. I turned a dial next to the door and the yellow stone floor started to heat beneath my feet. It felt like a ridiculous luxury until I saw the spa shower and infrared sauna.

This *lick of paint* was easily a seven-figure remodel. When the day finally came that I was alone, what was I gonna do with a storybook cottage in the middle of a trailer park? My heart squeezed in my chest. *What would I do about anything when that day came?*

I got ready for bed and approached the four-poster monstrosity as if it would come alive and swallow me whole. I tossed nine pillows to the floor, where they would stay indefinitely, pulled down the velvety comforter, and climbed beneath white silk sheets that were a whisper against my skin. *Did Dad find a show called* Pimp My Cottage *on Netflix?* I was frustrated with him for going so far over the top—as per usual—but questioning him would have to wait until morning. I had never felt so luxurious in all my life, and as I drifted off to sleep, I was a little ashamed by how much I loved it.

Dr. Felicia Ahmed of neurology specialists at Georgetown Hospital had the typical doctor's office. Cold, plain, neutral. Artistic print of peaceful landscape over easy-to-clean leather seats. But she came very highly regarded, so Dad and I were hopeful we'd get some answers.

She'd run a battery of tests, including a CAT scan that had to be done twice because Dad wouldn't stop singing "Highway to the Danger Zone" every time the machine started to move him inside. We were here today to get the results.

Dr. Ahmed adjusted a pair of violet-framed glasses that matched her violet pantsuit like they came as an accessory. I imagined her having drawers of glasses to match all her outfits. Finally peering over the paperwork on her carved mahogany desk, she smiled. "Mr. Virtue. How are you feeling?"

Dad shrugged. "I dunno. Fine. If I was feeling bad earlier, I've already forgotten it."

"Your tests all look pretty good. Your dementia is in the early stages. That's positive news because it means that we have the greatest chance to slow the progression down."

Dad shifted in his seat and sighed. I reached out my hand and placed it over his, my heart breaking to be talking about a disease that would eventually rob him of all his memories and cause his body to forget how to do the most basic of tasks.

Dr. Ahmed smiled at me now. "The CAT scan shows a little shrinkage of the brain at this stage, and only a small amount of vascular damage, but then Mr. Virtue does have a history of loud music with drug and alcohol abuse, so some of that's to be expected."

Dad chuckled. "No one is more surprised than I am that I'm still alive."

She twirled a gold pen in her left hand. "Considering the wild life you've lived, you're in excellent health."

Dad flashed a bull horns hand gesture, the rock-and-roll salute, and Dr. Ahmed flashed it back at him.

She pushed onward, holding up diagrams and charts and discussing levels and numbers that no one cared about.

My throat went completely dry. I wanted to scream, *Just tell us how long. That's what we're both thinking.*

Dad cleared his throat, his voice strained. "And you're sure there's no cure?"

Her eyes, already full of compassion, darkened with sadness. "I'm afraid at this time we don't know how to cure dementia. But with medication and some lifestyle changes you may be able to slow it for a while."

I wanted to ask what kind of changes, but grief cut my throat and stole my words.

Dad crossed his arms over his chest. "What kind of lifestyle changes are we talkin' about? Because I'm not eatin' broccoli or goin' vegan. Just kill me now."

I held in a chuckle. *Of all the things to be worried about, broccoli is his top concern.*

"You don't have to go vegan." She grinned and placed the diagrams on the table and smoothed them with her hands. "We know that sugar is enemy number one when dealing with a brain disease, so limit the sweets."

Fat chance of that.

Dad humphed.

She continued as if she hadn't heard him, which she had, because her lips twitched, and she had to lock it down. "You may also want to limit saturated fat."

Dad humphed again, lower.

"Who does the cooking in your house?"

Dad and I looked at each other. He answered, "Mostly Roy Rogers and the Colonel."

"Neither of us know how to cook." Dad's personal chef had stayed in Malibu.

The doctor pulled out a nutrition chart of foods to avoid and passed it to me. All our favorites were listed. Anger burned behind my eyes. Not at her or at Dad but at life. At dementia. This unforgiving monster that would take my father from me. I wanted to smash the paper into a ball and throw it at her. "What's the point of taking away everything he loves if it won't change the outcome?"

She was gracious and ignored that I'd just snapped at her like a moody teenager. "We may not be able to undo the damage completely, but we can fight it. Slow it down and give your father a better quality of life. Maybe even add years. Exercise, a healthy diet, and social interaction are some of the most important factors in battling brain disease. And in the meantime, we wait on the science."

Dad put his hand over mine now. "And you said there's medication I can take?"

She nodded. "Medical science is always advancing. Stem cell therapy may be the miracle of the future. And there are a couple of drugs on the market today that look very promising."

The doctor grew quiet and thoughtful. "You'll have good days and bad days. You may find that nights tend to be particularly difficult. Try to pace your energy so you'll have more consistent good days. Maybe more walks and reading. Avoid mosh pits and eighteen-hour days on the road touring."

Dad's face screwed up in disgust. "What do I have to read?"

"Dad," I chuckled, "no one's gonna make you read anything."

Dad blew out his breath in relief. "Okay. A man can only handle so much bad news."

Dr. Ahmed sat back against her leather chair and picked up her gold pen. "Do you have any questions for me?"

Dad thought for a moment then leaned toward her desk.

"Where can I get one of those metal tubes for my house? The acoustics in that thing were fabulous."

"You mean the CAT scan bed?"

His eyes grew wide. "Yes!"

"You did leave quite the impression on the diagnostic staff." Dr. Ahmed grinned and rolled the pen in her fingers. "Why don't I schedule you another session in about six months?"

Dad bit his bottom lip and leaned back in his chair, grinning. "Righteous."

Chapter 7

We headed home in Dad's cream-colored Aston Martin. He'd been quiet for the last twenty minutes, something that usually only happened when he fell asleep. "Are you okay over there?"

He nodded. "I guess some things you just have to walk through. It's not like I can opt out of the disease like an appearance on *The View.* Frickin' Whoopi Goldberg." Then he turned such sad eyes on me. "I hope I don't forget you're my daughter, baby girl. You're the best thing I ever did."

My chest felt like someone had reached inside to my heart and twisted. I blinked away tears. "I won't let you forget me, Dad. Don't you worry." *I'll fight it as long as I can.*

Dad's voice brightened. "What did you think of your bedroom? Fawn designed the bathroom with inspiration from two fairy tales. Something with birds and something without birds."

I put on my blinker to change lanes. "Well, that clears everything up. I'm thinking one of the stories is *The Swan Princess* because there is a definite swan theme."

"Nice. That's perfect. A swan's a bird, right?"

"It is."

"Nice."

I glanced over at my father. He was trying to make eye contact with each of the drivers as I passed them. "What exactly did you tell your interior designer about me?"

"Hmm? Fawn?"

"Yep. That's the one."

"Well, I told her that you loved stories. And that your favorite book is that storybook I brought home from Germany that time."

I slowed down for the toll booth to collect from my E-ZPass. "The Hans Christian Andersen?"

"Right. And that you wanted to be a veterinarian, but something went wrong and now you're playing music. But you won't let me help you, which is ridiculous, honey, because I can make one phone call and set you up with Stevie in a sound booth. I mean, Glen and Simon will back you up for free."

"Focus, Dad."

"On what?"

"What did you tell Fawn?"

"About what?"

"About me, Dad. Why do we live in Cinderella Castle? Why is every room themed from a fairy tale?"

"You don't like it? I could have her come redo it with an animal theme. Or we could do it up like we're in the Canadian Rockies. You like bears?"

"No, Dad. I didn't say I don't like it. You put a lot of money into it. I'm just wondering if she knows that I'm not currently in day care."

Dad twisted the seat belt absently. "Of course she knows that, baby girl. I showed her that picture of us playing together on stage a few weeks ago. I told her how wonderful you are to let me stay with you. I know no one wants to take care of some sickly old geezer when they're trying to live their life. It's a lot . . ."

His voice trailed off and I noticed the sadness and stress on his face from his reflection in the tinted side window.

A fist of shame punched me in the throat. Here I was complaining about something that had meant so much to him to do for me, and he's a multimillionaire living in a trailer park because he needs care, and I'm too scared of failure to move away.

The man worked hard his whole life. He has three different mansions and an apartment in New York City, and I've got him living at Lake Pinecrest. I reached over and put my hand on his arm. "Hey. It's not a lot. I'm really glad you're here and we can be together. I've got to tie up some loose ends having to do with my former partner in the police department, but then we can move to wherever you want. You want to go to your vineyard in Italy?"

Dad's eyebrows dipped. "Is that where it is? I thought it was in France."

I turned at the birch trees leading down to the lake. "You said you don't trust the French because of the mime thing."

His face clouded over. "Oh right. Frickin' mimes. There's no box!"

I laughed to myself. "Alright, well, you decide where you want to live, and we'll go there."

"I want to live here. With you."

"I know, but I'm saying I would go with you. You don't have to live in the trailer park. We can move into one of your mansions where you can get back to the lifestyle you're accustomed to."

"That doesn't matter to me, baby girl. The mansion gets lonely. And I'm tired of throwing parties just to have someone to talk to. I want to be with you." Then he started to sing a bubble-gum pop song. Mostly.

"I don't know what it is that makes me love, you know. I only know I never want you to go. 'Cause you started something that you can't see. Ever since I met you has a hold on me. I know that to be tru-ue, I know I want to be with yo-ou. "He grinned, pretty pleased with himself.

I pulled into the cobblestone driveway. "Uh-huh. But what about your friends, Dad?"

Dad screwed up his face. "What friends? The guys are all in Europe on the tour. Everyone else just wants something from me. Even the guys I went to high school with want to get paid now to be in my posse. Like I need a posse. We have each other, baby girl. And the ladies in the park."

"Oh, naturally we have the ladies, sure."

"And your husband."

"Nick isn't my husband, Dad."

"Plus, we have the dog and the cat."

"We don't have a cat."

"Yeah, we do. It came with the house."

I gave him a long look to see if he was kidding or hallucinating. "I think you're confused because you had a CAT scan."

Dad grinned and shook his head. "I am not confused, baby girl. This cat is black with white stripes."

I felt a tingle run up my spine. "Dad, so help me God, if you're letting a skunk into the house . . ."

He threw his hands up. "I'm not. You just wait. I'll show you."

Chapter 8

I PLAYED FRISBEE WITH RINGO FOR THIRTY MINUTES UNTIL ONE OF us was worn out. It was not Ringo. Then Dad and I walked into the Lake Pinecrest Clubhouse, and he was welcomed like Norm arriving at the Boston bar.

I, however, was greeted with "Did you bring the pumpkin pie like I told you to?"

"I didn't have time to make a pie, Agnes. We were in Georgetown all day."

The older woman scowled and threw her hand to her hip. "It was already made, Layla. I saw it on your kitchen counter last night."

"First of all, Agnes, I stole that pie. And second, I'm pretty sure Dad ate it while I was out because it was gone this morning."

Agnes rolled her eyes and called over her shoulder, "Don, did you eat that whole pumpkin pie?"

Dad, who was lightly disguised in a pair of dark glasses, a worn flat cap, and an oversized plaid barn coat, dropped another chicken wing onto his full plate and called back, "Yep."

Agnes gave me a look that said I was off the hook—this time. Then she called for her second-in-command. "Myrtle Jean, bring out the backup pie."

Myrtle Jean giggled and unboxed a bakery pie with a twinkle in her eye. "We call this the Layla contingency."

I grabbed a fork and stabbed a wedge of cheese and a cherry

tomato and groused, "Whatever. As long as I'm not getting a demerit for not contributing."

All day I'd looked forward to the community meeting even though it was a thinly veiled task force to micromanage the Thanksgiving dinner event orchestrated by the Lake Pinecrest mafia. I was excited about it—not because of Agnes's requisite rhubarb pie, or because it was the highlight of Dad's week where he got to socialize in a safe environment, but because I wanted to see Nick. He was the only part of these meetings that I enjoyed.

Nick loved the community meeting. Everything from the airing of petty grievances to the flagrancy of Clifford passing around shriveled blooms that he'd collected in various yards to illustrate that the owners had disregarded his schedule of appropriate deadheading. Nick couldn't wait to see what nonsense would unfold in the span of an hour. Usually, it involved me getting reamed out for some infraction of draconian regulations that he could tease me about later. Then we'd try to swipe extra cookies while Myrtle Jean was fawning over Dad.

I looked around the double-wide clubhouse for my friend whom I hadn't seen in several days, and my mood sank like my goldfish Petey when I was seven. Dad squeezed my arm on his way to a folding chair in his circle of friends. "Maybe he's just running late."

"Yeah." *Or maybe something is very wrong.*

I passed Donna, the plus-sized Black woman who used to be my friend. Well . . . *friendly.* She turned away to avoid making eye contact. She still hadn't forgiven me for keeping it a secret that the lead singer of an eighties rock band was my father, or for refusing to convince him to do a fundraiser for her grandson, Kelvin's, school.

The door banged open. My eyes snapped to the entrance. My pulse quickened. It wasn't Nick. It was a young blonde in a wheelchair whom I had never seen before. She rolled in, scanning the room timidly. Her face broke into a grin when she spotted Agnes.

Agnes beamed. “Good. You made it. Everyone! Attention please. This is Robin. She and her brother moved in this week. Let’s make her feel welcome.”

A chorus of greetings went around the room.

Donna’s eyebrows shot skyward. She poured herself an iced tea and gave Robin a wide-eyed look of surprise. “Jeanette Winthrop’s old trailer? I’m glad someone moved in there. Now maybe those newspapers will stop piling up.”

My former next-door neighbor, Benny, a Latino used-car salesman, drizzled ranch dressing over his buffalo wings and blew a raspberry. “Fat chance of that. I’ve tried to cancel that paper for two years and they just keep sending it. Nice to meet you, Robin.”

Robin flashed a bright smile to every person who greeted her. Dad approached with his hand out. “Hellooo. Trixie Hamm.”

I jabbed him. “Nope.” Then I tried to cover with a cough. “He’s kidding. This is my dad, Donald Hamm. Trixie is his sister.” I added through gritted teeth, “Who isn’t here right now.”

Trixie Hamm was Dad’s alter ego his first meeting here when I made him wear a more elaborate disguise for my peace of mind. Being nearly trampled to death by a mob of fans leaves a lasting mark on a kid.

He still had to wear a disguise when we go out in public, so people don’t recognize him as Don Virtue, but this had become a pretty low-key meeting for him these past months. A few of the residents knew who he was and didn’t care. Some of them wouldn’t know Don Virtue if he came in with the entire band.

Robin’s eyebrows shot up to her blond bangs. “Oh. Nice to meet you, Donald. And . . . ?”

I touched my hand to my chest. “Layla.”

She gave me a nod. “Layla. Well, Agnes told me there was rhubarb pie, so I want to get a piece of that before we start. Nice meeting you both.”

Dad and I went back to our seats in the rear of the white shiplap paneled room. Dad leaned into my shoulder. “Who is she kissing up to by eating that pie?”

I whispered back, "I don't think it's ever been cut before."

"Should we have a moment of silence?"

"What we need is the number for poison control."

Clifford Bagstrodt, our resident sourpuss in plaid dress slacks, cleared his throat with a lot of bristling and frowning and handed Robin a black folder. "This is your list of expectations and responsibilities for the neighborhood. We don't have an official HOA as per such." He cleared his throat again. "So, we manage on our own. I'm sure you will be a tidy addition to our little collective."

Robin took the proffered folder with a glowing smile and stuffed it next to her hip. "Thank you. Anything I can do to be a good neighbor. Anything you all need done around the house or yard, my brother is a whiz of a handyman."

Clifford's frown twitched in what may have been intended as a smile. He gave her a bow—Dad snorted—and Clifford proceeded to drag the old wooden podium to the center of the room, leaving yellowed flakes of shellac in a trail behind him.

I turned to my left to ask Nick if we'd be expected to curtsy for the new girl before leaving—but Nick wasn't there, and my heart dropped an inch lower in my chest.

Myrtle Jean waved a spatula menacingly at Clifford to vacate the spot where she had been about to plop her purple polyester-clad bottom onto a folding chair. "That'll do, Clifford."

Agnes took the place of honor behind the wooden stand and Clifford handed her a meat mallet to use as a gavel, which she rapped against the ancient podium. "Thank you for coming everyone. Tonight, we want to discuss fall decorations and the Thanksgiving potluck that is just one week from today."

The door opened with a bang and I gave myself whiplash. It wasn't Nick.

A woman I'd seen on the back of Fontainebleau was hunched in the doorway. Older and white, with dreadlocks in several shades of straw; her sallow skin, rail-thin frame, and the lines across her face spoke that life had been hard. I'd seen her a couple of times at potlucks, but this was the first community meeting she'd attended since I'd been here.

Agnes paused in her opening remarks, but she didn't greet her. The woman grabbed a plate of food then sat down in the back row across the aisle.

What was her name? Willow? Whiskey? Something weird like that. She had a look about her that I'd seen too many times. Meth. And she'd been at it a while too. She saw me staring and gave me the finger. I returned an apologetic nod. I knew that I lived in a glass house.

Agnes continued droning on about side dishes. "It's vitally important that you indicate what you intend to bring to the event. We don't need twenty-six cans of cranberry sauce with nothing to put it on. Two years of that was enough."

Myrtle Jean waved her spatula at us and made sure everyone got a squinty-eyed glare.

Dad's hand shot up and he called out, "The girl and I will cook the turkey."

I choked on my tea. "We'll do what now?"

He wiggled excitedly in his chair. "It'll be great, honey. I wasn't home for a lot of Thanksgivings. I want this one to be special. How hard can baking a turkey be?"

"I didn't know we were planning on coming." I glanced around the room to a sea of frowns judging me. I lowered my voice. "This isn't our house, Dad. It was going to be just the two of us. We were ordering that Wegmans dinner for four so we'd have leftovers. Remember?"

His glazed-over expression said that he had no idea what I was talking about.

I could hear Nick's voice in my head, teasing me. *Maybe he thinks all these white people are related to you.*

Agnes purred. "Wonderful. Don will bring the turkey." She narrowed her eyes at me, a challenge to disagree. "I'll pass around the sign-up sheet so everyone will get a chance to fill it in. Any questions?"

Foster raised his hand and Agnes cursed under her breath. “About Thanksgiving, Foster.”

He nodded.

“Okay, what is it?”

Foster stood in denim overalls, a flannel shirt, and a floppy felt hat. He needed some hay poking from his shirt and he’d look like a pudgy scarecrow. He pulled a piece of paper from his front pocket and unfolded it as I held my breath—wishing more than anything that Nick was here for what was surely about to come. “Hello, everyone. My name is Foster. I live on Versailles, and . . . for Thanksgiving . . . I want the management to designate part of the common ground as a playground for Pippi.”

I pumped my fist in the air. “Yes! Seven months in a row!”

Pippi was Foster’s miniature black pig who had more costumes than David Lee Roth. And, according to Foster, the keeper of secrets.

Agnes rubbed her temple with her thumb. “Foster, we’ve been over this. There isn’t enough money in the budget for a playground for a pet.”

Foster started to protest that Pippi Snickelfritz was not just a pet, when Donna raised her hand. “I’m sorry, but isn’t it Layla’s job to make these decisions now that she owns the trailer park?”

I felt the whites of my eyes turn to hard-boiled eggs. All heads spun to me, and I squirmed in my seat. *How did Donna find out?*

Dad appeared to shrink into himself, guilt rolling off him like a hot flash.

Marguerite waved the sign-up sheet that she had folded into a fan. “That’s true. If Layla owns the whole trailer park, it’s up to her to decide on the playground. And the budget.”

A few other voices joined in with the rebels. Clifford looked like he might be having a heart attack.

The right thing would have been for me to say that Agnes was in charge, although who put her in charge I had no idea.

When that didn’t happen, the smart thing would have been to keep silent.

Unfortunately, when I’m backed into a corner, I don’t do the right thing or the smart thing. I do the smart-mouth thing.

"What kind of budget does an imaginary homeowner's association have?"

Agnes smiled like the villain in every horror story. Wes Craven would have been proud.

Dad groaned, "Oh no."

Agnes picked up the meat mallet, walked out from behind her podium, down the aisle, and shoved it at me. "I cede the floor. The meetings are yours."

I tried to shove it back into her hands. "No, I don't want it."

She pushed it forward. "You're in charge. After all, you're fully moved in now. There's nothing keeping you from taking the reins. Or are you too busy with your music career to help out?"

Okay, that was a low blow. Anger and humiliation ran side by side up my spine. *Freakin' Agnes, always telling me what to do. I'll show you.*

I snatched the mallet with a huff and jumped to my feet. *On second thought, I'm glad Nick isn't here to see this.* I walked up to the podium and placed the mallet next to an open spiral notebook where Agnes kept her hit list.

Agnes took the seat next to Dad that I had just vacated. Myrtle Jean and Clifford immediately abandoned their posts and joined the audience. *I see how it is. Changing of the guard.*

I let out a breath. Before I could say anything else, Foster said, "My name is Foster. I live on Versailles, and I want the management to designate part of the common ground as a playground for Pippi. Pippi is a good girl, and she deserves a seesaw."

"Yes."

The room went silent.

Foster froze. His mouth open, his eyes twitching. The paper in his hands gave a little shake. Then he started to cry. "Yes?"

"Yes. You can have a playground for Pippi. Let me know what you need, and we'll get it started right after the holidays."

Agnes murmured loud enough for everyone to hear, "Good luck paying for it."

Foster stared at the paper in his hands. Then he dropped to his chair and gave me a quivery nod.

Immediately, twenty hands went up.

Benny asked to put a smoker down by the lake so he could make his famous brisket for our park events and not have to carry it from his house in batches.

"Yes."

Old Lady Henson asked permission to put in a vegetable garden.

"Yes."

Myrtle Jean asked permission to paint her trailer—to which Agnes sharply called her a traitor and a floozy. It didn't matter; she wanted it anyway.

"Yes."

The Alverezes asked if they could put a sign in their yard advertising their business.

"Yes."

The woman in dreads who had come in late stood and I thought she would ask for something, but she turned and walked out the door, not looking back.

My inner cop voice warned me that this would come back to bite me on the butt. People would always find a way to ruin things. But it felt good to have everyone love me for a change instead of being Layla the screwup. And Agnes had been far too controlling over simple things for too long. Let people have a little authority over their lives and their property. It's not like anyone was asking to fill the lake with sharks. This was a good thing. Not that everyone knew I owned the trailer park—*just wait until Donna asks for something. That two-faced rat*—but that the trailer park trio's reign of terror was finally over.

I ended the meeting, and everyone came to thank me personally on their way out.

Even Robin approached me with a smile. "I know I'm new here but give me a call if you need any help with anything. I want to get involved."

"Absolutely. I will let you know."

Agnes was on her way out the door and gave me a hearty wave. "And Don, don't forget about book club tomorrow night. We're reading *Lessons in Chemistry*."

Dad gave her a thumbs-up. "I'll be there, doll."

I called to her. "Agnes?"

"What's up?"

"What about all this food?"

She gave me a grin and a shrug. "You're in charge now, so you're the one who puts everything away and cleans up. I'm going home to watch *Bridgerton*."

Dad started out the door with her.

"And just where are you going?"

Dad jabbed his thumb toward our house. "I'm not in charge. I'm going home. Apparently, I have to study for chemistry now."

Agnes gave me a crooked grin under narrowed eyes and a shiver ran down my back. "Good luck, Layla. You have no idea what you've gotten yourself into."

Chapter 9

IT TOOK ALMOST AN HOUR TO CLEAN UP AFTER THE MEETING. Fortunately, most people took their leftovers home. I noticed no one took home that rhubarb pie with only one piece missing though, so I gladly threw it away. I was about to go next door to Agnes's house and tell her I needed the keys to lock up when I remembered I was given a set of keys the day we got the deed to the house. Sure enough, one of them was for the clubhouse door.

When I got home, Dad was searching the bookshelf that Fawn had filled with hardbound classics. "Baby girl, where do we keep the chemistry books? It's for an assignment."

"No, Dad. The book club is reading *Lessons in Chemistry.* It's fiction."

Dad gave me a scowl. "Are you sure? 'Cause I already ordered a kit on Amazon."

"I'm sure."

"Is it a movie?"

"I think it's a miniseries." I reached for the remote and pulled it up for him.

Dad lay back on the couch, breathing a sigh of relief, and put his feet on the coffee table. Ringo hopped up and curled into his side.

I was irritated so I went to my room. How did I get roped into operating those ridiculous community meetings? And if I'm in charge now, do we have to have those meetings at all? Can't I just do away with them? Why didn't I think of that at the meeting? I could have announced it was the last one. *Go live your lives and be happy.*

What we needed in case of an emergency was an email system so I could pass vital information to park residents without having to actually talk to any of them. I opened the notebook Agnes had left and thumbed through it. There was a long list of who owed lot fees. The list of who did not owe lot fees could fit on a stamp.

She also had entries on every resident in the park along with a list of what they were doing wrong. *Layla Virtue. Reclusive. Belligerent. No community spirit. Doesn't take her trash cans in by six P.M. on trash day. Grass always too long. Her father paid her lot fees for the next three years.*

Apparently, I was one demerit away from being kicked out. If only I'd known that before the meeting. This is what we in the police world called evidence before the fact. Because I was sure that one day Agnes was going to get murdered for nonsense like this.

Then there was the budget page, or should I say the bankruptcy page. Because there was no money. A community electric bill, water bill, and tax bill were all due at the end of the year. And I had just agreed to build a playground for a pig.

I looked down the column of names and addresses for the woman who I couldn't remember. Whimsy St. James. That was it. I knew it was something weird. She'd been living in the park for six years now. No infractions. How was that possible?

I climbed into bed and turned out the lights. Maybe tomorrow I could ask Nick how to get everyone in the park on email. That would give me an excuse to talk to him anyway. Unless he was mad at me. *Is he mad at me? What did I say?* It's usually women whom I offend and I have no idea how. Maybe he's mad that I moved over here and took Ringo with me. I hope not. I've got to find out soon because things just aren't the same without him.

* * *

The next morning, I woke up with Ringo across my legs. "Hey, buddy, what happened to your dog bed, huh? How about Ringo's bed? That looks comfy. Why don't we go get in that?"

Ringo gave me a groan that said he was fine right where he was, and I should be more tolerant of a little nerve damage.

So, I extracted myself out of bed with absolutely no help from the eighty-five-pound Lab. I took a spa shower with ten jets pummeling me with hot water. If you didn't mind the feeling of being trapped in a hurricane, you could be clean in less than a minute.

I dressed, put on some mascara, and headed to the kitchen looking for the box of Pop-Tarts I'd brought over from the trailer.

Dad was at the table, eating a bowl of Raisin Bran. "I fed the cat."

I pulled out the pastries and ripped open the sleeve. "Dad, we don't have a cat."

"Yes, we do, baby girl, and it was just in here."

I looked at the floor to where Dad indicated, and an empty plate sat. Ringo stood next to the plate, licking his mouth. "You're not helping this delusion, buddy."

There was a knock on the door. Dad and I looked at each other, wondering what to do. Nobody outside the park knew we lived here except Castinetto and the girls. I opened the door to find Marguerite wearing a lime-green sweater and a salty grin. Her rooster, that Dad had named Steppenwolf, hung from her body in a baby sling. I was still a little miffed about being railroaded last night so the pleasantries were not effusive. "What do you want?"

She handed me a piece of rough-edge notebook paper where she had printed a list of seven things that she wanted to do in her yard—including setting up a chicken coop, and a request for ten hens.

"What do you need ten hens for?"

She rolled her eyes. "Duh. Eggs."

"Don't they sell eggs in the store?"

"These eggs are better."

"The ones from the store don't make your yard smell like chicken crap."

She frowned at me. "Are you telling me no after you told everyone else yes last night?"

I sighed. "Let me give your request for Steppenwolf's brothel some thought, and I'll get back to you."

Coming up the walkway behind her, Foster was carrying an ancient Trapper Keeper binder while pulling a wagon. In the wagon was a miniature black pig dressed in a white sweater and a knit hat shaped like the bottom half of a turkey. "How you, Layla? I brought some ideas for Pippi's playground. You can tell she is very excited, especially about the castle."

Pippi gave me a squeal.

Marguerite passed them on her way down the sidewalk. "She's crabby, so good luck."

I took the binder and paged through it. "Foster, these are very elaborate plans. I'm not sure the Fairfax Children's Park has this extravagant of a setup."

The corner of Foster's mouth took a downward slant. "Layla, you promised. You said Pippi could have a playground."

"Well, yes—a seesaw and maybe one of those spinny things. Of course I'm on board with that. I'm just saying this"—I waved the binder—"might be a little aggressive."

Dad hollered from the table behind me, "Do you want me to put you in touch with Fawn?"

Oh dear God. "No! No. That's not necessary." I thumbed through the binder again. "It looks like Fawn's influence is already here anyway. I don't suppose you have any money to put toward this project, Foster?"

His expression went blank. "You said the community is going to pay for it."

"I don't remember saying those exact words."

Dad chimed in again. "It was implied. We all heard it."

"Yes, Dad. Thank you. Okay, Foster, let me have these for a few days, and then you and I will get together to discuss what we do next." *Maybe we could have the mother of all bake sales.* "Is that okay with you, Miss Snickelfritz?"

Pippi snouted a partially eaten apple and it rolled toward me in the wagon.

Foster interpreted that as "She brought you a thank-you gift."

"Well, thank you, Pippi." I took the apple, slightly used, from the wagon and placed it on the table by the front door.

We said goodbye, but not ten minutes later there was a thud and some scratching. This time Robin was at my front door, and when I opened it, she was whacking the frame with a stick. "Your house is not wheelchair accessible."

I looked at her and then looked at my steps. "That's because I'm not in a wheelchair."

She sighed peevishly and looked around my yard. "Yeah, but you're the management, and I have a complaint. And I should have easy access to you."

That email list has to be priority number one. "Okay. I've been management for twelve hours. Ramps don't appear overnight. What's the matter?"

"I just came to let you know, those people that you said could advertise their business in their yard, they live across the street from me. I shouldn't have to look at that monstrosity every day."

Dread inched its way up my scalp. "What did they do?"

Robin made a blasé face and rolled her chair back. "I'll let you head over there and see for yourself." She wheeled herself to her van and started the process of the lift gate taking her inside.

I grabbed my keys. "Dad, I'll be back in a little bit. Make sure you take your medicine." I got in my Jeep and drove around the lake toward Robin's trailer. I passed two cars and a couple on foot heading for my house. I feared that word had gotten around that the new owner was granting wishes.

I knew right away which lot we were talking about because the owners had placed a four-foot-by-six-foot neon green billboard in their yard advertising that they made custom signs and empanadas.

Myrtle Jean, Agnes, and Clifford were doing one of their daily laps around the lake. Agnes called out, "Good morning, Layla. Lovely day." They cackled as they disappeared between the trees.

I knocked on the door of the silver Airstream, but there was no answer.

Old Lady Henson came out of her front door one lot over. "Oh good. It's you. I hope you're going to do something about that eyesore."

"I will take care of it, ma'am."

She wrapped her crocheted shawl around herself and sniffed disdainfully. "Nothing like this ever happened when Agnes Harcourt was in charge. You can believe that."

"Yes, ma'am." A vibrating rumble caught my attention as a backhoe ambled down the road and stopped in front of her mailbox.

She waved the driver forward. "This way, Wendell. Everywhere you see grass, dig it up. I have to get the parsnips in the ground before Thanksgiving."

"Whoa!" I put my hands up and waved down the Bobcat driver. "I thought you wanted a little plot in the back for some tomatoes. You can't turn your entire yard into a vegetable garden. Half of that grass isn't even yours."

She shrugged. "Zucchinis need room to spread out."

My temple was starting to throb in that way it did when I was a beat cop. The vein spelled out a message in Morse code. *You should have known better.* "Ma'am, I should not have given you permission to plant a garden without getting all the details. That's on me. Can you please put this off until I can come up with a practical solution that won't tear up the yard and possibly break a water main?"

"When will that be?"

"Let me get through Thanksgiving."

Her lips pursed to the side. "What do I get if I don't make a big stink about this?"

"How about I'll absolve your past due lot fees?"

She pointed to the sky and drew a fast circle. "Wrap it up,

Wendell. I'll give you a call next week and we'll try again. Tell your momma I said thank you for the apple butter."

The driver saluted and threw the Bobcat in reverse.

Dad sent me a text message. **There are four people here for you with requests. At least there were when I started typing this—now there are six.** Then he sent me a birthday cake emoji.

I sighed. I'd been in charge half a day and I was ready to move away and start over on the other side of the country. I texted back. **I'll be right there**.

I wrote a message on the back of an envelope for the signage couple to call me and wedged it in their screen door. Then I drove back around the lake.

I passed Donna in front of her trailer sweeping her porch. She held my eye, and I was sure the message she was sending me was *You should have done the fundraiser.*

My phone dinged and I checked the screen then dropped it onto the passenger seat. I pulled into my driveway where a dozen park residents stood. Some had their arms crossed angrily. Others were waving papers and shouting about some grievance or other. One of them waved a pitchfork. Or maybe I imagined that. I passed all of them, marched into the house, and got the decorative box from my nightstand. I showed it to Dad who was still watching *Lessons in Chemistry*. "Was this expensive?"

He shrugged. "I dunno."

I took it into the kitchen, and with a steak knife, carved a slot into the top. Then I took it to the front porch and held it up. "Until I get email set up, submit your requests and complaints in writing and drop them in here." Then I set the box on the porch and got in my Jeep before they could rage against the machine.

I was the machine.

I had made a grievous error in judgment last night, but I had no time to deal with that now. Because on my way around the lake, Scarlett had texted me that she had cornered Abigail Keller at coffee, and if I wanted to question her, I'd have to come now.

Chapter 10

Sundrop Roasters was our pre- and post-AA spot. It smelled like burnt toast—which I was not a fan of—but had a passive-aggressive bookshelf, a giant teal couch, and lots of colorful armchairs and pillows to get lost in, which I liked. And a hundred paper stars hung from the ceiling lit up like Chinese lanterns at a festival.

Scarlett and Charisse were sitting on the couch with four drinks lined up on the surfboard coffee table. A husky brunette in an orange sweater was trapped in between them, her square glasses slightly fogged from the heat of stress.

Charisse flashed me a smile. "Hey, girl. Fancy meeting you here."

I put my purse down on one of the fuchsia leather chairs. "Oh you know. I just came for a caffeine fix. Who's this?"

The young woman who must be Abigail had the same confused and slightly stunned look on her face as a jumper I once talked down from the American Legion bridge.

Scarlett patted Abigail's knee, which startled her a bit. "This is a good friend of mine who used to take care of Ambrose before he accidentally spray-painted her car, Abigail Keller. Abby, meet Layla."

I took the seat across from her. Her eyes were flecked with gold and tinged with terror. "Hi, Abby. I feel like I've seen you somewhere."

She shrugged. "I don't know. Maybe in here? I usually stop in after yoga."

Scarlett grinned. "Isn't that funny? Here I was trying to make plans with Abby, but we never connected, and her Instagram feed shows that she's been coming in here every day after her yoga class down the street. What a funny coincidence."

Abby shifted uncomfortably in her seat and looked at the door like she was considering a prison break.

"That is a funny coincidence."

Charisse nudged a violet mug toward me. "They gave us one too many hot chocolates. Want one?"

"Don't mind if I do." I picked up the warm mug and cradled it in my hands. "Actually, you know what?" I looked at Abby. She steeled herself like she was about to negotiate her way out of a hostage situation. "I think I saw a reel that you were in on Instagram. You were with a group of women at one of my favorite bars." *Of course I never met a bar I didn't love.* "The Gibson. How were the Cupid Cocktails?"

Her wonky eyebrows twitched as one side of her lip curled. "I have no idea what you're talking about."

Charisse nudged her. "Sure you do, honey. Your girlfriend was getting married on Valentine's Day."

Her eyes widened and she cocked her head to the side. "Oh. That must have been Britta's bachelorette party. I don't remember anything from that day except she wanted to go on a bar crawl for an Instagram blast so she could gloat to her ex on social media that she was getting married."

I blew across my cocoa. "But you do remember the Gibson, don't you? Instagram specials?"

Scarlett pulled out her phone and held it up. "You know what? I think I have Britta's reel right here."

Abby watched the video for a moment then covered her eyes in horror. "I don't remember any of that. We went at it all afternoon. We were totally trashed by the time we were done, and I don't even know how I got home."

Scarlett chuckled. "I remember those days. Once I got so drunk I woke up in the Newark airport."

Charisse laughed. "That's nothing. I woke up in a taxi in front of some Indian guy's house after he'd gone off duty. His wife fed me breakfast and made him drive me home for free."

I snickered, then asked Abby, "Do you have any pictures from the bachelorette party?"

She shrugged. "I doubt it."

Scarlett reached for her hot chocolate. "Are you still seeing that boy you were with? *Chavon*, I believe? Did you ever tell your father you two were in the Poconos and not babysitting for me that weekend you went away? You were still in high school, weren't you?"

Abby's cheeks turned into two ripe apples. She pulled out her phone and started tapping and scrolling. When she got to the right date, she handed her phone over. "Why do you care so much?"

I started scrolling through her photos and lied like a perp in the interrogation room. "The Gibson was a favorite place of mine. I miss the old staff, you know? Nobody from back in the day works there anymore." I froze with my finger over the screen. "Well, almost no one."

A sudden flash of memory fired off. I was being led down a hallway by this woman. She opened the door for me and said, "Have a seat, hon. He's been waiting for you."

I turned the screen to show Scarlett and Charisse. They gasped. Serving Abby and her friends was the older redheaded waitress we'd met the other night.

I showed Abby. "Do you know this woman?"

She shook her head that she didn't.

"Can I get a copy of this?"

"Sure. I guess."

I took my phone out of my pocket and sent myself the photo from Abby's screen. Then I handed her phone back to her. I leaned against the seat and sipped my hot cocoa. "You all seemed to be partying pretty hard. I hope none of you drove in that condition."

Her eyes widened. "Wait a minute. Now I remember you. You're that cop who came over to the table and warned us not to drink and drive because we were getting too rowdy." After swiping through a couple of screens, she played a video that had not gone up on Instagram.

I was on the screen, looking menacing in my body armor. And very sober. Abigail and her friends were mocking me.

"Oooh, I'll take you in for public intoxication. Oooh. Don't come at me being all fierce because you gotta work on a Saturday afternoon. I'm getting married on Valentine's Day. Okay, Officer. This is my bachelorette party. We're not breaking any laws so back off."

One of the other women in the video frowned at the bride. "That's not funny, Britta. Knock it off. She's just doing her job. The bartender already warned us to quiet down, or he'd ask us to leave." Then she said to me, "We're taking Ubers."

Britta turned the phone back on herself. "Fine. Whatever. Can we buy you a drink to apologize, Officer?"

Off-screen I heard myself say, "I'm on duty. Just be careful."

The video ended. I sent myself a copy and I handed the phone back to her.

Abby stared at her hands in her lap. "I'm really sorry about that. We were so rude."

"It's fine. You've been very helpful."

She checked the time and clutched her purse. "I have to go. I have errands to run before my roommate gets home. Mrs. Weatherspoon, it was good seeing you. We'll have to do it again. I'll call *you* next time."

She flew out of the door and Charisse deadpanned, "I don't think she's gonna call you."

Scarlett's lips flattened. "Yeah, I'm pretty sure she blocked me."

We watched Abigail run across the parking lot to a little Mini Cooper. Scarlett rolled her eyes and yelled at the window, "If you don't want to be stalked, then don't put your every move on Instagram. No one needs to know what you ate for breakfast."

I nodded. "That's reasonable." I sipped my hot chocolate. "So, where is Bree? You would think she'd be here since that Instagram reel was her discovery."

Charisse's eyes darkened.

Scarlett's voice held a measure of sadness. "She's not answering my calls."

I pulled out my phone. "I'm texting her to tell her what we learned." The message said delivered but not read. That was a bad sign. Even when she was in her online classes, Bree still checked her phone like an actor waiting for a callback.

Charisse picked up her hot chocolate. "Girl, you know, that waitress bold-face lied to me. She said she was hired on Valentine's Day. Why would she do that?"

"There's only one way to find out. We have to go back."

Chapter 11

I DIDN'T WANT TO GO TO THE GIBSON WITHOUT BREE SINCE SHE was the driving force behind Operation Layla Remembers—her name for it, not mine. But she never answered any of our text messages, so we made plans to make plans Sunday night after AA.

Before I left the coffee house, I sent an email to the address for Astoria Holdings that Jorge had given me the other night. It bounced back, saying the mailbox was full. I tucked the napkin back in my purse until I knew what to do with it. Maybe Rami could track down the owner.

I stopped at Nick's trailer on the way home from the coffee shop. I couldn't stop worrying that something was wrong. The lights were off, but his car was still there. I banged on the door, and he yelled from inside, "I don't want to see anyone, Layla. Just leave me in peace."

"I'm worried about you. Is it the dog? Do you miss Ringo? I could bring him over."

No answer.

I stood on his front step wrapped in helplessness. "Come on, Nick. Just talk to me."

I heard voices coming up the road. Myrtle Jean Maud and Clifford Bagstrodt were out for a stroll. *That's cute. Are they a couple?* "Nick, you gotta come see this."

Clifford caught my eye. "Just the woman we wanted."

Uh-oh. "What's up, guys?"

They strolled up the walkway and approached Nick's front step. Clifford produced a clipboard and unleashed two crisp pages of notes. "We have a report of malfeasance for you."

"You have a what?"

Myrtle Jean gave me a grave nod behind a silver pair of cat-eye readers on a beaded chain. "Squirrels."

"Squirrels?"

Clifford made a pronouncement as serious as a crime scene technician reporting a mass-casualty event. "I'm afraid so. Someone on Buckingham has put out a squirrel feeder."

I looked from Clifford to Myrtle Jean to see which one would crack first because no way I wasn't being punked right now. They wore twin expressions of solemnity.

Myrtle Jean answered first. "I'm afraid it's true. And once you start feeding the vermin, you know what happens next?"

"They rate you on Yelp?"

Clifford rocked back on his heels and twitched his mustache. "You think this is a joke, missy? They bring diseases and procreate."

"I see. You do know that we live in the woods?"

Myrtle Jean removed her readers. "And just what does that have to do with the price of tea in China?"

"They don't actually need anyone to feed them. They have a near-endless supply of acorns alone."

Myrtle Jean and Clifford passed a look of horror between them.

Clifford asked her, "Are you thinking what I'm thinking?"

She gave him a solemn nod and her jowls made a gentle quiver of agreement. "We bring in the big guns."

Then Myrtle Jean turned to me. "We would like to formally request you bring in a bonded pair of falcons to keep the squirrel population at a reasonable level."

Without breaking eye contact with the dynamic duo, I back fisted the door behind me. "Nick. Please tell me you're hearing all this."

Silence.

Clifford shook the paper for me to take it.

It's not like we lived in a drug-addled neighborhood of domestic abuse and B and E. There was very little crime in the Pinecrest Mobile Home Park compared to most of Northern Virginia. And I would know. "I'm not interested in creeping around the park, hunting for people breaking the rules. As long as no one is hurting anyone else, let them do what they want in the privacy of their own homes."

Clifford and Myrtle Jean threw their heads back and laughed like I was a comedian at the DC Improv. Clifford tucked his pages back into his clipboard and gave it a good pat. "When we're overrun with vermin and you change your mind, don't say I didn't warn you."

Myrtle tossed her nose in the air and gave a disapproving sniff. "I can't stay and chat. I have a date tonight." Then the two of them were off. There was no telling how long it would take them to circle the lake if they didn't have to stop and write a violation report every few feet.

I took the ignored, beaten-up flyer about the park meeting from Nick's door and scrawled a note on the back for him to please call me and mentioned that I needed his help with something ASAP. Then I rolled it up and stuck it in the door handle.

I returned home to find Dad still watching *Lessons in Chemistry* before going to Agnes's book club. "So, what do you think of it?"

Dad paused the show and made a face. "Why is no one weirded out that this dog can talk?"

"I don't think anyone actually hears the dog, Dad."

"Uh, I just heard him right before you came in."

"I mean in real life. That dog is an actor playing a fictional dog . . . one who lets you know his thoughts."

Dad narrowed his eyes. "Well, I hope he got paid well. He had to learn a lot of lines."

I took out my phone and thumbed through my texts. "I'm sure you're right." I had a message from Paula reminding me of a last-minute gig she'd signed me up for to fill in with the Tristan Trio at some fancy country club. She said she'd left my outfit with my father. *It had better not be livestock related.*

"Did my manager leave something here for me?"

Dad pointed to my room. "It's on your bed. Is your gig at a Halloween party?"

A prickle of dread snaked through my stomach. "No. That was two weeks ago. Why?"

He shrugged. "'Cause I'm pretty sure you're going as Morticia Addams."

"Great."

I found a floor-length black evening gown that would fit Xena, Warrior Princess laying across my bed. It was covered in about fifty pounds of sequins. I texted Paula. **There is no way this is going to fit me.**

She texted back. **Non-negotiable. You have to match the others.**

Frickin' Paula.

With a groan and all the upper body strength that I had left, I climbed into the thing. It was like wearing a chandelier. The sleeves had their own zip code. I put on some makeup and slicked my hair back. I doubted my blue tips would blend in with the string trio I'd been signed up to accompany. I slipped on my highest heels to minimize how much drag I created and returned to the living room with a hiss of *shhhkkk shhhkkk shhhkkk* following me. "I feel like I'm walking through a swimming pool."

Dad paused with his Coke aloft and threw his head back and laughed.

I shot him a droll look. "Next time we go to the grocery store you're wearing this."

His amusement slid into alarm, and he clamped his lips shut. Ringo's tail stopped midwag, and he dropped his chin to his paws.

"I'll be back before midnight. I don't expect it to be a late one. I want you to have fun at book club, but remember to be careful."

"Would you relax. It's a bunch of old broads eating cake and talking about tearing down the patriarchy. How much trouble can I get into?"

"Half your songs would throw gasoline on that fire."

"It was the eighties. The chicks loved me."

"Well, they've been rethinking things. I'm nervous about you getting so active in the community when I'm not there to keep an eye on you. If word gets out that you're living here, we'll be surrounded by paparazzi and people with their hands out, and you won't be able to go anywhere."

I would love to be able to hide Dad in this house like a bank account in the Caymans, but I didn't want him to live the rest of his life like that. I wanted him to enjoy himself. Even in a book club where I knew he'd have no idea what was going on because no way was he ever gonna read a book.

Dad's lips pressed together like a duckbill. "Okay, Warden. Calm down. I'm just going next door. I'll be back in time to feed Bono."

"Bono's coming to dinner tonight? Here? I thought he was playing a festival."

Dad shook his head like he was talking to a toddler. "I mean Bono, the cat."

"We don't have a cat."

"Yes, we do."

"And if we did, you couldn't name him Bono."

"Why not?"

"Because all the other cats would make fun of him for being pretentious."

Dad considered my words and nodded. "You're right. I'll keep thinking of names."

"You do that." There was a knock on the door. I hoped it was Paula so I could give her a piece of my mind for dropping off this sequined tarp. Or at least ask to be paid by the pound. Except, when I opened the door, I found Detective Castinetto on my front porch.

His eyes took a long roll down the length of me. "Did you shrink in the wash or is there a bottom half joining you?"

"Har har. What do you want?"

Dayton's lip quirked just a smidge before he waved an interoffice envelope. "I have something the department wants your help with."

"What is it?"

"A case they've stalled on."

"Uhhh. I think not."

His eyes widened in confused surprise, like it had never occurred to him that someone wouldn't want to work with the police. "Why not?"

I picked at the sequins fighting for dominance on my shoulder. "Does the term *Internal Affairs* mean anything to you?"

His hand rested on his hip just over his badge. "Look. I don't like it either. I think it's a big mistake getting you involved. You didn't exactly leave the department on good terms. Have you even finished your court-ordered therapy?"

"Not gonna happen."

"And with that lovely attitude . . ." Castinetto sighed. His eyes rolled back, like he was fighting an internal battle just to be in my presence. When he'd collected himself, he took another approach. "Apparently, after all the help you gave us a few weeks ago with the McCracken homicide, the commissioner wants you to personally look into this case."

"Why?"

He wouldn't meet my eye. "This one is . . . challenging. Your special skills could be useful. And it's not like you'd be working for the police officially. You're just a concerned citizen asking questions, like the last time."

"The last time you said I was nosy."

He shrugged. "When it ends in an arrest, you're a concerned citizen, and you get a commendation."

"What's it about?" I reached for the folder, and he snatched it away.

"Another murder investigation. We're stuck. All the suspects have alibis, and there appears to be no motive."

"Then why do you think it was murder?"

"Because the guy was found in a Catholic church confessional with his head bashed in."

"Fair enough. But that still doesn't explain why me?"

Castinetto looked away. "He had enough heroin in his system to OD."

My stomach bottomed out. "So, it's my connections to Hurtado that you're after. Even though my entire team died—or appeared to have died—when I tried to take down the drug ring."

"Archie Wilkins had a lethal amount of heroin in his system. That falls under narcotics, which is your area of expertise."

"What about the new narcotics unit? Why aren't they looking into this?"

"That whole department is seriously understaffed and underfunded since Stratton Park. Half of the team is . . . gone."

"You mean dead."

"Well, yes. And no one wants to transfer in after what happened due to the bad press. The commissioner wants you to see what you can dig up. Unofficially."

Anger heated me like a sunburn. "Are you freakin' kidding me? The DEA team should be a top priority. Is he just going to let Hurtado and his scumbags have free reign on our streets if I don't get involved?"

And why did it have to be me? After the months of turmoil Internal Affairs put me through with their criminal investigation, they found nothing they could charge me with but still wanted to demote me. That was why I left. They were sending a message that they couldn't prove I was guilty, but they didn't think I was innocent either. It meant a lot to me that the commissioner believed I was innocent of orchestrating the sabotage that killed my team. Most of the cops from my old precinct were not as generous and they had a way of reminding me of their feelings on the matter.

Castinetto held up his hands. "I'm just the messenger. I don't want you to be involved. But if you still have informants on the inside, they could be useful. The department doesn't have the resources to cultivate another CI this late in the game."

I turned away from him so he couldn't see the despair I was wrestling with. I was out. And I wanted to stay out. I had more than enough problems of my own with Dad's illness, my sobriety, Nick's troubling behavior, and the ridiculous situation I'd gotten myself into with the trailer park idiots.

"I have this for you too." He pulled a small envelope out of the inner pocket of his suit jacket. "It's your photo. No one knows I looked into this for you other than Rami."

I snatched it from his hand.

"Okay, next time lead with that."

"Don't get your hopes up. Rami found nothing."

"What do you mean, nothing? It has to be doctored in some way."

"There are no fingerprints other than yours. And no, it isn't altered as far as she can tell but . . ."

"But what? Spit it out, Castinetto."

His neck tinged pink. "Look, I'm not judging you. You've been through hell and back. But are you sticking to your story that you didn't make this? Take an old picture of your boyfriend and put a phony election sign on it?"

Anger heated up my sequins and threatened to melt my polyester. "I told you I don't know the first thing about Photoshop, and now you think I'm so expert at it that I can fool Rami? She can deconstruct the most advanced deep fake, but she can't tell when an amateur layered on an election sign?"

"I've done some checking. I know you're friends with people with skills. You're no dummy, Virtue. I'm just concerned that you're letting your emotions lead you astray again. We don't want another meltdown."

He was about to get a meltdown, alright. I was about to combust all over him. "Go nuke yourself, Castinetto!"

I threw the door in his face. It wasn't until later that I realized I hadn't taken the folder he'd brought me to consult on.

Chapter 12

THE GRAND BALLROOM OF THE FOX CHASE COUNTRY CLUB HAD put on the Ritz. Linen-clad tables and plush, cream-colored carpeting with a green flourish surrounded a polished herringbone-patterned wooden dance floor. Each table had a hollowed-out white pumpkin filled with peach roses, pampas grass, and pheasant feathers as a centerpiece.

How is it that Paula only gets me upscale venues when I'm filling in for someone else? On my own, she sends me to the Seahorse Lounge, which hasn't had a good spruce since the Cold War.

I passed a chalkboard easel that had WELCOME INSTITUTE FOR MENTAL HEALTH written in fancy script and approached two identical older women in gowns that matched mine with the exception of theirs being appropriately sized for their large frames. They were setting up a harp and a squat poufy pink chair, which I imagined was called a tuffet, in the stage area. A plump Amazon with white hair and hazel eyes gave me a wide smile. Trapped in that giant body was the tiny voice of a child. "You must be Layla. I'm Tabitha Tristan—I play the harp, and this is my sister Tessa on the violin."

Tessa twiddled her large fingers. "Our sister, Tatiana, is home sick."

Tabitha put one hand on her sister's arm. "She knows that, silly. That's why she's here. I see you got the gown. Good. It's important for our brand that we match."

Tessa giggled. "Well, as much as we can anyway. You're about thirty years younger than us so that's bound to stick out."

Tabitha nodded at her sister. "Not to mention the hair. Well, we can only do so much, can't we, sister?"

She giggled in response. "Yes, you are so right, sister. After all, we are a triplet trio. Layla will just have to look like one of our daughters, won't she?"

"Oh yes. Yes, indeed."

My head was spinning from their banter. I couldn't imagine a third one just like them. I gave them both my best networking smile—at least that's what I call it when it's totally fake, but I want it to be genuine. "Thank you so much for giving me a chance. I will try to blend in with your violin and harp and just provide the background notes."

I eyed the harp. "You were of course aware that I play electric guitar?"

They both nodded with grins on their faces, and I had a vague memory of cartoon chipmunks pecking at the edge of my brain.

I imagined myself trying to play medieval Renaissance music on my Gibson Les Paul Special and sent a silent apology to the Rock & Roll Hall of Fame. *I guess there's a first time for everything.* "Where do you want me to set up?" I tried to hoist the combo amp over the tuffet, but sequins weighed down my arms.

One of the sisters—I'd already forgotten which was which—took the amp from me. "Oh yes. We've heard all about you from Paula. We think you'll be perfect for our little string trio."

I mumbled more to myself, "Oh k-aay."

"So, Layla, are you ready for the holidays? We've had our tree up since Halloween."

I plugged in my guitar and started a sound check. "I'm not even ready for Thanksgiving."

The sisters giggled like I was the funniest little munchkin. "Oh my. Thanksgiving is less than a week away; you'd better get cracking. When do you get your Christmas tree . . . or put out your menorah?"

They watched me with big smiles, mirroring each other's excitement. "If I get a tree at all, it's usually Christmas Eve when they're practically giving them away."

The light went out of their eyes, and they suddenly looked a little concerned that I might be a mental patient. One of them threw out her skirt and flounced onto her tuffet. "Maybe we should just get started since people are arriving."

I put my guitar case at the back of the stage and dragged myself to the microphone with nerves growing in my belly. "Do you have a set list or sheet music you want me to follow?"

The harp player cracked her knuckles. "Just try to keep up." She nodded offstage and the lights dimmed, encasing us in a soft pink spotlight. Then she plucked out the initial notes to "Paint It Black" on her harp and I knew I'd be okay.

The ballroom filled with tuxedos and evening gowns while we went through a classic rock repertoire that would make Dad weep. The ladies had a particular penchant for AC/DC and went right from "Thunderstruck" into "Back in Black." At one point Tessa whispered to me, "Would it be okay if we played Society's Castoffs' hit 'Sins of a Lover'? You do know it, don't you?"

Do I know my dad's biggest hit? Please. That's how I got him to buy me my first car. "Yes, I know it."

"Awesome. Why don't you take the lead?" The sisters nodded to each other, and I started the opening chords. It was going really well. If Eddie Van Halen played the harp, Tabitha Tristan would have given him a run for his money. Plus, I was in the zone. *Tonight just might be the best gig I've ever played.*

As soon as we cranked out the final notes, they wanted to play The Scorpions' "Still Loving You." My heart thudded to a stop like it had dropped out of my chest. "Can that be my one veto song?"

Tabitha grinned like I'd given her a compliment. "We don't have veto songs, honey. I gotta follow where the harp leads me." She plucked the strings a little harder to make her point.

With shaky hands, I tried to focus on the music. "Still Loving You" was my and Jacob's make-out song. I hadn't heard it since he died. Or supposedly died. *Is he dead?*

My head was swimming, and I was too slow to change chords. I plucked the wrong string, and the note rang in my ear like a twang. *Is there less oxygen in here than before? Who is playing with the air?* I looked around. *Is anyone else getting hot?*

I started to sweat, which made the polyester adhere to my body in unfortunate lumps.

I need to get out of here. Through my peripheral vision, I thought I saw Jacob walk past the stage on his way to another table and my stomach tried to leave my body through the sequins.

Tessa leaned toward me and played her violin in my ear to get me back on track. She had no idea what she was dealing with.

Another Jacob walked past me from a different direction. I couldn't seem to suck in my breath all the way. My ears were ringing, and I glanced at Tabitha. She frowned. I made a face that was supposed to say, *I'm sorry. Please don't beat me with your harp.*

The song ended and the lights dimmed. *Thank God. Intermission.* I took off my guitar and walked around the stage, trying to vacuum more air into my lungs.

Five waiters wheeled out carts with big copper pans on burners. In a flourish they added brandy to the pans and five pillars of fire erupted in front of me.

I felt myself going out, so I dove behind Tabitha and threw my head between my knees. Nothing happened but applause. *These people are sick. Don't they know they're in danger?*

One of the sisters whispered my name. "Are you okay back there? A little stage fright is okay, honey, but you don't need to hide."

The other sister added, "They're serving dessert, and they have a little presentation, so we need to leave the stage now. Do you need a drink?"

If you only knew. I opened my eyes and peered around the sisters' voluminous dresses. No one was paying any attention to me. They were being served something in fancy dessert glasses. I straightened up to my full height of about six inches shorter than the two triplets and slunk myself off stage behind them.

We took seats in the back of the room and the ladies ordered champagne. "Ginger ale for me, please."

One of them, Tessa, I think, leaned over to whisper, "Are you okay?"

"I'm fine."

I am far from fine.

She grinned and her eyes squeezed to little slits. "Okay, well, I don't believe you, but I won't pry." She looked at her sister and I thought I saw them pass an eye roll between them.

A white-haired man in a tuxedo tapped on the microphone. "Welcome, welcome to A Night of Thankfulness with the Institute for Mental Health. We want to thank everyone for supporting our annual fundraiser for PTSD awareness."

You have got to be kidding.

"Six out of every one hundred people are affected by post-traumatic stress disorder after being exposed to a traumatic event."

I scanned the crowd, worried that I would be pulled on stage as exhibit A. Calculating the distance to the exit, I was ready to run if I thought they were coming for me, but this dress would seriously slow me down. My body armor weighed less.

The white-haired man took the microphone off the stand and began to work the crowd. "People who are exposed to a prolonged, human-inflicted trauma are more impacted by PTSD."

He described the symptoms of PTSD, and while my personal checklist would have gotten me BINGO had we been playing, my mind flew to Nick and his recent downgrade in mood. I didn't know anyone who had experienced prolonged trauma more than he had from doing several tours of duty in the Middle East.

"Many of you know that this time of year is especially difficult for those dealing with depression. High holiday expectations can rarely be lived up to. Family and work events often bring added social and financial pressures or feelings of loneliness. Those already dealing with mental and emotional trauma can find themselves overwhelmed. The holidays can be a triggering event for drug and alcohol abuse and even suicide."

The tone in the room shifted. Or maybe it was just me as my spine turned to ice and I became hyperfocused on the speaker.

"When someone is acting out of character for how you know they usually are, it's a warning sign. Avoidance, isolation, losing interest in activities, changes in sleep. Increased irritability, aggression or risk taking. Even a dangerous sudden improvement in mood from depression to glee. All are red flags that you need to get involved. Silent cries for help that so often go unnoticed. Ask questions. Be a pest. On average, one hundred and thirty-five people commit suicide a day, with a growing vulnerability in older Americans and veterans. Twenty-two veterans a day die by their own hand."

The ladies next to me *tut-tut*ted. "Such a shame."

I checked the time. "When is the event over?"

One of the ladies whispered back, "We've been asked to play for another hour after the speech."

An hour. I wanted to run out of there and get to Nick as fast as possible. I knew something was wrong with him, but was this an omen of things to come, or was I being ridiculous? Maybe he was just tired of me bugging him.

Every cell in my body screamed that we needed to get to him. Fast.

"Have you ever considered billing as the Tristan Duo when your sister is sick?"

Identical faces scowled at me.

"Why would we do that?"

"Just wondering."

The man was asking for donations now. "And don't think the danger is over when the holidays end. Statistics show us that the suicide rate goes up on New Year's Day. Be good to yourselves, look out for each other, and give generously."

The audience began to clap. The two triplets started toward the stage. I heaved myself up to follow them and spent the longest sixty minutes of my life playing psychedelic rock, starting with an ode to Pink Floyd and "Comfortably Numb," which I thought was a really strange choice considering these were mental health workers.

When the ladies took their final bow, I couldn't get out of that ballroom fast enough. I pulled my plug and planted my guitar in its case, then hoofed it out to the Jeep and tossed the amp in the back. I tried calling Nick as I backed out of my spot.

No answer.

I hung up and tried four more times, which he probably never heard because by now he'd blocked me.

I sped out of the lot with my hands gripping the steering wheel. No matter how much weaving through traffic I did, I still caught every light. My fingers thrummed against the top of the door, willing the cars in front of me to get out of the way. I pulled into the park and skidded to a stop at Nick's trailer. Everything was dark.

Eleven-thirty. He's probably asleep.

Be a pest.

My pulse thundered in my ears as I approached the door and knocked. "Nick, it's Layla. I need to talk to you."

Silence.

Sweat ran down my back as I stood breathless at the door.

The wind stilled as if it knew something heartbreaking had happened, and it dreaded the moment I became a part of it.

I tried the handle. Locked.

My heart thudded in warning. *You can't handle this.*

I banged louder and my voice came out in a sob. "Nick! It's important."

I put my ear to the door, groping for any sound to confirm life. A footstep, a snore, a complaint about my meddling. All I received was deafening silence.

Chapter 13

SLEEP WAS NOT FORTHCOMING. NOT EVEN IN THE CLOUD BED. I should have called the police about Nick and made them do a wellness check. If something had happened, I would never forgive myself. I should at the very least have checked the Seahorse Lounge across the street instead of giving in to my fear that Nick would be so annoyed he wouldn't want anything to do with me anymore.

I finally crawled out of bed at six A.M. figuring sleep just wasn't gonna happen so I might as well go do something else. I padded to the kitchen and found Dad at the table eating a ham-and-cheese sandwich. "Hey, Dad. You're up early."

"I made lunch."

"It's the middle of the night."

Dad's lips flattened. "That explains why all I can find interesting on TV are old movies and something called *Saved by the Bell.*"

"*Saved by the Bell* is a classic."

Dad rolled his eyes. "I refuse to watch anything about a character named Screech. I thought it was just a dark afternoon."

"How do you explain that glowing white ball in the sky?"

One eyebrow raised. "Eclipse?"

"Okay. Where's Ringo?"

Dad shrugged. "I dunno. Isn't he with you?"

My brain couldn't make sense of what Dad was saying but my heart sounded the alarm and started to race. "No. He was here last night when I got home. Did you let him out?"

Dad put his sandwich down and stared at me, his face ashen and his eyes wary. "I don't think so. I went outside to check the mail earlier, but I don't think he went with me."

I called out, "Ringo! Rin-go! Here, boy!"

Dad yelled, "Treat! Treat!"

Nothing.

I started to cry—which was ridiculous. I mean, I hadn't even looked for him yet. Why was I getting so upset? I threw the front door open and yelled, "Ringo!"

I was pacing the front yard in the dawn light calling his name like a maniac.

Dad put his hand on my shoulder. His voice calm and reassuring like when I was seven and lost the stuffed kangaroo I couldn't sleep without. "I'm sure he hasn't gone far. Let's go look for him."

I ran inside and grabbed the keys, pushing the remote start. Dad and I climbed into the Jeep and backed down the driveway, our eyes peeled for a black Lab in the shadows. "Ringo!"

"Where are you, you scoundrel?"

We crawled around the lake calling him every few seconds, my feeling of dread building like a pot about to boil over. "What if something happened to him? Aren't there coyotes around here? What if he got hit by a car—oh no, Dad. What if he's on the side of the road hurt?"

"Whoa. Just calm down. There's no traffic over here. Don't let yourself go there." Dad blew out a frost-laden breath. "I saw a show about how sometimes when people move, their pets get confused and go back to the old house. Maybe Ringo's at the trailer. Let's go look there."

"That's a great idea."

We slow-rolled to the old trailer in silence, desperate to find a black dog sitting on the front porch, but our porch was empty. I threw the car in park as a tear slid down my cheek. *I knew I'd be a bad mom. I should never have taken him from Nick. I ruin everything.*

Steppenwolf ran out to the Jeep and gave a half crow. Marguerite emerged through the yard behind him. "Hey, Don. What you doin' over here?"

"We're looking for the dog, doll. Have you seen him?"

A sharp bark drew my attention several feet away. There was my dog. Wagging his tail and grinning at me from under Nick's trailer. He hopped up on the porch, looked back at Nick's door, and pawed it.

Dad spoke through a laugh. "Hey, hey. There's the rascal."

"Can you hang with Marguerite until I get back?"

"Sure thing, hon."

I jumped out of the Jeep and ran to Ringo, wrapping my arms around his neck, burying my face in his fur. "Why did you leave me? I was so worried. You could have been hurt. Don't ever do that again."

Ringo licked my face. Then he looked at Nick's door and whimpered.

I rapped sharply on the door, partly out of desperation, partly from anger. "Enough, Nick! I don't care that it's early. Open up or I'm breaking a window!"

The knob turned and the door opened just enough for me to see that Nick was wrecked. He was wearing dirty sweats and a rumpled green bathrobe. His pale blue eyes were bloodshot and sunken into dark circles, his face ashy beige. He hadn't shaved in days. Nick was drop-dead gorgeous, but the man before me was practically skeletal.

"My God, Nick."

Ringo pushed his way past him into the trailer.

"Look, Layla. I've been working a lot of long nights. Last night I drank too much and passed out. I'm not good company right now."

I stared at him in silence for a moment. "No."

I pushed in under his arm and entered his trailer, ignoring his protests. Someone had turned over his bookcase, and all his tech manuals were open, lumped in a pile on the floor. There was a fist-sized hole in the wall next to his desk, and the photo of his platoon lay smashed on the table. A pile of glass shards sat in a dustpan next to the broken frame. I looked into his eyes and saw shame. I recognized it immediately. I'd seen it many times in the mirror.

Ringo shoved his snout into Nick's hand like it was made of bacon.

"Sit down. I'm making you some tea. Do you have tea?"

Nick nodded unenthusiastically and went to the couch, Ringo glued to his side.

I went into his kitchen and filled the teakettle. Dirty dishes were piled on the counter. A bowl of half-eaten oatmeal was doing its best to turn into concrete. I found a clean mug and a box of Lipton. While the water heated, I emptied the dishwasher and refilled it, scrubbed the counters, and took out the trash. "Do you take milk?"

I opened the refrigerator and found it empty.

"Never mind." I put two scoops of sugar in the mug and filled it with hot water over the tea bag. Then I plopped a spoon in it and went to the living room.

Ringo was lying in Nick's lap like a giant furry baby, his head on Nick's shoulder. My heart broke a little bit more.

I set the mug on the table in front of Nick and cleaned up the rest of the broken glass. I found some crackers and peanut butter in the mostly bare pantry and made some little sandwiches with them. Then I took the plate out and set it next to the tea he hadn't touched.

Ringo eyed the peanut butter but laid his head back on Nick's shoulder.

"What's going on, Nick?"

He breathed through a ragged sigh.

I picked up the tea, blew across it, and put it to his lips. "Drink."

He flicked his eyes to mine and blew on the tea and sipped.

"How long you been wearing those sweats?"

"It's too late to wash them; they can only be burned now."

"That's what I thought."

He took the mug from me and sipped again.

"Are you suicidal, Nick? Are you planning something?" My voice broke. "Because I'm not okay with that."

His eyes softened but he didn't look at me. "No. I just . . ." He trailed off.

"What?"

His voice cracked. "One of my platoon mates killed himself a few days ago. That makes four of them now. Gone."

My eyes welled with tears. I put the tea on the table and took his hand in mine, weaving our fingers together. "I'm sorry."

He nodded. "This is a rough time of year. We didn't come home the same people who left. No one understands. That's a hard change for parents and wives. They want big family gatherings where everybody is happy." His words strangled in his throat, and he stroked Ringo's fur. "Some of us can't manufacture happy where it doesn't exist."

More than anything I wanted a word to make it all better. But if I'd had one, I'd have used it on myself a long time ago. My feeble attempt at comfort would only fall short so I didn't even try. I squeezed his hand.

He squeezed mine back, but his eyes didn't meet mine.

We sat in silence until Ringo whimpered and gave me a nudge. "You don't have to walk through this alone."

Nick gave me a weak lip twitch that he was trying to pass off as a grin.

"And Ringo has obviously decided to return to his birth father and help by letting you cradle him like a huge baby."

Nick breathed out a sincere chuckle. His free hand stroked Ringo's ear. "I'm sorry I've been avoiding you. I just need some space. I never wanted you to see . . . all this."

"When I woke from a night terror in your yard in my underwear we slid way past all of this."

He rolled his eyes to mine and the grief there threatened to pierce my heart.

I held his hand, rubbing the back of it with my thumb. "You think I haven't been flat on my back looking up at the bottom? I've wanted to end the pain many times. I didn't believe there was anything that could bring me joy ever again. But I was wrong. Because then I met you. My life is so much better now because you're in it. I don't want to lose you."

Nick tightened his grip on my hand. "I'm not going to do anything. It's just really hard right now."

"Why don't you come stay with me for a few days? I'm just across the lake. I have a whole loft above me that is probably decorated for Cinderella, but if you look past that I'm sure it's not horrible."

His eyebrows dipped, his expression the closest I'd seen to the old Nick in days.

"Oh yeah. You think I'm kidding, but you haven't met Fawn, Dad's interior designer to the wealthy elite and Dr. Seuss."

Nick chuckled—for real. "No, I'm not up for being around anyone. I'll be fine. I'm just tired."

I stood, a clutching ache of worry robbing me of the sliver of peace I so desperately wanted. "Okay. I understand. But please. Please. If you feel like you are spiraling or having dangerous thoughts . . . Please come to me. Just so you're around someone who can be there for you and keep you from doing anything stupid."

He nodded. "I will."

"And text me every day so I know you're okay. Promise?"

"I promise."

Ringo let out a heavy sigh and rolled his chocolate eyes to mine. *I feel you, buddy. I'm not buying it either.*

I tried to steel my voice to hide the emotion that threatened to overwhelm me. "And in the meantime, could you please keep Ringo for a few days? I have some errands to run, and a couple holiday gigs, and I don't want him home alone in the new house."

Nick's expression said that he didn't believe a word I was saying but he'd go along with it. "Sure. I can do that."

"Okay." I headed for the door. "And eat those crackers. God didn't make you this hot to waste away."

He snorted. "Yes, dear."

I closed his door behind me and burst into tears.

Chapter 14

"ERKA, ERKA!" STEPPENWOLF STRUTTED OVER TO NICK'S PORCH and pecked me on the toe.

"Ow! How would you like to be made into nuggets?"

A sandy-haired rookie cop, whom I had not seen since I assisted with the coffee shop takedown of the birthday party clown killer, leaned around the side of my trailer to peer at me across the grass. "Is that you, Officer Virtue?"

I quickly wiped my eyes. "What do you want, Beasley? Shouldn't you be off shadowing Castinetto through Northern Virginia's finer diners and drive-throughs?"

His face broke into a crooked grin. "He's moved up to Bob Evans and Freddy's Frozen Custard."

"Oooh-la-la."

Adam chuckled and held up an interoffice folder. "He said he forgot to give you this last night."

I tromped through the fallen leaves over to my trailer and took the folder. "I thought he didn't trust me."

He hooked his thumbs onto his utility belt. "You know how he is—Mr. Suspicious. My uncle says Castinetto once locked his own mother in the interrogation room until she confessed to littering."

I broke the seal on the folder. "He does like to be in charge. I'm surprised he'd go along with the commissioner seeking my help with an investigation."

"My uncle has faith in you. He wants to give you a chance to prove yourself."

"I didn't realize the commissioner knew my name other than it being attached to the Stratton Park scandal."

Adam toed a clump of weeds with his boot. "Not everyone believes you were responsible for Stratton Park." Adam's eyes narrowed and he nudged the edge of my recycling bin. "And well, those that do, think consulting on a case will keep you too busy to be nosy and do your own investigating."

"The department overestimates my interest in clearing my name."

"Detective Castinetto just thinks it's wrong to take the case away from good officers to involve someone with . . . your issues . . . who isn't even on the force anymore."

"Well, that's rude, but whatever."

His eyes grew wide, and he waved his hands like he was trying to erase the words hanging in the air. "Not that I agree with him, mind you. Besides, I think he has his own agenda. He's been having a lot of closed-door meetings with the captain." He bit his lip. "I probably shouldn't have told you that."

I thumbed through the investigation documents. "Nothing I didn't already know, Beasley."

"Whatever you said to him yesterday really wound him up. He's been moping around the station like his best friend died."

"From what *I* said?"

Adam nodded. "He keeps muttering about not doing you favors anymore. What the heck did you ask him to do?"

I tucked the papers back into the folder. "Nothing."

"You know, if you ever need anything from the department you can ask me. I owe you a lot, Officer Virtue. I'm sure if things hadn't gone the way they did I'd have been on the narcotics team with you. And you know I want to help clear your name if I can."

"I appreciate that, Beasley, but it's all under control. Think of your own career and don't get singed by the dying embers of mine."

Adam's radio squawked and he responded that he was en route to an accident around the corner. "Gotta go. See you around, Officer Virtue."

"Later, Beasley." I considered collecting Dad and going home to look at the crime scene photos, when Steppenwolf assaulted me with another half crow. Then he kicked some dirt at me and pecked my recycling bin.

Marguerite came around the corner shaking a tumbler of dried corn made out of a plastic two-liter Pepsi bottle. The rooster took off running in her direction. "Layla, whatchu doing over here so early?"

I tucked the manila envelope under my arm. "Nunya."

She clicked her tongue. "You are sour. This is why you don't get huevos rancheros with me and Don."

I looked past her and past the screened-in porch to where Dad waved from Marguerite's picnic table. He lifted a fork and gave me a thumbs-up.

"Sure. It could be that. Or maybe it's because I'm not a good-looking wealthy bachelor."

Splotches of pink crept to Marguerite's cheeks. She tossed her long silky black hair and gave me a one-shoulder shrug. "I dunno that he's rich."

I narrowed my eyes at the Latina. "Your huevos are getting cold."

She made a rude hand gesture and wiggled back to her yard, Steppenwolf pecking at her heels.

I took out my keys and opened the trailer door. I would look at the police report here while Dad was wined and dined by Lake Pinecrest's plus-sized Sofia Vergara. I'd only moved out three days ago and somehow my bare little trailer no longer felt like home.

It was stuffy. And sad. I felt like I was intruding on someone else's domain. Someone with no personality who loved the color gray.

I dropped my keys on the empty TV stand inside the door. The TV was in my bedroom over in the fairy-tale cottage. One of the only things I owned that made the trip around the lake. I'd hung it over the fireplace in place of those flowerpots—don't tell Fawn.

I grabbed a grape soda from my emergency stash in the fridge and took a seat on the gray couch. Removing the police report from the envelope, I spread the pages across the flag stone coffee table.

Homicide was two weeks into the investigation when they'd hit a wall. *I don't know what the commissioner expects me to find if Castinetto's team couldn't find it.* I slipped Castinetto's business card off the paper clip and into my purse.

An eerie shiver caressed my neck as I read through the incident report and tried not to think about what I was actually doing. Being a cop was a part of my past life. Now here I was again, playing a detective. Imposter syndrome punched me in the gut while the shame of losing my team flew at me in a sharp burst of regret.

Name: Archie Wilkins. Married. White. Male. Date of Birth: October seven, 1966. Employment: Pixieland Academy Private School. Teacher. Manner of Death: Homicide. Location of Incident: Our Lady of Mercy Catholic Church.

There were quite a few crime scene photos attached. I went through them several times looking for anything that could have been missed. Poor Archie was definitely killed in the church and moved into the confessional postmortem. Blood spatter doesn't lie.

Weren't Catholics usually given a few Our Fathers and Hail Marys to reset their souls back to zero? "Jeez, Archie. What could you possibly have confessed to get this kind of reaction?"

Archie Wilkins was found bludgeoned to death with a giant golden candlestick in the penitent side of the confessional booth in what was looking like a twisted Roman Catholic version of Clue.

He still had his watch—a fancy German brand with an inscription—and his wallet with a couple hundred dollars and a few credit cards. The church donation box was apparently untouched, presuming it only contained thirty-six dollars, seventeen cents, and a stick of Big Red cinnamon gum before Archie was killed.

He was discovered by the priest, Father Gary Matthews, as he returned from doing visitation at Fairfax Hospital. A handwritten note on the side of the report said, "The priest's alibi checks out."

Other people of interest who had been interviewed were the church secretary, Archie's wife and daughters, and Archie's coworkers at the primary school. No motives. Everyone loved Archie.

Funny how murder victims are always the most loved people in every community.

The tox screen showed a lethal amount of heroin and fentanyl in Archie's system, but he'd been bludgeoned before it had stopped his heart or there would have been no blood at the crime scene.

Did he take the heroin himself right before someone whacked him over the head? Or did the killer administer the heroin afterward? And why?

My phone buzzed and I pulled it out of my back pocket. It was a text from Scarlett. **Can you come to the morning meeting? Something is up with Bree.**

I sent her a reply. **What's wrong with her?**

She's ghosting everyone. If she doesn't show, we're taking the meeting to her.

Icy fingers of fear reached around my heart once again. **I'll move heaven and earth to be there.**

Which in this case was just a matter of collecting the crime scene papers and getting Dad out of Marguerite's clutches.

I locked the trailer and placed the empty grape soda bottle in the recycling bin for Steppenwolf to spar with later. Then I walked back to Marguerite's. Dad was laughing at something she'd said as she topped off his coffee.

"Hey, baby girl. You wanna try this cafay campeche?"

"What?"

Marguerite playfully smacked his arm. "*Café con leche*, Don."

Dad breathed out a laugh. "What she said."

"I'm sorry I can't. We gotta go."

Dad picked up the coffee and downed it in one gulp. "Delicious, doll."

Marguerite giggled at Dad, then cast me some stink eye. "Well, I'm sorry you have to go so soon."

"He's been here all morning. He can come back and play another time. I have to get to a meeting."

Dad's eyebrows lifted. "The kind of meeting I can go with you on?"

I nodded. "As soon as we get you . . . spruced up."

Dad passed a look to Marguerite. "She means disguised."

I sighed. "Ixnay, Dad."

Marguerite grinned. "You want to borrow the outfit I wore to my niece's quinceañera? I was more petite back then."

"Is it a dress?"

She shook her head. "Nope. Pants and a jacket. Very tasteful."

Dad shrugged. "Sure, doll. That'd be great. You know how the girl overreacts to me going out in public."

I was slightly irritated at the dig, and I would have told him so in the Jeep along with a reminder that we don't tell the trailer park ladies our private business. Then I saw him emerge from Marguerite's wearing a hoochie mama outfit and all was forgiven.

Chapter 15

I EVENTUALLY STOPPED LAUGHING, AND WHEN I CAUGHT MY BREATH, I decided Dad's fancy special occasion pantsuit had been penance enough. Mostly.

Marguerite had dressed Dad in shiny silver bell-bottoms with a flashy red tank top and matching sequined jacket. She'd put his long gray hair up in a side twist and clipped it with an enormous red flower.

Dad pouted all the way to the Jeep. The irritation creased across his forehead, making him scowl. He glanced at me and rolled his eyes before climbing in.

"Whatcha wearin there, Don?"

He smacked his lips. "I dunno. It looks like something Charo wears in her act. A little more eyeshadow and I'd look like Bowie. I'm having flashbacks to that gig we played in Amsterdam." He picked at the silver lamé hip-huggers. "What is this made from? A space blanket?"

Another tinkle of laughter escaped from my throat. "At least you got that bolero jacket to cover your plunging neckline."

Dad pulled at his tank top. "I must have a whole box of Kleenex shoved in here."

I backed out of the driveway and headed for the main road, trying to see through the tears. "I think I busted a prostitute in that same outfit. Didn't Marguerite say she wore that to her niece's quinceañera?"

Dad pulled down the visor mirror and pursed his lips. "I don't know what that is, but it must be some kind of Latin disco. I'm pinned out the wazoo."

"Well, what'd you expect?" I turned on the highway and glanced at his waist. Marguerite had attached safety pins every couple of inches to keep the voluptuous pants on my father's love handles.

He shifted his weight and rubbed the side of his stomach. "I think that gal forgot to close one of 'em. Something's poking me right in the breadbasket."

"I'll take a look when we get to the meeting. Maybe I can move them around."

He reached into his cleavage and pulled out a lipstick. He puckered his lips and applied a thick coating of bright red before making an air kiss to blot them together.

I pulled out my phone at the light and took his picture, sending it to the girls along with the message **On our way.** I didn't check it for the rest of the drive, but the constant pinging of return messages told me Charo had created a stir.

We parked in the side lot instead of using the valet. Dad didn't have his wallet, and I could have had ten wallets, but they'd all be empty.

Dad strutted through the lobby toward the AA room as hotel guests going to breakfast stopped to stare. I gave a little wave to the concierge who by now knew us as meeting people.

Scarlett and Charisse were camped on the first row with their eyes glued to the door. They both erupted in ginormous smiles as Charo 2.0 crossed the threshold.

Charisse shook her head and gave Dad a long appreciative look. "Well, just look at that."

Dad gave a spin before alighting on the chair and demurely crossing his legs.

Bree ran in from the hall, breathless. "Did I miss Aunt Trixie? Oh. My. Lord." One hand flew to cover her mouth, and she giggled. The sound warmed me through, and judging from the looks on Scarlett's and Charisse's faces, they were as relieved as I was.

Dad nudged me in the side. "I'm getting cookies. If I have to come out dressed like a cruise ship dancer, I'm having as many as I want."

"Help yourself, *Aunt Trixie.* I'll get us some cocoa. Okay, *Aunt Trixie?*" I gave Dad a nudge.

At first he raised an eyebrow that said, *What the heck are you talking about?* But then the lights came on and Mrs. Doubtfire emerged. "Ooooh, cocoa would be lovely, dear. Thank yooo."

Dad chatted up half the room in his Aunt Trixie voice while I joined the girls with the cocoa. "I finally talked to Nick."

Scarlett passed me a cookie. "What was his deal?"

"One of his platoon mates committed suicide. He's not in a good place, but I can't get him to accept my help."

Charisse put her hand on my back. "I can't imagine what he's going through. Or what he's putting you through. You must be so scared."

Bree's eyes darted between us, and she seemed to shrink into her chair.

I nodded. "And we got Dad's doctor's report Thursday afternoon. It wasn't good."

Scarlett watched Dad trying to figure out the hot cocoa dispenser before Jonathan stepped in to help. "How fast do they think he'll decline?"

I shook my head. "She won't say. Apparently, it varies. Getting out is good for him, even though cookies are not."

Bree frowned. "Aww. He loves cookies."

"I'm not taking them away. My father has had a lifetime of getting what he wants whenever the mood strikes. Trying to change that now will only frustrate him. He knows he's forgetting things, but so far, it's a mild decline from his usual burnt-out spaciness, so it's not causing him a lot of distress. I know he's scared though. It's why he'd rather stay with me than move back to his mansion."

Jonathan called the Saturday morning meeting to order so Dad sashayed over to take his seat. I handed him a cup since he'd forgotten his at the table.

"What's that?"

"Hot cocoa."

His eyes lit up. "Oooh, they have cocoa?"

I smiled and nodded, having just watched him drink half a cup while talking to Varish. "Isn't that nice?"

Charisse raised her hand that she wanted to share, and she took to the front of the room. "Hi. I'm Charisse and I'm an alcoholic. I've had a rough week. One of my dearest friends seems to be struggling. She's been hiding from me, and she won't let me help, and that's caused a lot of anxiety. And with anxiety comes all the old temptations."

Scarlett nodded solemnly while Bree stiffened beside me. We all knew Charisse was talking about her, but she wasn't being passive-aggressive. Just honestly sharing her struggles. One of the challenges with making friends inside the program was that they became both your source of support and your source of trials. It was a delicate line to share your struggle when someone in the room was causing it.

It was also why I had no intention of sharing my struggles with Dad's dementia with him sitting right in front of me. One or both of us was bound to start crying and I didn't want our mascara to run.

Charisse didn't look our way until she changed the subject. "In other news, I thought my divorce was moving along pretty amicably. But then the other day I went home to an empty house. And I don't mean empty in that my grown kids weren't there, and Michael wasn't home. I mean empty in that Michael has stolen all my furniture. I still have a few things that came from my mother when she passed on, and the things I came into the marriage with, but all my furniture is gone. I had to have my locks changed. How am I supposed to go home and sit in an empty room and stare at our family portrait? What am I supposed to do with the china we bought together as newlyweds?"

Scarlett leaned into me with a devilish grin. "If you have a shotgun I have an idea for the china."

"Uh-oh."

Charisse continued, unfazed. "Thank God I got sober for me and not to save my marriage because I'd have drunk a vat of wine over the last couple of days if that were the case. The holidays are gonna be rough."

Charisse took her seat and Scarlett whispered, "We should go shopping after the meeting. We can fill your house with new things you like."

Charisse nodded. "Let's do it. Won't that be fun, Bree?"

Bree gave a tight nod. Her arms locked across her chest. "Sure."

Charisse nodded. An unmistakable sadness returned to her eyes. "It's a date."

Bree was quiet while a few more of the regulars shared. Tapping her foot and occasionally shaking her head like she was having a conversation only she could hear.

Varish finished his share and headed for his seat. Bree shot up to the front, nearly knocking him over. We braced ourselves. "My name is Bree and I'm an alcoholic and drug addict."

"Hi, Bree."

"This is a very hard time of year for my family. It's the anniversary of my brother's death."

Scarlett muttered, "Oh no."

"My parents are trying to make the holidays special, but I know his death is at the front of all our minds. I've been struggling with a lot of guilt." She looked at Charisse. "I know I've made everyone worry, but I just need some space right now. Everything is fine. I need time with my family to grieve. I'm allowed to have that."

She didn't make eye contact with any of us as she returned to her seat. I had the nagging feeling that what she shared was dangerous. We all deserved time to grieve, but isolation was the breeding ground for temptation. And Bree's share had more than a dull edge of passive aggression to it. Something was wrong. And it went deeper than she was letting on.

Dad raised his hand, and I felt the room close in on me. Oh no no no no. What's he gonna say? Does he remember who he's supposed to be? *What could go wrong? Pretty much everything.*

He took to the front and cleared his throat. "Hello, my name is . . ."

The four of us called out in unison, "Trixie!"

Dad grinned and gave us a thumbs-up and changed his voice to a very passable Julia Child. "Trixie Hamm with two M's. I'm an alcoholic."

"Hi, Trixie."

"I've been clean and sober for three years now. Joining AA was the best decision I ever made. I could never have done it alone. I spent most of the eighties high and sometimes I didn't know what town I was waking up in or what hotel I was being kicked out of. My manager threatened to quit on me once a week. When I got too dangerous to be fun, many of my friends turned their backs on me. Then a buddy of mine invited me to my first meeting. He probably saved my life.

"But now I'm having memory problems."

Dad glanced my way with a look that asked if that was okay to share and I gave him a nod.

"My biggest fear is that I'll forget my daughter and the life we've had together. And that I'll forget I'm sober and start drinking again. That's why I live with my . . . Layla. She'll keep me straight. She's used to putting other people's needs ahead of her own. The first to rush into danger and the last to move to safety. I hate that I'm going to be a burden on her. I want to do all I can to make her life better for after I'm gone. I love her more than words can say. She's my rock and I trust her with my life."

My heart stung in my chest and I wanted so badly to do a better job of keeping him safe.

Dad gave a wide grin to the room of recovering alcoholics while I sobbed into my napkin. He gave me a curious look as he approached his seat, his silver lamé bell-bottoms making a *swish swish* as he moved. "Did I say something wrong?"

I grabbed his hand. "Not at all. You did good, Aunt Trixie."

His opinion of my abilities was a little inflated. I could barely take care of myself. As each day passed, I could hear the tick-tock of dread getting louder, warning that when things got tough, I would let him down. I would let them all down.

Chapter 16

We piled into the Jeep to take Dad home so he could change out of his Ziggy Stardust clothes—his words. Plus, he was fading fast. It had taken all of his energy to share at AA.

"Baby girl, did we ever find the dog?"

"Yeah. He's at Nick's house."

"Oh good. Pick up some cat food at the store while you're out. That rascal stole the ham out of my sandwich the minute my back was turned."

Scarlett leaned forward from the back seat. "You have a cat?"

Dad answered, "Yes" at the same time that I said, "No."

I flicked my eyes to the rearview mirror and sent a silent message to the ladies in the back seat.

I pulled up to the cottage and the ladies were stunned for a beat. After Dad said goodbye and disappeared into the house, Scarlett said, "Wow," in that way that meant *What the heck am I looking at?* "Look at that roof."

Bree's eyes grew to saucers. "That. Is. Fabulous. Is that Tinker Bell's lantern by the front door?"

"Yep."

"What does it look like on the inside?"

"It's just as striking as the outside. Trust me. You'll have to come back when Dad isn't worn out, and I'll show you details that would make Tim Burton giddy."

Charisse nodded silently, like she was trying to think of just the right words. Finally, she went with, "It's like one of the houses in Marie Antoinette's Hamlet in Versailles."

She wasn't fooling anyone with that diplomatic answer. "I think you mean the Mother Goose House in a theme park."

Charisse breathed through a laugh.

Bree pressed her hand against the window. "I love it."

Scarlett moved up to the front seat. "And you say his interior designer did all the work?"

I put the Jeep in reverse. "Yeah. I suspect she was on hallucinogens. I still haven't been up in the loft."

Bree asked, "Why not?"

"I'm afraid. And I've been preoccupied with Nick, and Dad, and the community meeting where, somehow, I became in charge of everything, including building a playground for a pig, and the Thanksgiving potluck that I wasn't even going to. Then Dad told everyone that we'd bring the turkey. I can't tell if it's the dementia or the past drug use, but he seems to be under some delusion that the trailer park people are family."

Bree smiled at me in the rearview mirror. "That's kind of nice though, isn't it? I mean you have all those people to be with."

Scarlett snorted. "Spoken like someone who has never made a big holiday dinner on their own. Graham is determined to have the full Norman Rockwell experience. And now he's invited his parents to come all the way from Knightsbridge in London. I don't know anything about roasting a turkey. The one time my mother tried to make a turkey, we found the bag of innards still inside after it was cooked. We were so grossed out we couldn't eat it. That was the year of the ramen Thanksgiving."

Bree sighed wistfully. "My mother used to make the big dinner. My grandparents would come. Uncle Phil and Aunt Carol and their three kids." She stared out the window as we passed a strip mall that had set up a Christmas tree lot. "Her heart isn't in it this year. Dad suggested we order a family meal from one of the grocery stores for the three of us. How sad is that?"

Seeing as how that was my plan A, it didn't sound half-bad to me at all.

Charisse breathed softly. "Maybe we're putting too high of an expectation on ourselves to make it the perfect holiday for our loved ones. I've somehow gotten roped into making a full Thanksgiving dinner for the kids who are stopping by for *two whole hours* on their way to Michael and Dollie's. What am I supposed to do with an entire turkey after they leave? And where are we supposed to sit? Michael stole the dining room set. Maybe I should just get Boston Market pot pies and folding chairs and call it a day."

I pulled into the furniture store lot and turned off the Jeep. "Worst-case scenario, we buy you a Ping-Pong table and you can make the kids toast and popcorn."

Charisse flashed me a wide smile. "That's totally my new plan."

The moment we walked in the door, we were accosted by a hungry-looking salesman whose name badge read STEFANOS. We begged off and said we'd like to look around for a while. We did the first lap in awkward silence, the sadness of what we were there for—the dissolving of a marriage—weighing on us all. On the second lap, Charisse took notes on the back of an envelope while Scarlett and I gave commentary on which pieces we thought worked together while Bree shuffled meekly behind. We asked her a few times what she thought of this or that, but she'd only shrug and look away. By the time we were back at the front door, Bree broke down in tears.

"I'm sorry for how I acted at the meeting. I know you were just sharing what you were going through, and I shouldn't have been such a butt."

Charisse pulled the girl into a hug. "It's fine, honey. We are all just worried about you."

Scarlett immediately joined them. "And isolating isn't the answer. You can grieve just fine with us close by."

Bree sniffled. "I know that."

I edged over and the three of them pulled me in, wrapping their arms around me. "I understand loss, guilt, and shame being intertwined. Don't cut us off because it hurts."

She nodded against my neck. "I'm sorry."

The salesman cleared his throat. "Do you ladies have any questions?"

Charisse mumbled inside the huddle, "Really?" and Bree giggled. Then Charisse handed the salesman the envelope. "I want these pieces, and I want them delivered to that address as soon as possible."

Stefanos looked from the envelope to Charisse wide-eyed, calculating his commission. He blinked a couple of times to be sure he was seeing the numbers clearly. Charisse handed him her American Express and he took off running like he'd stolen it.

We hung out on the sectional by the door until he'd wrapped up the details. Forty minutes—and a box of fancy thank-you chocolates from Stefanos—later, we headed to the swanky home goods store so Charisse could load up on all the things her ex had stolen.

We did make a quick detour for a late lunch at Burger 21 because they had amazing milkshakes, and we'd had enough stress over the past couple of days that milkshakes were a requirement. But once we arrived at the department store, we each grabbed a cart and headed inside.

"If Dollie wants the twenty-year-old set of towels Michael has dried his naked butt on, let her have them. I'm getting everything new. I've got five years of bonuses saved up and I know just how to spend them."

Scarlett's eyes sparkled with mischief. "Maybe we could get some things to spruce up your place, Layla. Like a bowl of golden apples or some red dancing shoes."

"Psssh. I don't have any money. I have a Jeep payment and a dog now. I'm trying to decide if I should splurge on cat food for an imaginary cat that's probably a possum just to make Dad happy." I put my coat and purse in the front of a basket and wheeled it after Charisse. "Oh, I almost forgot. Castinetto came by and asked me to consult on a homicide for the department. Well, actually Adam Beasley gave me the case file this morning. Castinetto pissed me off so bad when he was trying to deliver it that I slammed the door in his face."

Scarlett grabbed an Instant Pot and put it in a cart. "What'd he do now?"

"He brought back the picture of Jacob someone sent me and even though forensics said it's not altered he still accused me of Photoshopping it."

The three women stopped in their tracks and stared at me. Scarlett smacked me on the arm. "Are you kidding me? Why are you just now telling us?"

Charisse grinned and added an electric kettle to her cart. "To be fair, we've had a lot going on today."

Bree pulled up alongside us with a cart holding a toaster oven, food processor, and one of those fancy pod coffee machines George Clooney got paid to like. "Can we see the picture?"

I pulled it out of my purse and held it up. They grilled it like they were examining for hidden messages.

Charisse nodded slowly. "So, that's Jacob."

"Yep."

Scarlett tilted her head left and right. "No offense, but he looks like the punk kid in every teen movie."

"Mmm. Yeah. We had a desk sergeant who called him Bender."

Bree asked, "Who's Bender?"

Charisse clucked her tongue. "*The Breakfast Club.* We really have to do a better job of educating you on the important things."

Bree grinned and put her hand on my shoulder. "What are you going to do?"

I returned the picture to the envelope in my bag. "I have to try to find him."

Scarlett's eyebrows shot up past her glasses. "Then what?"

"That depends."

Was it my imagination, or did I see a flicker of fear in their eyes?

Bree stuttered. "Y-you would just talk to him though, right? You wouldn't hurt him?"

I took a moment to consider it. "We'll see."

Scarlett nudged her basket forward and grabbed an air fryer.

"What if you find out he's been looking for *you*? You moved into the trailer park right after Stratton Park. Maybe he doesn't know where you are."

"That's true. But I shouldn't be that hard to find. Castinetto found me right away."

Charisse picked up a case of flatware and sucked some air through her teeth. "But what if you find out he survived because he faked his death? Maybe he's working with the drug ring."

I held up two patterns of dishes and Charisse pointed to one of them. "I just might kill him myself if that's the case."

Bree gathered a bunch of pretty table linens that matched the dishes and placed them in her cart. "We have to get your memory back fast so you will know what to do. If Jacob tried to kill you once, what is to stop him from trying again once he knows you're looking for him?"

I nearly dropped the mixing bowl set I was holding. "That had not occurred to me."

Scarlett took the set from my hands and placed them in her cart. "Okay. Everything will be okay. What's Detective Castinetto's case about?"

I moved my basket forward and looked at the baking supplies. I had no idea what any of them were except the rolling pin, so I grabbed one and held it up. "It's a homicide that's creeping into the cold-case category. A mild-mannered private-school teacher was bludgeoned to death and stuffed in a confessional of Our Lady of Mercy Catholic Church."

Bree's eyes widened at the rolling pin I was waving around as I said Archie was bludgeoned. I quickly placed it in the cart. "Sorry."

Charisse paused with her hand on a Bundt pan. "Are you talking about Archie Wilkins? I knew him. At least we'd met before when his wife and I were on a fundraiser committee for the Kennedy Center. What a tragedy. The police don't have any leads?"

I grabbed a chef knife from a display. "Nope. No enemies." I considered the ten-inch Wüstof, but my only frame of reference for knives was postmortem matching stab wounds to a murder weapon, so I put it back on the display and grabbed a Vitamix instead.

Charisse reached for a white KitchenAid stand mixer. "He was loaded. You'd think it would be easy to find a motive in all that money."

"You'd think. I'm going to try to visit the widow and ask some questions."

"You want me to go with you and make an introduction?" Charisse offered.

"Yeah, if you know her. It's not like I can pull out a badge and say let me in."

"Let's do Sunday afternoon. I'll set it up."

Scarlett was tapping on her cell phone. "You know, Our Lady of Mercy is right around the corner. We could stop by and take a look at the crime scene when we're done here."

Charisse grabbed her cart and swung it around. "Then we'd better hurry up. I can shop for everything else online. I can't see where someone was murdered on Amazon."

I grabbed the Wüstof and added it to my basket. "At least not yet."

Chapter 17

OUR LADY OF MERCY WAS AN IMPOSING GOTHIC-REVIVAL CHURCH from the mid-1800s set in a quiet residential neighborhood. With its gleaming white stucco brick, three-story central tower and spire, and large stained glass rose window, the dimly lit, aluminum-sided convenience store across the street seemed really out of place.

It wasn't a rich neighborhood, but not what you would call a bad neighborhood either. The sun was going down, casting long shadows over the manicured grounds.

Scarlett mused, "This place is deserted. Maybe Catholicism is out of favor these days."

Bree pointed to a sign next to a life-size marble statue of a man with a halo and a staff. "The next Mass isn't for two more hours. Maybe that's why no one's here."

We walked around the building, taking note of the well-lit front door, variety of stone angel statues in the azalea garden, and carefully tended graveyard.

"I've listened to my fair share of true crime podcasts," Charisse said, "and a random act of violence is much more likely in a populated area with more foot traffic and places to hide."

I nodded, while looking through the bushes at the convenience store across the way. "Random acts of violence are more rare than you'd think, but there are many motives for murder where decent people get pushed too far and snap."

I pulled out my cell phone and called Castinetto. "Hey, I'm at the crime scene. Did you get CCTV from the convenience store? It wasn't in the report."

While he was checking, a white-haired man in round glasses and priest togs came out a side door in front of us and heartily waved. "Yoo-hoo."

We each raised a tentative hand as if operated by the same nervous puppeteer.

"Service isn't for a little while yet. Would you like to come in and have some tea?"

Scarlett spoke through a tight smile. "Is this really happening?"

Bree mused, "It's just like a British crime drama."

I glanced at Charisse, who shrugged, too dumbfounded for words apparently. "Sure, we would love some tea."

"Gotta go." I hung up my phone and put it on silent, figuring Castinetto could leave a message when he called back.

We followed the elderly priest in through the side door. He led us down a beige linoleum hallway while calling over his shoulder, "I'm Father Matthews. What brings you to Our Lady of Mercy?"

We turned into a large green office. A blue sofa and two pink chairs faced a desk covered in papers and books. The entire wall behind the desk was a bookcase made of wood so dark you wouldn't see it if the lights were out. Hardbound volumes of ancient church hymnals filled the bookcase and spilled out onto the floor next to the desk.

"Well, to be honest," I said, "I'm looking into the death of Archie Wilkins."

Father Matthews's eyebrows shot up. He waved his hand in the direction of the sofa. "Is that right? Sit. Sit."

While Bree, Scarlett, and Charisse crammed together on the sofa, I took one of the empty chairs.

The priest ran his hand over his jaw in thought. "Are you with the police?"

Scarlett replied right away. "Yes."

I wanted to keep quiet but thought lying to a priest might

break one of the Ten Commandments, and I couldn't afford the bad press with God. "Unofficially."

Father Matthews picked up the phone receiver on his desk and pushed a button. "Gladys, please bring tea for five to my office. And some cookies. Yes, the good ones. No, they weren't snooping. They're with the police." He looked our way. "Anyone take cream in their tea?"

Bree gave a weak smile and raised a hand.

"Yes, bring some cream, Gladys."

He hung up the phone and took the other chair next to the sofa. We made small talk until a little white-haired lady in a blue knit dress with a lace collar and string of pearls entered the room, lumbering under the weight of a tray holding a teapot, five cups and saucers, sugar, and cream. There were no cookies.

Father Matthews did not get up to assist. "Why didn't you bring it on the cart?"

She set the tray on the coffee table, and in her little old lady voice croaked, "This was faster."

Father Matthews lifted his palms and shrugged. "Ladies, this is the parish secretary, Gladys Beacon. She keeps everything running like a machine here."

Gladys smiled primly. "Except this room. He won't let me touch his desk, so don't blame me for the state of it."

The priest grinned. "Thank you, Gladys."

Scarlett put her hand to her neck. "I love your pearls. They're beautiful."

Gladys reached for the strand. "Thank you. My daughter bought them for me for Mother's Day a few years ago. I wear them every day to think of her. Well, let me know if you need anything else."

The church secretary silently slipped from the room pulling the door, and Father Matthews poured the tea. "So, what do you want to know that the police haven't already asked?"

He handed me a cup and saucer and I put a spoonful of sugar in my tea. "Did you know Archie Wilkins?"

He finished passing out tea to the others and poured a cup for himself before settling back in the chair like we were there for a lovely visit and not four women who might suspect him of murder. "Not really. Mr. Wilkins did not attend services here. I only saw him a couple of times at special events."

Scarlett tapped her spoon against her cup. "So, he wasn't a regular at confession?"

The priest shook his head. "I don't believe I've ever taken his confession. Of course I am getting older and with that a touch forgetful. As far as I know, Mr. Wilkins only attended Mass when his students were in some program or another."

"So, some of his students attend here?" I asked.

"Oh yes. The primary school is just a couple blocks away, so naturally there is some overlap of families."

"Do you know which of the children were in his class?"

The door banged open, and Gladys entered with a plate. "Silly me, I forgot the cookies. I think I'd forget my head if it wasn't attached." She crossed the room and set a selection of Pepperidge Farm cookies on the table. "Anything else, Father Matthews?"

"I think that'll do it."

Gladys took a step back and folded her hands at her waist, her eyes sparkling with a touch of mischief.

The priest gave her a long look. "That will be all, Gladys."

She grimaced and reluctantly left the room.

"That woman needs a bell around her neck." Father Matthews quietly stirred his tea, the spoon clinking the sides of the china teacup. "I don't exactly know which were his students, but I do know that a few of them attend our catechism classes. There are two other primary schools nearby, so we have families from all three neighborhoods. It's hard to say which kids go to which school."

I smell a backpedal. "Did anyone have problems with Archie? Anyone have something against him?"

Father Matthews bit his lower lip and bobbled his head neither yes or no.

Charisse put her cup on the table. "I would imagine you

would have the inside track with the stuff that comes out in confession?"

He gave us a kindly grandpa type of smile. "I can't reveal anything from confession."

I leaned toward the priest. "I understand your vows, but a man is dead. And as this is your church, and your confessional, and as you found him, you are the most likely suspect. Since the police haven't found a better suspect, I'd hate to see them focus all their suspicion on you."

Father Matthews blanched like he was regretting giving us the good cookies.

Bree sipped her tea. "We just want to find his killer so he can be brought to justice, and his family can have closure. Especially this time of year, around the holidays. It must be very hard on his family not to know what happened to him."

I knew the priest was holding back, but Bree's words had gotten to him. He was working his lip like chewing gum. "I thought the police suspected the attack was a robbery gone wrong."

I took a cookie from the tray. "Do you feel like this is a high-crime neighborhood?"

He breathed out in a puff. "Well, no. But we have had several thefts from the donation box in recent months."

"Did you report those thefts?"

He put his teacup on the table and folded his hands in his lap. "No. They didn't take much. Usually less than fifty dollars."

"Do you have a problem with addicts or gang members on the property?"

He shifted in his seat like he was sitting on a tack. "Gang members—no."

Bree placed her teacup in the saucer with a gentle clink. "What about drugs? Anyone hanging around the building who shouldn't be here? Anyone acting strange? Nervous? Paranoid? Overly excitable?"

Father Matthews blinked twice and dunked a Milano into his tea. "Drugs are a problem in the best of families. And there is the occasional teen vandalism, but nothing serious."

"Do you have security cameras outside?"

"No. We've never needed them before."

I passed a cookie to Bree. "So, the odds of this being a random attack are pretty slim, wouldn't you say so, Father Matthews?"

His lips rolled inward, and he pressed them together until they were white. "I would guess so."

Scarlett lifted both of her hands. "So, that brings us back to the question, Did Archie have any enemies in the church?"

The priest sighed. "It's probably nothing . . . but a couple of my parishioners—I can't say who—have been struggling with a lot of stress recently, and they've had . . . dark thoughts . . . about . . . how to . . . handle it." His next words were rushed like he thought he'd already said too much. "Which isn't necessarily anything new or weird. But . . . in the past week . . . since Mr. Wilkins's demise . . . they've been . . ." He shrugged and bit his lip. "Happy? Relieved even. Their problems seem to be over." He was lost in thought for a moment. "I'm not saying anything untoward has happened . . ."

I finished his thought. "But the timing of it is an odd coincidence?"

He nodded.

"I understand."

Gladys returned holding four brown paper lunch bags. "I'm so sorry, dearies, but Father Matthews has to get ready for Mass now. I've packed up some cookies for each of you to take with you as a little treat."

Not one to miss a hint, we stood and gathered our things.

I reached my hand out to the priest. "Thank you for your time. I know it was difficult for you."

Gladys placed the cookies in my outstretched hand before Father Matthews could shake it. "You can call Father Matthews if you need anything else. Just Google us for the number. Come on, I'll walk you out."

She led us down the hall, chattering all the way to the door. "Father Matthews is such a good man. It's a shame something like this had to happen in his church. Of course that poor, poor

Mr. Wilkins. His family must be in a right state. And so close to the holidays too. Well, reach out anytime you need us. We'll be here." She threw the door open and gave us a twinkle of her fingers. "Bye, lovelies."

I stood in the side yard with half a Milano in one hand. "What just happened?"

Charisse grunted. "I do believe we've been dismissed."

Bree unfolded the top of her paper bag and peeked inside. "And with parting gifts too."

I stuffed the remaining shard of my cookie in my mouth and my eyes caught a flap of movement on the Jeep. Someone had left something on the windshield. I crossed the lawn and reached for the folded paper under the wiper blade, extracted it, and flicked it open. My stomach gave a little quiver as my eyes rolled over the message.

BACK OFF OR YOU'RE NEXT!

I looked around to see if anyone was lurking, watching me, waiting for me to find their threat. A few leaves skittered across the gravestones. Other than that, nothing.

"Girls, get in the Jeep. Now."

They complied without argument. Scarlett leaned across the seat and nudged me. "What's wrong?"

I showed her the note. She glanced around the parking lot like I'd just done. "Well, they're gone now."

"Yeah. And no security cameras mean I have no way to find out who left this."

Charisse pulled her bag closer to her side. "Do you want to call the cops?"

"Definitely not." Castinetto would pull me off this assignment faster than you could say *civilian.*

Bree quickly pulled on her seat belt. "What are we going to do?"

I put the threat on the dash inside. "Nothing yet. But now we know they're watching the church."

I drove back to the John Adams so everyone could get their own cars. Bree was quiet the whole way. She kept fidgeting with the cuffs of her sleeves.

"That was a good question you asked Father Matthews about the drugs," I said.

Bree looked out the window and watched the cars as we passed them. She mumbled a thank-you.

Scarlett nudged her and gave her a smile. "I thought the priest would spill his tea when Layla said he was the prime suspect."

Bree's mouth made a flicker of movement before she turned away.

My eyes caught Scarlett's in the rearview mirror.

Even though we'd thought we'd had a mini breakthrough at the furniture store, a dark cloud still hung over Bree and none of us knew what to do about it.

We had just finished loading Charisse's haul into the back of her SUV when my phone buzzed a message from Myrtle Jean Maud.

You're needed at home.

Why?

I never got an answer.

Chapter 18

I DIDN'T HANG AROUND THE HOTEL PARKING LOT WAITING FOR A reply. I said goodbye to the ladies and hopped into the Jeep. I tried to keep my trembling stomach under control on the drive home, but the tea and cookies were surfing on a choppy sea of nerves.

What if something happened to Dad? We were at the beginning of this dementia journey, but what if I already couldn't leave him alone? How was I supposed to work and go to meetings if he needed a babysitter? And who could I trust to stay with him who wouldn't take advantage of him?

I passed three bars on the way home that were lit up like Vegas nightclubs. I gripped the steering wheel and kept my eyes on the road, reciting the Serenity Prayer.

Finally, I turned at the birch trees and started the trek down to the house.

Maybe Dad pulled a Ringo and thought we still lived in the old trailer. I should have asked Myrtle Jean which home.

I didn't have to worry about that for long, because a black SUV sat at the curb in front of my house and the head of Dad's security team, Ronnie Voa, waved from the driver's seat.

There was also a scooter, a van, and a little red Audi in the driveway, so I parked behind Ronnie. He met me at my Jeep. "What's going on?"

"I got a call earlier from one Agnes Harcourt. Don requested a detail until further notice."

"Why? What happened?"

Ronnie gave a hint of a head shake. "It seems we may have a stalker situation. We aren't taking any chances with Mr. Virtue, given his history. I'll have someone stationed out front until we hear from you that the coast is clear. Let me know as soon as you can what we're dealing with."

"Will do." I climbed out of the Jeep and headed for the front door.

Inside my house was a flurry of activity. Aromas of a variety of spices competed for attention. I dropped the cat food and cookies on the counter and followed a slew of tittering voices. All the usual suspects were in the greenhouse dining room. Agnes, Myrtle Jean, Marguerite, Old Lady Henson, and even Clifford and the new girl, Robin, who'd gotten her wheelchair inside.

Dad sat at the head of a long table holding up a bottle of root beer, toasting the trailer park peeps scattered around him. A bevy of casseroles lined a granite counter. Lasagna, chicken enchiladas, pork and cabbage, scalloped potatoes, and a lemon Bundt cake.

"Baby girl, you're home!"

"I am. Did I miss an invitation to this party?"

Dad chuckled and waved his hand. "Join us. The gals brought some food, and this guy made a killer cake. What'd you call it again?"

Clifford bristled. "A Victoria sponge."

Dad smiled. "Yeah yeah. A Victoria sponge cake. You gotta try it, honey."

"I will. Maybe in a bit. It's good to see you, Robin."

She grinned and pointed to the back door leading out to the lake. "Agnes led me around the back to gain entry. You should have told me the back was wheelchair accessible."

"Had I known . . . Dad, can we talk for a minute?"

"Sure thing, darling." Dad pushed his chair back and followed me out to the living room. "What's up?"

"I don't know. You tell me. Why is there a security detail out front?"

He pursed his lips and made a face. "Psssshhh."

"Don't give me Psssshhh. Something happened or you wouldn't have called Ronnie."

He shoved his hands in his pockets and cocked his head. Noticing the box on the counter, he rocked forward. "Hey! You got cat food! Sweet!"

"Dad! Focus. Ronnie."

He sighed and dropped onto the arm of the plush couch. "Fine. I didn't want to worry you, but I got a weird message that was taped to the front door."

"What kind of message?"

He shrugged. "I don't remember. But at the time it freaked me out."

"Well, where is it?"

"I don't know where I put it."

"I need something, Dad. What did it say?"

He looked around the room as if hoping it would pop up and do a dance. He started to nod his head to a tune only he could hear. Then he threw his chin in the air and cried out, "Blackmail!" which snowballed into about eighty percent of an old Robert Palmer song. "You are blackmailing me. Taking all my money. We don't think it's funny. The way you've started badgering me."

"So, someone's trying to blackmail you?"

Agnes rushed around the corner, either her knees or her leather pants creaking with every move. "Don. Shhh!" She reached up into the bookshelf and pulled down one of those handmade threats pasted together from magazine words like you'd see on a crime show. "This was stuck on the door earlier. He didn't want you to get upset with him so he called me and asked what he should do."

I took the slightly crumpled demand and held it out. **Leave a hundred thousand dollars under the canoes by Thanksgiving or I'll go to TMZ with the story that Don Virtue lives in a trailer park**.

Dad covered his face with his hands. "I'm sorry, baby girl. I didn't mean to cause so much trouble for you."

I sat across from him on the edge of the coffee table. "Dad, this isn't your fault. You have nothing to feel bad about."

"You told me not to go to the community meetings."

Agnes's hand shot up to her beehive. "You said what!"

My throat felt raw, like I had strep and made the mistake of drinking a ginger cayenne health shot. It only takes once to learn that lesson. "You deserve to live your life without getting foolish threats and ridiculous demands." *A hundred thousand dollars. Seriously? He probably has that much in his underwear drawer. Ooh. On second thought, that's not good either. I should check on that.*

"Why don't you go back to your party, and I'll take this out to Ronnie. He'll do some digging and set a watch over those canoes. Everything will be fine."

Dad peeked at me through his fingers. "Are you sure?"

"Absolutely. And we'll get through—"

Dad wasn't listening anymore. His eyes grew wide, and he pointed to the kitchen. "There's the cat!"

Agnes and I spun toward the kitchen, but nothing was there.

I scanned every corner in my sight. "I don't see anything."

Dad's face screwed up. "He was there just a minute ago. I could have sworn he had a cookie in his mouth."

I looked back at Dad to see if he was teasing me—he wasn't. Then over at Agnes to see if she was in on it—she seemed genuinely confused. She gave me a backward glance as she led him back to the greenhouse. "We'll catch that cat, Don. Don't you worry."

I blew out my breath. I had to get him out of here and back to his gated community where I could keep him safe. Maybe a few visits with Keith and Phil and Uncle Steven would bring him some clarity and clear up this invisible cat situation. I took the threat out to Ronnie and gave him the rundown of the sitch. He confirmed my suspicions that anyone could have recognized Dad from one of our outings and followed us home. We came up with a plan for security cameras and twenty-four-hour surveillance, then I went back inside to make some calm tea to help me sleep.

First someone shoves the photo of Jacob under the door at the old trailer. And a few hours later we're being extorted for a hundred grand to keep Dad's privacy safe. What were the odds? Could those things possibly be connected? There was no overlap in our circles—other than Dayton Castinetto. He used to hang around my private school selling weed to the rich kids behind the gym. Back then it seemed like the whole world knew I was the daughter of Don Virtue. We'd never talked about it, so I wasn't sure that he knew. If he did, I could believe he would try to rattle me into a confession by creating the photo of Jacob, but blackmailing Dad? For what purpose? Just to hurt me?

Before I could get Dad somewhere safe, I'd have to find Jacob and get to the bottom of whatever he was involved in. That meant working with Castinetto, but could I trust him? I suspected that someone on the force had been working with the drug lord we were trying to take down and they used me as their scapegoat. Anger and humiliation rolled over me once again. If Jacob was working with Hurtado the whole time, what did that say about me? About my instincts as a cop? As a girlfriend? And if it wasn't Jacob, then who?

A cackle erupted from the greenhouse and put a smile on my face. Dad and his fan club. As I was pouring steaming water over the tea, my eyes fell on the bag of cookies Gladys Beacon had sent home with me. The top was shredded, and the bag was ripped open. A Chessman cookie stuck partway out. I did a fast look around the kitchen again but found nothing.

Something else to keep me awake half the night.

Someone pounded on the front door and startled me awake. I reached for my Glock out of habit, frustrated to find a statue of a frog on the nightstand instead. I grabbed my cell phone and checked the time. Two A.M. Another sharp knock on the door. A hundred bad scenarios flooded my mind as I jumped out of bed. I snared the fireplace poker on my way to the front door, flicked on the overhead light, and threw the door open.

It was Ronnie Voa with Nick. "Sorry to wake you."

I nodded absently. My eyes fixed on the man who meant so much to me. Relief flooded my mind to see him standing there in the flesh—living, breathing—as my heart broke to see the hopelessness that clung to him like prison blues.

Nick looked like he'd been run over twice since I'd left him yesterday morning. The lines in his face were deeper. The shadows under his eyes darker. Ringo stood at Nick's side and gave me a soft whimper.

"Nick. What's wrong?"

He swallowed hard. "I'm not in a good place."

Chapter 19

"It's fine, Ronnie. I've got this." I quickly ushered Nick and Ringo inside and shut the door before Nick could freak out and change his mind. He already looked like a wild horse trying to bolt. I moved to the kitchen, and they followed me. "Coffee, tea, or cocoa?"

"I don't care. Whatever you want."

"Cocoa it is. Come in and have a seat."

Nick pulled out one of the chairs around the table and Ringo dropped into a ball at his feet with a groan. I poured milk in a saucepan and put it on the stove before adding the powdered cocoa packets.

Nick ran his hand over his hair and shook his head like he couldn't believe he was doing this. "I'll just be here tonight."

"Nonsense. You'll stay as long as you need to. Let's just take it one day at a time."

Nick looked away from me and nodded.

We were silent as the milk heated, the only sounds Ringo's light breathing and the hiss of the propane burner. I placed a steaming mug of chocolate in front of Nick, and he gave me a wan smile. I sat across from him with my mug and waited.

He blew across his cocoa and took a sip. "I considered it tonight."

My heart shattered. I wanted to tell him off for even considering taking his life and hurting someone I cared about, but he was here, and he was safe, so I waited for him to tell me what was going on in his own time.

"Logic tells me that things will get better, and I won't always feel like this. But right now, it's like someone drilled a hole in me and everything good has drained away. The air is too heavy. With every breath I lose a little more of myself. I don't know how many more times I can go through losing someone."

Ringo sat back up and put his head in Nick's lap. Nick reached for him and ran his hand over the Lab's back.

My heart gripped with pain for Nick. I was very familiar with hopelessness and how it cut you from the inside and stole all the light around you.

Nick cradled the mug close to his chest. "I don't want to be alone right now."

I reached across the table and squeezed his arm. "You're not. You've got me and I won't let you go."

Dad padded into the kitchen in black silk pajamas. "Hey, your husband came home. I knew you guys could work it out. Are you staying for dinner, guy?"

Nick raised an eyebrow. He glanced at me. "I should be."

Dad opened the fridge, took out a bottle of orange soda, and twisted off the cap. "Righteous. Want to order a pizza?"

"Dad, it's nearly three in the morning. Not the afternoon."

Dad paused with the soda halfway to his lips. "Are you freakin' kidding me? No wonder I'm so tired." He sighed, put the soda on the counter, and headed back to his room. "I'll see you in a few hours."

As he disappeared around the corner, we could clearly hear him butchering Peaches and Herb. "Reunited don't it feel too good. Reunited like I knew they would."

Ringo watched Dad retreat, looked at me, then at Nick, then put his head in Nick's lap.

I gave Nick a look. "So that's happening?"

His eyes softened. "Have you seen the neurologist yet?"

"Yep. It wasn't good news." I filled Nick in on Dad's diagnosis and all the doctor's instructions. He chuckled when I said Dad was supposed to eat healthy meals that were low in fat and sugar.

"Where is he gonna get those from?"

I answered with a crooked smile. "Chik fil-A has a salad, don't they?"

Nick snorted. "The fact that you don't know makes me worry about the both of you."

We stayed up talking until the first rays of sun tickled the windows and Nick seemed to level off emotionally. I caught him up on all that he had missed—the trailer park meeting fiasco and my sudden apparent in-chargeness and all the chaos I had caused in a few short days. He was almost giddy about the playground for Pippi. I told him about the new girl, Robin, who'd moved in with her brother, and the rare appearance of Whimsy. "Dad's volunteered us to bring the turkey for the potluck because he obviously has magical turkey baking powers now."

"Don't worry about that one. I can make the turkey for you. It's the least I can do."

"That'd be great." Warmth filled my chest. Thanksgiving was four days away. Nick would be here for at least that long. He was already looking lighter just from hearing how many ways I could get myself into trouble.

I'd learned a long time ago while driving around as a beat cop with a partner that one way to get your mind off your troubles was to share someone else's. So, I pulled out the picture of Jacob and passed it to Nick along with the story of how I got it.

"Shoved under the trailer door?"

"Yep."

"After you'd moved out?"

"Yep."

"And you say Castinetto didn't ask where you lived when you called it in? He just showed up at the trailer?"

The hair prickled on the back of my neck. "That's true, but no one on the police knew that I had moved. I had to give Castinetto my new address as part of the harassment report."

"Well, you can definitely rule out the neighborhood. It sounds like everyone here knows you've moved on up." He held up the photo of Jacob. "How do you feel about this?"

"I've been through every emotion twice. I don't know what to think. And he could be anywhere in the world. I have no idea where to look."

"He's at Ben's Chili Bowl."

"What?"

"In this picture. He's at Ben's Chili Bowl on U Street. That's the foot of the panda statue in front of the building. I used to eat lunch there once a week when I worked downtown. Whoever took this picture only caught the edge of the red building, but they got the panda foot."

I stared at the photograph. I'd thought it was a blue Ugg boot. I'd looked at this picture a hundred times since last Wednesday, but I'd been so focused on the election sign that I'd completely missed the connection to the artsy panda in front of the historic DC eatery.

"My God, has he been in my backyard this whole time?"

"Why don't we head down there this week and see if anyone recognizes him? Maybe he lives in the area."

"That would be awesome. Thank you, Nick."

Nick yawned and took a look around. "Is it just me or is there a definite theme to this room? Like any minute someone is going to break into song with rabbits?"

"I don't break into song before ten A.M."

Nick full-on laughed. "I can just see you in here with bluebirds singing on your shoulder as the mice help you make a pie."

"I wouldn't get too cocky, mister. We haven't seen your room yet."

The smile vanished into a smirk, and I knew there was nothing I wanted more than to finally explore the loft.

Nick's eyes narrowed with a hint of challenge. "Let's go."

Chapter 20

We ran up the spiral staircase. The loft was a jungle of ferns, and still the most tasteful area of the house. We were standing in a cream-and-white apartment with a stone fireplace, a comfortable couch loaded with silvery-green accent pillows, and a queen-sized bed with a cream duvet under the peak of the roof. Exposed wooden beams warmed up ivory stucco walls and matched two mission-style dressers and a large carved maple desk. Nick sucked in a breath. "Whoa. That's a lot of plants."

"Man, I was hoping for the Seven Dwarfs' bunk beds, or Rapunzel's tower, but this is downright tame compared to my room."

Even Nick's bathroom was tasteful. Silver-and-white checkered flooring, a white claw-foot tub next to a natural stone shower. "Ugh. I'm so jealous. This is going to be like living in a nature preserve. The craziest thing you have in here is the fern-patterned wallpaper."

Nick touched a stack of silver towels and a bittersweet look passed through his eyes. "You didn't see the cuckoo clock, did you?"

A grin split my face. "No. Where?"

He chuckled. "Right over the bed."

I never realized how evil I could be until that moment. I laughed like I didn't have a care in the world. "Okay, well that makes me feel better. In a few hours I'll show you my room and give you the rest of the tour. Then you'll see that you've got Shangri-la up here."

"I think you mean FernGully," he chuckled.

I gave Nick a hug good night. He tried to make it seem casual, but he held on too tight and too long, reminding me that this wasn't a sleepover. "If you need anything, at any time, my room is at the bottom of the spiral stairs. I'm so glad you're here."

He released me and his eyes were glassy. "I'll see you in a few hours."

In my room, Ringo was curled tightly in his bed snoring away. He was worn out. The poor little guy must have been glad to be home. He'd worked so hard all day.

I climbed back into bed and snuggled down into the covers.

What felt like a minute later, I got a gentle shove on my shoulder. "Baby girl. Wake up. There's a lady here to see you. I think she's your manager."

"What?" I checked the time. Half past nine. "No. Tell her to go away. I've only had a couple hours of sleep."

"She says you have a gig. She's been calling you."

I checked my cell phone call log. Seventeen missed calls. "Oh crap. I put my phone on silent at the church last night and forgot to take it off. What's that smell?"

"Nick's making pancakes."

"Hey! You remembered his name."

Dad grinned and knocked on his head. "I think the medicine is working."

"Layla Virtue! Get your butt out here!"

Dad's grin slid into pursed lips. "Uh-oh. The lady sounds mad. You don't want to piss off your manager or she'll send you to revenge gigs in Podunk arenas."

I threw back the covers and chuckled. "Arenas. Right."

I padded out to the living room where Paula paced back and forth like a puma in a royal blue power suit. The color made her eyes pop. Or maybe that was the anger. Her ash blond bob bounced and swayed with every turn around the coffee table. She spied me and her eyebrows dipped into a crease running down the middle of her forehead. That crease had become more pronounced in the two months we'd been working together. She held up a dry cleaner's dress bag. "Where have you been?! I've been calling since last night. You've got twenty minutes to throw this on and get over to the Hot Stuff Kitchen for their Boogie Wonderland Brunch."

Dad perched on the arm of the couch and Ringo stretched at his side. I thought they were there to offer backup, but apparently they just wanted to be nosy.

I reached out and took the dress bag. "Did you tell me about this gig?"

"I would have if you'd answered your phone. You're playing in an ABBA cover band. Their Björn and Agnetha have the flu."

"Which one am I?"

She opened her tote bag and pulled out a CD. "It doesn't matter. And here. Learn these songs on the way to the gig."

I took the CD and stared at it. "I don't have anything to play this on, Paula."

Paula scrolled through her phone. "Well, you'd better figure it out. Because the Hot Stuff Kitchen has live music every weekend and I've been trying to book through them for months."

I peeked inside the garment bag and gasped at the yard of blue satin ruffles. "I've already got plans today."

She threw her hands to her hips. "Plans to do what? You suddenly sign on with a label while I was working this deal for you?"

"No, I'm consulting with the police and I'm meeting one of my friends to question a suspect."

Paula had already stopped listening. She reached behind the chair and handed me a shopping bag.

"What's this?"

"Your go-go boots. Now tick-tock. You're going to be late."

A snicker drew my attention to the front of the house. Nick was watching us from the kitchen, Dad's KISS THE COOK apron around his waist and a spatula in his hand like a scepter. "Hurry up. I can't wait to see this outfit."

I stormed to my room to change while Paula cozied up to Dad

and tried to convince him that he needed new representation. I had half a mind to let her book him for something just because she deserved the headache, except it would breach his contract with Jimmy.

I texted Charisse that something had come up and I might be a touch late. Then I pulled up the ABBA station on Spotify and pressed play.

I dumped the contents of the garment bag on the bed and smoothed out a blue one-shoulder spandex bodysuit with a mile of ruffles down the one arm, a white belt of stars, and a silver cape. In the bag were over-the-knee silver platform boots, and a compact containing silver and blue eyeshadow.

Some days the murder victims seem to have gotten the better deal.

Chapter 21

NICK AND DAD COULDN'T STOP GIGGLING WHEN I'D EMERGED from the bedroom. Nick asked if my outfit came with batteries, and could I keep the boots because they were kinda working for him. Then he rolled a pancake around a sausage and made me take it to go. I ate it in the Jeep with the satin arm ruffles tucked into my bra strap.

I arrived at the Hot Stuff Kitchen only ten minutes late and the cover band's keyboard player, Gary, let me know he was less than pleased and would have words with Paula. Right away I recognized the scowling face of Mohinder, the Neon Dreams bass player I'd worked with in the past. He was filling in for "Björn" on electric guitar so all I had to do was sing. Singing was not my strength. I was a guitar player. With singing I didn't know what to do with my hands.

Mohinder made like he was introducing himself when really he wanted to pass me a message. "You're not going to have another freak-out, are you?"

"I'm not *planning* it. Besides, that's only happened twice."

He did not look impressed.

The Hot Stuff Kitchen was a kitschy seventies-themed diner. Silver-and-aqua booths on the perimeter, bistro tables and sweetheart chairs in the center. All facing a stage that rotated acts between disco and drag queens.

Gary introduced me to Sheila, the Anni-Frid to my Agnetha,

and immediately launched into "Take a Chance on Me" before my mic was hot.

Sheila nudged my arm. "Just follow the prompts on the iPad there on the music stand."

The words came fast, and I was a half second behind everyone else. Then Sheila expected us to strut around in synchronized poses that involved a lot of pointing and hip rolls. *What am I doing up here?*

She made an exasperated hiss. "Your agent said you were familiar with the act. Exactly what dance are you doing right now?"

I pulled a move I thought was probably from *Dance Fever.* "Freestyle?"

"Ugh. Try to copy me."

Does that include the scowling? I'm gonna kill Paula.

Gary transitioned into "Dancing Queen," and I caught my breath. That was an oldies station staple and God knew my father kept the seventies and eighties music flowing twenty-four hours a day when he was home from a tour.

Sheila announced a break, and I tried to follow her off stage.

"Where are you going?"

"You said take five."

"No, *I'm* taking a five. You're singing 'Fernando.'"

"Isn't that a duet?"

"Not today. Now get back up there."

Gary started the opening notes, and I reached for the neck of Mohinder's guitar. "Hey, trade with me. You take the solo."

"Not on your life."

Look, I did the best I could, okay. "Fernando" is a really emotional song that I don't entirely understand. Who was that guy? And exactly what war was he fighting? Between Sheila's iPad karaoke teleprompter and waitstaff bringing the diners bottomless mimosas, we'd run a full set list of ABBA hits, and I'd faked my way through about eighty percent of it without a flashback or freak-out. My dignity was in tatters from marching and posing, but little did I know that would not be my most embarrassing move of the day.

That came after the crowd insisted on several encores, including "Lay All Your Love on Me"—which, thinking of Jacob, made me feel some kinda way—and I was now running a full half hour late and would have to interview Archie Wilkins's widow dressed as a Super Trouper.

I parked my Jeep in front of a three-level Georgian brick colonial. Four two-story white columns flanked a Wedgewood-blue front door. Archie Wilkins had lived in a nice upper-middle-class neighborhood. The kind where kids go to private school, moms were on the PTA, and peanut butter and jelly was a novelty and not a staple.

Mrs. Wilkins answered the door wearing a tweed skirt and cashmere beige twinset with an emerald brooch. She'd probably had the same shoulder-length hairstyle for forty years and hadn't considered changing anything because it was what all the other PTA moms were wearing, and it was still acceptable.

She did look a bit taken aback by my satiny, ruffled presence and I was half tempted to say, "Trick or treat." "I apologize for my appearance, Mrs. Wilkins. I'm Layla Virtue on behalf of the Potomac County Police. I believe our mutual friend Charisse is already here."

Mrs. Wilkins continued to assess me, open-mouthed and wide-eyed, until her manners got the better of her, as they always do in people of good breeding, and she invited me in.

An enormous vase of sunflowers sat on a mahogany console table in the center of her expansive two-story marble entryway. Silver-framed photos of the Wilkins family on various trips around the world were lined up like royal soldiers. Skiing in Switzerland, posing like marble statues in the Roman Colosseum, waving from the Great Wall of China, sailing a yacht in French Polynesia. I had many of the same photos in a box somewhere at home. All with Dad. No two with the same woman at his side.

She led me past a wall of mirrors covered in condolence cards made by small children into a white marble kitchen where

Charisse sat with two young women drinking tea out of bone china teacups. The farmhouse table was covered in an array of chintz place settings and tiered trays of sandwiches and sweets. A crystal vase of English roses sat in the middle of the table next to a china teapot patterned in frolicking Scottie dogs.

Charisse had an unfortunate moment of choking that coincided with my appearance. She gave me a look that I interpreted as *What in God's name are you wearing?*

I pulled a face that said, *Girl, I have no idea.*

Mrs. Wilkins offered me a chair and made the introductions. "These are my daughters, Sophie and Grace. They have been the strength by my side since Archie . . ." Her voice trailed off and she picked up her Earl Grey.

I said hello to the two young women, both of whom had their noses turned up like I was a dirty vagrant with my hand out. Sophie appeared to be the older of the two, matching her mother in all ways tweed and cashmere, but with her brunette hair in a messy bun. Grace had either just come from horseback lessons, or wanted to appear as such in tan breeches, sable riding boots, and one of those little black velvet jackets.

My mother had signed me up for riding lessons one miserable week when I was thirteen. The breeches gave me a wedgie and the horse bit me on the stomach. I missed the jacket though. "It's nice to meet you both. I apologize for my outfit; I've just come from a costumed event that ran long."

None of the Wilkins women were mollified, but Charisse was hiding her smile behind one of those Biscoff cookies that I was not offered.

I placed my bag on the floor and took out a notebook and pen. "Thank you for meeting with me. I'm very sorry for your loss. I know this must be a horrible ordeal for you." When none of them said anything in response, I cleared my throat. "What do you do for a living, Mrs. Wilkins?"

The woman touched her hair and then her brooch. "I'm a stay-at-home mom. Archie always felt it was very important for me to be here to guide the girls and attend to their needs."

I smiled at the girls, who were closer to my age than they were school age.

Sophie sniffed like she suspected I smelled unpleasant. "What difference does that make, what my mother does with her day?"

I gave the woman a tight smile. My partners on the force knew that meant you had one strike. "I'm just trying to get a better understanding of the family dynamic."

Mrs. Wilkins went on. "And of course I also do a lot of charity work with my various clubs and institutions."

"Hmm." I nodded to encourage her.

Charisse placed her cup in the saucer. "Marion is on the board of the Arts Council and Humane Paws—an animal rescue organization in DC. And of course the Kennedy Center where we met."

"That's fabulous. That must keep you very busy."

Marion shrugged but a light pink flushed her milky white cheeks. "I like to be useful."

Now the younger daughter, Grace, crossed her arms tightly over her chest. "What did you expect? That Mom sat around all day watching soap operas and game shows?"

Why so much hostility? "I didn't expect anything."

Marion gave an uneasy look in her daughters' direction and smoothed the cloth napkin in her lap.

"I understand Archie was a primary school teacher."

Marion nodded. "Pixieland Academy. Second grade." She reached for a photo album next to a tray of sandwiches. Opening it, she tapped a picture of a balding mild-mannered man in a sweater vest and bow tie. He made a demure smile laced with humility for the camera. "That's my Archie."

"How long had he worked for the private school?"

Sophie breathed through an acrid chuckle. "Why don't you ask them?"

I gave her another tight smile. Strike two.

Marion twisted the napkin in her lap. "Almost twenty-three years. He could have retired after twenty, but he loved it so much. And the children loved him. We've received almost a hundred sympathy cards from former students." Her lip trembled and she bit down to still it.

"That says a lot about Archie that so many of his students would reach out to offer condolences."

Marion nodded and sniffed, reaching out to caress the photo of her late husband once more.

"Did Archie have any enemies?"

Grace clunked her teacup against the saucer with a loud *huff.* "We've already told the police this. Everyone loved my father. He was the kindest man you'd ever meet."

I ignored her and kept my eyes on Marion. "Mrs. Wilkins, did Archie ever do recreational drugs?"

Marion's mouth popped open like a baby bird, but Sophie cut her off. "Are you an idiot? My father? Do drugs? The man was a saint. His attack was obviously a senseless random act committed by one of the drug addicts that hang around that church. Have you even spoken to the priest yet? What's his name?"

"Father Matthews," Grace supplied.

"Yeah, Father Matthews."

I glanced at the older girl. Her nostrils flared, her eyes were sharp and glaring, accusing me of causing all the pain they were forced to relive. "We have, yes. And I understand that your family does not routinely attend Our Lady of Mercy?"

Their expressions dared me to challenge them. "Christmas and Easter."

"I understand this is very painful for all of you. If you girls want to wait in the other room, I'm only here to speak with your mother at this time."

Sophie rolled her eyes. "Right. And let you bully her into saying something that you can use against her? No, thank you."

Charisse gave me an apologetic look and shook her head ever so slightly.

Marion's cheeks flamed, but she kept silent.

"Did Archie have any recent altercations? Someone who wasn't an enemy, but upset with him about something that may have seemed trivial at the time?"

Marion's shoulders shook like she was trying to shake off a bad memory. "No. No enemies. No altercations."

Charisse reached out a hand and placed it over Marion's. "Do you know why Archie was at Our Lady of Mercy that night?"

Grace was not quite as hostile as her older sister, but her words were just as cutting. "You obviously didn't know him at all. Our dad did a lot of charity work for the unfortunate. He was probably at the church for something to do with that. He gave money to animal shelters and volunteered his time at the Good Samaritan food pantry. Always involved in the community to help the kids whether they were in his class or not. He was more than a teacher. He was a father figure to those children."

While she was talking I looked around the kitchen. A rack of French copper pans hung over a professional six-burner range. The refrigerator and freezer were so large they wouldn't fit in my trailer. Every countertop appliance was top-of-the-line, and I knew that because we'd just bought them all for Charisse. No teacher I'd ever met lived in this extravagance. Was Archie making drugs in the basement? "Your house is beautiful. If you don't mind my asking, how do you afford this luxury on a teacher's salary?"

Charisse's eyes popped and she gave me a questioning look, unsure of where I was going.

Both daughters launched at me with a vitriolic attack. "How dare you!"

"You don't have to answer that, Mom. We're the victims here."

"My father made good investments. He was wise with their money."

"Just what are you accusing us of?"

Sophie pushed her chair back. "I think you should go now."

I passed an appraising look over Marion. She had twisted that cloth napkin into a tight rope. She looked from me to her daughters and back to me. In a trembling voice she said, "We didn't offer you any tea."

Sophie jumped to her feet. "She doesn't need tea. She's leaving."

Marion shrunk back into herself. She smoothed the napkin on her lap. "I'll walk you both out."

I closed my notebook and picked up my bag.

Charisse gathered her things. "Marion, I'm so sorry we upset you like this. I hope we can do lunch one day. My treat."

Marion led us toward the door while Sophie shouted after her, "If you come back here we'll report you for harassment to the lead detective in charge of the investigation!"

Charisse took Marion's hand. "Let me know if you need anything in the coming days." She gave me a pointed look as she went out to her car to wait.

I offered my hand to the widow. "Thank you so much for your time, Mrs. Wilkins. I know it was difficult, but I really just want to get to the bottom of what happened to your husband."

Marion looked over her shoulder toward the kitchen. She grabbed my hand and pulled me close. "I can't talk now in front of my daughters. Can you meet me tomorrow night at my grief support group session?"

"Of course."

"Come alone." Marion reached into her tweed pocket and pulled out a card. "Here's the address and the time." I passed a brand-new Lexus in the driveway while walking out to my Jeep.

I smelled something rotten before I had the chance to open my door. I cupped my hands around my eyes and pressed against the window. Roadkill. Someone had put a dead possum on my driver's seat. It wasn't just the church they were watching. It was me.

I opened the door wide, then went to the back of the Jeep and grabbed the tire iron. Then I went to the passenger side and opened the glove box, taking out a pack of baby wipes I had for Ringo's muddy footprints. I flicked the flat possum off my seat and through the driver's side door with the tire iron, then used the baby wipes on every surface until I was willing to get inside.

I started the Jeep and pulled around until Charisse and I were side by side.

She rolled down her window. "What was that all about?"

"Nothing important."

Charisse's nose wrinkled. "If you say so. I can't believe how hostile the girls were. I didn't think the family were suspects."

"They weren't. But they are now."

Chapter 22

I DID A DRIVE AROUND THE TRAILER PARK BEFORE GOING HOME. Foster had installed a banner made from an old sheet and craft paint saying FUTURE HOME OF PLAYGROUND PIPPI in the empty lot at the end of his loop. I spent a few minutes trying to talk him and Pippi down and explain that we had to make sure we could legally use that plot of land for the playground. Trying to explain utility lines and zoning laws to Pippi was pointless. She already had her heart set on that patch for her seesaw.

I was able to convince the Alverezes to take down their billboard and put up a more appropriate yard sign the size of a recycling bin in the spirit of being good neighbors and getting reduced lot fees. I'd planned to appeal to logic that no one in the park ran a business needing a custom sign and that maybe their advertising efforts would work better in a business zone, but that plan was dashed the moment Benny showed up and ordered a sign for his yard advertising that his used-car dealership had special financing through Christmas.

Marguerite was putting together what looked like a ten-by-ten-by-ten cage for what I could only assume was the chicken coop I had not signed off on. She tried to cover it with a plastic tablecloth when I rolled by. "How are you planning to disguise the chickens if I say no?"

"I dunno whatchu talking about."

"Really, because I can see the cat costumes on your picnic table."

Marguerite placed her arm casually over the stack of cat ears and tails. Things had gotten out of hand very quickly and I hadn't been in charge for a week yet.

I drove around the lake for home, passing Whimsy St. James who cut into the woods the moment I appeared. Two doors down, Myrtle Jean was on a ladder putting multicolor swatches of paint on her baby blue double wide, while Agnes sat on her front porch hollering that all the colors were putrid. She was not wrong. Myrtle Jean appeared to favor shocking violet and lime green.

I gave a quick salute to Ronnie's guy keeping watch out front and ducked into my house like a seventies ninja with a ruffled sleeve, as Ringo had already alerted both ladies next door to my arrival and I didn't want to be asked to give an opinion neither of them would appreciate.

Dad and Nick were on their hands and knees in the kitchen searching the lower cabinets. Dad had a flashlight, and he was banging it around the saucepans and colanders.

"What exactly are you two doing?"

Nick gave me a look of exasperation over his shoulder while Dad's voice echoed from under the sink. "We're looking for that cat."

"Uh-huh. Why?"

"Because that rascal stole my Ho Hos."

I looked at Nick. He sighed.

"Nick. Have you seen this cat?"

Dad answered, "Of course he has."

"Sure." Nick screwed up his face and shook his head no.

"Okay. I'm gonna go change and then I'll set up your medicine, Dad."

Dad's arm shot out from the cabinet, and he gave me a thumbs-up.

I took a shower and scrubbed the blue eyeshadow and glitter off, then blow-dried my hair and changed into jeans and a white sweater. I passed Dad on the couch watching a football game—Ringo curled into his side, a fire blazing before them—and went back to the kitchen. Nick was adding spices to a big round pot on the stove.

I pulled out the chair closest to watch him. "Whatchu making?"

"My world-famous chili."

"World-famous?"

"Well, it's famous in my grandma's house and Afghanistan."

"Alright. That counts. Aren't you tired?"

"You'd think so, but I slept so much before coming over that I feel strangely energized. How'd the ABBA gig go?"

"I learned two important things. I don't know the words to ABBA songs. And neither does anyone else who attends a disco brunch."

Nick laughed and stirred the chili. "That's good to know in case you get invited back." He grabbed a grape soda from the fridge, popped the cap off, and handed it to me. "What's the deal with the box from the shire on the front porch?"

"Why?"

"People have been coming by all day and putting things in it."

I groaned "That box is a cry for help." I filled Nick in on my brilliant plan to handle park requests and how the first few I'd approved had gone so far. When he stopped laughing at me, I went out to the front porch and brought the box in.

I pulled the lid off and made a quick assessment that there were more than thirty requests in there. "Do you know how to set up an email account for the park residents?"

Nick's mouth dropped open. He clutched his heart and gasped. "You don't know me at all."

I started pulling out papers and stacking them. "Alright. Don't get yourself worked into a lather. I don't know the first thing about tech stuff. We had an IT team at the precinct that handled that for us." I pulled out a red plastic thumb drive and placed it on the table.

Nick moved into the chair next to mine. "Yes, I can set up a parkwide email for you. But how are you gonna check it?"

I took a long drink of my soda and looked sideways at him. "Internet?"

He snorted. "You need to get a computer. And you'd better hope all the residents at least have a cell phone that gets email, or you'll be going around delivering flyers about the *unappealing expressions on community jack o' lanterns* just like your predecessor."

I groaned. "How did I let Agnes stick me with this?"

Nick picked up a stack of requests and started thumbing through them. "'Cause your backbone went away with your badge."

I gave him a dirty look even though he was totally right. "Here's a request to stock the lake with fish but only cod because it's the only fish that tastes good battered and deep fried."

Nick laughed. "Good luck with that. Cod's a saltwater fish. Here's a request to ban all motorcycles from the Fontainebleau Ring, and here's another request to put in a special asphalt pad on the Fontainebleau Ring to park three motorcycles."

"Fabulous. This guy wants approval to add a living bamboo fence around the perimeter of his lot for privacy. How tall does bamboo get?"

"Fifteen feet."

"Oh heck, no. These people are insane. This one wants me to put in a tennis court. Don't they know their lot fees barely cover the basic utilities? And this one is just a bunch of unflattering profanity about me."

Nick held up a blue scrap of paper. "Carl Gruber wants a pool with a diving board and Jacuzzi and a sign that kids are not welcome on Tuesday afternoons."

"What happens Tuesday afternoon?"

Nick grinned. "Apparently, that's when he likes to entertain the ladies."

"Gross." I held up the last request. "Finally, one I can accommodate."

Nick raised an eyebrow.

"Please have that cranberry sauce that comes out in the shape of the can at the potluck."

His face broke into a megawatt smile. "Yeah. That one's mine."

"You little turd."

Nick laughed and picked up the thumb drive. "What about this?"

"I don't know what I'm going to do with that."

"You know I brought my laptop over while you were getting your Dancing Queen on. We could go upstairs and check it."

I pushed away from the table. "What are we waiting for?"

Nick turned the heat off under his chili, and I followed him through the living room. Ringo's head shot up over the back of the couch and his tail started to thump against the cushions. Dad was fast asleep with his mouth hanging open. "Stay there, buddy."

We ran up the spiral stairs to the rainforest. Nick had not just brought over his laptop. He'd brought over enough tech to run a small country. He pulled out a very fancy blue-and-black leather chair and took the thumb drive, plugging it into a machine.

"I have to run some scans first. This will only take a minute."

I paced behind him trying not to be obvious that I was looking around his room. He'd left almost no evidence that he'd spent the night here. The bed was made just like when he arrived and there were no dirty clothes or wet towels.

"Alright. Let's open it up."

There were only three files. All pictures. Nick clicked on the first and it opened another mishmash ransom note like Dad had received last night. My blood ran cold as I read the words. **The clock is ticking. Don't mess with me or I'll ruin you. 100Gs by Thursday! I'm watching you, Don Virtue.**

"What in the world is that?" Nick asked.

"Someone is threatening to go to the media with the story that Dad lives here if Dad doesn't put a hundred thousand dollars under a canoe by Thanksgiving."

Nick's jaw flexed and his knuckles turned white on the mouse. He clicked on another picture, and it was Dad, sitting out on the back deck with Ringo. The last picture was Dad getting into the Jeep. He was dressed in his regular clothes so we must have been going to the doctor's office. "A hundred thousand isn't a lot of money for someone with your dad's wealth."

I pulled over the wooden desk chair next to Nick. "So, what are you saying? Dad should just pay it?"

"No! Definitely not. But whoever is blackmailing him is thinking really small. Like, could it be a kid?"

"Addicts think small. Maybe it's someone looking for money for drugs. Or maybe they thought this amount wouldn't be worth his while to go to the police over."

Nick gave me an appraising look. "And they clearly don't know you're a cop."

"Former cop."

"With cop friends."

"Cop friend."

"Leave this with me and I'll see if I can uncover some metadata."

"What's that?"

"It means I have ways to find out who's behind this."

"When you do, you'll need to hold me back."

Nick put his hand on top of mine. "Someone will need to hold us both back."

Chapter 23

THE LADIES AND I STOOD OUTSIDE OF THE GIBSON SUNDAY NIGHT. We'd just come from an AA meeting across town to bolster ourselves to go back into the bar. I had a new resolve to find Jacob after discovering he might have been just a few Metro stops away in DC the whole time my life was falling apart. *My God, I'd done events downtown. I could have run into him anytime. And why wasn't he looking for me?*

Anyone with access to a TV, local newspaper, or Internet headlines knew I'd survived Stratton Park. The IA investigation into the explosion at the warehouse was all anyone here could talk about until news broke that the pandas were coming back to the National Zoo.

There were days I couldn't get out of bed, the grief was so heavy. And Jacob was at freakin' Ben's Chili Bowl having lunch. "This waitress better be full of information or I'm gonna lose my mind."

Scarlett handed me a mini Hershey bar. "Alright. Calm down. Let's not pull our earrings off until we know her story."

Bree popped a chocolate into her mouth and let out a grunt of pleasure. "Does Ambrose know you've been stealing his Halloween candy?"

Scarlett scoffed. "Ambrose is seven. He doesn't know that I know about his stash in the garage. I've been complaining about the Now or Laters in the house candy to throw him off."

Charisse dropped her peanut butter cup wrappers into her Fendi bag and snapped it shut. "Are we ready?"

I nodded. "Let's do this."

We approached the wide green door of the swanky cocktail bar where I'd freaked out just a few days ago. Determined to keep my cool tonight, and filled with stolen chocolate, I yanked that sucker open and marched right in.

The crowd was light. Just one man in a suit with a takeout bag at the bar. There were few business meetings on Sunday nights, and the Instagrammers were home getting ready for school tomorrow. We spotted the older waitress from the bachelorette party reel chatting up a booth in the corner. We stared at her until she waved. "Just sit anywhere, girls."

Scarlett stepped toward her. "Actually, we came to talk to you."

Her painted eyebrows shot to her copper hair. She came at us with a quizzical look on her face. "Is that right? Well, what can I do for you?"

Charisse pointed to an empty booth away from the others. "Can we sit?"

"Yeah, yeah. Of course. But you know I'm on the clock, so you'll have to order something."

Bree gave the woman a friendly smile. "I'm sure we can get some mocktails. You do have mocktails don't you . . . ? And maybe some bar food. What's your name?"

"No mocktails. It's against policy." She grabbed four skinny menus from a stack on the ledge and took an order pad from one of her bulky apron pockets. "And it's Nancy, hon. What'll you have?"

As soon as Scarlett's butt hit the wood, she held up her phone and played the reel. "That's you, isn't it, Nancy?"

The waitress squinted at the screen and moved back to see it better. "Yep. Sure is."

"Well, the thing is, Nancy"—I kept my voice light and hopefully noncombative even though I was full of anger and chocolate—"that video was taken before you started here back on the twelfth of February. You said you came on after the turnover to new management."

She considered us for a moment, then looked behind her in both directions. Then Nancy pushed Bree deeper into the booth and slid in next to us. "Keep your voices down. That's a secret and Gwennifer has a big mouth. She'll report me just to get my hours."

Scarlett put her phone face down on the table. "So, what gives, Nancy?"

She leaned back against the dark wood and gave us a lazy shrug. Then she crossed her legs. "What's it to you? Why do you care when I started here?"

I took out my phone and played the video clip I'd taken from Abigail with me talking to the bridesmaids in my riot gear.

Nancy tucked her pencil behind her ear. "Yeah. I remember you. You don't see too many cops with blue streaks in their hair." She gave a gravelly chuckle, like she'd just come in from a fifty-year smoke break.

An image opened in my mind of this lady leading me down a dark hall. She'd commented on my blue hair then too.

"Heck, we don't see too many cops in here at all. This is a classy place. The management fired everyone at the end of shift that night. Something about missing cash from the drawer, and top-shelf booze walking away—I dunno. I only kept my job because they needed me to train the new hires on the ancient computer system none of them knew how to use, and then they forgot about me. No one here knows I'm OG, as the kids say. It's amazing how an old lady can just disappear in plain sight, isn't it?"

I looked at her long and hard. She didn't flinch under my scrutiny. Even gave me a slight nod of challenge as if to say, *What else you got?* "Do you know what happened to the rest of the staff from that night?"

"Why? Someone owe you money?"

"I have some questions and need information from someone who worked here."

Bree flashed her iPhone. "Like maybe this guy."

She leaned away from Bree's phone to better see the photo of the Viking bartender that Bree had made her lock screen. "That's Angel. Great bartender."

Charisse took out a little notebook. "Angel who?"

"I don't know his real name."

Scarlett set her phone on the table. "Where can we find this Angel? You must have his address in the employment records. Where did you send his last paycheck?"

Nancy pulled herself out of the booth. "No idea. The bookkeeping isn't on the same system as the ordering and POS. He's probably working at another bar in the city. I guess you gals could start hopping around. You'll know him from the angel tattoos on his arms."

One of the customers in the back booth waved at Nancy and held up his empty glass.

She waved back at him. "I'll be right there. Good luck, honey. I hope you find what you're looking for." She was already giving her customer a playful hard time before she'd walked away.

I looked around the table. "Well, I guess we Google bartenders named Angel now."

Bree held up her cell phone. "I'm on it, but I'm not seeing anything on TikTok with Angel tagged."

Scarlett shook her head. "Nothing on Facebook either. He must go by another name."

Charisse gave a wide grin. "His name is Seth Masters, and he won first place in a mixology tournament two years ago."

"Where'd you find that?" Scarlett pushed.

Charisse returned a smug grin. "LinkedIn."

I was properly impressed. "Nice, Charisse."

The other two girls were more skeptical than I was. Scarlett leaned back against the booth and crossed her arms. "Alright, smarty. Where does he work now?"

Charisse's eyebrows dipped. "Hmm. That's strange. He hasn't updated his profile since the Gibson."

Nancy was giving us a weird look from across the room and I felt our welcome was worn out unless we started ordering something dangerous and expensive. I slid out of the booth and grabbed my bag. "Don't worry. I have someone who is dying to help me clear my name. I'll give him a call and ask him to do some digging."

Chapter 24

My morning wrangle with Dad had worn me out. He'd put three bowls of food down for "the cat" and they were all currently empty, which only reinforced the fantasy. Ringo licked his chops and looked more than a little guilty, giving away that he at least sensed that the salmon Fancy Feast wasn't really meant for him. Not guilty enough to not eat it again, mind you. I had no doubt the minute my back was turned the fourth bowl would be emptied.

Nick seemed determined to earn his stay with us by making a constant buffet of food. This morning it was a protein-packed, low-fat frittata—whatever that meant. I tried getting Dad to back me up that Nick didn't have to do all the cooking, but Dad couldn't stop saying *fri-ta-ta* and giggling. He eventually left the kitchen singing, "Brick Howwwse. It's all hanging out. Bow chica chica wow wow."

After playing Frisbee with Ringo for about an hour, Nick and I made plans to go into DC later today, but first, I wanted to visit the school where Archie Wilkins taught second grade. Maybe someone there knew of a reason the world's nicest man would be bludgeoned with a candelabra and shot up with heroin.

At first, I thought GPS had taken me to the wrong address. The building before me looked like a schoolhouse back in time on a prairie. A large two-story red wooden building with pristine white windows and doors. A bronze bell hung gleaming from the central three-story tower and Laura Ingalls waved from the front porch. Okay, I made that last part up.

I knew the charming little schoolhouse had a state-of-the-art security system, because two armed guards met me in the parking lot before I'd made it past Mrs. Archer's fourth-grade scarecrow project on the side lawn. They tried ushering me back to my Jeep without so much as a how do you do when a statuesque, middle-aged woman in a tailored pantsuit appeared, and they stood down without her saying a word. Maybe she had a special whistle only rent-a-cops could hear.

The woman gave me a professional-grade smile. "I'm sorry about that. Jayne Moorefield. Principal. We don't allow drop-in visitors who aren't parents. The security of our students is of utmost importance at Pixieland Academy."

I shook her outstretched hand and noticed the lack of a wedding ring and a very classy French manicure. "I believe it. Layla Virtue."

"What can I do for you, Ms. Virtue?"

"Layla—please. I was hoping to ask you some questions about Archie Wilkins."

To her credit, Jayne didn't flinch. She appraised my blue hair and glanced at my Jeep, sizing me up right away as not a cop. She took a moment probably to consider whether or not I was with the press. "And who do you represent, Layla?"

"I'm helping the police with their inquiries." I fished Dayton Castinetto's business card out of my purse and handed it to her, not wanting to think of the hissy fit that would follow if she actually called him.

"But you're not a cop."

"Not anymore. Think of me as a sub."

She examined the card and nodded. "Follow me."

We passed Crabbe and Goyle stationed by the front door. I gave them a little finger wave on my way into the polished front lobby. They did not return the gesture.

Principal Moorefield took me past a raised counter of busy admins into her office and offered me a chair. Diplomas and awards lined her walls along with framed pictures of her with student classes dating back fifteen years. "That's nice. You can see how they grow and change through the years."

She smiled at the photo marked from this year. "Mmm. Well, we only take them as far as fifth grade here, and when they start middle school, they never return to say hello."

"I'm sorry. That must be hard for you when you get attached to them."

She nodded, a hint of sadness in her eyes. "I never had kids of my own . . . So how can I help?"

I took out my notebook and pen and placed them on the edge of her polished desk. "I was hoping you could tell me about Mr. Wilkins."

She crossed her legs and leaned back in her padded pink desk chair. "Archie was a wonderful teacher and human being. The kids loved him. Voted favorite teacher every year. I can't believe something so horrific could happen to such a sweet man. He's dearly missed."

"What kind of teacher was he?"

"Archie focused on the academic basics. He used to say that the whole world was open to you if you knew how to read and write. These kids are very fast learners." She reached into a drawer and pulled out an embossed linen page listing the requirements and fees for enrollment. "Here at Pixieland Academy we have a very selective admissions process. We require IQ and cognitive testing, as well as an impressive extracurricular profile. Our students are the most gifted in the country. Both the student and their family members are vetted through essays and a tough interview process."

"What kind of essay is a preschooler required to write?" My eyes zoomed in on the number of zeros listed under tuition and I had to blink twice. "Oh that kind."

A frown crossed Jayne's brow. "We hire only the best educators, and our curriculum and standardized test scores make us the envy of private schools around us."

"I'm sure they do." I threw her a smile to hopefully coax her back away from a defensive stance. "Exactly what kind of salary goes along with that envy and responsibility?"

Jayne smoothed the crease in her burgundy slacks. "Is that relevant?"

I nodded. "It would help me get a better picture of Mr. Wilkins's life, and why someone might want to kill him."

Her face paled, only slightly, but she recovered. Instead of answering me outright, she wrote a number down on a scrap of linen paper and passed it across the desk. "This is our average teacher's salary. Archie was here for more than twenty years so naturally he would be making a bit more."

I could see why she didn't want to say the number out loud. You could pay two public school teachers with that amount. It didn't explain the lavish home Archie had. Not in Northern Virginia. And definitely not in that neighborhood. Or the extravagant vacations every year. He must have been a wiz at investing because that would be tough to achieve on his salary alone.

I tucked the scrap into my notebook. "How are the kids taking Mr. Wilkins's absence?"

Her shoulders relaxed and she cupped her hands in her lap. "They don't really understand what's going on, but they miss their teacher. Parents do talk, and they don't always shield their children from the conversation, so they have a way of finding things out. Then those kids tell other kids . . ." She sighed. "At least they're processing their grief in art therapy, through journaling, and meditation. I brought in grief counselors just to make sure each child got the support they needed."

"So, I have to ask. Have there ever been any complaints about Archie Wilkins? Twenty-three years on staff. No parents have ever gotten their nose out of joint about an assignment or bad grade?"

She shook her head vehemently. "Never."

"No concern about inappropriate behaviors?"

Her eyes widened. "Certainly not. Mr. Wilkins was not that kind of man. And we are a quality institution built on integrity. We've never had as much as a hint of impropriety."

She reached behind her and pulled out a ringed binder, opening to a section for the second grade. It was filled with snapshots from Archie's classes. He always had on a cardigan sweater and jaunty bow tie like a time traveler from a hundred years ago. "The children absolutely adored Archie. And every classroom has a class monitor not just so that each child gets the attention they deserve, but for accountability."

I flipped through the pages. Archie giving lessons, overseeing art, journaling, and recess. I considered the smiling faces and community spirit presented within. But then you don't put the pictures of kids being scolded or looking scared into the binder, do you? No one catalogs their bad days for posterity. "How about the rest of the staff? Anyone not get along? Petty jealousy? Competitiveness?"

She took the binder from my hands and replaced it on the shelf behind her. "We've had a scuffle or two amongst colleagues in the past, but never with Archie. He was always the most genial of men."

"What about drugs and alcohol? Did you ever see Mr. Wilkins under the influence?"

Jayne laughed. "What? Archie? He abhorred drugs. Even at the staff cocktail receptions, Archie Wilkins volunteered as the designated driver, making sure everyone got home safely. No, I'm afraid you're looking for a motive in the wrong place. Archie even ran the food drive every holiday to get the kids involved with the Good Samaritan food pantry where he volunteered. He wanted to teach them that charity begins with your neighbors."

That was a nice sentiment, although I doubted those receiving charity from the food pantry were neighbors of anyone attending this extravagant private school. "Do you think I could see the classroom where he taught?"

"I'm afraid that's not possible. The children are taking early exams before the holiday. But if you'd like to come back on Wednesday at eleven, we're having our Thankfulness banquet, and I can give you a quick tour and show you the classroom then. Mind you, you could only observe."

"Sure, I get it. In the meantime, can I get a roster of students in say . . . the last five years of Archie's classes?"

Worry passed through her eyes. "Well, our parents hold high positions in the community and rely on a certain amount of privacy."

"The list would be for my reference only. My only interest is in finding out who killed their beloved teacher. I could get a warrant, but no one wants to go through all that stress over the holidays—right?"

She rubbed Castinetto's business card. With a sigh of resignation, she reached for the phone on her desk. "Dawn, please bring me the last five classroom rosters for second grade. Thank you."

A minute later, a slim woman with dark skin came through and handed the principal a few typed pages. Jayne read them over and handed them to me. There were only twelve names listed for each year. "I trust that you will keep this confidential?"

"Absolutely."

I read through the list and recognized some of the names as the who's who in Potomac County. If you were a mover and a shaker you obviously sent your kids or grandkids to school here. Which did cause me to question how a man as connected as Archie Wilkins could be murdered without a community memorial or public outcry for justice.

I thanked her for her time and went out to the parking lot. Her security team were stationed at the front door. They gave me tight frowns as I passed.

I headed for my Jeep, but something shiny winked from the front tire, which I could clearly see was flat. Someone had plunged a small knife into the wheel. I went back inside and up to Shaggy and Scooby to wipe the smug looks off their faces. "Someone knifed my front tire. I don't suppose you noticed anyone around my Jeep while I was in with the principal, did you?"

They flew into action like one of the president's kids had been kidnapped. Sealing off the perimeter. The kids had to stay indoors for recess. One of them took a hundred photos if he took one. The other consulted the security system. Nothing conclusive was caught by the camera. The tire that had been knifed was hidden by the car I'd parked next to, and no one entered the property to make the attack. The perpetrator could only have come through the woods next to the parking lot.

After my tire was changed with my spare, I was sent home with an apology. Someone really didn't want me looking into Archie Wilkins's murder—that was already clear. But how did they always know where I'd be?

Chapter 25

"YOUR FATHER THINKS SOMEONE BROKE IN AND STOLE HIS BAG OF Doritos." Nick handed me half a grilled cheese sandwich with one end wrapped in wax paper so I could eat it while driving us to the Metro Park and Ride.

"He probably ate them and forgot."

Nick took a bite of his half of the grilled cheese. "I suggested that, and he proved that he hadn't eaten them by showing me the lack of cheese dust on his fingers."

I nibbled the end of the buttery, cheesy bread. "Mmm mmm mmm mmm mmm."

He snorted. "I'll take that to mean you like it."

I pulled the triangle away from my mouth and a string of cheese snapped and caught me on the chin. "I want to marry this sandwich." I put my blinker on while switching lanes. "Some days Dad seems *Don Virtue level spacey* and other days he seems to be declining so fast I worry that I won't be able to take care of him on my own."

"Which one is it today?"

I turned the Jeep into the parking lot. "I have no idea. I'm just glad Agnes is with him."

We finished our sandwich and got tickets for the closest stop to Ben's Chili Bowl. Once on the train, we settled into a comfortable spot where we wouldn't be overheard. I knocked Nick's knee with my own. "So, how are you doing?"

He took a few seconds before he answered. "Better. I'm still grieving and sad, but it's not overwhelming me."

"Good. And sleep?"

"I got about six hours last night, which is better than my recent habit of sleeping for thirty-six hours after staying up for three days straight. It helps to have to make breakfast for Don so he won't fill up on cookies."

The train stopped to let on a few more passengers. "He loves his cookies. Be careful though. If you keep making Dad breakfast, he'll start to put in special orders."

Nick grinned. "I can handle it. It feels good to be needed."

I searched his face. "I always need you. Don't forget that."

His gaze fixed on me for the time it took for the train to close its doors and leave the platform. Then he squeezed my knee. "I won't."

I spent the rest of the journey filling him in on my disastrous time at Archie Wilkins's house with his timid wife and overprivileged daughters. Nick took great pleasure in laughing at me and expressing the right amount of irritation at the mom-blocks known as Grace and Sophie until we had to change trains at L'Enfant Plaza. I told him about my visit to Pixieland Academy where Archie was apparently beloved by all. A few stops later we arrived at the U Street station and got out across from the iconic DC eatery. Even though the harsh daylight blinded me after being underground, I still spotted the panda statue right away and felt like a fool all over again for missing it.

We crossed the street, and I pulled the snapshot out of my bag. Nick examined it and looked around. He placed himself in position and pointed. "I think the picture was taken from over there. See how they got the panda's foot in the frame but not the red-and-orange building?"

I held my fingers together to make a box. "All I see is the white-and-gray wall behind you. If I stand here, I don't even see the mural in the alley."

Nick looked past me. "The photographer must have been next door. Let's go see if they know anything."

We went inside the restaurant next to Ben's Chili Bowl and showed the photo around. No one recognized Jacob. Then we tried showing Jacob's picture in some of the surrounding restaurants and shops on the street but had no luck there either. I was starting to lose hope. "Maybe this was a foolish idea to think someone would recognize him from walking by one time. I shouldn't have dragged you into this, Nick. I'm sorry. What a waste."

Nick put his arm around my shoulders. "Alright, don't go full Eeyore on me. Come on. I'll buy you a gyro from that food truck."

"Okay. I'm upset, but I could still eat."

Nick chuckled. "That's the spirit."

A yellow box truck with YIANNI'S GYROS AND SOUVLAKI painted on the side was parked in front of the Lincoln Theatre. The window opened as Nick approached. He ordered a gyro with everything, and we waited.

When the food arrived, I asked the chef, a Middle Eastern man in a Washington Capitals jersey, "How often are you on this corner?"

He passed Nick his change. "A few times a week."

I pulled out the photo of Jacob. "I don't suppose you've ever seen this man?"

He squinted at the picture and nodded. "Yeah, I know Kevin. He loves my chicken souvlaki."

Kevin? We'd been asking around for an hour with people looking at me like I was crazy, and hearing someone recognized him just now still sent a shock wave through me. *So, he's going by Kevin?* A million emotions sliced me all at once, leaving little cuts of mockery. *Maybe you never knew him at all.*

For a moment, I thought I could hear the warehouse explosion. The ash floated gently around me like gray snow. My former partner and lover was alive, and so close that he might as well have lived in the trailer next to mine. *Then why haven't you come looking for me?*

I sucked in some air. Ringing started to fill my ears.

Nick took my trembling hand in his and I took a four-count breath. And another.

When it was obvious I was barely holding on, Nick took over. "Do you know if Kevin lives or works around here? We're old buddies from high school and I've been trying to find him."

Yianni leaned out of the window and pointed down the block. "Yeah, man. He's almost always at the bar down the street called Muddled. You can always catch him there for happy hour. They've got a great IPA selection."

Nick gave me another look then turned back to Yianni. "Thanks for the information. That helps a lot."

"Sure thing, man." The window slid into place with a *clack*.

Nick waited a moment then squeezed my hand. "You alright?"

"Not really, no."

"Do you want to go to Muddled or sit here and eat this gyro?"

"I dunno. I lost my appetite." Waves of anger and sadness washed over me. A part of my brain was still fighting with reason. *I saw him die.* Not take his last breath exactly, but I watched the explosion suck him into the warehouse. I'd read the coroner's report that confirmed he'd been burned past recognition. If that wasn't real, then who helped him fake it? And why?

"I want to go to Muddled."

"Then let's get to it." Nick let go of my hand and passed the gyro to a homeless woman sitting in front of the theater. She blessed him several times until he was slightly embarrassed by her gratitude. His face pinked slightly as he told her to take care of herself.

I pulled out my phone and used the GPS to locate Muddled, two blocks north. We took off down the street in search of the cocktail bar.

Muddled was your typical corner bar with red brick walls, an open ceiling of exposed pipes and ductwork, and an outdoor beer garden surrounded by potted boxwoods. It was a chilly Monday afternoon, so the beer garden was unpopulated.

We found a twenty-ish redhead in jeans and a tight black

T-shirt emblazoned with a golden dragon behind the bar filling a glass with beer on tap. "Sit anywhere. I'll be right over."

I approached the bar. "That's alright, we're just looking for someone. Maybe you could take a look at something for us." I held out the photograph and placed it on the bar.

She passed the beer to a server and met us down at our end. The harsh light hinted that her age was closer to thirty. Her hands whispered that thirty might be in her rearview mirror. She picked up the photo and gave it a long look. "Sorry, no."

"Are you sure?"

She dropped it on the counter. "I'm sure I've never seen him before. He your old man or something?"

A guy in jeans and a black polo came through the swinging door to the kitchen and passed her a paper bag that was stapled shut. "Order for Liz. And, Kiara, let me know when you're ready to swap out the ale and I'll give you a hand."

She gave him a nod. "Thanks, Raj." She walked down the bar to a woman nursing a beer and handed her the bag.

When she turned her attention to us, I pushed the photo back to her. "No, nothing like that. We were just told we could find Kevin here."

She glanced at the picture, then slid it back to me. "Sorry. Can't help you. You're welcome to hang out and see if your guy materializes."

I tucked the photo in my pocket, disappointment wrestling with relief. Maybe Yianni was an idiot. "Thanks anyway."

Kiara called over her shoulder that she was ready to swap out the keg, so Nick and I showed ourselves to the door.

I stood in the fall sunshine next to the biergarten and tried not to think about drinking. My emotions were frayed, and I needed my dog.

Nick shoved his hands in his pockets. "Now what?"

"Let's go home and regroup."

"I have a better idea."

"What is it?"

"Let's go get you a laptop so you can break the chains of oppression and enter the twenty-first century, and we can discuss what to do next about Jacob the friendly ghost."

I laughed out loud. "Okay. And while we're at it, don't you need a turkey or something?"

Nick put his arm across my shoulders and chuckled. "Yeah. Or something."

Chapter 26

TWO HOURS LATER WE PULLED IN BEHIND DAD'S ASTON MARTIN, a new laptop on the seat behind me, and the back of the Jeep full of brown paper bags from the local grocer containing a huge turkey with all the fixin's for several side dishes that I'd never heard of. Sweet potato streusel? Broccoli Ritz casserole? Green stuff? My Thanksgiving side dish knowledge began and ended with TV dinners and commercials that ran the month of November.

I grabbed the box of stuff Nick had picked out at Best Buy. "I gave Dad's credit card a good workout, but this community meeting nightmare is his doing so it serves him right. I was pretty happy living in obscurity in my old trailer across the lake."

Nick didn't chuckle like I'd expected him to. "There's some guy on your front porch. Do you know him?"

I looked through the Jeep, following Nick's gaze. "That's Adam Beasley. Some rookie cop who thinks he's going to single-handedly redeem the name of Officer Virtue."

Adam gave me a goofy wave.

Nick snorted. "Do you think he can?"

"Not in a million years, the dumb cherub. My officer cred flat-lined a long time ago."

Adam rambled down the pathway to the Jeep and grabbed a paper bag from the back seat. "Hey, Officer Virtue. Let me help."

Nick headed into the house with the groceries, leaving us alone in the front yard.

"What are you doing here, Beasley?"

"I was knocking on the door of your trailer, but no one was there. Your neighbor across the street told me where to find you."

Frickin' Donna. "Yeah, sorry about that. We moved a few days ago."

"Detective Castinetto wanted me to check on your progress. What? What did I say wrong?"

"You gave me the case files forty-eight hours ago and it was the weekend. How much progress does he expect?"

Adam grinned broadly and shrugged. "I dunno. I just do as I'm told."

"Why didn't he just call?"

"Then I can't make sure you're staying clean." The blood drained from Adam's face, and from the heat rising in mine, I'd say I collected it.

Nick had returned, took a long look at me, and silently took the laptop from my hands before I turned it into a weapon.

I grabbed two grocery bags to give my hands something to do that wouldn't get me arrested for assaulting an officer. "Is that what this is about? Castinetto wants to make sure I'm not getting drunk on the job?"

Adam grabbed another bag and followed me up to the porch where I passed mine off to Nick. His words were rushed and dripping with regret. "I wasn't supposed to say that. You know how he is. He wants everything done by the book. It's not that he doesn't trust you . . . he just thinks that it's not safe for you to do police work anymore."

"You tell Castinetto to go—"

"Good, you brought the turkey up and saved me a trip." Nick took the last bag out of my hand and gave me a look meaning *Be careful with what you say to a cop.*

If he wasn't going through a rough time of his own, I'd tell him where to go right now too. "Look, Beasley. Tell Castinetto that I'm working on it. I've got a couple leads. If he can get me that security footage from the convenience store I asked for that would be great."

Adam handed his bags to Nick's waiting arms. "Okay. I can do that. Is there anything else I can help with? Off the record?"

"Yeah. You know what? See if you can track down an address for a bartender named Seth Masters who goes by Angel. And keep it to yourself, okay? It's personal. No need to bring anyone else in the department into this."

Adam saluted. "You got it! I'm your man. I'll let you know what I find as soon as possible."

"Great. Thank you."

Adam gave me a goofy grin.

"You should go now."

Adam shook himself. "Right. I'm going." He practically skipped down the sidewalk, calling over his shoulder, "I got you."

Nick giggled when I muttered under my breath, "Stupid little cherub."

"He does look a little like Baby Huey, doesn't he?"

"Dumb as a box of rocks, but he has friends in high places. And that freakin' Castinetto. Who does he think he is? My sponsor?"

I followed Nick inside and called for Dad. He was elbow-deep in the grocery bags. "Where are the cookies?"

"That's just the food for Thanksgiving, Dad. You can't possibly be out of cookies already."

"I've been sharing them with the cat."

"Dad . . ."

"Don't blame me. That cat is a thief. I had a whole bag of Oreos that went missing."

I sighed. "Did you take your new medicine today?"

"I took whatever was in the little cubbyhole for Friday."

"It's Monday. Did you take just Friday? Or Friday and Monday?"

Dad's face slid into a blank expression. He cut his eyes to Nick. "Do you know the answer?"

I felt Nick tense beside me. "I'm sorry, I don't."

Dad gave me a sheepish grin. "What's the worst that could happen? I stop peeing altogether?"

Nick's eyes widened in alarm. "I think that would be a problem."

Dad considered this. “Hmm. You might be right. I don’t know, baby girl. What do you want me to do?”

I didn’t have an answer. This was as new to me as it was to him.

Nick pulled out his phone and started tapping the screen. He showed it to me. “We can get a timed pill dispenser that only gives you the medicine when you need it.”

Dad craned his neck to look at the screen. “Hey! I’ve seen those. I think we had one at Rob’s house. You spin it like a roulette wheel and a new pill pops out every ten minutes.”

“It’s not a party game!”

He crossed his arms and laughed. “It totally is.”

Nick gave me a sideways look. “We can program it for the exact time and the pills won’t come out before.”

“Okay.” I handed him Dad’s credit card. “Get it.”

Dad grabbed a soda from the fridge and sat at the table to watch us unload the groceries.

I was in a terrible mood. I was still reeling from the blow that Jacob is alive. Sorry. *Kevin* is alive. The can of worms *that* opened up was all bad. Then Beasley set me off with that dig from Castinetto. Every once in a while, I thought I felt a strange attraction vibe with Castinetto. Then he pulled some crap like this and I remembered he only had eyes for himself in the mirror.

Why did I let myself get sucked in to working with him again? I only took this consulting job as a favor to the commissioner since he asked for me personally. Okay, that was only partly true. If I was honest with myself, I really wanted to prove that I wasn’t the screwup the whole precinct thought I was.

I put the loaf of bread Nick bought for stuffing in the cabinet with the mushroom soup and green beans and slammed it shut. My hands were shaking. “Whatever happens, don’t let me drink. Okay?”

Dad was playing on his phone. “You want to watch that *Chemistry* show with me? Maybe you can explain what the heck is going on.”

“Maybe in a little bit, Dad. I’m too antsy to sit still right now.”

Nick put his hands on my shoulders. “What can we do to get your mind off it?”

"I'd like to figure out who killed Archie Wilkins so I can shove it in Castinetto's face. You want to go to the food pantry with me? Archie volunteered there and they might be willing to tell me more about him than his uptight private school."

Nick nodded. "Let me get a couple cans of soup and we'll go."

"Why do we need soup?"

Nick opened the cabinet and took out two cans. "We can't go to the food pantry empty-handed. We need a donation."

"Sorry, I didn't realize. I've never been on the moral high road before."

Dad rolled his eyes. "So dramatic. You were a cop, weren't you?"

"Yeah, but we just took our donations to the precinct and threw them in a box for the captain to deliver."

Nick laughed. "Settle down. It's just soup." He looked back into the cabinet. "Didn't you put the stuffing bread in here?"

"Yeah?"

"Well, where is it?"

"What do you mean?"

Nick pointed to the open cabinet. The bread was gone. We both looked at Dad.

Dad grinned and raised his soda to us. "Told ya."

Chapter 27

DAD PITCHED A FIT SAYING THAT HE WAS BORED AND WANTED TO come with us, so I eventually said yes. After he changed out of his yellow leather jumpsuit and into something less headbanger with more of a *dad mowing the lawn* vibe. We'd save the ballgown for when he'd be interacting with people directly. He put on a pair of Nick's sweatpants and a gray T-shirt, and I put his hair up in a man bun then hid it under my PCNU hat. Nick gave him a pair of run-of-the-mill sunglasses and we were off. As long as no one noticed his thousand-dollar sneakers we'd be fine.

You know, if he kept quiet. Perfectly fine.

The Good Samaritan food pantry was the midpoint anchor of a 1970s strip mall in-between a weed dispensary and a Vietnamese nail salon. The dimly lit interior was set up like a normal grocery store without any bells and whistles. Most of the food lining the industrial metal shelves remained in the cardboard boxes they were shipped in, with dishwasher-sized boxes of donated canned foods running down the center aisles. A chalkboard sign advertising weekly cooking lessons using basic pantry items found around the room sat on a table full of recipe cards.

They were pretty busy gearing up for the big holiday. People of all ages and backgrounds pushed carts with wobbly wheels up and down the aisles. Dad pushed his glasses to his forehead and reached for a cart.

I grabbed his arm. "We've already been shopping. Remember?"

His mouth formed an O, and he nodded. Then winked. "I'll just look around."

"Keep a low profile. Okay?"

Dad dropped the sunglasses back to his nose and wandered toward the produce section with bins full of apples from one of the orchards in Loudoun County.

Nick placed our cans of mushroom soup on a shelf marked THANKSGIVING DONATIONS with a meager stockpile of condensed soups, stuffing, gravies, green beans, yams, and cranberry sauce. "I'll keep an eye on him."

Relief washed over me as Nick followed Dad to the cookie aisle.

A balding man in acid-wash jeans and white sneakers came around the corner with a stack of recycled paper bags. He placed the bags at the end of the nearest checkout lane. "Need some help?"

"Is there someone in charge that I could speak to?"

He took a step closer. "I'm Peter Frye. I run the Good Samaritan. Is there a problem?"

"No. Not at all." I put my hand out. "Layla Virtue. I'm helping the Potomac County Police with their inquiries into the death of Archie Wilkins."

He shook my hand. "A shame. A real shame what happened to Archie."

I nodded. "Did you know him well?"

He rocked back on his heels and shoved his hands into his pockets. "Not real well. Archie only volunteered on Saturdays, but he'd been here for several years. Dedicated."

I looked around. "What did that volunteering entail, exactly?"

Peter lifted his palms, and his eyes made a slight roll. "Same as everyone else. Unpacking boxes that come from retailers, organizing donations, stocking the shelves. Sometimes he'd run the checkout, although that wasn't his favorite job."

"What was his favorite job?"

"He liked to check people in. You know, check their pay stubs, their food stamps. It gave him a chance to chat. Offer up some encouragement. Keep their spirits high."

"So, Archie was a talker?"

Peter reached over and separated the gelled cranberry sauce from the chunky variety. "You bet. Especially when one of his kids happened to come in. He was a second-grade teacher, you know."

"Of that fancy, expensive private school? What were any of those kids doing in here?"

"We don't judge anyone for having a need. And it's my understanding that they take an underprivileged scholarship student every once in a while."

"Mmm-hmm. Okay. So, the kids come in. Then what?"

"Well, Archie'd say hello. Chat for a bit. The kids were always happy to see him."

"What about the parents? Grandparents?"

Peter's eyes rolled skyward. "I think his rapport was more with the kids. The adults would usually head off and do their shopping as quickly as possible once they saw Archie would entertain the troops, so to speak." He chuckled at his own joke, then stopped abruptly and cleared his throat.

Off in the distant bowels of the food pantry, I heard Dad begin to butcher Def Leppard. "Pour brown sugar on me! Ooh, hot and sweet."

He's in the baking aisle. Get him out of there, Nick. I coughed and gave Peter a tiny smile. "Did Archie ever have problems with anyone?"

"No. Of course not. You don't volunteer here unless you really care for the community."

"And Archie cared for his community. For everyone?"

A slight blush peeked out of the neck of Peter's ivory sweater. "Yes, of course."

I pressed a bit. "There was no one who had a problem with him?"

"No. Not Archie."

So, someone bludgeoned and drugged the nicest guy on the

planet. "Okay, you ever see anything suspicious in the way he treated someone else?"

Peter tapped the wheel on the Thanksgiving food cart with the toe of his sneaker. "Well, to be totally honest—and I hate to cast any aspersions upon the dead . . ."

I nodded understanding. People never wanted to say anything bad about the dead. I don't know why. The dead aren't in a position to care anymore. "You never know what could help the police find his killer and bring them to justice."

Peter swallowed. "You see, sometimes we get high-dollar goods when they near their expiration dates. Large bottles of olive oil. Gourmet sauces. Boxes of chocolates. We keep the high-dollar donations at the front because they go very fast. Everything here is free if you have a need. That's why we have to check their pay stubs, government papers, welfare card."

I looked around and noticed nothing had prices. "I get it."

"Our patrons give small donations if they can, but nothing is required."

Now we're stalling. "Sure. But what does that have to do with Archie?"

Peter sighed. "There was this woman who would come in—weekly for a while there. Archie would move all the high-dollar donations under the counter as soon as he saw her."

"Why?"

"He said she was a drug addict, and he didn't want to be an enabler. Drugs were a bit of a hot button subject for Archie." Peter shrugged. "She wouldn't be the first addict to frequent the Good Samaritan. Everyone is welcome here."

Dad's voice sang out over the low hum of fluorescent lights and machinery. "I'm gonna be riding on the gravy traaaaain."

I was sure that Syd Barrett never intended his Pink Floyd song to reference whatever packet or jar Dad was looking at right now. "And how did this woman act around Archie?"

"She would keep well clear. Hover around, waiting for another lane to open or for Archie to go on break before she checked out. I think she could sense Archie's disdain."

"What was her name?"

His eyes darted nervously, and he wrung his hands. "Oh . . . I don't know . . ."

"You said you check IDs? Pay stubs? Welfare cards?"

"Well . . . yes, but . . ."

"Come on, Peter. You don't want the police to come back with a search warrant and shut down the food pantry for an official investigation, do you? Right before the holidays?"

Peter wouldn't look me in the eye. He picked up the stack of paper bags he'd placed when I arrived. "No, I don't want that."

"Okay. So, who is she?"

He sighed. "Her name is Carol Hodge. And I haven't seen her in weeks."

"See. That wasn't so hard." Carol Hodge. I don't think I know of any Carols from my meetings. And I'm pretty sure there was no Hodge on Archie's classroom roster.

"Baby girl, this place is awesome!"

Nick was back up front with Dad and a short woman who was grinning like the Joker from Batman. Dad held up a package of Entenmann's chocolate chip cookies. "These are free!"

"Oh, Dad, no. Those are not for you."

Nick held up a hand and gave me a face that meant *Just wait.*

The woman's smile somehow grew even larger. "It is the least we can do. Thank you so much, Mr. . . ." Her voice trailed off and she giggled. Then she put her fingers to her lips and twisted like she was locking them tight.

Oh no.

Nick gave me a pointed look. "We should probably head out. Are you finished here?"

"Yeah, yeah, yeah. Let's go. Thank you, Mr. Frye. We'll be in touch if we need anything else."

He waved a hand and nodded, clearly steeped in confusion.

I got Dad safely in the Jeep and cranked it to life. "Okay. What happened?"

Nick gave me an apologetic grin. "Well, they know who Don is now."

I glanced in the rearview mirror where Dad had a cookie in his mouth and one on deck in his hand. "Wha . . . ?"

My throat made a weird sound, like I was being waterboarded. "Because of the singing?"

"I think the autograph really sold it." Nick shook his head. "That, and the ten grand he just donated."

Dad mumbled through a mouthful of chocolate chips, "It'll help a lot of people, baby girl. And the nice lady promised she'd keep it a secret."

"They always do."

Peter Frye ran out of the front door with the Joker in tow. He appeared to be crying tears of gratitude. She looked ready to hurl herself onto the Jeep.

I threw the Jeep in reverse and backed out of there so fast, if I was still on the force, I would have given myself a ticket.

Chapter 28

My phone pinged a Google Alert. I handed it to Nick. "Check that for me please."

"'Don Virtue of Society's Castoffs makes large donation to local food bank. DC Fox News.'"

I scowled into the rearview mirror. "That's why we make our donations through Jimmy in Nana's name. Right?"

Dad shrugged and pulled another cookie from the box. "Do we?"

My phone pinged again, and I sighed.

Nick's shoulders slumped. "You're not going to like this."

I took the ramp for the toll road. "I'm sure I'm not."

"Someone on TikTok just posted a video appealing to Don to come donate to the homeless shelter they volunteer in."

"Yep."

Dad leaned forward in his seat. "Where is it?"

"Don't answer that."

Another ping. "Here's a picture of Don in the food pantry. Probably from the security camera. It's grainy. You can't tell it's him."

"It won't matter. Trust me."

My phone made a new sound.

"That's a text from Scarlett."

I flipped on my blinker to change lanes. "What does it say?"

"'911 Bree. Meeting.'"

"Tell her I'll be on my way after I drop you off."

Nick tapped out my response and placed the phone in the cup holder to let it ping on its own the rest of the way home.

My anger was rising, but Dad looked very small in the back seat. In a few minutes he wouldn't even remember why I was mad.

After dropping Nick and Dad off, giving an update to Dad's security detail, and flipping through two dozen new requests from the trailer park psychos, I snuggled my Ringo for a few minutes. He'd embedded himself into my side as soon as I opened the door. "You are the world's sweetest boy. Do you know that?"

Ringo answered with a lick on my chin.

I went to get in the Jeep and found that someone had keyed "Bit" into the side of my door while we were in the food pantry. We must have come out before they could finish. I took a picture with my cell phone for the insurance claim. If they thought they were scaring me off, they didn't realize I was a former cop. These threats were a dime a dozen to me.

I headed out to the McLean AA meeting to support the girls, but after this morning I needed to go for my own recovery reasons. On the way, I called Castinetto and filled him in on what I'd learned at the school and food pantry.

"Not bad, Virtue. Maybe you won't screw this up after all."

"You can't see me right now, Castinetto, but I'm flipping you off."

"Very professional."

"And I need you to look into Carol Hodge. Let me know if she has a record."

"I'll see what I can find out."

"And don't forget that I want to see the security footage from the convenience store. What's the holdup on that?"

"I don't know. I've asked for it twice. Let me see if I can rattle some cages."

The thought crossed my mind that Castinetto might be blocking me from investigating. He made his opinion about my involvement in the case loud and clear. I was like salt in his lemonade.

"Someone is trying to scare me away from looking into Archie's death. You don't know anything about that, do you?"

"No. Scare you away how?"

I told Castinetto about the different threats I'd received while working for him.

"I knew it was a bad idea to let you be involved, Virtue. You're off the force. And a lot of people are still pissed that you were in a bar instead of backing your team up when they were sabotaged."

His voice softened. "I think we should take you off the case for your protection. You're not going to get anything productive anyway."

"Don't you dare take me off the case, Castinetto. I may only be a consultant, but clearly I've made someone nervous, which means I'm on the right track. If you want answers to what happened to Archie Wilkins, then leave me alone and get me that security footage."

I ended the call just as I pulled into the hotel parking lot. I chose to self-park instead of valet because that was ten dollars I could put toward an electric fence around my property until Make-A-Wish season passed.

The meeting was halfway over by the time I arrived. Scarlett and Charisse were waiting for me, worry etched across their faces.

One of the regulars was sharing about her sister-in-law wanting to do a vegan Thanksgiving, so I had to skirt around the back of the room not to interrupt her meltdown. Charisse waved me up to the seat between her and Scarlett. When the share was over, Charisse whispered, "Bree hasn't shown up again, or answered any of our calls."

Scarlett leaned across her and hissed, "It's not like we're saying she has to go to every meeting."

Charisse put her hand on Scarlett's arm. "But she hasn't missed a meeting in months up until two weeks ago."

Scarlett adjusted the silk bow on the shoulder of her purple blouse. "This isn't like her."

Charisse groaned. "She's been working so hard at the program. The poor baby's OD'd twice. It's a miracle she's even alive."

We grew quiet while a man shared about his stress over which two kids from his three ex-wives he would have to let down over the holidays since they all lived in different states.

He sounds like he spread the love around as much as my dad. It's a wonder I turned out as good as I did. Of course I am sitting in an addict recovery meeting with the first friends I've made in over thirty years, and I'm being shaken down by a pig in a tutu for a playground. I should probably tell this guy he's doing better than he thinks.

When his share was over, I leaned into the girls and whispered, "She said the other day that her family was having trouble dealing with her brother's death around the holidays. Have either of you ever met her parents?"

Scarlett shook her head. "No. But I know they had to move recently because they couldn't afford their house anymore. I took her home one night and she told me their insurance dropped them, and outpatient programs and therapy bled them dry."

Charisse crossed her arms and hugged herself. "Bree carries those heavy burdens every day. But lately it's like there's a shadow over her countenance. Her eyes just don't have the same light, you know?"

A gnaw of fear rumbled through my belly. I'd seen Bree pull at her sleeves when she was stressed. The occasional peek of silvery scars revealing themselves. We didn't talk about it, but we all knew. It was the unspoken fear we shared and why the ladies were so quick to be concerned when Bree's behavior became erratic.

Jonathan closed the meeting with the Serenity Prayer and people started milling about.

The words about suicidal behavior from the gig the night I played with the Tristan Trio floated across my memory. "Why don't we go over and check on her?"

Scarlett's eyes widened as she considered the idea. "A wellness check?"

Charisse hissed through her teeth, "She could be offended. Remember how she reacted the other night?"

I grabbed my purse and a cookie. "I don't care. I can't tiptoe around this anymore. If she's in danger I want to get ahead of it. If she gets mad, she gets mad. At least she'll be safe. Women have stopped being friends with me for far less."

Charisse tucked her leather purse under her arm. "Then what are we waiting for?"

Scarlett dug her keys out of her bag. "I'll drive."

So, we ditched the meeting and drove over to a sleepy town house neighborhood in Annandale. Scarlett parked her Porsche in a visitor spot under a golden hickory tree. She pointed to a three-story brick town house. "When I dropped her off, she went into the one on the end there."

We sat in the car and watched the unit like we were hoping Bree would appear and wave us in. I took a breath, pictured Bree in my mind, and opened the car door.

I marched up the front steps with the others behind me and hit the doorbell. When no one answered I banged the knocker. Nothing. "Could they be out of town?"

Charisse checked her phone. "Since yesterday? Kind of last-minute."

I knocked again. "We know you're in there! Open up!"

A soft voice called over to us from a few feet away. "Hey. What are you all doing here?"

Bree stood in front of an identical brick town house one row over. A little bulldog on a pink leash was sniffing the ground around a bare azalea bush.

The door in front of us flew open and an old woman in curlers and blue nightgown stood facing us. "Whatdoyouwant?"

I looked over at Bree. "We were looking for you."

Her nose scrunched up into little wrinkles. "That's not my house."

Scarlett murmured, "My sense of direction has never been good."

I threw Scarlett a look of exasperation.

The woman in the door tapped a Lucky Strike cigarette out of a near-empty pack and placed it between her lips. "You have two seconds to tell me what this is about or I'm calling the cops."

"I'm sorry. I think we have the wrong house."

In one swift movement, the woman flicked her lighter, lit the cigarette, and slammed the door in our faces.

Charisse quickly abandoned us and walked down the steps toward Bree. "Well, which one is yours, honey?"

Bree tugged on the leash. "Hurry up, Alice." She pointed her elbow down the walkway of the unit she stood in front of. "This one."

Scarlett followed Charisse's lead. "We came because we were worried about you."

Bree huffed, "Jeez, guys. It's like one meeting, okay? It's not like I left the country."

I tried a negotiation tactic. "Everyone here loves you, Bree. We just want to be a part of your life. You want that, don't you, Bree? Can't we sit down and talk this over?"

Bree's eyes locked with mine with a touch of irritation. It was a tense moment until Alice sniffed my leg, smelled Ringo, and peed on my Doc Martens.

My cop voice abandoned, I backed away from the little bulldog. "Ugh! These cost me a fortune!"

Bree pulled the leash. "Alice! No! Layla, I'm so sorry." Bree's lip quivered. She bit it, but the tears forced through her resolve. She started to sob, her whole body shaking. "I'll pay for the new boots. She didn't know any better. She's just a puppy."

I was momentarily taken aback. I'd only seen this kind of overreaction one other time when a 220-pound gangbanger was arrested for holding up a Walgreens in the drive-thru lane because his nan needed her heart medicine.

Charisse and Scarlett stood motionless. Scarlett's eyebrows knitted in consternation, Charisse's mouth agape.

"Bree, it's fine. I'll just Windex them. Really." I took a step toward her. "What's this all about?"

Bree crumpled into my arms to take the hug that I should have offered. "Everything is so messed up. It's all my fault."

"That can't possibly be true."

Scarlett and Charisse wrapped their arms around us while Alice pranced in circles and trapped us in her leash. Scarlett smoothed Bree's honey-gold locks away from her forehead. "I don't believe that at all."

Charisse patted Bree's back in a slow soothing rhythm, her words like chicken soup. "There there, honey. Tell us what happened."

Bree sniffled. "I heard my parents arguing about Thanksgiving. They're stressed about money. I know they're buried under bills from my rehab. They'll say it was worth every penny just to have me doing better and still with them, but I can hear my mom crying at night. I know she misses Ryan. Why did their good kid have to be the one that died?"

I pulled back to look Bree in the eyes. "Bree, I've seen a lot of families torn apart by drugs. The one thing I know for sure is that parents will do everything in their power to save their kids. There is no way that your parents regret spending that money for you to be well."

Bree pushed her face into my neck and nodded. "The holidays make everything so much worse."

I tightened my hold on her. "I know they do."

With one check my dad could fix the surface problem, but money never heals the heart. Love heals.

Friendship heals.

The flicker of an idea started to take hold on me. "Why don't we all have Thanksgiving dinner together? I've been roped into making the turkey for the community association in my trailer park. And by me, I mean Nick, because in addition to being fine, that boy can cook, and I can't boil water."

The girls all laughed, and Bree wiped her eyes then pulled Alice's leash to get her to unwind.

"Our potluck isn't until four. We can coordinate times so Charisse, you can still have time with your kids. And, Scarlett, you can still reenact the Pilgrims' first Thanksgiving."

Scarlett squeezed her eyebrows together. "That's gonna be a disaster."

I grinned. "And, Bree. Invite your parents to come. They can bring something if they want—or not. If they like sour rhubarb pie I can pretty much promise one will make an appearance unless I get enough signatures on my petition."

Bree's eyes filled up again. "I would love that. Not the pie I mean—eww. But having dinner all together."

"Then that's the plan. If you can get Alice unwrapped from around our legs maybe we can go get coffee before I have to visit Archie Wilkins's wife's grief support group."

Scarlett pulled the leash away from her suede designer boots and stepped out of the tangle. "Uh. I think you mean *we.* 'Cause we're totally going with you."

"She told me to come alone."

Charisse rolled her eyes. "She don't tell us what to do."

Bree's face brightened. "Yeah. What if I want grief support?"

Charisse jabbed her thumb in Bree's direction while she tried to step out of Alice's leash. "There you go. We'll be there for Bree."

Scarlett grinned. "It's not our fault that sound travels."

That was solid logic. I just hoped Mrs. Wilkins saw it that way.

Chapter 29

BREE'S MOTHER WAS SO EXCITED TO BE INVITED TO THE COMMUnity Thanksgiving that she had to come hug each of us twice. If I'd ever wondered what Bree would look like in her fifties, her mother, Susan, was the answer.

By the time we were able to say goodbye and pack into Scarlett's Porsche, we were running late. We transferred to my Jeep at the hotel and did a quick Starbucks drive-through where I got a starter coffee. Also known as hot chocolate in a cup that sat too close to the coffee beans, so every sip tasted like what I assume a mocha is.

I parked across from the address Marion had given me yesterday afternoon. The grief support meeting took place at Fibre Space, a tall blue-brick building in Old Town Alexandria. One entire outside wall was covered with a mural featuring a Jane Jetson-style woman in a space helmet floating on a giant blue ball of yarn, knitting needles at the ready. Inside was filled with rows and rows of yarn in every color and thickness imaginable.

We said we were there for the support group and a kindly woman in an intricate lavender sweater told us each to pick out a skein. Only Bree knew what that was and she handed us each a ball of yarn from a practice barrel. Scarlett and Charisse chose knitting needles, and Bree picked a hook stick she said was for crochet. I had only seen knitting needles once in my life and they were sticking out of some guy's neck at the time. Apparently, knitting can only do so much to relax you when your husband is a serial cheater.

We were led to a ring of metal folding chairs arranged in a circle. Each one had a colorful seat and back cushion made out of yarn. The girls sat across the circle from me and made small talk with a couple of other early attendees while they turned their yarn into something useful. I fiddled with my yarn, having no idea how to do anything productive with it. I knotted loops around my wrists and yanked, testing the tensile strength to see if it would make decent handcuffs, until Charisse cleared her throat loudly and gave me some side-eye because everyone was staring like I had someone tied up in my basement.

I tied the yarn in a loop and thread it through my fingers into a cat's cradle while keeping one eye on the door for Marion. At least the others in the room no longer looked like they wanted to flee.

Finally, Marion crashed through the door in a designer pink tweed suit. "I'm so sorry I'm late. The housekeeper had an emergency, and I had to heat up dinner for the girls by myself."

She immediately scanned the back of the room. Her eyes rested on me and a determined look crossed her face. She grabbed a ball of yarn and some knitting needles and wound her way to the folding chair next to mine, which for some reason no one else wanted to sit on.

She noticed Charisse and gasped. "I thought I asked you to come alone."

Charisse covered with a surprised face and a *Fancy meeting you here while I'm supporting my friend Bree* speech.

Grief support was a lot like AA except no one introduced themselves with a reminder of their addiction, and they all created something out of yarn while they shared.

All night I waited for Marion to share, but she was tight-lipped and focused on her violet knitting. Her eyes kept flicking to Charisse then to me. The unasked question: *Can I trust you?*

Bree, however, opened up to the group and dove right in to talk about her brother and how he had died at seventeen. "He was like totally a straight A student, you know. Already had early admission to Cornell. He was really gonna be someone. I can't help but feel robbed that he was taken from me before we could be friends, you know. Now all of my parents' hopes and dreams are focused on me, and I can't live up to their expectations."

The ladies fluttered around her and cooed their condolences like a flock of mourning doves.

They were mostly older women. Many had lost parents. A couple sisters. Two had lost children. My thoughts went to Dad. *Would this be me in a couple of years?* I wasn't ready for that. The more my heart was squeezed, the more air left the room. When one of the ladies spoke of losing her mother to Alzheimer's I thought I'd break down completely, but I held it together on the outside. This wasn't why I was here. I would cry later at home, with Ringo.

When the evening was over, my blue yarn was twisted into knots around my fingers. I was trying to figure out how to escape it when Marion grabbed my arm and hissed, "Follow me."

I unwound myself and followed her a few feet away to the far side of the store. Not exactly the chamber of secrets.

"Thank you for meeting me. My daughters mean well, but . . . they're protective like their father."

That painted a rather grim picture of Archie. "So, what'd you want to tell me?"

She reached over to a lime-green yarn, fat and fuzzy like a caterpillar, and rubbed it with her finger. "My husband didn't have any enemies."

Well, this meeting could have been a phone call. "Okay."

She gave me a sharp nod like her disclaimer was out of the way. "Something unpleasant happened a couple of months ago. I ran into someone I'd met at one of Archie's programs at the grocery store. I said hello, but she looked down her nose at me like I was vermin. Refused to speak to me. Just turned and walked away. I thought surely she must have mistaken me for someone else."

She swallowed hard, like the words had made a bitter taste in her mouth. "But then a few days later, the same thing happened at the library when I was dropping off some books for their annual book sale."

"Same person?"

She fanned herself with a crochet magazine. "Different. A little, old, white-haired lady said I should be ashamed of myself. She shook her fist at me and stormed off. I've never felt so much like a social pariah."

A rack of patterns behind her head swayed and three sets of eyes peered at me over a Fair Isle knitting display. I waved a magazine and shooed them while Mrs. Wilkins rubbed the lime-green yarn again. "Ashamed of yourself for what?"

"I have no idea. I went home most distressed, and had to make myself a vodka martini. I mean, we've never hurt anyone. We keep our yard tidy. We give a substantial amount of money and time to charity. It was so unsettling. I told Archie what had happened, and he said it was probably nothing, but I wasn't to go back to either place again."

"What? Not ever?"

Behind her, all three ladies tried to make themselves look natural while thumbing through different yarn books, but I clocked their raised eyebrows.

Marion's watery blue eyes filled with tears. "Archie thought it was best."

"He told you not to go back to the store or the library? How were you supposed to get groceries?"

She absently twirled her wedding ring on her finger with her thumb. "Archie was very protective. When he heard what had happened, he said we'd have Jasenka, our housekeeper, do all the shopping from then on. That was what we paid her for anyway. I just wanted to pick out a nice First Communion card for Archie's students. That's something I think one should do themselves. Not ask the help to pick up something so personal. Don't you think so?"

"Sure. Just out of curiosity, how many other places did Archie tell you not to return to?"

Her face pinked. "It wasn't like that. I just had to avoid my second favorite spa and the tennis club. But those weren't really a big deal. I don't care for tennis anyway. He hated to see any of his girls upset. He said my job was to be a good mother, organize the help, and take part in social functions while he took care of the finances."

Charisse dropped a yarn caddy she was trying to disappear behind, causing Scarlett to dive under an afghan on display. Bree spun in a circle looking for an exit and lunged into the next aisle.

Marion's head swiveled toward the sound of the clatter.

Charisse picked up the caddy and said, "Oh good. It's on sale." Then patted it and moved toward the front of the store.

I sighed at our lack of subtlety. "That was very traditional of him."

Her eyes relaxed. "It was. Thank you for saying so. Archie took such good care of me. I never even saw our finances. He handled everything."

She pulled a fat, legal-sized envelope from her purse. "That's what I wanted to talk to you about. I brought copies of our bank statements and investment portfolio so you could see that our standard of living was because of Archie's fiscal management. You asked me how we could afford to live the way we do on a teacher's salary, and I don't want there to be any question about something untoward. Archie was a good man."

I took the envelope. "Thank you. I'm sure this will be very helpful."

She grabbed my free hand. "Please. Just find out who killed my husband." Her voice started to quiver. She turned and headed for the door.

The ladies and I waited a minute in silence, then we reconvened in my Jeep. I ripped open the envelope and pulled out three months of bank statements and an investment report. "These look like normal household expenses for a high-income family. I don't see anything overtly extraneous that would account for a yacht or trips around the world. I also don't see a mortgage or a car payment."

Scarlett tapped the bottom of one of the pages. "The same amount of money was going out that was coming in each month. He didn't have anything left over for a mortgage or car payment."

Bree peeked over my shoulder. "There are a lot of big donations to charity. The Good Samaritan, Humane Paws, Compassion Foundation Worldwide, the Kennedy Center."

"That tracks with everything that Marion told us." I handed the investment portfolio to the expert. "What does this mean?"

Charisse gave it a long perusal and whistled. "Well, I don't know how Archie made his money, but it wasn't through these investments. If this is any indication of how he handled his finances, I'd say he was lucky he hadn't declared bankruptcy."

I tucked the documents into the envelope. "I have a feeling these are just the statements Archie wanted his wife to know about. He's got money hidden somewhere."

I dropped the envelope into my bag and reached for my seat belt. A gunshot sounded to my left followed by a rock of impact against the Jeep. Someone was shooting at us. I floored it and tore out of the parking spot thinking only that I had to get my friends safe. I ran the red light and cut off a sedan. The owner laid on the horn. I didn't care. We careened around the corner, and I switched lanes to pass a hideously orange colored mini-SUV then switched back around a sports car. I spun the car around the turn into an alley.

Scarlett screeched at me, "Slow down! We're fine!"

Charisse called up to me from the back seat, "No one was hit. Don't kill us trying to get away."

I skidded into an arc next to a dumpster and threw the Jeep into park. "Everyone's okay?"

The ladies nodded. "Everyone's okay."

"No one is hurt? Are you sure?"

Scarlett reached for my arm. "Layla. No one is hurt. Do you want to check the Jeep now or wait until we get home?"

I took a breath to steady myself. Then another. "Now."

I threw open my door. "You all stay there!"

I walked the perimeter around the Jeep and found a bullet-sized hole in the rear quarter panel. I got down on my belly and rolled over, looking under the Jeep. The bullet missed the gas tank and went clear through the other side. Either that was supposed to be a warning, or whoever shot at me was a bad marksman. Or someone was just trying to piss me off. They succeeded with the last one.

I climbed back in. "We're fine."

The ladies all examined my face for signs that I was lying.

"Someone shot the Jeep, but the damage was minimal. I'll put in a police report when I update Castinetto."

Their faces were ashen. This was a brave front for my sake.

Charisse folded her hands into her lap. "All right. Then let's go home."

No one spoke until I was back on the highway, and Bree said, "Where did you learn to drive like that?"

"Mario Kart."

It took a solid thirty seconds before she laughed.

Chapter 30

I DROPPED THE LADIES AT THE HOTEL TO GET THEIR CARS AND TAKE Bree home, and drove to my house lost in thought about Archie Wilkins and his money. There were very few motives for murder—people were pretty basic. Jealousy, humiliation, vengeance, greed. Money was always at the top of the list. For being the world's nicest guy, Archie sounded more controlling with each new person I spoke to.

Coming down the winding road, I passed Whimsy St. James trekking through the woods. Her blond rasta dreads were tied up with a blue bandanna and she had a stripped branch she was using as a walking stick. I slowed down to say hello, but she only glared my way for a moment without stopping.

I pulled into my parking spot as a scattering of leaves danced across the driveway. The yaps of my canine alarm system sounded the moment my tires hit the cobblestones. All the lights were on in the house. Maybe Dad was having another party. He was used to a party lifestyle. I'm sure he missed it. I had to get him back to the life he was familiar with before the dementia took over and he could no longer enjoy it. Without the drugs and alcohol anyway.

I waved at the security guard and stopped on the front porch to check the looney bin, also known as the community request depository. Agnes appeared in the doorway with Ringo next to her jumping with excitement. I gathered a handful of papers and shut the lid. "Hey, buddy. I'm home now. I missed you too."

Agnes moved to the side to let the Lab tackle me and cover my face in kisses. "It's about time you came home."

"I wasn't aware that I answered to you."

"Your father has been going a little stir-crazy. We thought we'd keep him company."

The melody of one of Dad's hits from the eighties wafted out on notes made from his electric guitar.

"That was nice of you, I guess."

"Plus, I wanted to check on the preparations for the community Thanksgiving."

"I stand corrected. Now we've slid into nosy. I've got it under control, Agnes."

Ringo gave me a lick and nudged his head under my hand to get a free pet.

Agnes stroked her streaky beehive. "Do you though? This potluck is an important occasion for a lot of our residents."

"I don't think it's as important as you think. I'm sure they'd all rather be at home where they can nap and watch TV without fear of Clifford questioning their future recycling plans."

Agnes pouted so hard, her face shriveled into itself like a prune.

Ringo gave a little whimper and nudged me toward the door and his idea of safety.

"You're in charge of everything now, missy. It would be a shame if you let all these people down because *you* want to be left alone." Agnes tossed her head and spun back into the house in a huff.

I rolled my eyes even if no one was there to see me do it. "Let's go inside and warm up, Ringo."

Ringo did a hop of excitement and led me into the living room. Dad was in front of the TV with all the women he was collecting, a fire blazing in the hearth. Agnes was propped on the arm of the couch in between Dad and Robin in her wheelchair. Myrtle Jean was telling a story about her cat and Dad was insisting he'd trained his cat to take food from his hand just that afternoon.

I went to the kitchen to avoid that hysteria, and Nick was sitting at the table with a mug of something steamy. Ringo went to his side and put his head in Nick's lap. "Hey, you."

Nick gave me a wan smile. "It's been a day. Your dad was worn out after the trip to the food pantry. He took a long nap, but the doorbell woke him up. People've been escorted up to the house by security all afternoon."

I dropped the stack of requests to the table. "And what about you? You alright?"

Nick gave me the hint of a shrug, then stood and went to the cabinet to get another mug. "The sadness comes in waves, but I'm a million times better here than I was at home alone. You want tea or cocoa?"

Ringo's tail started to thump against the kitchen chair like he thought Nick was getting a box of treats down.

"What are you drinking?"

"Tea."

"That sounds good. Did you have dinner?"

Nick filled a copper kettle with water and lit the stove. "Don had some chili and cornbread earlier, but I was waiting for you."

I opened one of the notes from the box and flattened it. "Why don't you sit? Let me get through these and I'll get us some bowls."

Nick pulled two bowls from the cabinet. "I'll get it. You can read the new demands to me."

"This one's nice. 'With all the money you have, you can afford to pave our roads. I wrecked my suspension on the pothole on Buckingham. You're lucky I don't sue.' *Anonymoush.*"

"Cousin to Scaramouche." Nick shook his head while he ladled chili into a teal bowl. "That's just lovely. What else?"

I opened the next one. "'I'd like permission to breed two alpacas so I can start an Etsy shop making sweaters.'"

Nick placed a bowl in front of each of us. "Ask for a sample sweater before you decide."

"Sure. No use getting an alpaca before we know if they can knit."

Nick reached for a fat paper and unfolded it with a snicker. "You've been sent an official blueprint for Pippi's playground."

I blew on my chili and looked across the table. It was a hand-drawn diagram in purple pencil that looked like it had been inspired by a treasure map on the back of Cap'n Crunch. "Oh good. That'll save me from paying for an architect." I grabbed the paper and slid it across the table for safekeeping. "I bet that moat around the wooden castle is gonna be expensive."

In the other room, Dad started playing his acoustic guitar. I recognized the tune from the one he and I had started working on in the trailer.

Nick chewed slowly as he listened. "Hmm. That's pretty."

I smiled to myself and nodded. "It sounds like he's improved it again. Every time he works on it, he adds a subtle change."

"It's funny that he's known as a headbanger. A lot of his music is really beautiful."

I broke a corner off the piece of cornbread we were sharing. "Metal was the market in the eighties. The band followed what was popular to sell records. I think Dad would rather have focused on ballads, but it's songs like 'Savage Authority' that pay for the tour."

Nick opened an envelope and pulled out the enclosed paper. The joviality slid from his face.

"What is it?"

He let out a shaky breath and turned the paper to face me. It was another pasted conglomeration threat. **Time is running out, Don. Send the money or I'll tell the world that your daughter's drinking is why Melissa died under her command.**

I stood up so fast, my chair fell backward. Dad flew into the room followed by Agnes. "What's the matter, baby girl?"

Nick deftly folded the threat with one hand and moved Pippi's map closer with the other. "Did you see this blueprint?"

Agnes's eyes narrowed as she looked from Nick to me.

Dad's eyes lit up. "Wow! That's gonna be rad. What is it again?"

I tried to steady my voice as I righted my chair. "That's the proposed layout for the pig's playground."

Dad laughed. "It's awesome."

Agnes stared at me for a minute, then she put her hand on Dad's arm. "I bet everyone would love to hear you play your guitar, Don."

Dad rocked on his feet. "Yeah? Righteous. I got a new song me and the girl were working on. Wanna hear it, sugar?"

Agnes looked over her shoulder at me as she led him from the room. "I'd love to."

Once we heard the first notes, Nick turned the envelope upside down and a photo of Dad playing cards with Agnes, Myrtle Jean, and Robin taken from the back deck fell out. I used the sleeve of my sweater to grab the ransom note and photograph, slid them into a ziplock bag and ran out the front door up to the security van with Nick on my heels. The security guard was out of the van before we were off the porch.

"What happened?"

"This happened. And it happened sometime today because Nick and I emptied the box yesterday afternoon."

He looked over the photo and the threat, his brow wrinkled and tense. "No one has been on the property all day except for park residents that your father and Agnes Harcourt preapproved. I've checked every ID. People who said they were here on official community business have been filling that box on the porch all day."

"Well, you don't take orders from Agnes Harcourt or my father. I know he's the client, but he has special circumstances and she's just a busybody."

The security guard nodded sharply.

"You take direction from me, from Nick, or from Ronnie. That's it."

"I am so sorry, ma'am. I did catalog every person who came today, and the only new face was that new gal with the dreads who looks like she could OD anytime."

"Did she happen to go around to the back of the house?"

"Not that I saw, Ms. Virtue. And the cameras at the back haven't picked up any activity."

Nick added, "That could have been taken with a telephoto

lens from across the lake. Cameras wouldn't have picked up anyone that far away."

The security guard gave Nick a curt nod. "I really can't apologize enough. And I'll let Ronnie and the team know that we're moving the security to level Orange. The threat is coming from inside the park."

And apparently, they knew about Melissa.

Chapter 31

I WAS STANDING OUTSIDE OF THE WAREHOUSE AT STRATTON PARK. Melissa was crouched behind a white pickup truck. Where was everyone? They should be waiting for my command. Melissa yelled something to me that I couldn't hear. I yelled for her to repeat it. She kept pointing at the building.

Jacob showed up on the loading dock shouting.

I called out, "What are you doing? Where's the team? You were supposed to wait for me to give the order."

He waved me away.

"Jacob! What did you do?! Did you sell us out?"

His mouth was moving but I couldn't hear him over the gunfire. Or was that my blood pounding in my ears?

"Why didn't you come for me?!"

He didn't answer. He turned and looked over his shoulder. An explosion rocked the world and pulled him into the warehouse. I flew backward and hit my head. I was looking up at falling ash against a gray sky. I'd killed them. I'd killed them all.

Everything faded and I woke up in my room. It was just a nightmare. *I can't take this anymore.*

I got out of bed and went to the kitchen, took a bottle of scotch from the cabinet next to the fridge, and poured myself a double. The soothing warmth caressed me, promising that everything would be okay now.

But it wouldn't.

I looked at the empty crystal glass in my hand. *What have I done?* My heart thudded in my chest and my throat burned like I'd coated it with acid. *Why did I just do that? What is wrong with me?*

In a weak moment, I'd thrown away my sobriety as if Stratton Park didn't matter. I swore I'd never drink again after killing my team. How could I let them down? How could I let myself down? Disgust filled me as the glass fell from my hand and shattered. I wiped a lick away on my cheek. "No, Ringo. Get away from me before you get hurt."

Another lick on my cheek was followed by a whimper. The kitchen faded away and I started to come to. I was still in bed. Ringo had plastered himself on my chest. He nudged me on the chin. I reached a hand out and placed it on his head. "Hey, boy."

The bed started to shake with his tail wags.

I patted the sheets next to me. "Over here, buddy."

Ringo moved off my chest, but he didn't go far. I unwound myself from the damp sheets and sat up. I looked around the room and everything was freaky weird from a fairy tale—so . . . normal. Relief washed over me. *Thank God. Just a dream.* Ringo gave me a smile. "Good boy."

I checked my cell phone. Scarlett had sent me a text.

What's your plan for today?

Dunno. Rough night. Had a drinking nightmare.

Those are the worst.

I took a quick shower and got dressed. After I let Ringo out to bark around the yard just in case a squirrel was thinking about stepping foot on our property, we went to the kitchen where Nick was making waffles.

He pulled a toasty brown raft off a silver waffle iron that I'd never seen before in my life. "You okay? You were yelling in your sleep."

"That depends." I opened the cabinet that had the scotch in my dream just to make sure. Assorted mugs. "Was there a broken glass in here this morning?"

Nick looked around the floor. "No."

"Then I'm fantastic."

Nick put his hand out. "Give me your cell phone."

I pulled it out of my back pocket, unlocked it, and passed it to him.

He started tapping on the screen. "I set up the park email for you and now I'm going to add it to your phone." He handed it back.

"That was quick."

"What can I say? I have mad skills."

Dad wandered into the kitchen, smiling. "Is it morning?"

"It sure is."

"Yeah! Three days until Thanksgiving."

Nick handed Dad a plate of waffles. "Two days."

Dad grinned broader. "Two days until Thanksgiving."

I passed him the bottle of syrup as he sat across from me. "Are you sure you want to have Thanksgiving dinner with the trailer park people?"

"Aw yeah, baby girl. They're our friends, aren't they?"

Nick gave me a look as he sat, placing plates of waffles in front of him and me.

"Well, some of them are. Some of them might be trying to extort money from you."

Dad shrugged. "I have enough money. Maybe we should just pay it."

"No way, Dad. I want to put this scumbag in jail. Not reward them for knowing how to cut letters out of magazines to scare old men."

Dad froze with his forkful of waffles on the way to his mouth. "Hey! Who are you calling 'old'?"

I poured syrup on my waffle, with my eyes on him. "I dunno. Which one of us lost at poker to Eric Clapton and had to name his daughter, Layla?"

Dad's eyes rolled up to his forehead like he was thinking. "That sounds like me."

"Well, it certainly wasn't Nick."

Nick reached for the butter and gave me some side-eye. "You don't know everyone I hang out with."

I glanced at the stack of request-demands from the community, then out the window at Ronnie Voa's van, and jabbed my waffle. "I've just been thinking, maybe we get you away from here for a while."

"You mean like a vacation? For the four of us? Who will feed the cat?"

"The imaginary cat will be fine. But I mean just for you, Dad. Maybe you could go to your villa in Italy until we find out who's been sending the threats."

Dad put his fork next to his plate. He looked back and forth at me and Nick. "I don't want to go without you, baby girl. What if I forget who I am in Italy? Who will help me? I only know how to say like four things in Italian and three of them will get me arrested."

"I know. But I'm only talking for a little while. Just to keep you safe."

His eyes took on a glassy sheen. "I'm safe with you. How much safer can I be than with my daughter the cop?"

Nick caught my eye and cocked his head. *He's got you there.*

Dad reached for my hand. "Don't make me leave. I'm afraid if I'm away from you, I'll forget who you are."

A lump formed in my throat. I was a washed-up cop without a gun, with a security team who let a possible assailant walk up to my house, and I wanted to have a drink every day of my life. How was I supposed to keep my father safe? I couldn't even stop his own mind from destroying him. "Of course you don't *have* to go. I just thought it might be a nice change for you."

Dad grinned and picked up his fork. "That settles it. I'm staying here."

Nick reached under the table and squeezed my knee.

I heard the slam of car doors and the gaggle of voices coming down the walkway before the doorbell rang. "What are they doing here?"

I opened the front door and Scarlett rushed past me with

Charisse and Bree in tow. "We're here. What do you need? Jeez Louise. Would you look at this place? Is that an alarm clock hanging from a hook hand?"

"Yep. If you get close, you can smell the crocodile."

Charisse pulled me into a hug. "Don't worry. We all have falling-off-the-wagon dreams. It's normal." She looked over my shoulder and gasped. "Wow. A Snow White- themed chandelier." She let go of me and headed into the kitchen to inspect the gold chandelier dripping with crystal blue birds, red apples, green leaves, and pink rosebuds.

Bree walked around the living room with her mouth hanging open. She reached out and touched the mermaid carved into the bookcase and whispered, "I love it."

"Well, since you're all here . . . Who wants to see the insanity?"

They appeared at my side in an instant, Charisse with bacon in her hand.

I gave them the full tour except for the loft. They were charmed by everything. Especially my bathroom. Charisse asked for Fawn's number.

Bree looped her arm around mine. "You can never sell this, Layla. It's far too wonderful."

I hugged her arm close and patted her hand. "That won't be the only reason I can never sell it."

Nick came around the corner and grinned. "I made more waffles if you're hungry."

Charisse clapped her hands. "Alright now. I could go for some waffles."

When Nick had returned to the kitchen, Scarlett nudged me on the arm. "How could you not tell us Nick moved in?"

"He's just staying here for a few days."

Charisse crossed her arms over her chest. "A man who looks like that and knows how to cook, I'd never let him leave."

I nodded. "That's why I put a lock on the outside of his door."

Bree's eyes widened. "You did?"

I snickered and started for the kitchen. "No."

Dad was thrilled to have company. He'd already forgotten our talk to have him temporarily move away. And Ringo was making his rounds getting his ears stroked and his back rubbed. Even though I was relieved to have them here, the stress from my dream had not entirely left my body.

I was about to start the dishwasher when there was another knock at the door. I opened it to find Adam Beasley in uniform on the front step with my security guard.

The security guard raised an eyebrow. "This gentleman says he's an officer, but he doesn't have a badge."

"Beasley, where's your shield?"

Adam shrugged. "I think I left it on my desk." Reading the shock on my face he added, "I got jelly on it."

I sighed and gave the guard a nod. "He's legit—ish."

The security guard nodded and turned to head for his post.

"Beasley, what can I do for you?"

He held out a slip of paper. "I got you that address for Seth Masters."

"Who?"

"That guy you asked about."

I took the paper from him. "Oh right. Thanks. Nice work."

"Don't tell Detective Castinetto I brought you that. He threatened the whole department that no one was to go near you, or they'd be sent down to traffic."

"Wow. He really doesn't trust me, does he?"

Adam bit his lip. "Well, I overheard him talking to the chief about removing you from the case. Something about a disaster waiting to happen. I probably shouldn't have told you that."

My face heated with anger. Ringo leaned into my leg and rubbed his head into my hand. "It's fine."

Adam reached for the Lab, but Ringo didn't leave my side. "Have you made any headway with your memories?"

"Nope."

"Let me know if you do. I'm sure you'll remember something we can use to clear your name."

I gave the rookie a look. He was awfully interested in my memories. Did the station have a pool going for when I'd get them back? "Thanks, Beasley. Go get that badge before you do anything else." I shut the door and looked at the slip of paper in my hand. I might not have my memories or the respect of the police, but now I had a lead who might know what happened the night of Stratton Park, and that was good enough for today.

I returned to the kitchen and waved the paper. "Beasley's tracked down Angel."

Scarlett pushed away from the table. "What are we waiting for? Let's go question him."

Chapter 32

SCARLETT OFFERED TO DRIVE, BUT WITH SOMEONE ATTACKING ME I couldn't chance something happening to her Porsche, so the four of us took my Jeep. A black SUV with tinted windows seemed like it was following, so I cut into a strip mall and parked at the Dairy Queen. The SUV didn't pursue. I had to wait for Scarlett and Bree who went inside to get ice cream. They came back to the Jeep with chocolate-dipped cones and then Charisse and I changed our minds and needed to go in and get ice cream. We got back on the highway and continued our journey, but this time too many cars were on the road to know if anyone was actually following us.

I turned into a three-story, red brick apartment complex in Shirlington and no one came after me. Each building had a central entry point with a green awning over the walkway. The second and third story had large windows on either side of the breezeway, creating a menacing face effect. Boxwood hedges, neatly trimmed into cubes, edged the brick in rows like a cop mustache. Few cars dotted the parking lot; the nearest one had a Gold's Gym bumper sticker.

I watched both exits for a solid five minutes until I felt we were in the clear and could approach the apartment. I locked the Jeep and set the alarm.

* * *

I knocked on the door of Apartment 2-D and heard footsteps. After a momentary pause, a series of chains and locks jangled and clicked. The door opened to reveal a very large man with a pointed Viking beard and biceps the size of baby watermelons. He was wearing tight little bicycle shorts over legs that could crack walnuts behind his knee. Immediately my mind flashed a memory.

I stood at the bar in the Gibson and the Viking said, "Be careful back there. They aren't all who they seem."

The memory faded and, in my stupor, I lost all sense of finesse if I'd ever had any to begin with. "Hi."

His eyes grew large and round like someone was inflating them from the other side. His lips parted but no sound came out, like he couldn't believe what he was seeing. He finally shook himself alert. "Hi."

"Do you know who I am?"

"Yeah." He stared at me so intently that I thought he might reach out and touch me to see if I was real. "I always knew you would come." He scanned the ladies who were with me. If he was surprised by them, he didn't let on. He stepped aside and waved us in.

His apartment was immaculate. An oversized leather couch sat facing an oversized flat screen TV. The entire dining area was dedicated to a home gym. Three of the walls were covered in floor-to-ceiling mirrors reflecting four complicated weight machines.

"Should I call you Angel or Seth?"

He sat on the edge of a weight bench, facing the couch where the four of us had clumped together, and crossed his arms, flexing the angel on his biceps, contorting her face to surprise. Seth Masters was a walking BowFlex ad. "Angel is fine."

A fat orange tabby cat wound its way through the room, stopping to sniff each of us, before jumping into Angel's lap.

Bree reached for the tabby, rubbing her fingers together. "*Ssp ssp ssp.* What is your kitty's name?"

Angel stroked the cat's ears. "Chutney. I found her behind an Indian restaurant." He glanced at me and frowned.

"What did you mean by you always knew I would come?"

"I remember you from the night of the explosion. I never saw you leave the bar, and I was worried something had happened to you. Then I saw the news and how you were at the warehouse that exploded. Eddie was a friend of my cousin."

My chest crushed with pain. I took a shaky breath. "Eddie was a good guy. He joined my team after his son died of an overdose."

Angel gave me a nod and looked away. "His wife is alone now."

Bree walked over to the weight machine and gave Angel a hug. "The poor woman. We're so sorry for your loss. I know Layla has been just devastated over the passing of her team. She lost four good friends that day."

He gave Bree a grateful smile and nodded. He considered me for a moment, his dark eyes piercing mine. "They said on the news that you had amnesia. I knew if you remembered the Gibson, it was only a matter of time before you'd track me down."

"I only want to ask you a few questions."

"I'm ready."

"You told me not everyone at the bar was who they seemed. What did you mean?"

His hand paused over Chutney's back, shaking ever so slightly. "I don't remember that."

"Are you sure? It's the only thing I do remember."

He stroked the cat's fur slowly. "I'm sure I have no knowledge of anything strange going on at the Gibson. Next question."

As far as lies go, that one was a whopper. And Angel had zero poker face. Even the angel on his bicep looked guilty. But I couldn't afford to antagonize him on the first question, so I let it drop. "I don't remember much from that night. Was I drinking?"

"I didn't see you once you were in the VIP room, but all you ordered was ginger ale."

The cat jumped down and slinked over to Scarlett's purse to

check it out. She picked her purse up and set it on her lap. "You have an amazing memory. That was nine months ago."

"I've had a lot of time to think about it. Plus she made a big deal about being on duty. You almost ran a bachelorette party out for getting too rowdy."

"Sorry about that."

He shrugged and stroked his beard. "I was about to ask them to leave anyway. We'd had complaints from the corporates."

"Who took me to the VIP room?"

"Nancy was in charge of the VIPs. She'd been there the longest and that was just the way it had always been."

That tracked with what I remembered. "Do you know who was back there?"

"Nope. Nancy came out and got a bottle of our best tequila on the house, so it must have been someone important."

The cat tried to sniff Charisse, but she snapped her fingers and pointed at it. The cat froze in place.

"What went on in the back room? Who was there?"

"I dunno." He turned to me. "But you pitched a fit when you got back there."

"Pitched a fit how?" I asked.

He crossed his arms over his chest. "I heard yelling all the way out to the bar."

"Did you overhear anything that was said?"

"Only one word. *Castinetto.*"

All the blood rushed from my head and made me momentarily dizzy. *No. That can't be right. Why in the world would I say Castinetto? He wasn't even in the narcotics unit. Surely he wasn't in the room, was he?*

Dayton Castinetto is a pain in the rump, but I always thought he was a good cop. He didn't think much of me though. He accused me of doctoring the photo of Jacob. And he never did believe that I didn't have more to do with Stratton Park than I'd put in my official report. "Are you sure? You're sure I said 'Castinetto'?"

"That's all I got. We were busy that afternoon. The Instagram specials were a big hit, and people were coming in droves to make videos about them before Valentine's Day. Not to mention all the takeout orders that go through that place. No one wants to eat alone at the bar anymore, so they get it to go. I had just given one of our regulars their to-go order when I thought I heard a gunshot. I ran to the back to see what was going on and find out if I needed to call an ambulance. The door opened for a moment and Nancy ran out of the room. She said it was getting ugly in there and told me if I was smart, I wouldn't ask any questions. That's when I heard you yell 'Castinetto.' I never saw you again."

Bree touched his shoulder. "That must have been so scary."

He nodded. "It was. I thought for sure I'd have to give a statement to the cops, but none ever came."

Charisse leaned forward in her seat. "Didn't you worry that someone was dead? What happened when the people in that room left? They'd have to walk right past you. And what happened to the gun? Weren't you afraid you'd have to ID someone? Or were a suspect?"

Scarlett put her hand on Charisse's. "Okay, podcast queen. Calm down."

Angel answered me as if I'd asked the questions. "I couldn't ID anyone. I never saw anyone's face other than yours. They came and went by the back door in the alley."

I sighed and muttered to myself, "Of course there's a back door."

Angel pulled an arm across his chest and stretched. "I was fired at the end of the night. We all were. We were told the bar was under new ownership and they wanted to bring their own people in. If the cops came looking for a statement, I don't know what they were told."

Scarlett murmured, "I smell a cover-up."

"Angel, do you have any idea who I was meeting with?"

He fidgeted on the workout bench.

Bree squatted to be eye level with the big man. "You said that VIP door was open for a moment after the gunshot. Did you see anything that could help us identify who was in there?"

Angel sighed. He clicked his tongue, and the cat came over and jumped back in his lap with a chirp. “I got a quick look before Nancy closed the door. I don’t know who you were talking to, but I saw him from the back, and I saw what he was wearing.”

“And what was that?”

“Same thing you were.”

Chapter 33

"I WAS IN MY FREAKIN' RIOT GEAR!"

I stood under the green awning observing the Jeep while Bree held my hand and said comforting things like "It's okay. We're here for you."

Meanwhile, Scarlett marched back and forth in front of us fast punching the air. "I knew you were set up!"

Charisse kept swiping her cell phone screen. "There's so many podcasts about dirty cops."

"We don't know for sure that it was a cop. You can buy a lot of things that look like riot gear at Army Surplus, police auctions, the Internet . . ." My words sounded weak even to me. If it looks like a rat and smells like a rat . . .

Bree patted my shoulder. "I know, honey. But this is no time for denial. Angel heard you say 'Castinetto.' "

"Okay, that is concerning, I'll give you that. But I need more proof if I'm going to take him down. And when I say 'take him down,' I mean he won't be able to walk again. Because no way I'm going after another cop through official channels.

"I need to remember what happened. If he was in that back room—why was he there? And what did he do to me that I can't remember? And what does he have to do with Jacob being alive?"

Charisse stopped swiping. "Do you think he helped Jacob fake his death?"

Bree stopped patting. "After the fit he gave her for Photoshopping that picture. Boy, that's a dirt bag move."

Bile rose up in the back of my throat. "If he did, there will be hell to pay."

I made the ladies stand under the awning against the building while I inspected the Jeep. All the attacks had happened while we were investigating Archie Wilkins's murder, but I couldn't be too careful. My assailant could be following me everywhere. My cop instincts kicked in to protect the civilians, plus these were the first real girlfriends I'd had my whole life. Keeping them safe was my first priority.

I waved them forward while scanning for shooters. They ran to the Jeep and hopped in. We didn't stay in the parking lot like sitting ducks. Cars were harder to hit when they were on the move, so I pulled out onto the main road.

Bree said she had to go home to take a final exam and Charisse had a meeting she couldn't miss because it was the last one before the holiday. I suspected they were also a little worn out from being on high alert all morning, so I dropped them off at their homes.

On the way back to my house with Scarlett, I couldn't shake off my irritation and dread. "Frickin' Castinetto. Why would I be talking about him at the Gibson? Could he have been there?"

Scarlett shrugged. "It does sound like there was another cop in the room. Maybe Castinetto called the meeting."

"For what purpose? It would take something huge for me to go to a clandestine meeting over taking down Hurtado. We worked on that sting for months—cultivating a fake relationship, infiltrating his cell, getting him to trust us. It would take a lot more than Castinetto, I'll tell you that. Do you know how much crap he has given me about being drunk on the job when I should have been at Stratton Park? He always says it like he's concerned about me, but I can read between the lines, you know?"

"Definitely."

"I'm calling him."

Scarlett put her hand on the dash to steady herself as I took a turn with a little too much rage. "You're what!?"

"Oh yeah. Let's see what he has to say now."

I put the call through the Jeep's speakers so Scarlett could listen in.

"Castinetto here."

"It's Layla."

"I know. I was just about to call you. Everything okay?"

"Yeah. Did you think it wouldn't be?"

There was a pause. "Well . . . you do have a gift for getting yourself into trouble. So . . . I never know what to think when your name flashes up on my screen."

A Potomac County cop car pulled onto the highway behind me. "Where are you right now?"

Castinetto had a suspicious tone to his voice. "At the station. Some of the information you requested just came in. Where did you think I was?"

"I dunno. Shouldn't you be out with Beasley mentoring him?"

"Beasley's on traffic duty for the rest of the week because he tried to turn his dash cam off when he went to lunch."

"What do you mean 'he tried to'?"

"I mean he called in a ten- fifty-four and forgot to turn it back on until he got to Hooters and thought he was turning it off."

"A ten-fifty-four? What kind of livestock was on the road?"

Castinetto rested his hand on the butt of his gun. "Yeah, there was no livestock. He thought it was the code for a bathroom break."

I didn't have a rational response to that, so I sighed and thanked God I wasn't on the force anymore. "What information did you get?"

"I got you an address for a Carol Hodge who used to frequent the food pantry. No priors."

"Great."

"I'm sending it to your phone now. I'm still working on the security footage for the convenience store. There's been some delay. I should have it tonight."

"'Kay. Cool. By the way, I don't suppose any officers have placed a weapons discharge report recently?"

Scarlett gave me an indignant nod.

There was a weighty pause before Castinetto said, "Wait. Did someone shoot at you?"

"I dunno, Castinetto. Know anyone who would do that?"

"Jeez, Virtue. You're freaking me out. Did someone shoot at you or not? Where are you? Are you okay? Do I need to send someone to take your statement? Set up a watch detail?"

"Let's just say that I'm perfectly fine, but my Jeep's Blue Book value took a big drop. And if you find out who's been sending me threats at your crime scenes, you tell them to aim better next time. Because when I come for them, I won't miss."

I hung up while Castinetto was stuttering about wanting me to come in so he could check out my Jeep. Right. Like I was gonna go to my old precinct where everyone hated me just so he could make a big show of examining my Jeep and possibly give himself an alibi. *He can bite me.*

"I'll drop you off so you can get your car and then I'm gonna pay a visit to Carol Hodge."

Scarlett made a face. "What? I'm not going home now. Bump that. I'm going with you. Ride or die, girl."

"As you wish."

We plugged in the address Castinetto had sent me. Carol lived around the corner from Charisse's swanky home goods store. We pulled up outside a white vinyl-sided bungalow with a sad skinny scarecrow in the front yard. Three jack-o'-lanterns were rotting on the front step.

I parked right in front of the house within full view of the street from Carol's picture window. "Keep your eyes on the Jeep while we're inside, okay?"

Scarlett gave me a thumbs-up. Then she took her iPhone out of her bag. "I'll do better than that. I'll film it the whole time."

I picked up a stack of mail stuffed in the screen door, rifled through it, then knocked. A wispy thin woman with sunken eyes opened the door. She was wearing a sweater that looked to be two sizes too big for her. "Can I help you?"

I handed her the stack of overdue bills. "Are you Carol?"

She looked warily between me and Scarlett. "Who's asking?"

"I'm Layla Virtue. I'm helping the police with their inquiries into the death of Archie Wilkins."

Her head cocked to the side. "Layla Virtue. Why does that name sound familiar?"

Scarlett shifted her hands out in a ta-da move and told a whopper of a lie. "She was Miss Virginia."

Carol's face brightened. "That must be it." Then her smile faltered, and her hand covered her heart. "Poor Mr. Wilkins. Yes, come on in."

As we followed Carol through the door, I cut my eyes to Scarlett and mouthed, "Miss Virginia?"

She grinned and mouthed back, "She won't know."

We stepped into a tiny blue living room populated with cheery yellow furniture and a pale wood bookcase full of children's classics. Her home was clean and smelled of fresh-baked cookies. Scarlett moved to the front window and held her phone facing the Jeep.

A buzzer in the kitchen dinged. "Those are my snickerdoodles. They're Clara's favorites. She'll be home from school soon and I like to have a little treat waiting for her now that I have more energy. I'll be right back."

She grabbed a cane and limped to the kitchen. She returned a couple minutes later with six cookies on a plate she placed on the wooden coffee table. "Please sit. Help yourselves."

Scarlett gave Carol a clever ploy for why she couldn't join me on the couch. "I'm admiring your yard. You must like to garden."

Carol took the chair opposite mine. "I used to. I haven't had any energy for the past couple of years. My beds must be overgrown with weeds by now."

I took a cookie and held it. "How old is Clara?"

Carol's whole face lit up. "Eight going on thirty. Smart as a whip. She didn't get that from me, that's for sure."

"Eight? What is that . . . third grade?"

Scarlett nodded.

Carol gave me a quizzical look. "That's right. You obviously know she's a student at Pixieland Academy or you wouldn't be here with questions about her teacher."

Scarlett and I passed a meaningful look between us.

"She's not on the list of students from the past few years. Does she have a different last name than yours?"

"Sorry, yes. My husband passed away when she was a baby, and I went back to my maiden name. She's registered as Clara Stableman."

"And she was in Mr. Wilkins's class last year?"

Carol nodded. "She loved him. He was always so kind to her. Just the nicest man. I didn't resent him."

"I didn't ask you that."

Her eyes darted from me to Scarlett. "I just assumed that's why you were here. The Child Protective Agency visits?"

Scarlett managed to keep her face from showing surprise. "Of course. Tell us about those."

Carol picked a cookie off the plate and broke it in half. "I don't know . . . I must have done something to offend Mr. Wilkins. At least I'd always assumed it was him that placed the anonymous tip about my drug use."

She broke the cookie in half again, placed a piece to her lips, and changed her mind. "The agency cleared me of suspicion and ended the investigation. Even introduced me to some great resources that helped us get through the worst of it, like the food pantry. Of course Mr. Wilkins was there too. Looking down his nose at me."

"And by 'worst of it,' you mean detoxing?"

Carol's face pinked slightly. "No. I mean chemotherapy. I have stage two uterine cancer. I thought you would have seen that in the report."

I nodded. Ashamed of the line of thinking I had been going down. Although I had met many addicts over the years and very few single moms fighting cancer. "Why did you think it was Archie who registered the complaint?"

"He turned cold toward me around that same time. Overnight. He would write notes on Clara's homework that she was doing remarkably well considering her home life. He wouldn't return my calls when I'd contacted the school to set him straight. And he would hide things when I shopped at the food pantry. I'd see him move the fancy goods under the counter whenever I came in. I don't know what he heard, but it changed the way he treated me."

"Did you tell the principal?"

"No. I didn't want to make trouble for Clara. I already felt like I was on a watch list. They know I'm a single mom and my late husband's life insurance pays for Clara's tuition. She was late a few times because I had trouble getting up in the morning. And she tried to make her own lunches, God bless her, because I was so nauseous all the time. Apparently, one day she took cake that a neighbor had made us for her entire lunch and that led to questions about her life at home."

Scarlett chuckled. "I have a sneaky seven-year-old, and if he could pack his own lunch he would take advantage in a hot minute."

Carol relaxed and leaned toward Scarlett. "And she really didn't mean to make me look bad. She's been such a good girl. I take four different drugs just to deal with the side effects of the chemo. We tried to keep a sense of humor about everything. I would tease Clara, *Don't grow up to be a druggie like me.* But she never misses a single day of school and turns in all her homework on time. And in a school like Pixieland Academy, you can't afford to fall behind."

Her voice took on a bitter edge. "There was no reason to suspect she wasn't being cared for. He could have just called me and asked what was going on instead of trying to ruin my life."

My phone buzzed in my purse that a call was coming in. I put my arm over it to muffle the sound. "By having Clara taken from the home?"

Her lips clamped down and she crushed the cookie in her lap. "And he really was the nicest man—to Clara. He told her she could be anything she put her mind to, if she just stayed off drugs and didn't follow in my footsteps."

"Harsh."

She nodded in agreement, pain and bitterness shining from her eyes. "I had no reason to want him dead."

My phone started to buzz again. Whoever was calling me was being insistent about it. I pulled it out and checked the screen. Nick. "Would you excuse me for a moment?"

Carol waved her hand. "Of course. Please."

I answered it. "Hey, Nick. What's up?"

"Layla, I don't know how to tell you this, but I can't find your dad anywhere."

Chapter 34

"WHAT DO YOU MEAN YOU CAN'T FIND HIM? DID YOU CHECK outside?"

Scarlett abandoned her job of filming the Jeep and was at my side in a flash. "Who's missing?"

"Dad."

"Layla." Nick sounded exasperated. I noted the panic in his voice that he was trying to hide from me. "I've checked the entire house and yard. I was in the loft doing some work and your dad must have gone out. The security detail never saw him leave but they knew something was wrong because someone spray-painted over the back cameras. Agnes and Myrtle Jean haven't seen him. I tried calling him and found his phone on a pizza box in the greenhouse. Do you want me to call the police?"

"Is his car there?"

"Yes."

"Okay. That's a relief. Don't call the police yet. I'm on my way." I hung up the phone and grabbed my purse. "Carol, thank you so much for meeting with us. I'm sorry we have to end this abruptly, but I have an emergency at home."

Carol stood and wrapped her sweater tightly around her. "I understand. I hope everything's okay."

Scarlett and I gave her a wave as we hustled out the door. "I'm sure it will be."

That was a big fat lie. My hands were shaking so hard, I had trouble turning the key in the ignition.

Scarlett put her hand on my arm. "Just breathe. He couldn't have gotten far. Maybe he went out for some air and got lost. Let's just see if he's on the road around the trailer park."

The engine cranked to life, and I nodded. "I hope so. I'm just worried that whoever's been sending threats has him."

"Why would they take him? He has until Thanksgiving to deliver the money."

I turned onto the highway and nearly sideswiped a UPS van. "Maybe they're getting impatient. I should have done more to keep him safe."

"Don't second-guess yourself. You're doing a lot. And this is all new to you too. Let's just focus on getting to the neighborhood and looking around. If he isn't there, we'll put in a silver alert. He'll probably beat you home."

"Okay. You're right. Let's just get home."

Twenty minutes later I turned at the birch trees and started the slow wind down to the lake. We didn't pass Dad along the way, but Agnes and Myrtle Jean were out walking. "We're looking through the woods for him, Layla. He's got to be here somewhere."

When I got to the house, Ronnie Voa was standing in my yard. "I've got three men patrolling the streets around the park. We'll find him."

I nodded and did a U-turn in front of Agnes's trailer. Scarlett and I backtracked down the road and took the turn to my old trailer. We passed Nick over by Benny's house. He had Ringo in the front seat of his car. "Anything?"

"He's not on the road. We were about to go check around the lake."

I threw the Jeep in park in front of Donna's house. Donna was sweeping her sidewalk. Scarlett and I hopped out and I marched up to Donna with more anger than I would normally show a perp outside the interrogation room. "Are you sending threats to my house to scare my father because he didn't do the fundraiser for Kelvin's school?"

Donna leaned against her broom. "First of all, you better step off. And second, am I what?"

"You heard me. My father's being blackmailed for a hundred grand. The perpetrator is threatening to tell the media that he lives here. Sound familiar?"

Donna's eyes narrowed to slits. Her head tilted and she considered me carefully.

I forced my balled-up hands to relax. "We're not paying the demand. And if you're so gung-ho on destroying what little peace he has left, you might as well include that he has dementia and he's slipping away." My voice cracked and I cursed myself for being weak.

Donna's eyes softened in remorse, but she didn't offer a confession.

Ringo turned his head toward the trees and barked. He ran ahead and Scarlett, Nick, and I followed.

There was Dad, sitting on a picnic bench by the canoes. Robin sat in her wheelchair next to him. Ringo leapt on Dad, paws on his legs and covered his face with kisses.

"Hey, buddy."

Tears of relief and frustration broke through my brave facade. "Dad! Everyone is out looking for you."

Dad had the decency to look sheepish. He turned his face away from me.

Robin gave us a tight grin. "I found him down here at the water's edge. I think he was lost. I was just about to bring him home."

"Thank you, Robin."

I squatted down next to him. "What happened, Dad?"

He breathed through an embarrassed laugh. "A guy came to the back door and said you needed me right away. He said you were in trouble. I thought he was one of your friends."

Nick pushed forward past Scarlett. "What'd he look like?"

"I dunno. Tall. Super skinny. Fuzzy blond hair."

That sounded an awful lot like Whimsy if Dad thought she was a man. "How did you get past security?"

Dad's eyes took on a blank expression, his struggle to remember playing across his brow. Then he threw his head back and started to sing. "I'm sailing today! Set us both a course on the frozen sea. 'Cause I've got to break free!"

"Are you telling me you took a boat?"

His expression sharpened. "That's it. We took a boat."

Scarlett looked around. "What boat?"

Dad pointed to the canoes that were chained up tight. "One like those. When we got over here, he let me out and took off. That's when this gal found me."

Robin gave me another tight smile. "He was just sitting on the bench when I found him. No guy or boat in sight."

I knew Dad was given to the occasional hallucination; the hard thing was determining if any of this had really happened or if he'd imagined the whole thing. It could have been something he saw on TV in the middle of the night. "Thanks, Robin. I'll take him home now. Come on, Dad. Let's go."

Nick pulled me aside. "I'm going to do another drive around to see if anyone has a canoe in their yard. I'll meet you back at the house."

"Okay." I squeezed his arm. Scarlett and I got Dad and Ringo into the Jeep. When Dad swung his legs in, I happened to notice the bottom of his pants and his shoes were dripping. "How did you all get wet, Dad?"

Dad looked at his feet. "The boat leaked."

Scarlett and I passed a look between us. Could he be telling the truth? I let Scarlett watch Dad for a minute while I inspected the stack of canoes by the rental hut. The chain was so rusty the lock would shatter if someone forced a key, and the canoes were all dry. I would check with the security team to see if they got anything.

I returned to the Jeep and Ringo gave me a snout punch on the cheek. "Thank you, buddy."

We were halfway around the lake after several stops to let the trailer park people know he'd been found when Dad started to cry. "I'm scared, baby girl. What if I wander off and you can't find me?"

I reached for his hand. "We'll make sure that doesn't happen."

Scarlett leaned forward from the back seat. "When I was a pharmacist, some of my patients had memory issues. Their kids had sewn GPS trackers into their shoes in case they wandered. I bet we could do that for you."

"Where do you get something like that?"

She shrugged. "Internet, I guess. You can get everything else there."

"Good idea. I'll ask Nick. He's the keeper of the Internet knowledge."

Dad waved out the window as we passed some of the park residents on the road. "Your husband is really smart."

I glanced in the rearview mirror at Scarlett and caught her raised eyebrows. "Nick is just a friend, Dad."

"Are you sure? He lives in the house."

"That's just for the time being."

Dad was quiet for a moment. "Well, I hope he stays. He cooks a lot better than you do."

"I know that's right."

"What if I forget that I'm sober? I can't go through that hell again."

"I won't let you forget that."

Scarlett nudged my arm. "We could take him to a meeting tonight."

"Where?"

"There's a new group meeting in Second Chance Church where we used to go."

Dad clapped. "That would be fun. Let's do it."

"You think an AA meeting sounds like fun?"

"If I'm with you and the foreign girl back there."

I blew out an uncomfortable breath, but Scarlett just giggled.

We slowed when we saw Agnes and Myrtle coming out of the woods. "We've got him."

Myrtle Jean patted her chest. "Thank goodness. I was so worried. I thought I'd have to get my Claude involved. He's former law enforcement you know."

Agnes rolled her eyes at Myrtle Jean, then gave Dad a long look. "Next time, tell me when you want to go out and I'll go with you."

Dad looked chagrined. "Yes, dear."

Well, I did not like the sound of that at all. "We're definitely going to a meeting, because now I want a drink."

Chapter 35

"ARE YOU SURE I HAVE TO WEAR THIS, BABY GIRL?"

I steadied my voice. "Well. At least you're not dressed like a lady."

Dad was standing in the living room dressed in a satiny saffron-colored tracksuit with a matching fuzzy bucket hat. He hiked the waistband up over his belly and folded it over. "I look like Snoop Dog and Martha Stewart had a baby and that baby is old."

Agnes rubbed her hand down Dad's arm. "I think you look sharp, Don. Very sexy."

Dad's lip curled and his eyebrows raised. He wasn't buying it. "You're just saying that because this was your husband's leisurewear."

Scarlett held a hand over her mouth to keep the glee from spilling out. She opened her mouth to say something, snapped it shut, and shook her head with another laugh.

Agnes stood back and gave Dad a long appreciative look. She purred, "You don't fill it out in the rear as well as Boris did, but at least you won't stretch out the belly any farther. You can still see where the seams are pulling apart after his Baja Gordita phase. That man went from Gomez to Pugsley overnight." She sighed.

Nick sat on the sofa with Ringo in his lap. He had a storm brewing behind his eyes. He'd driven the whole park and didn't find a boat or canoe anywhere. We were both worried about Dad's safety, his privacy long forgotten.

"Are you sure you don't want to come with us? It's an open meeting."

Nick shook his head. "I've some work to do while you're gone. Tomorrow I'll be baking pies all day."

Dad's face brightened. "Ooh, what kind of pie?"

"Apple, pumpkin, pecan."

Dad pumped his fist. "Righteous! Can I help?"

"What do you mean 'help'?" I asked.

"I mean watch."

Nick grinned. "Yeah. You can help."

"Sweet!" Dad clapped his hands. "Alright, let's go get this party started!"

I gave him a look. "And by party, you mean AA?"

Dad's face fell. "Is that where we're going?"

"It was your idea."

"I thought we were going to hang with Run DMC. Isn't that why I'm dressed like this? I'm one gold chain away from being signed by Def Jam."

"No, Dad. We're going to a meeting. Now grab your sunglasses and let's go."

Dad grumbled all the way out the door that Jam Master Jay was probably expecting him.

"Oh good Lord."

Scarlett giggled. "We'll be fine. Once he gets to the meeting, he'll remember why he's there."

"You sound a lot more optimistic than I feel. Dad's a basket case by this time of day."

Nick stood and stretched. He gave me a lazy grin. "You're doing a good thing. I'll update the security team. They'll be here in a few to install new cameras around the back. And I'll make us my grandma's chicken and rice casserole for when you get home."

"Okay. I'll be back soon."

Agnes gave me a sly look as we headed for the door.

I gave her a dirty look right back. "It's not like that."

She sashayed out the door ahead of me. "Then you're an idiot. Bye y'all."

The only thing that had changed at Second Chance Church was the smell. Same frigidly cold room. It was like a concrete cell with a linoleum floor. Same old folding chairs being held together by rust and wishes—although set in a circle instead of rows. There were some familiar faces, but now the room smelled of chili with beans and canned lavender air freshener.

Scarlett waved her hand. "Oof. Maybe Miranda was on to something when she wouldn't allow anyone to wear perfume."

"You always wore perfume."

"Yeah, but I have good taste and Miranda irritated me."

We took seats near the ice machine that seemed to be going through the change of life. It groaned in distress every few minutes.

Dad crossed his legs and leaned in to whisper, "Hey, what's my name?"

Scarlett pursed her lips. "Who do you feel like?"

Dad assessed the room, nodding. "Hmm. How about Carmello?"

I looked across the aisle. "Is it because that lady is eating a Caramello bar?"

Dad grinned, showing both rows of teeth, pretty pleased with himself.

"Yeah. Why not? Carmello."

The meeting was called to order, and we listened to a few shares before Dad raised his hand. "Hello. I'm . . . Heath."

Scarlett looked at me and pressed her lips together thoughtfully. "Close enough."

"And I'm an alcoholic."

"Hi, Heath."

"I've been sober for three years. Some days are harder than others. Lately, I've been struggling because I'm told I got some brain disease stealing my mind, and I don't have that much left to steal."

A few people chuckled, making Dad grin, even more amused with himself no doubt.

"I'm scared this thing is going to move fast and I don't have a lotta time left. The fear that I'm going to lose my daughter anyday has me craving my old friends Jack and José."

As Dad continued to tell the group what he was going through, my mind was stuck on the last thing he'd said about wanting to drink. I had to protect him better. I was away too much, looking into this nonsense with Archie Wilkins. I wasn't a cop anymore. I shouldn't even be involved, whether I wanted to prove myself or not.

And Jacob. How much time was I wasting on chasing a ghost? But it wasn't like I could just put that behind me and move on. I needed to know.

Did Jacob set us up and leave me to take the blame? Or did Castinetto? My God, maybe I'd been playing right into Castinetto's hand. If I was going to find out the truth, I'd have to play along. If I confronted Castinetto now, I'd just show all my cards.

Dad put his arm around me, and I realized he was done with his share. I gave him a smile. "Good job, Dad. I'm proud of you."

He smiled so big, little wrinkles formed in the corner of his eyes.

Scarlett reached across me to pat dad's shoulder. "That was great, Heath."

Dad looked pleased. "I thought so too. Why am I craving chocolate?"

I chuckled. "It's a mystery."

A twitchy guy in an army jacket and ripped baseball cap raised his hand then put it down. Then he put it up again. "I'm Daniel. I'm an alcoholic. I was sober for eleven months and twelve days and I threw it all away. My ex-wife is giving me crap about child support. Then the state took my license away until I get caught up. I got fired from my job for being late because I missed my bus. It's been a crap month.

"So naturally, under stress I sabotage myself."

Scarlett nudged me. "Been there."

I nodded. "I live in that town."

Dad leaned in. "I wrote that song."

Scarlett pointed at Dad. "You win."

Daniel took his ball cap off, releasing a frenzy of tangerine-brown hair. He twisted the cap in his hands. "I just relapsed down at this trendy bar that I had no business being at. One of my old buddies I ran into on the bus suggested we meet there. I should have told him I'm in recovery, but I already felt like such a waste of skin."

My heart pinged with sadness. This guy could be my twin with less fabulous hair.

"So, I met Keith at Muddled and we started talking. And drinking."

Whoa. The hairs on the back of my neck stood to attention. Maybe this guy saw Jacob.

"That night lasted a whole week. I spent every dime I had and showed up at my old house where my ex-wife lives with her new boyfriend and shot out all the windows with my deer rifle. I spent the night in jail and my ex filed for an emergency custody order. So here I am again, homeless, jobless, about to lose my kids. Sober for thirty-six hours."

We gave Daniel a round of applause. It took so much strength to get this far after an astounding failure like he'd just had.

Like I'd had.

The moment the meeting was over I hissed at Scarlett, "Watch Dad." Then I bolted across the room for Daniel.

"Hey. Got a minute?"

Daniel looked around. "Yeah, I guess. I'm sleeping here tonight, so technically I'm home already."

I pulled out my phone and brought up a picture of Jacob and me at a Christmas party a year ago. "By any chance, have you ever seen this guy?"

He took a look. "Yeah, that's Kevin. He works at the bar where I just set my life on fire."

"He works there?"

"Yeah. Bartender."

"You're sure?"

Daniel chuckled bitterly. “Believe me, I gave that guy so much of my money over the past few days I should get visitation with *his* kids.”

“Do you know how long he’s worked there?”

Daniel shrugged. “No idea. But you could ask the other bartender. Kiara. She’s Kevin’s girlfriend.”

Scarlett’s indignation sounded in my ear. “His girlfriend!”

I turned my head. She and Dad were right behind me. I gave her a look.

“What? You said keep an eye on him. He’s right here.”

“Apparently, I should have been more specific.”

Daniel frowned, catching on to the fact that this was unpleasant news for me. “I hate to be the one to tell you this, but they touched each other so much behind the bar, they could charge for the show—so they’re definitely a thing.”

Flashes of memories bombarded my mind, and I couldn’t think of what to say. Jacob getting out of the shower and teasing me to hurry up and get dressed so we could get to work on time. Jacob bringing a chocolate muffin to my desk because he knew I missed breakfast. Jacob telling me he loved me. Jacob asking me to move in with him. Jacob getting angry because I said I wasn’t ready for commitment.

Suddenly, Dad’s hand warmed my back.

Scarlett answered for me. “Thanks so much, Daniel. Good luck with your recovery. Hang in there.”

Then Dad added, “See you around, man.”

“Yeah, you too.”

Dad’s hands on my shoulders turned me toward the door and we were in the Jeep before I knew it. Scarlett was in the driver’s seat, and I just let it happen. Dad and Scarlett chatted all the way home, but my mind couldn’t form words. Jacob was everywhere I looked.

We pulled into the driveway. The security guard was waiting to give me a report when we arrived. “No more incidents today. And we’ve got some new security cameras out back, but I still want to post a guard at the back door.”

"Thanks," I replied numbly.

He handed me some letters and a manila envelope without a return address. "And here's the mail that was delivered today. The mail carrier's ID checked out. Do you want me to open and check the package for you?"

"No, it's fine. If it's anything to worry about I'll bring it out to you."

Scarlett gave me a hug in the driveway and told me to go right inside and let Nick and Ringo stay with me. "I'll see you tomorrow. Unless you need me sooner. Just call."

Dad walked with me to the porch. I followed Dad inside before Ringo could topple me from the excitement that I'd returned.

The house smelled amazing. The secret ingredient in Nick's grandmother's chicken and rice must have been magic. Dad floated into the kitchen. "Oooh-weee, something smells good."

Nick had the table set. A casserole dish was keeping warm on top of the stove. "How'd it go?"

I handed him the envelope. "With Dad, it went great. And there was a guy who relapsed at Muddled a few days ago. He saw Jacob. Evidently Kiara is his girlfriend."

Nick's eyebrows lifted. "Kiara the bartender who's never seen him before?"

"Yep. The same."

Nick clucked his tongue, sympathy in his eyes. "I'm sorry."

"Yeah. Me too. Looks like I'll be heading back to Muddled tomorrow to break Kiara's knees."

Dad lifted the lid on the casserole. "Wow, the police have really changed their rules since my day."

Nick waved the envelope. "What's this?"

"I dunno. Came in the mail today."

I cut my eyes to Dad who was filling his plate with the magic chicken and rice and whistling.

Nick opened the envelope and slid out the contents. He leafed through them. "It looks like police documents." He handed the pages to me.

The first two pages were heavily redacted. But the next, were the unredacted originals. One was part of an evidence file. The top was stamped Stratton Park. Underneath was a copy of my tox screen. Next to the panel that included a check for Rohypnol and GBH was written *canceled.* "What the—I was told the sample was lost. Who did this?" Or a better question, who had the authority to do this? At the time, I outranked both Castinetto and Jacob.

I pulled out the second page expecting more information about me, but this was a ballistics report. The bullets pulled from Eddie's and Oscar's bodies were a match for Jacob's service pistol.

On the bottom of the report someone had scrawled a message.

Trust No One.

Chapter 36

Ringo was stuck to me like Velcro for the rest of the night. I paced around yelling for a solid twenty minutes while Dad and Nick watched me from the couch while calmly eating chicken and rice.

Eventually, Dad gave me a pat on the back and went to his room to watch TV. Nick corralled me to the table and made me eat something. "You're going to make yourself sick if you don't calm down."

"I can't let them get away with this. And I don't even know what *this* is."

"I know. But you can't do anything if you don't take care of yourself. I bet you haven't eaten since breakfast."

"Well, you're wrong. I had a snickerdoodle at Carol Hodge's house."

Nick's eyes grew wide in mockery, and he held his hands up in false surrender.

"Alright, fine." I picked up my fork. "But I make no promises that this subject will be dropped when I'm finished with this plate."

That was an hour ago, and all I'd managed to accomplish was doing the dishes and getting into bed with my Labrador body pillow. I tossed and turned for I don't know how long. Images of Jacob shooting Oscar and Eddie tormented me. I was desperate for sleep, but full of anxiety over the nightmares that awaited me.

* * *

I woke with my heart pounding, the sheets wrapped around me like hands gripping my throat. My phone ringing a special tone programed only for when the girls called me. I snatched it off the nightstand. Quarter past midnight. The screen flashed Bree's name.

"Hello?"

"Layla?"

"What's wrong?"

Silence.

"Bree? What's going on?"

Bree sobbed into the phone. "I'm so sorry."

I sat bolt upright. "What do you mean? What did you do? Do you need an ambulance?"

Bree sniffled. "No."

"Did you take something?"

"Not yet. But I don't know how much longer I can hold out."

I put her on speaker and texted Scarlett and Charisse while I pulled on sweats and sneakers.

Bree. 911. Going over now.

"Just stay calm and tell me what's happening. I'm on my way." I grabbed my keys and my bag.

Ringo raised his head and watched me closely.

"Come on, boy."

He jumped off the bed and followed me out to the Jeep while Bree told me what she was looking at between sobs.

"I came home and found my dad crying over a Christmas ornament that Ryan made in school."

"Oh no."

"I wanted to make him something nice with a picture of all of us to give him a happy memory, so I was going through a box of old pictures of me and Ryan that I had under my bed."

"Okay." I backed out of the driveway and sped up the road to the highway.

"I found a baggie."

"Of what?"

"Ecstasy."

"Alright. Don't do anything. Just keep talking to me."

"I must have hidden it there when I was in high school."

"Sure." I was on the highway now, and I knew it would take me almost twenty minutes with light traffic to get to Annandale. *What I would give to have lights and a siren right now.*

"My mom had gotten into the habit of searching my room whenever I was out."

"Understandable."

"After they found me . . . unresponsive . . . from a heroin overdose . . . my dad Narcaned me. I was rushed to the ER." She sobbed again. "My brother stayed with me all night. He never left my side. I was taken to rehab the day I was released. They didn't even want me to come home on the chance that I would do it again."

Ringo nudged my elbow from the back seat. "Almost there, buddy. I'm bringing you a special friend, Bree. Just hold on."

She sniffled. "I can't believe I'll never see Ryan again. The last time he saw me my life was a dumpster fire. I keep looking at these pills and thinking what's the point. I'll never be worth saving. Nothing can ever bring Ryan back."

"Listen to me, Bree. Ryan would be so proud of where you are now. All you've accomplished since you've been clean. You're going to be a college graduate soon. That's a big deal."

Bree sobbed, "I'm a phony, Layla. I have no idea what I'm doing in school. Everyone else gets it, and I'm struggling to keep up. I just know I'm going to let my parents down again. I can't watch my mother cry another tear over me. One of these days my mistakes are going to destroy her."

"That is absolutely not true." A lump of terror sat high in my chest. My phone was flashing messages from the others, but I didn't want to stop driving to check them. I prayed that one of us would get to her before it was too late.

"The only thing you could do to destroy your parents is try to kill yourself again, Bree. As long as you're alive they have hope."

The phone went silent.

I switched lanes, my exit coming up fast. "Still with me?"

Her voice was a whisper. "How did you know?"

"Honey, I'm a cop. I've seen way too much, way too often. I know you wear long sleeves to cover your scars—and it's okay. We all have scars. Some of yours are on the outside. And we all love you."

"You do?" Her voice broke along with my heart.

"Absolutely. You're the kindest person I've ever met. My life wouldn't be the same without you. Tell me more about your brother. I'm almost there."

She told me a few more stories about Ryan, and what he was like. Her voice was getting thin, and dread was climbing my chest. Then the line went dead.

I tried to call her back, but the phone rang like it was turned off.

There were no open parking spots in front of her house when I arrived a few minutes later, but Scarlett's Porsche was double-parked behind Bree's minivan. I threw the Jeep into park right behind her. Ringo jumped out and ran up to Bree's door even though he'd never been here before. I raised my fist to knock, but Scarlett opened the door before I connected.

"We're in here."

Ringo rushed ahead. I followed Scarlett into a little dining room.

Bree was sitting at the table, a steamy mug in front of her. Charisse had her chair butted up close with her arm around the girl.

Ringo nudged Bree's arm until she petted him, speaking in puppy tones. "Hey, buddy. You came to see me."

Her eyes rose to mine and filled with tears. She got out of her seat and came to me, folding herself around me, shaking.

I held her tight. "It's alright. I'm here."

Bree's mother came out of the kitchen and placed a mug in front of me. "Thank you for coming. I can't tell you how much it means to us that she has other people who love her and understand what she's going through."

She gave me a look of heartbreaking gratitude that shattered a part of me.

"I can see that Bree is in good hands, so I'll say good night and leave you to talk." With a single nod and her eyes wet with emotion, she left us. A door down the hall closed quietly behind her.

Bree pulled back and wiped her eyes.

"How did you do? Did you take them?"

She shook her head no. Then she walked over to an ornate box on the coffee table and pulled the baggie out. "I didn't know what to do with them, so I waited for you."

Three little poison discs rested inside. "Where's the bathroom?"

She pointed down the hall and I walked in through the first door, opened the packet, and dumped them in the toilet. "Is this everything?"

"Yes."

I flushed and waited for them to disappear, then flushed again.

Bree gasped. "I didn't think you were allowed to flush drugs or medicine."

"We're gonna allow it. If you ever find anything else, don't think. Just flush it immediately."

She bit down on her lip and nodded. "Okay."

I put my arm around her, and we headed back to the dining room where Scarlett and Charisse waited. I had never been so relieved in my life. They may have saved Bree from doing something desperate before I could get here. As far as I was concerned, they were heroes.

Bree reclaimed her seat at the table and cupped her mug; Ringo's head was in her lap instantly. "I don't know how to thank you . . ." Her words trailed off as her lip started to tremble.

I put my hand on her arm and Charisse put her hand on mine followed by Scarlett. "You being here and staying healthy is enough."

She gave us a watery smile and nodded.

Scarlett pulled a deck of cards out of her purse. "Who's up for gin rummy?" She shuffled the deck a couple times while we spaced around the table. "Just so you know, Ambrose got into my cards, and now the four of hearts is an Uno card, and the queen of spades is a Pokémon."

We laughed, but the three of us had our eyes on Bree to see her laugh while we did so. We played cards and ate cookies for hours while Bree told us stories of her brother, sometimes through laughter and sometimes through tears, always through Ringo's fur because he'd managed to stuff his eighty-five-pound self into her lap. But we made it through the night.

In the morning, I texted Nick to let him know where I was, so he didn't think I went on a rampage. About twenty minutes later, just as Bree's mom was putting scrambled eggs and bacon on the table in front of us, I got a text.

Only, it wasn't from Nick. It was from Castinetto.

Seth Masters is dead.

Chapter 37

"HOW DID CASTINETTO EVEN KNOW WE VISITED SETH MASTERS? Or knew who he was? I told Beasley to keep that between us, the stupid, dumb, baby cop."

Bree put a spoonful of scrambled eggs on my plate before passing the dish past me to Scarlett. "Poor guy. He was so sweet."

Scarlett took some for herself then passed the dish to Charisse before sneaking Ringo and Alice another piece of bacon under the table. "At least eat something before you call him half-cocked and hangry."

I jabbed an egg and chewed angrily. Another text came in from Castinetto.

I'll be at your house in 30.

"Great. He's coming over."

Charisse paused with bacon on the way to her lips. "He's coming here?"

"No, to my house."

Bree picked up her orange juice and shotgunned it. "Well, hurry up and eat then. We gotta get over there before he does."

"You all don't have to come. You've been up all night."

Three sets of eyes looked at me like I'd suggested we shave our heads.

Charisse huffed. "You're not shaking us."

Bree's mother chuckled softly and put her hand on my shoulder. "I'll pack four cinnamon buns to go."

* * *

We were all in my kitchen waiting for the high-and-mighty detective who may have been playing me for a fool this entire time. Nick flitted around the room opening cans and chopping things. Dad had positioned himself at the end of the table with the best view of the activity without actually being close enough to do anything useful.

I was on a razor's edge of anxiety and full of suspicion. "What is Castinetto up to?"

Nick set a mug of cocoa in front of me without saying a word. His other hand grazed the width of my back as he walked away. The girls clocked it and passed looks to each other.

Dad asked, "Who's Castinetto?"

"The cop who came to the trailer when someone tagged the side with spray paint."

"I think he likes you." Dad reached for his glass of orange juice. "He sure made a fuss over your safety when he was there."

"I think you're misreading those signals, Dad. He's a cop. He gets off on being in charge."

Dad shrugged. "Would I lie to you?"

"No. Of course not. I'm not saying that. It's just . . ."

Dad wasn't listening anymore. He was in his own world drumming his fingers on the table and singing the Eurythmics' "Would I Lie to You." Almost.

"Did I say somethin' that isn't true? I'm telling you, babe, I wouldn't lie-ee-iee-iee to you."

I looked across the table at the girls and bowed my head.

Ringo started to bark and prance around. At first I thought it was because of Dad's singing; then I realized someone was here. I flung the door open to find Pippi standing on my front step. She was wearing a little orange sweater that had PUMPKIN embroidered across the front. Ringo pushed past me, excited to play with his friend, and started chasing the black pig around the yard. I stepped outside and looked around for Pippi's sidekick. "Foster?"

Ronnie Voa's guy waved to me from the curb.

I pointed to the pig. "Is she here by herself?"

He shook his head no, and Foster appeared from the side of the house. He had a few wildflowers in his hand and he was being escorted by the back security guard. "Hey, Layla. How you?"

"It's fine. I'll take it from here. Foster, what are you doing here?"

"Pippi was excited for Thanksgiving tomorrow, so we came to see if you needed anything."

"Oh. Well . . ." I felt a little chastised. I was ten shades of irritated before I opened the door and ready to bite the head off of anyone who stood there. Plus, I had eaten like a pound of bacon that morning and suddenly wasn't feeling real good about that situation. "Nick has everything in hand for our contribution. You just need to bring whatever you signed up for."

Foster's face pinked and his nose twitched. He looked at his feet. "I didn't sign up for anything."

"Okay. Well, what do you want to bring?"

He toed the edge of the welcome mat that was advertising a blatant lie. I'd prefer it if everyone just stayed away. "I have some crackers I could bring."

"Alright. That's perfect."

"Layla Virtue!"

I turned my head toward the high-pitched cry of Myrtle Jean Maud. She had on a thick white Irish sweater over a tan plaid skirt and glossy brown boots. She was marching through the side yard with both Agnes, who looked like a drag queen in pink zebra patterned leathers, and Clifford, who was wearing a tweed three-piece suit with a cravat. On a Wednesday morning. In a trailer park.

"This can't be good. Why don't you wait inside, Foster?"

The trio made it all the way to my sidewalk, through Ringo and Pippi running circles around the bushes, before telling me the reason for this drop-in-pestering. Myrtle Jean lifted a clipboard aloft. "We're here to do a final check on the Thanksgiving preparations."

I heaved a sigh—partly for my benefit and partly so they would know they were vexing me. "What?" I said, flatly.

Agnes rolled her eyes. "Now you know very well, Layla Virtue, that we have zero confidence in your ability to pull this off."

"How generous of you."

She waved me away like I was a mosquito. "We spent all morning passing around the notices about the new email system; now we're here to help with the potluck plans."

Clifford bristled and rolled his shoulders back. "This Thanksgiving shindig is a Lake Pinecrest tradition, and it must be done with the gravitas it deserves."

I locked down most of my mockery, but my eyes did half a roll before I could stop them. "It's paper plates and red Solo cups, Clifford. Not a state dinner at the White House."

Clifford's throat gurgled, like he'd swallowed his tongue.

Myrtle Jean handed me her clipboard. An attached list of "needed dishes" remained mostly unchecked. Her papery cheeks quivered. "These items must be at the dinner for it to be a success."

I read down the list. "Chestnut stuffing, mashed potatoes, macaroni and cheese, squash casserole, green bean casserole, braised cabbage, yeast rolls. Don't you think this is excessive? No one will even be there but you three, and you lot have signed up for rhubarb pie, pickled beets, and a Jell-O salad."

Agnes shook her head. "Layla, Layla, Layla. I should never have let you be in charge."

"As I recall, it was determined that I was in charge because I own the trailer park. And since Dad didn't buy it from *you,* I have to wonder who put *you* in charge in the first place."

Clifford huffed. "Insolence!"

Myrtle Jean put her hand on his arm to quiet him. "Such disrespect, Layla."

Agnes puffed one of her cheeks. "That's not important." She tapped the clipboard. "Corn pudding. *That's* important."

I checked the list again. "Well, the only other things that have been signed up for are three cans of cranberry sauce and a bottle of Mr. Peppo."

All three of them grimaced.

"Don't look at me. You're the ones who made this list. Maybe people don't want to do this dinner. Did you ever think of that?"

Ringo chased Pippi through the center of us then stopped to bark at someone coming down the road. Once again, I thought it was Castinetto, but it was Robin in her van. She had Marguerite riding shotgun and holding Steppenwolf.

"Did someone turn on the nuisance signal over my house?" I handed Myrtle her clipboard. "I can't control what people bring, and I can't make people come. I'm not even sure I'll be there. With these threats my dad has been getting I don't feel like it's safe for him."

Clifford shrugged. "Well, if he can't make it."

Myrtle Jean smacked him on the arm. "Of course he needs to be there."

"Why do you care? I thought you had a boyfriend."

Her cheeks flamed. "I do, but he's in Paris. For now."

Agnes pressed her lips together. "Myrtle Jean is right. Don is an important member of our community. We're not going to let anything happen to him. As long as I'm still living here, I'll make sure he's safe."

"What do you mean as long as you're still living here?"

Agnes's face softened. She cocked her head in half a shrug. "If you'd read the sale papers I gave you with the deed to the property, you'd know. I'll be leaving soon. I got free rent on the double wide in exchange for managing the trailer park. Since I'm not the manager anymore, I'll be moving at the end of the year."

Robin was being lowered from her lift gate. "Wait, who's leaving?"

Agnes casually looked over her shoulder. "I am."

Marguerite threw off a few words in Spanish that I recognized as expletives, then she glared at me. "What did you do?"

"Nothing. I just found out."

Robin rolled forward to the porch. “Great. There goes the neighborhood.”

“Hey. Maybe you should wait until you’ve been here longer than fifteen minutes before you start criticizing me.”

She made a rude gesture and headed down the path to the back of the house.

Everyone began yelling at me at once. Ringo ran to sit in front of me as guard.

Castinetto’s yellow sports car slowly rolled into my driveway.

“Alright! Cool it! The cops are here.”

They scattered like I’d shot a starter’s pistol. Only, they went the wrong way—into my house.

“For the love of God, go to your own homes!”

Castinetto parked and gave me a slow smile. “Did you get your bodyguards to come back you up?”

I heard the door behind me open, and the smile slid off Castinetto’s face.

I looked over my shoulder just as Nick put his hand on my back. “Everything okay out here?”

“Yeah. I’ve been expecting him.”

Dayton’s eyes flicked past me and widened.

I looked behind me, and every person in my house had their face plastered to a window. “Ignore them. It’s like visiting hour at the zoo. What do you have for me?”

He searched my face for a moment. “Seth Masters was killed last night. Took a bullet to the head. It looks like he interrupted a robbery.”

A robbery. Right.

“Traffic cameras in the vicinity picked up your Jeep turning into his apartment complex.”

“That doesn’t mean I was at his house.”

“The neighbor’s Ring camera shows you entering his house a few minutes later.”

“Okay. That doesn’t mean I killed him.”

The tips of Castinetto’s ears turned red. His voice went sharp. “No one is saying you killed him, Virtue.” His eyes flicked to

Nick, and he looked away. He composed himself and turned back with his hand on his hip under his service pistol. "Some kids on bikes used a crowbar and stole the camera from the neighbor's doorjamb a couple hours after you were there before he was killed, but everything had already been recorded in the cloud."

"Kids on bikes?"

His voice was flat. "Yeah."

"And you believe that's a coincidence?"

"No."

I stared at him for a long minute until he turned away again.

He started to pace a bit. "Look, we both know that wasn't a robbery. Seth Masters was targeted, and I think it had something to do with your visit."

"I didn't even know him. How do you know we weren't there to buy protein powder?"

"I know why you were there, Layla!"

Ringo growled and Castinetto stepped back.

Nick squeezed my shoulder. "Does she need a lawyer for this discussion?"

Dayton's lip curled a bit, and he gave Nick some side-eye. "Why are you here?"

"I live here."

The color drained from Castinetto's face.

I hadn't realized how much whispering was going on in the house behind me until the silence swallowed every sound, including the wind through the leaves, in that moment.

Castinetto's eyes turned hard. The muscle in his jaw flexed. He stepped back and gave me a stare. "You need to stop investigating what happened at Stratton Park before you get hurt. Leave it alone. Just stick to the Wilkins murder case."

"And what if I don't? Are you afraid of what I'll find?"

A flash of something passed behind his eyes, too fast for me to grab hold of it. He turned and strode to his sports car without another word.

I spun around in time to see everyone scatter.

Nick chuckled. "Subtle."

I marched into the house in full rant. "If you people are going to come over here with your demands, the least you can do is give me some privacy when the cops are here!" I headed into the kitchen without breaking stride. "We're going through a difficult time, and I could use a little support!" I threw open the cabinet to get a medicinal cookie. "Next time—AAAAAHHHH!"

I was midrant when something flew out of the cabinet and attacked me.

Chapter 38

IT STOOD ON ITS HIND LEGS, HISSED, AND WAVED A COOKIE IN MY face before taking off.

Agnes pointed. "It ran under the table!"

Nick threw his arm across me. "Get back!"

Ringo had it in his sights immediately and chased it through the living room and around the coffee table where everyone screamed.

Charisse yelled, "Sweet Jesus, what is that!"

Pippi squealed and booked it for the front door. Followed by Foster who called after her, "Wait for me!" and slammed the door behind them.

Dad cried, "Hey, that's my cat!"

I grabbed a broom. "That's not a cat, Dad. How do you not know a raccoon when you see it? And it's the world's fattest raccoon because it's full of Fancy Feast and eating your Sausalito cookies."

The raccoon lumbered to the fireplace where it stood on its hind legs, its arms spread out to full width, half a chocolate chip macadamia cookie still in one of its paws. Its eyes roved over us, looking for the weakest link.

Dad whined, "How was I supposed to know? I thought it was one of those funny new breeds. Why would a raccoon be inside the house?"

The trailer park people clumped together by the bookcases

and pushed Bree forward. Bree jumped on the coffee table and yelled, "Eww! Layla, do something!"

Scarlett stood by the dragon-shaped lamp, cool and calm. "Do you have a shovel? One good whack and I'll have this problem solved."

Dad's eyes were pleading. "No. Please don't hurt him."

I raised the broom. "Get the door, Nick!"

Nick ran to the front door and pulled it open. Whimsy St. James was crouched, placing a can of cranberry sauce on the front porch next to the stone hedgehog. Ten people yelled with one voice, "Watch out!"

I swatted the raccoon toward the front door, and it took off lumbering with the cookie in his mouth. Ringo chased him at full gallop.

Whimsy's eyes nearly shot from her head, and she flung herself into a boxwood shaped like Pinocchio. Once the raccoon passed her and ran for the bushes, Whimsy cast an angry look at me, kicked the can of cranberry sauce, and took off.

Nick shut the door and threw the lock, and we took a moment to collect ourselves.

I knocked the broom against the fireplace. "I'll call animal control."

Nick nodded. "I'll check for entry points."

Dad slumped down in his chair. "Man, I miss that little guy."

My phone buzzed in my back pocket and, whether because of adrenaline or exhaustion, I jumped into Scarlett. I checked the screen and let out a groan. "Jayne Moorefield reminding me we had an appointment to see Archie's classroom and meet the kids. I could use your help if you're up to being a little sneaky."

Scarlett's lips formed a wicked grin. "I was born for moments like this."

I was shrugging into my jacket at the front door when Bree grabbed her purse, ready to roll. "Okay, let's go."

I held my hand up. "You need to go home and get some sleep. No—don't argue. I know we're a team. But this fancy private school is locked down and they won't let us all in there anyway.

I'll drop you off on my way and tell you what they said tomorrow." I nodded toward Charisse. "And don't you have things to do for Thanksgiving with your family?"

Charisse groaned.

Nick grabbed his keys. "Why don't I take the ladies home so you can get right over there?"

I looked across the room at Dad, then at Agnes.

She nodded and put her hand on his shoulder. "Let's watch a movie, Don."

"Thank you, Nick."

Charisse yawned. "I don't like it, but I need to figure out something for tomorrow when the kids come over."

Bree looked at me and her lip trembled.

"You've got this."

She rolled her shoulders back and nodded. "I got this."

Charisse grabbed the girl's hand. "And we're one call away."

Scarlett hugged Bree closely. "If you need me, I'm there in a heartbeat. Graham will have to be happy with the Mrs. Smith's I have hidden in the back of the freezer in the garage."

"Okay. That settles it. You two go get ready for your family dinners, and we'll meet here tomorrow at four for Thanksgiving, trailer park-style."

Jayne Moorefield was waiting for me at the glossy white door. She looked at her watch and frowned. "I thought we said eleven A.M."

"I'm so sorry. We had a wildlife incident in my house." *And half a dozen other pests.*

She clucked her tongue. "Well, okay then. But we let out at noon for the holiday, and I don't want any distractions when the parents are here."

"Understood."

She made a quick pivot, and her brown wool skirt flared under her fitted jacket. She was still chastising me as her brown pumps clacked down the hall. I could have told her I couldn't hear anything she was saying but I didn't want to interrupt her in case this was a ruler-whacking school. I'd been whacked by enough nuns for a lifetime.

We rounded the corner, and I followed her to a door that said GRADE TWO above it. She knocked, then opened the door into a bright classroom with three rows of desks filled with quiet, curious faces watching me. A shiver ran down my spine.

The walls were covered with colorful drawings and teaching posters for reading and math. Each child had a construction paper turkey made from tracing their hand on the desk in front of them. I guess no matter how fancy the school, there are still only so many art projects for Thanksgiving.

A woman in a white blouse with a beautiful purple scarf stood at a chalkboard. Each child wore a red blazer with a golden insignia over the pocket. How well I remembered hating those blazers even though mine was gold with green trim. We looked like deranged little Realtors.

"Class, this is Ms. Virtue. She's here to observe. Please give her a warm welcome."

This was followed by a chorus of *Hel-lo, Ms. Vir-tue.*

I gave the kids a smile that I was sure did not match my body language. One of the boys in the back had unbuttoned his shirt at the collar and his jacket hung open. His hair was gelled so sharp, you could grate cheese on it. He narrowed his eyes slightly and gave me a naughty grin. I looked deeper at him, and he giggled and looked away.

"Layla, this is the classroom monitor, Mrs. Jaya Kapoor."

I held my hand out and Jaya clasped it. "Such a shame . . . what happened."

I nodded, noticing the kids shifting in their seats and making faces at each other. They knew exactly what was being talked about.

Jayne Moorefield took a seat at the desk and told me to go ahead and look around. I was making over the self-portrait artwork on the wall when there was a knock on the door. One of the security guards.

He raised his eyebrows and Jayne asked, "What is it?"

"Ma'am, we have a situation."

"Can't you deal with it?"

He gave her a pointed look. "It's a potential new student. The parent needs to make a decision today. I really think you need to be involved."

Jayne stood with a huff. "Fine. I'll be back as soon as possible, Ms. Virtue. Until I return, Mrs. Kapoor can get you whatever you need."

Once Ms. Moorefield left the room, the kids started chatting amongst themselves and giggling.

Mrs. Kapoor clapped her hands. "Silence! Eyes up front."

I took advantage of the principal's absence to ask a couple impromptu questions. "Hi, kids. I'm Layla. I want to talk to you about your teacher, Mr. Wilkins."

The boy in the back called out, "He's dead. Murdered."

There's an informant in every group, and I'd clearly found mine. "I know. And I'm sorry. What I want to know is: Did you like Mr. Wilkins?"

All the heads bobbed up and down.

"Did anyone ever see Mr. Wilkins outside of school?"

No one stirred.

The boy in the back called out, "Why does your hair have blue paint in it?"

"From keeping secrets."

Every kid in the room started pulling their hair in front of their eyes to check. A girl and a boy each put their hands up. I called on the girl first. "I saw Mr. Wilkins at church for the fall play about the Indians."

The boy immediately dropped his head to a pout.

"Is that where you saw Mr. Wilkins too?"

He nodded.

"Can you tell me the name of the church?"

The boy shrugged but the girl's hand shot up again. "Our Lady of Mercy. That's where we go."

I whispered to Jaya, "What's that one's name?"

She whispered back, "That's Ava Green."

"Our Lady of Mercy. Okay. Anyone else?"

Another girl raised her hand tentatively. "I saw Mrs. Wilkins at the library."

"How did you know it was Mrs. Wilkins?"

"My nana told me."

"Anything unusual happen?"

"Nana yelled at her that she should be ashamed of herself for what she was doing to people."

"Okay." I nodded to Jaya.

She whispered, "Charlotte Adams."

Three more hands went up. I pointed to a boy who said, "I saw Mr. Wilkins at the grocery store, and it was weird."

"What was so weird about it?"

"I didn't know he bought food." The boy covered his mouth, and the class giggled.

I looked at Jaya.

"Noah Pearson." She lowered her voice. "Of the Pearson Oil family. Very rich."

"How about you?" I asked my boy in the back.

"My dad and I saw Mr. Wilkins in the parking lot, but I'm not supposed to tell anyone."

"Why not?"

"Because my dad was really mad at him and said some bad words I'm not supposed to know."

The other kids immediately pounced with a group "Oooooh" and a bunch of snickering.

"Well, thank you for trusting me."

I looked at Jaya again and she whispered, "Benjamin Whitcomb."

After a moment when no hands went up, Benjamin offered up his friend. "Elijah's dad yelled at Mr. Wilkins too."

A boy with dark curly hair shot Benjamin a scowl. "That's a secret."

Benjamin threw his hands out in exasperation. "Do you want blue hair?"

Elijah sank lower in his seat. "My dad yelled at Mr. Wilkins that he was a turnip and didn't have any more blood."

I thought about that for a minute, rolling the words around my mind. "Did he maybe say you can't get blood from a turnip?"

Elijah's face lit up and he nodded vigorously. "That's it."

Jaya groaned and her shoulders drooped. "Elijah Hart."

"Did you ever have any problems with Archie?"

"Never. I can't imagine where all this is coming from."

I addressed the class again. "Did anyone have any problems with Mr. Wilkins?"

Faces scrunched in confusion and feet kicked under the desks. Many of the kids shook their heads.

"I'm going to ask you to do something for me. I want everyone to shut their eyes very tight. Yes, even you, Benjamin. Okay. Now I'm going to ask you something very important and I want honesty. And no peeking."

Benjamin squinted through his fingers.

Ava ratted on him. There was one of those in every group too. "Benjamin's peeking."

"If you peek, Santa will know."

Benjamin's hands shot back up to cover his eyes. And Ava did the same.

"Okay. Raise your hand if Mr. Wilkins ever did anything that made you uncomfortable or weird."

Jaya's breathing stilled and the room grew quiet. Not one hand went up. I waited just an extra moment.

"Did he ever say anything about your parents that made you feel funny or sad?"

Nothing.

"Wonderful. Why don't you all talk amongst yourselves while I chat with your room monitor." I turned to Jaya. "Ms. Moorefield told me they drew pictures and journaled about Archie's death."

"That's right."

"What did they say in their journals?"

She adjusted her scarf. "I don't know. I'm not allowed to read them."

"What do you mean?"

"Mr. Wilkins was very protective of the kids' privacy. No one was to read the journals but him."

"Sure, but he's dead."

She flinched at my unfiltered truth. The boy in the back repeated my words. "He's dead."

I locked eyes with him, and he gave me a naughty smile again.

Jaya wrung her hands. "Well, that's true. I just assumed when their new teacher started after the holidays she would take over the journals."

"I'd like to see them."

"I don't know if that would be allowed."

"I promise they'll be safe with me. And they might help me find out what happened to Archie. Besides, you don't want the cops taking you down to the station for questioning, do you?"

Her eyes softened. "Well, okay. If you promise to keep them safe." She took a set of keys from the top drawer in the desk and unlocked a closet on the side of the room. Inside were rows and rows of journals cataloged by year. "Which ones do you want?"

"I want everyone who's in the class right now. And also, get me the class from last year."

She pulled the different notebooks and handed them to me. "Can we keep this just between us for right now?"

"Absolutely. No one else needs to know." I stuffed the bulging stack into my bag and tucked it under my arm. "I'm wondering, in a school where everything is uniform and precision, why are the journals all different?"

She locked the closet and returned the keys to the desk drawer. "Mr. Wilkins let each child have artistic expression when choosing their journal. He said it should be as personal as what they write inside."

"Did he now."

The door opened and Ms. Moorefield entered with a bead of exasperation on her lip. "I apologize. A prospective parent with some admission questions that couldn't wait until after the holiday."

"No problem. I understand completely."

The school bell rang, signaling the period was over. Jaya clapped her hands. "Class, gather your things and line up for dismissal."

The children did as they were told and formed a straight line at the door.

I thanked Jaya and Ms. Moorefield for their time and assistance and followed the kids out to the main foyer with the sole purpose of seeing who went home with whom. The children marched in a straight line to the main foyer then broke into runs.

Ava ran to either a big sister or an au pair.

Elijah kind of pout-stomped over to a thin, willowy man in a bespoke suit. He looked very familiar. I knew I'd seen him somewhere before, but I couldn't place him. Then I spotted Gladys Beacon from Our Lady of Mercy standing in the parent line. She put her arms out as Charlotte ran to her. She spotted me and her head cocked to an angle. I put on a pleasant smile and wandered over casually. "Hello again."

"What are you doing here?"

"I just came by to express my condolences to the class."

Gladys's voice softened. "The dear man. What a shame. He will be missed."

"He won't be missed by all."

The cutting remark came from the man to my left. I turned in time to spot the dad holding Benjamin's backpack and hand turkey. Benjamin looked at me and the naughty smile was back.

"I take it you did not worship Mr. Wilkins like all the other parents?"

The man snickered. "I never met a greater busybody in my whole life. And any parent who says otherwise is a liar." Before I could ask him what he meant by that, they slipped out the door.

I asked Gladys, "Who was that?"

"Pssh. That was just Nigel Whitcombe. You've probably seen him on channel five. He's the local Fox News weatherman. Don't pay him any mind. He's not been himself since his wife left him for a dance instructor."

"Ava Green says her family goes to Our Lady of Mercy. Is that an au pair I saw picking her up?"

Gladys's lips flattened. "Au pair . . . mistress—it's all the same to some people."

"Do you by any chance know Elijah's parents?"

Gladys gave me an incredulous look. "You mean Congresswoman Hart and her husband? I'd say everyone knows them. I'm surprised you don't. The woman ran on a platform to end drug trafficking."

"Hmm. I remember that. Speaking of drugs . . . Are you aware of any drug addicts hanging around the church?"

Gladys huffed out a long sigh. "Father Matthews, God bless him, thinks the best of everyone. But some people can't be redeemed. There are more unsavory characters in the church than he wants to admit. He's had to practically double his time in the confession chamber."

"Anyone in particular?"

"I couldn't possibly break his confidence with that information."

Another classroom was let out as Carol Hodge appeared in the doorway. A little girl with hair the color of sunshine ran to meet her with her arms out.

Gladys *tsk*'d. "That's a tragic story. Poor little thing already lost her father, and it seems her mother may not be with us long. But if anyone had a right to be angry with Archie Wilkins, it was her momma. What he put them through."

The church secretary shook her head and guided her granddaughter from the building, leaving me wondering what else she might know.

I followed the stragglers out to the parking lot and gave a discreet salute to Mrs. Scarlett Weatherspoon, prospective new parent.

She flashed me her newly acquired tuition packet, and with a grin and salute of her own, climbed into her Porsche and took off for home to thaw a Mrs. Smith's pumpkin pie.

Chapter 39

"Are you sure you have time to do this, Nick? You've been making pies all day. You must be tired."

Nick shrugged into a tan suede jacket and grabbed his keys. "I'm sure. You've been wigged out since AA when you learned Jacob's girlfriend is the bartender at Muddled."

"I don't like being lied to."

"You've done nothing but pace back and forth slamming doors since you got home from the school. Ringo is so tired from pacing behind you that he didn't want to play Frisbee when I offered to take him out. Let's just go back to Muddled and check it out. Unless you're too exhausted. You haven't slept in almost twenty-four hours."

I grabbed my coat off the rack and got my bag. "No. You're right. If I go to sleep now, I'm just gonna have night terrors anyway. Dad's in his room watching reruns of *Saved by the Bell.* Let's go now."

I stopped at the security van to check in. "We'll be out for a while. How are the new cameras?"

The security officer tonight looked like she was Demi Moore's body double from *GI Jane* twenty-five years later. Short, cropped gray hair and a neck tattoo that would make even me speed my pace in a dark alley. She showed me an iPad with views of all the security cameras around the outside of the house and another with views of the canoes down by the pond. "Good to go."

"Thank you. Don't let anyone in the house without calling me." Against my better judgment I added, "Except Agnes or Myrtle Jean. They're Dad's best friends in the park, and if he gets confused, they'll calm him down."

She gave me a thumbs-up, and Nick and I went and got into his car.

Nick waited until I got my seat belt fastened before he started the engine and pulled onto the street. "Do you have a plan for what you'll do if you see Jacob? Do I have to be ready to back you up in a street fight or take you out for milkshakes? I'm good with whatever but I do like a plan."

"Truthfully, I haven't let myself be totally convinced this Kevin is my Jacob. I keep thinking it's a coincidence. There are doppelgangers out there. Jeez, Dad pays one to get spotted when the paparazzi gets too close. So, part of me expects to find Jacob's body double, and he won't have any idea who I am or what happened at Stratton Park."

"Okay. Sounds reasonable."

"Let's keep that milkshake idea on the back burner though."

Nick chuckled. "You got it."

"How are you doing?"

"Better. I'll probably move back into my place Saturday morning."

"Oh."

"What?"

"Nothing. I mean, I guess that's good. You've got your own life. You know?"

With all the special lessons I'd had in my privileged lifetime—dance, ice skating, gymnastics, diving, competitive shooting, guitar—*Dad, obviously*—I should have taken acting lessons. Because right now I knew I was not pulling off casual aloofness about Nick leaving. Nick was the bright spot of my day. I was used to working with a partner and I guess I missed having someone around who had my back all the time.

He glanced at me for a moment then eyes back on the road.

"I appreciate what you've done for me, but I don't want to cramp your style. You need your privacy."

"Sure." I wanted to say, *Not from you,* but my voice betrayed me. "And so do you."

After a moment, Nick replied, "Sure."

We drove in silence the rest of the way to DC and parked in a pay lot. I paid for one hour with the app on my phone and we walked around the block to Muddled.

Nick pulled the door open and made a strangled sound in the back of his throat. "So many people."

"Are you okay?"

He sighed. "It's definitely the holidays. Everyone is getting prebuzzed before they have to face family tomorrow."

The trendy bar was beyond packed. There was a band set up against the far wall playing live music. A few clusters of people who didn't have seats stood around the stage area with glasses of wine or bottles of expensive imported beer, trying to hear each other over the noise. We had to push our way up to the counter where an older blonde in a tight T-shirt and miniskirt was pouring shots. "I'll be right with you."

I looked around and didn't see a waiter who looked like a quarterback with sable brown hair serving drinks. I only saw a short waiter that looked a lot like he was an extra hobbit in *Lord of the Rings.*

Nick was also looking around. He raised his voice for me to hear him. "I don't see Kiara."

I shouted back, "Maybe she's in the kitchen."

The blond bartender handed off her tray of shots, then came over to our edge of the bar. "What'll you have?"

I flashed her the photo of Jacob. "Is Kevin here tonight?"

She glanced at the picture and shook her head. "Kevin's off."

Nick asked, "What about Kiara? Is she in?"

"Nope. They're both off."

I swallowed the potato-sized lump in my throat. "Together? On a night this busy? My boss would never have given me the night off on a holiday."

The bartender cleared a couple lager glasses and wiped the counter. "Yeah, I'm not that lucky either. But when your father owns the bar, you and your fiancé get to take off for Thanksgiving."

I'm pretty sure I felt the blood drain from my face down to my knees. In the corner of my mind, a bell started to ring, and I felt unsteady on my feet.

Nick grabbed my hand. "I've been trying to catch up with Kevin for weeks now. We used to work over at the Gibson together."

The bartender nodded. "Yeah, I know it. Ricky owns both places. Sometimes I sub in at the Gibson when they're short-staffed."

The bell was growing silent as my cop senses sharpened. "Ricky? As in Ricky Hurtado owns both bars?"

The blonde's eyes grew twice their size. She bit her lip and reached for a shammy cloth. She began a frenzied polish of the bar top while checking behind her. "Um. No. I have no idea who that is. You must have heard me wrong."

Nick and I passed a look between us. "Then who owns the bars?"

She shrugged awkwardly, trying to appear nonchalant. "Both bars are owned by some holding company. I forget what it's called."

"Astoria Holdings?"

"Yeah. That's it."

A familiar burning sensation rose up from my chest. Ricky Hurtado, the drug lord we were set to take down at his warehouse in Stratton Park the day my life was ruined, owns the bar I lost my memories in, *and* the bar Jacob works for.

Jacob works for Ricky now. Did he work for him back then too? Good God, Jacob. What have you gotten yourself into?

The door opened and a young couple came in and shook off the cold. The man pushed his way up to the bar and ordered two beers on tap.

I gave him a look that I was not to be trifled with. "Dude. We were here first."

The waitress gave me a weak smile. "You need to order something or go. I'm already over my occupancy limit as it is."

"Just tell me this. How long has Kevin worked here?"

"Nine months. He was a Valentine's Day hire. Which I only know because Kiara won't shut up about how they met on the most romantic day of the year."

Chapter 40

"ARE YOU SURE YOU WANT TO BE ALONE RIGHT NOW?"

I turned into the Lake Pinecrest development. "You've been an amazing friend tonight, Nick, but I need to process this information. If Jacob was working for Hurtado the whole time he was my partner, I'm a bigger fool than I realized."

I'd loved him. And I'd tortured myself every day for not agreeing to move in with him. Was it all a lie? Was he just playing me to feed information to Hurtado?

"Uh, you wanna slow down a touch? You almost took out that tree."

"If he faked his death to get off the force, why is he a bartender just a few miles away in DC? I know it's outside of our old precinct, but he's not hiding that well. Internal Affairs should have found him. If he were in WITSEC he'd be dead by now." My hands clenched the steering wheel till my knuckles turned white. "I might beat him senseless."

Nick gripped the dash. "I believe you. But you and I—we're friends, right? And this is my car you begged me to let you drive. Maybe you could try to not kill me before I can get that turkey in the oven, or you'll have nothing to take to the community potluck."

"Frickin' potluck. How did I get strapped with being the ringleader for this circus?"

Nick chuckled, but his voice had a slight twinge of fear to it. "Because your rock star dad bought you a trailer park."

A vision of my father passed through my mind and my heart swelled with compassion. I tapped the brakes and took a breath. "Why can't I just have a pony like all the other rich little girls?"

"Probably because you wouldn't cooperate by telling him what color."

"That's true. And I am kind of afraid of them since one bit me unprovoked." I pulled up behind the security detail and parked. I passed Nick the keys. "Thank you. For everything."

We locked eyes for a minute.

Aware that the security guard's stare was on us, the moment was shoved aside. We headed into the house, but I stopped to check the box of requests because the lid was askew, and I obviously felt I hadn't been punished enough for the day. Ringo called for me to hurry up, whimpering that he was going to pass out from excitement if I didn't come in immediately.

Nick leaned against the doorjamb. "What is it? You're making a face like you want to take another run at that oak."

"It's a list of things from Agnes that she says I need to bring tomorrow because they weren't on the sign-up sheet. Butter, salt and pepper, ice . . ."

Nick rubbed the stubble on his chin. "I, uh . . . used all the butter today in the pies."

I flicked my eyes to his. "It's not like I have ice either. And I'm sure not taking the hand-carved Dopey and Grumpy salt and pepper shakers to the community room."

"What are you going to do?"

I yawned. "I guess I'm gonna run to the store. Freakin' Agnes."

"Well, if you're going . . ." He gave me a cheesy grin.

"What else do we need?"

"We need butter, and that raccoon ate the last of your dad's cookies. You know how he gets when he can see the bottom of the bag."

"Okay." I stuck the lid back on the box and headed to the Jeep. "Text me if you think of anything else."

Nick went inside to calm the clinically depressed Lab who groaned in agony when I didn't join him, and I hopped in the Jeep and backed out of the driveway.

I wound my way back up the lane to the main road. Traffic was lighter than usual for this time of day. People had taken off early for the holiday and were either flying high in the skies or already where they were going to be. So, it was really noticeable when a dark SUV pulled out from the shoulder and started tailing me.

I switched lanes just to be sure I wasn't imagining it.

The SUV switched lanes. No license plate. Dark tinted windows so I couldn't see who was inside.

I moved into the left lane and made a U-turn going back the way I'd come. I made sure not to move my head when I looked in the rearview mirror to not tip my hand that I was onto them, but I tilted my eyes to check the view.

The SUV followed me.

I turned into a strip mall and passed a Starbucks and a Subway. I slowed down in front of a hair salon. The SUV slowed down and idled a few car lengths back.

I checked to make sure no civilians were around, then I put the Jeep in reverse and slowly rolled backward.

The SUV lurched, then with its tires squealing, pulled off to the side and flew past me. No license plate on the back either.

I put the Jeep in drive and started to push forward, but had to slam on the brakes because some guy with an armful of subs stepped out in front of me. I blared on the horn. He mouthed an apology.

By the time he'd crossed the parking lot the SUV was gone.

I drove around for a few minutes but didn't spot it again. Finally, I gave up the search and pulled onto the highway to continue my journey toward Harris Teeter, with routine checks for the SUV in my rearview mirror.

The grocery store parking lot was packed like a blizzard was in the forecast. This quick trip was gonna be a nightmare. I parked so far away I might as well have walked here from home.

I hiked up to the door and grabbed the only cart just as some lady took her bag from the basket and let it go.

Inside the store was a madhouse. You'd think Thanksgiving had suddenly announced it was coming early and caught everyone by surprise. I wheeled my cart toward the cookie section, grabbed a few bags of Dad's favorite lineup, and put them in the basket. Then one more for me and Nick. *I hope Nick likes lemon.*

An eerie feeling crawled up my neck—like a whisper from the grave. I turned my head and thought I saw a familiar set of broad shoulders disappear around the corner.

I pushed the cart forward to follow, but they were gone. I looked both ways to catch another glimpse, but there were too many shoppers crowding the aisles to be sure of anything.

Castinetto's voice mocked me in my imagination. *You're losing it, Virtue.*

I pressed on toward the dairy section. There was not a box of butter to be had. One lone container of soy butter sat gloomily at the back of the shelf like the last kid to be picked for dodgeball. I was weighing in my mind how desperate I was to escape the scorn of Agnes the Thanksgiving taskmaster when someone grabbed the soy butter and wheeled triumphantly toward the registers.

I called after them, "I didn't want that gross fake butter anyway."

On the edge of my periphery, again I thought I spotted Jacob, this time standing behind a display of corn chips. My neck snapped as I tried to get a better look.

The image evaporated like a mirage.

I wheeled my cart around the shopper next to me like I was speeding into the turn at Nascar. The woman gave me a sharp look and muttered something that made me wish I still had a badge to flash.

I hurried down the perimeter of the store, checking aisle by aisle for the traitor who might have killed our friends. I was one hundred percent sure that he was here. When I got to the paper towels, I'd lost fifty percent of my confidence. By the toothpaste, I'd lost eighty-five percent. When I ended up in the alcohol, I spun my cart and took off the opposite way out of self-preservation.

What was wrong with me? The bartender said he was home with his fiancée. Not trolling the grocery store, spying on the woman he left to pick up the pieces of his bad judgment and possible treachery.

I pushed the cart to the self-checkout and bought the cookies, then went and got into my car heading for home.

I drove with my eyes darting to the rear and side mirrors. No one followed me. I didn't relax until I started the wind down to the lake, but once I crossed the threshold into the house a spike of irritation shot through me like lightning.

"I forgot the freakin' ice."

"Is that you, baby girl?"

"Yeah. I'm home."

"Look! We got a cat."

I stood stock-still in the foyer trying to understand what I'd just heard. Surely Dad wasn't in the living room with the raccoon. I called out tentatively, "We got a what?"

Myrtle Jean's voice was added to Dad's. "Come see, Layla."

Nick came around the corner, trepidation shining in his gorgeous blue eyes. "Okay, just stay calm. It's really a cat this time. And Don *loves* it."

I set the bags of cookies down in the foyer and followed Nick to the scene of the crime. There was Dad, sitting crisscross on the couch with his feet tucked up under him. A ridiculously fluffy cream-colored cat with a seal-brown mask and tail curled in Dad's lap.

Dad's eyes shone with joy as he stroked the cat's fur. I could hear purring from across the room. "Isn't he beautiful? And he's not a raccoon."

"Yeah. That's probably his best feature." I looked from Dad to Myrtle Jean to Agnes. They both watched Dad with similar pleasure in their eyes.

Myrtle Jean turned to me. "He's a seal point Himalayan and he's two years old and already neutered. I got him from the shelter. Your dad was so disappointed earlier when his cat turned out to be . . ." She nodded, her papery jowls trembling with the movement.

Agnes filled in for her. "A fat raccoon."

Dad turned his face up to mine. "I just love the little fella. Can we keep him?"

Oh God. How do I say no to that?

Ringo leaned against my leg and looked at me.

"Ringo, do you want a cat?"

Ringo grumbled that he did not.

"Ringo will get used to him. Won't you, Ringo?" Dad put the cat on the floor, and it slinked over to the Lab and stretched to rub his face against Ringo's.

Nick chuckled. "I think Ringo just rolled his eyes."

Dad's eyes were pleading. "I promise I'll take care of him."

Uh-huh. What happens when he no longer remembers he has a cat? A crush of sadness hit me, and before I knew what I was doing I agreed. "Okay, but we need to go get some things for him, like food. And a litter box." *Ugh.*

Myrtle Jean bounced off the couch. "I got you all of that. You don't need to get a single thing until he runs out of food. I even got him a little catnip mousie."

Dad held up what looked a lot like a dead mouse and grinned.

I flinched, and Nick's hand began to warm my back.

Myrtle Jean clapped. "This will be so much fun. We can have play dates with Marshmallow."

Dad nodded. "Yeah, doll. Who's Marshmallow?"

Myrtle giggled. "That's my baby, Don. You met her."

Dread inched its way up my spine. "You did say that cat is neutered, didn't you?"

Agnes chuckled. "You'll find out soon enough."

We ordered a pizza for dinner, while Dad went through a whole list of names for his cat—*How did I let that happen?* And so far, he had stuck on Elton. Now if he could only remember it. Myrtle Jean and Agnes left after I fell asleep sitting up at the table with half a piece of pizza in my hand.

Once Dad and the cat were safely tucked away in his room, Nick and I shared a long look before going our separate directions.

Ringo followed me into the bedroom, and I stripped down to my underwear and crashed instantly, dead to the world.

I vaguely became aware that Ringo was barking and I shushed him. He barked again and I threw a pillow at him, muttering something about squirrels and going back to sleep, before drifting off again.

A hand clamped down on my mouth. Adrenaline kicked in and my pulse shot up like a carnival ride. My eyes flew open as I grabbed at the assailant on top of me. I knew I should fear for my life, but all I could think of was why wasn't Ringo barking and was he okay?

My assailant hissed sharply, "Shut up! Be still."

It took me a moment for my eyes to focus, but even then, I had trouble believing what I was seeing. Jacob?

I wanted to throw my arms around his neck and kiss him.

Then I remembered Melissa bleeding out in the parking lot, Eddie's and Oscar's funerals, and the last few months of torture I'd been put through while he was skipping around DC without a care.

I wanted to put my hands around his neck and squeeze until he passed out.

His hair was poking out every which way like he'd just removed a balaclava. And there was that close beard he was sporting in the photo. On second thought, it didn't look good. It looked stupid.

"I'm gonna remove my hand. Are you gonna stay quiet?"

I nodded, my mind running through possible scenarios of how to incapacitate him. I reached for the frog prince on the nightstand and prepared to strike him on the temple.

He slowly moved his hand from my mouth, smoothing my hair back and tucking it behind my ear. "Stop following me, baby. You're gonna blow my cover on an operation that's over a year in the making."

His voice came out soothing, like he was calming a child, but it plucked the wrong string in my nerves and only served to irritate me. "Riiight. That's why you killed our team and faked your death. Where's my dog?"

"He's fine. I put him outside after he bit me. The dumb dog wouldn't take the tranq bone I brought to keep him quiet. When did you get a dog? I thought you said you wanted your life to be low maintenance. That's why we couldn't move in together."

"That's what you want to talk about right now? How our relationship failed. How about we talk about your new fiancée? What is going on, Jacob?! What'd you do to the security detail out front? And the cameras? How did you get in here?"

"Let's just say your guard is gonna have one hell of a headache when he comes to."

Anger rose in my chest like a volcano about to erupt. "What did you do, Jacob? You were *undercover* with us. Now you expect me to believe you were also undercover with one of the Alphabets? In your dreams. Were you working against us the whole time? Oscar, Eddie, and Melissa are dead. And you left me to take the blame. I trusted you, you lying scumbag!"

Even in the low light I could see his eyes flash fire. "That wasn't my fault. There's so much more going on than you could possibly understand."

"Did you ever really love me, Jacob?"

He leaned forward and kissed me lightly. "You're only alive because I love you."

His thumb ran down my jaw seductively, then he climbed off me and stood at the side of the bed. He was completely dressed in black. His voice was cold and hard as steel. "I've been following you for days. Quit asking around about me. Just stay away, Layla. I don't want to hurt you, but this is too big an op to let you interfere and blow it."

Liar.

I hurled the frog prince and caught him on the temple. He yelled and clawed at his face.

Nick's footsteps crossed the ceiling and came running down the spiral staircase.

Jacob ran from the room, knocking into Nick and throwing him backward into the wall. Nick pursued while I jumped out of bed and pulled on sweats.

I ran to the back door and called for Ringo. The Lab was at my feet in a moment. He licked my face. "Thank God you're okay."

Nick returned, out of breath. "He got away through the woods. The back security guard and I tried to cut him off, but he had someone parked around the lake and they were ready for him."

I started to shake. Not out of fear. Out of rage. "That lying piece of trash!" Ringo stuffed his head in the palm of my hand.

"Hey, what's going on out here?" Dad appeared in his bedroom doorway, the cat in his arms. "Something woke Santana and me up."

I tried to calm my voice, but it came out unnaturally singsongy. "Everything's fine, Dad. You can go back to bed. We've got a big day tomorrow."

Dad rubbed the cat between the ears. "Oh yeah. Wait until you learn about Thanksgiving, Santana. You're gonna love it."

Dad disappeared back into his room, and I started to pace. "That traitor. Warning me to stay away or I'm going to get hurt. Undercover for who? By whose order? You know how many tears I wasted on that lying, conniving, scumbag? It makes me sick."

Nick sat on the edge of the couch and let me rant while Ringo followed me back and forth.

"How dare he not be dead with the rest of the team. He said he loved me. Liar. I might just kill him. Oh crap. Ronnie's guy is hurt. We need to call—" The doorbell rang.

I grabbed a fireplace poker and headed for the door with a Ringo shield.

Ronnie's guard stood on the front step and started apologizing. Blood trickled down the side of his head.

I put my hand up. "You need an ambulance."

"No, I'm fine."

"You're not fine. You're bleeding. And you probably have a concussion. Come sit down."

"Ronnie's on his way. I'll head to the urgent care when he arrives."

The back guard appeared at the door. "I got a plate number but it's probably been stolen. I'll stand guard out front until Ronnie arrives. Don't answer the back door."

Nick pulled out his cell phone. "I'm calling an ambulance. I'll cover for you until your backup gets here."

He came in and sat on the kitchen chair while Ringo and I got him an ice pack. Then I went to get my cell phone with Ringo stepping on my feet all the way to my room. "It's okay, buddy. I'm fine. Jacob tricked you." I stopped and dropped to my knees and held Ringo's face in my hands. "I'm sorry I was so tired and didn't realize you were trying to warn me. It wasn't your fault."

Ringo licked me on the chin.

I hugged him close until we both felt better.

I got my cell phone off the nightstand to text Castinetto and paused. What if he's dirty? What if Jacob's telling the truth? Of course he attacked my security guard, so there'll be a report. I have to say something or I'll look suspicious. Dad's health is too important to put him through an investigation right now. And Castinetto has seen the photo. It's not likely to be a surprise that Jacob is alive.

Just keeping you in the loop for the official record. I just had a visit from Jacob where he attacked and threatened me. I'll fill you in after the holidays.

Castinetto was at my door twenty minutes later.

Chapter 41

"YOU DIDN'T HAVE TO COME OVER HERE IN THE MIDDLE OF THE night."

Castinetto was dressed ridiculously for a cold November night, like I'd caught him playing basketball at the rec center. "You said you were attacked."

"I was. Aren't you cold?"

"Yes! Can I come in?"

I moved out of the way to allow him entry. He passed me, but Nick stood in the foyer with his arms crossed over his chest like a mildly annoyed grizzly and Castinetto could go no farther.

Dayton stood in front of Nick and tried to sound cool, but I could hear something strained in his voice. "Could you move out of the way?"

Nick didn't flinch and his voice stayed icy calm. "After you."

What the heck are they doing? "Alright, Castinetto, you want a statement, don't you? Let's go to the kitchen so we don't wake up my father again."

Castinetto stayed where he was.

Nick had a cocky set to his jaw that I hadn't seen since the bar that first night we met.

"Well, I'm going to the kitchen and making tea. In thirty minutes, I'm going back to bed whether you have your statement or not." I pushed past them both, not sure what weird game they were playing. I was used to seeing the cop stink eye turned on a perp, but Castinetto better not suspect Nick had anything to do with Stratton Park. I wouldn't stand for that.

They both joined me in the kitchen where Ringo was glued to my side before the kettle whistled. I took down three mugs and a can of tea. "Are you okay with this chamomile? I've only had like four hours of sleep in two days, and I have to go back to bed after this."

Dayton pulled out the chair with his back to the wall. "Chamomile's great."

Nick took the chair opposite Castinetto closest to me. "Whatever you make will be fine."

I plucked three tea bags from the can and dropped them into the mugs. I wasn't sure how much to tell Castinetto. The warning to trust no one still rang very loud and clear in my mind. The gunshots at my Jeep screamed AMEN to that! But someone had sent me files that could go a long way to clearing my name; if only I knew who it was. My only friend on the force was Adam Beasley and he was pretty useless when it came to investigating, so it was hard to see him digging up redacted files. But he did have friends in high places, so maybe.

I glanced at Castinetto. His scowl at Nick was pretty ragged. I decided that I would stick to the facts without giving him anything he could twist into evidence against either of us. "So, here's what happened. I woke up with Jacob on top of me in bed."

Both men answered at once. "He was what!"

I poured water over the tea bag in the first cup and looked at them both. "That's not really the shocking part of the story, is it?"

Castinetto smirked at Nick. "Where were you?"

I put the steaming mug on the table in front of him. "What difference does that make? I'm the one who was attacked. And Jacob's alive, man. Pay attention!"

Nick's eyebrows raised in challenge to Castinetto.

"Nick has nothing to do with this, so don't try to fit him into the frame somehow."

Dayton shifted his gaze to me. "Is that what you think I'm doing?"

"I honestly have no idea what you're doing. But I know you don't trust me, and I know you think I caused what happened at Stratton Park. So, let's just get through the statement, okay?"

Something passed through his expression that I had trouble pinning down. Was he irritated that I called him out for accusing Nick? I mean—read the room.

"Fine." Castinetto clasped his hands on the table. "What happened?"

I filled him in on what Nick and I had found out over the past couple of days, and how Jacob had threatened me to stop following him.

Castinetto took out his phone. "I'll put out an APB on Jacob, and we'll get you a restraining order."

"Mmm. What if we wait? What if he's working undercover for someone and I'm going to blow his operation?"

Dayton looked me in the eye. "Did he say that?"

I shrugged and tried to look casual.

Castinetto made a face like he didn't believe me. "Why are you covering for him?"

"What makes you think I am?"

"'Cause I know you."

I stared right into Castinetto's eyes. That weird feeling was back in my stomach. Sometimes, when he looked at me . . . Naw. "Don't you think any good cop would protect their own? I don't want to be responsible for outing a potential undercover officer. Do you?"

Dayton's lip curled. "In my almost twenty years on the force, we would never have killed our own and framed an officer for an undercover mission. I think he's lying."

Nick sipped his tea. "Working for an agency would explain how he faked his death. He'd need someone with either skills or authority to change dental records."

Dayton nodded. "That's true. But if an agency were going to recruit someone on your team to go undercover, why Jacob? You were the brains of the operation. That's why the captain put you in charge of the team."

Whoa. Why's he playing good cop all of a sudden? "I'll tell

you this. He got past my security team and my cameras tonight, and he wasn't that good of an agent when we put him undercover in Ricky Hurtado's cell."

"Whatever agency he's working for, they haven't liaised with us. And if they were going to help Jacob fake his death, why kill the rest of the team? Hurtado's guys got away clean as far as we know."

Nick lifted his mug to Dayton. "How do you know all this? I thought you were a beat cop who recently got promoted to homicide."

Castinetto's poker face broke only by the muscle in his jaw clenching. "The details of Stratton Park are common knowledge around the precinct."

Nick looked my way.

"That's true. And gossip runs around that department like an old-lady quilting bee."

Nick looked back at Castinetto. "Need anything else? Because we need to get back to bed."

Dayton searched my face for an answer I wasn't going to give him. I'd let him swing on that rope for a while. "I'd like to set up a detail to cover you until we can confirm Jacob's story. You've received a lot of threats this week and there's a good chance he's behind them."

I felt like a total fool, but that had not occurred to me at all. Maybe I'd been compartmentalizing my life too much. I was really losing my edge. And that last threat including Melissa was very department specific. "I don't need a detail. I've already got security out front. I've got Ringo—"

Ringo grunted and I interpreted it as *You got that right.*

"And Nick is a Marine. We're fine."

The warm glow of gloating was rolling off of Nick, but he still agreed with Castinetto. "I'd rather know that you're safe when I can't be with you."

"Today is Thanksgiving. We'll be at the community potluck. I don't want anyone to miss their holiday because of me. Let's just touch base on this in a couple of days. Give me time to consider what to do."

Castinetto narrowed his eyes and gave me a police scowl. That was ten times more impressive than a civilian scowl. It would have been really intimidating if he wasn't wearing a tank top. "Fine. But try to stay out of trouble until I can get someone to shadow you."

Nick leaned in and draped his arm around my chair. "Don't worry. I've got her back."

Dayton pushed away from the table. "I bet you do."

We walked Castinetto to the door and locked it after he was back in his car. I turned on Nick. "What was that all about?"

He gave me a shrug and a grin. "That guy has a real chip on his shoulder."

Chapter 42

I SUSPECT THAT I FELL ASLEEP IMMEDIATELY, BUT IT WAS ONE OF those nights when your mind is racing and you feel like you're awake, but time moves too fast for that to be true. Sometime before dawn I fell deep into the darkness.

Angel appeared before me, a gunshot wound in the middle of his head, his eyes hollow and empty. *This is your fault. One talk with you and I'm dead. I should never have trusted you. Trust no one.*

His face morphed into Jacob's. *You're a fool, Layla. How could you believe I loved you? And you call yourself a cop. You have no instinct at all. I've been following you for days.*

I pulled my service weapon and shot three rounds into Jacob, but all he did was laugh. *You don't even have your gun anymore.*

I was in the back of a dark SUV with my hands zip-tied. My head was pounding and everything was fuzzy. *Why are you doing this?* I tilted my eyes to the rearview mirror and caught the reflection of a Potomac County Narcotics Unit hat before everything went black.

I woke with a splitting headache and Ringo flanking me like a peel-off tattoo. I reached a hand for his velvet ears and gave them a rub. A rhythmic *thump thump thump* reverberated off the bed. I picked up my cell phone and checked the time. "Why is it seven in the morning, Ringo? Can't I just have one good sleep without nightmares?"

I pushed myself back and sat against the pillows. The frog prince lying across the room by the door brought back the memory of Jacob threatening me to back off as if I didn't matter to him at all. Tears spilled down my cheeks as fury and grief battled for preeminence in my emotions.

Ringo climbed in my lap nose to nose so he could give me kisses. "Okay, buddy. That's enough." He laid his head on my shoulder.

I remembered Oscar and Eddie and Melissa, and fury rose to the top. If everything Jacob said last night was true, then why did they have to die? And why not me? What was all that talk about us moving in together and starting a life if he was about to destroy me?

The dream I'd just had of being tied up in the back of the SUV started to come back, and along with it, the painful revelation that that was not a nightmare, but a memory. My pulse quickened as it flashed through my mind again. Something about the way the driver looked. I only saw the back of him, but he was familiar. Was it Jacob? That didn't feel right. Castinetto? I could clearly remember feeling confused. *Why was this happening?*

Ringo nudged my hand because I'd stopped petting him, then his ears tensed like he'd heard a noise. He jumped off the bed and went to the door, his tail wagging. When he looked back at me with a soft whimper I threw the covers off. "Alright. Let me get dressed."

Dad was in front of the TV with Nick. Nick was holding the remote, flicking through channels, trying to help Dad find something to watch since his hands were full of a ball of fluff that appeared to be taking a bath. Nick stopped on the news. "How about this?"

"Seen it."

He clicked again. "Here's an action movie."

"It's already started. I can't watch a movie that's already started."

I let Ringo out to do his business and came back to stand behind the couch while Nick ran through several good options that Dad was not impressed with. Until he landed on the channel with a giant inflatable Woodstock.

"Whoa! Stop. What's that?"

"That's a giant balloon, Dad."

"I know that, but why?"

Nick looked sideways at Dad. "It's the parade."

Dad stroked his cat's ears, and the cat stretched out and batted the remote in Nick's hand. "What parade?"

I let Ringo back in and he ran to the couch and hopped up next to Dad. "What do you mean, 'What parade,' Dad? It's the Macy's Thanksgiving Day Parade."

"I've never heard of it."

"You've performed in it."

"I have not. When?"

I reached back into the recesses of my mind. "Sometime in the late nineties when you released 'A Very Metal Christmas.'"

"Freakin' Christmas album. That was Simon's idea."

"Well, it sold like a quarter of a million copies."

"Oh. Maybe it was my idea. Whoa! Look at that. It's a fat bear eating noodles."

Ringo leaned into Dad and slowly fell into Dad's lap, pushing the cat into the corner of the couch.

"I think that's a panda, Dad."

"Why would a panda be eating noodles?"

"No idea."

Nick snorted. "That's Po." He laughed again, harder. "Why are you two looking at me like that? Do you two really not know *Kung Fu Panda*?"

I settled into the couch and grabbed the throw blanket. "Why would we know that?"

"It's a pretty famous movie for kids."

Dad chuckled and repositioned the cat in his lap on top of Ringo's head. "Then I think the question is Why do *you* know that, dude?"

Nick's voice rose higher. "I have nephews. It was everywhere when it came out. Jack Black?"

Dad flinched. "He's not here, is he?"

"Why would Jack Black be here, Dad?"

"To steal my cookies."

Nick and I laughed, but Dad kept muttering.

"It wouldn't be the first time. Freakin' Jack Black."

Nick settled back against the couch and took a corner of my blanket. "Well, I know what movie to recommend we watch later."

Dad pointed to the screen. "I think I dated her."

Nick put his hand on my knee. "Which one?"

"The redhead."

"Dad. You did not date Scarlett Johansson."

"I'm pretty sure I did. She was in some movie at the time. I had to break it off when rumors started floating around that she was a black widow. I mean, I like to have a good time as well as the next guy, but I don't wanna die for one."

The cat got up, turned in a circle, and lay back down.

Dad stroked the cat's ears. "Settle down, Hendrix."

It was hard to tell what was real with Dad and what he imagined while under the influence. But right now, warm smells of roasting turkey and something spicy with apples and cinnamon was lulling me into a sense of relaxed joy. This was good. I could do this every day. Life sucked right now, but with Dad, and Ringo, and Nick—I had a lot to be thankful for.

My phone buzzed on the table and a message popped up.

I lifted the phone and tapped the box. "Nick. What is this?"

Nick's voice had that dreamy quality of being totally relaxed and a little bit exhausted. "What's it look like?"

"I dunno. Spam? It says, 'Tick Tick Boom.' "

Dad pointed at the TV again. "What's with the giant yellow farmers?"

Nick sat bolt upright and grabbed the phone from my hands. "That's your park email."

The hair on my neck gave me a tingle, but I was too tired to let it go on full alert. I sighed. "So, it's another threat?"

Nick jumped up. "Yeah. But they just made a huge mistake." He jumped over the couch and ran up the spiral stairs.

I looked at Dad. "I don't know what that thing is, but I saw it on a birthday cake once."

The cat stretched again, walked across Ringo's back, and put one foot on my lap. His whiskers twitched and he scanned my reaction. A knock sounded at the front door, and I moved the blanket off my legs. "Sorry, Hendrix. That'll be the first pest of the day."

Ringo and I headed for the door and Dad called after me, "Who's Hendrix?"

Adam Beasley stood on my front step with the security guard.

"He's fine. I'll take it from here."

The security guard gave me a nod and returned to his surveillance. "Beasley. Whatchu doin?"

He held up a manila file stamped EVIDENCE. "I found this on Castinetto's desk."

Dread pummeled me. "Oh, Beasley. If your uncle wasn't the commissioner, you'd never have made it this far. You can't take evidence out of the precinct. Do you want Internal Affairs all up in your business?"

"But it's about you. Castinetto has proof that you tried to save Melissa Bayles the day of Stratton Park. Emergency techs found you unconscious in the gravel next to her. You were holding her hand. Why did they make it out like you were responsible for the explosion?"

I put out my hand and took the file. It contained photos from the crime scene. The last one was outside of the warehouse. I must have crawled through the broken glass across the parking lot to get to Melissa, but with her femoral artery severed she bled out before I reached her. I blacked out and woke in the hospital. I had never seen this photo before. It explained the cuts on my arms and legs. I still had a little scar on the palm of my left hand.

The smothering tentacles of grief and despair clutched at my heart and threatened to squeeze the life from me. I held the folder out to Adam. "Put this back immediately before you're caught with it."

"But I thought it could help. Maybe jar your memories a bit."

"All that shows is Melissa died, and I wasn't able to save her."

Adam hung his head.

"Go home, Beasley. Enjoy Thanksgiving with your family."

I shut the door before he was off the front porch. Ringo and I returned to the couch. He put his head in my lap.

Nick returned triumphantly. "We got 'em."

"You know who's been sending the threats to expose Dad?"

"You bet I do. I traced the email—don't ask me how—and know that it isn't admissible in a court of law, but it was sent by someone who lives at 24 Fontainebleau."

"Are you sure?"

"Absolutely."

"That's Robin's trailer."

Chapter 43

THE REST OF THE MORNING WAS SPENT COMING UP WITH A PLAN for how to neutralize Robin while helping Nick in the kitchen. Let's be honest, I was very little help with the latter. But I was a whiz with the plan to crush that little scheming witch who'd pretended to be Dad's friend the whole time she was blackmailing him.

The can opener was about the only sharp object Nick would let me touch after I nearly cut off a fingertip chopping the celery for him, so I opened another can of cranberry sauce and let it slide onto a plate.

Dad entered the kitchen dressed like a scarecrow, wearing blue jean overalls and a straw hat. "Look, baby girl, I'm one of those yellow blobs."

"Where'd you get that outfit?"

"What's-her-name brought it over."

"The silly one with the sweaters?"

"Smoker's voice."

"Agnes."

"That's her. I'm gonna go help her put up some decorations. I'll meet you over there."

"Ahhh. You know it's like two doors down, right?"

"Of course I do."

I shifted my eyes to Nick. "Of course he does."

"I'll be fine." Dad shoved his hands in his pockets.

Nick crossed the room and patted Dad on the back. "He'll be fine. Let him go."

"Okay." I wasn't sure that Nick hadn't lost his mind too. "Just be careful, okay, Dad? Wandering can be dangerous for you."

Dad grabbed his purple Stratocaster and opened the front door while butchering a couple lines from an Eric Clapton song. "Danger! I'm out in it tonight. Danger! I'm such a pretty sight."

The door closed behind him and Nick pulled out his phone. I ran to the window to make sure Dad was headed in the right direction. The security guard jumped out of his van and looked to me with his hands out. I patted the air and we both watched Dad cross the yard. He disappeared through the bushes. "Agnes probably has him now. Don't you think? Nick?"

Nick held up his phone. "So far so good. He stopped at her house. Now he's on the move again. In the right direction toward the community room."

"How do you know that?"

"I slipped a tracker in his back pocket before he left." Nick held up his cell phone and I watched a blinking blue light moving toward the community room.

I pulled out my own cell phone and placed a call to Ronnie Voa. "I'm sorry to bother you on a holiday, but we have some information about the blackmailer that can't wait."

Thirty minutes later, Ronnie was at my kitchen table, two laptops set up with a bunch of electrical devices attached to them. He tested the connection with a few clicks of his keyboard and nodded that he was pleased with the setup. "I've searched into Robin's past and found out she was in a car accident ten years ago that left her paralyzed from the waist down. Hit by a drunk driver."

I sucked in my breath. "Oof. That's terrible."

"That's where the sympathy ends. She and her brother have been scamming people ever since. Home repair and Internet dating scams. Usually it's the elderly who are quick to give up personal details and bank account information when the caller states they're with tech support or a government agency like Social Security. There have been several complaints filed about them, but it is suspected that the list of victims runs much longer."

"Why haven't they been prosecuted?"

"The Feds have never been able to collect enough evidence before she scorches the trail and they change locations. I've called a friend of mine who's with the FBI, Sloane Harlow. She's going to fast-track a warrant and meet me at the unit with a team and we'll go through their trailer while Robin and her brother are at the potluck. If we can gather enough evidence, an arrest will be made. If not, the FBI might set up a team to watch the two of them, so keep this under wraps for now."

We discussed a few more options for ways to expose Robin and her brother, then shook hands with Ronnie and walked him out just as Scarlett's Porsche pulled into the driveway. Ringo started wagging his tail once he saw who was there. The ladies got out in a cloud of perfume, having three conversations at once. They each gave me a hug and started in on how things were going with their own plans.

First up was Bree, who handed me a ceramic pumpkin vase full of colorful mums. "This is from my mom. She and my dad will be along in time for dinner. She wants to know if you need them to pick up anything on the way."

I looked at Nick who checked the status of his meat thermometer. He shook his head.

I didn't want to ask for ice, salt and pepper, or butter from Bree's parents. The whole point of inviting them was to give them a no-hassle holiday. "No, we're good."

Bree pulled out her phone and her thumbs flew across the screen. "I'll let her know."

"Who wants warm cider?" I offered.

All three ladies replied in the affirmative. Charisse took off a cashmere coat and laid it across the back of the ornately carved kitchen chair. "So, the kids came. And went. I put out a baked brie and some bacon-wrapped dates, and they didn't have more than a smidge. They didn't say it, but I know they were saving their appetites for Dollie's lame turkey."

Scarlett handed Charisse a warm mug. "Is that what we're calling Michael now?"

Charisse hooked a smile. "He's been called worse. Especially after I found out he had a burner cell so he could get calls from Dollie behind my back. I brought the baked brie with me. How'd Graham and his parents like your traditional Thanksgiving, Scarlett?"

Bree sipped her cider. "Ooh yeah. How'd you do?"

Scarlett clucked her tongue. "Well, seeing how Graham's British mother is the authority on all things American, I did everything wrong. The stuffing isn't supposed to go into the bird anymore. You're supposed to soak the turkey in saltwater overnight. And the sweet potatoes are supposed to be covered in marshmallows that she will then complain about and pick off."

I pulled out the chair and sat next to her. "Yikes."

"But that hardly compares with Graham's father's toast at dinner to 'the Americans' survival that was only made possible through the generosity of the indigenous people whom they subsequently exterminated.' "

Nick laughed out loud.

Bree's mouth dropped open. "Jeez. I mean he's not wrong, but how about a 'Thank you for making this wonderful family meal and including us in your tradition'?"

"He can think about that while he's on the toilet because apparently they all have some light food poisoning."

"Oh no." A giggle escaped my lips before I could stop it. "How did you manage to not get sick?"

Scarlett made a face. "I didn't eat anything. I saved myself for this meal."

Charisse asked, "Is Graham . . . mad?"

Scarlett's expression softened. "No. He's wonderful. He must be the most supportive man in the world. He told me through the bathroom door to have a good time with the Americans.

And Ambrose was sent to his room to play on his Switch, so I'm Mother of the Year right now. How'd it go at the school, Layla?"

"I finally found someone who didn't think Archie Wilkins was ready for sainthood. One of the kids' fathers made a comment as they were leaving. I have to follow up with him, but I brought home a dozen journals to read, so that's my homework."

Bree moved her cider to the side. "Let us help you. We can get through them a lot faster if we each take a stack."

Charisse grabbed her purse and took out a pen and notebook. "That's a great idea."

"I'm in." Scarlett pulled out a chair.

I collected the books from my bag in the foyer. "Alright. If you all don't mind scrubbing through the writings of a bunch of entitled kids looking for dirt."

Scarlett snickered and adjusted her glasses. "I do that every day."

Nick joined us, and we each took a journal and started to read.

After a few minutes, Scarlett took out a pen and paper and started to take notes. "Charlotte says her grandmother wants her mother to quit her job, but she can't because it pays for her school."

Charisse trilled, "Whoo, girl! These kids were spilling all kinds of family secrets."

Bree flipped a page. "And Archie was asking them questions for more information."

Nick tapped his journal. "He actually asked this kid if he could bring in his parents' wedding certificate for show-and-tell."

Scarlett thumbed through her pages, scanning. "Charlotte's mother had to go away and now she lives with her grandmother."

I found a juicy bit in my journal. "Ben overheard his dad on the phone saying that he got fired from his job because his assistant made a complaint. He can't say anything to Mom because Dad will lose *custardy.*"

Bree shook her head. "Ava's uncle is in the country illegally, and her mother tells her that she's not allowed to tell anybody they are from Colombia."

Scarlett put her pen down after a lengthy note. "Charlotte's excited that she'll get to visit her mother for Christmas when she's allowed family visits. Her grandmother is trying to get her mom released."

"Charlotte's grandmother is Gladys Beacon, the secretary at Our Lady of Mercy. She picked her up from school yesterday."

Bree twisted her hair. "Funny she didn't mention that when we were at the church."

Nick flipped a page. "Apparently, Elijah's mom hits Elijah's father, and he cries a lot. He can't go to the hospital because the news will come. The news? Does that make sense to you?"

I sighed. "Yep."

Scarlett read another page. "Charlotte also says her grandmother steals raspberries from Trader Joe's. Grandma says it's okay because God knows they charge too much for them and their money is better spent helping people like Mrs. Washburn who's about to lose her house on account of she can't work anymore because she doesn't understand the computer."

I breathed out a chuckle. "That's a lot of information. Where is Clara Stableman's journal? She would be in the stack from last year."

Charisse found it in the pile and handed it to me. I scanned until I found what I was looking for. "My mom is very sick. She can't get out of bed to make breakfast. She told me not to grow up and be a druggie like her."

Scarlett flipped a page in her journal. "Well, that's where the call to Social Services probably came from. I'd love to see what Ambrose would write about me and what he calls my dictatorship."

Bree read from a new journal. "Emma says her mom and dad are fighting a lot. Then she asks Mr. Wilkins what *infidelity* means."

Charisse grunted. "Noah says his grandpa is threatening to take away his father's trust fund if he doesn't get clean. Noah doesn't understand what is so dirty about his father. He looks clean to him."

We made notes on most of the journals and had to stop reading when the meat thermomcter alert went off for the turkey. Bree's parents arrived and her mother, Susan, hugged me like I was her long-lost daughter. It was nice. The hugs were growing on me. I almost hugged her back.

Our excitement was building as we all buzzed around the kitchen gathering the casseroles and making the journey across Agnes's and Myrtle Jean's yards to the community room. I fully expected to find Dad in there alone with three trailer park terrors, but the door flew open to cheers and applause. To say I was stunned would be a huge downplay. The room was packed wall to wall. And the table was covered with casseroles and a long row of aluminum chafing dishes covered in foil.

Dad gave a laugh. "Hey, hey! The gang's all here. Let's eat!"

Nick placed the turkey, and Agnes handed him a knife. He set about carving while I introduced the girls to what had to be most of the trailer park residents. I didn't know all of them and Agnes filled in the blanks.

Bree was so excited to help serve the meal, she was giddy. Her mom gave me my third hug since she'd arrived. "Thank you for this. It's good to see Bree out of her head and away from her own problems for a while."

I squeezed her arm. "She's been there for me a lot too."

Agnes made a point of introducing me to several of the residents who would have been all alone today. They either had no family left, or none in the area. One older Black woman from Buckingham took my hand and told me, "This is the only Thanksgiving I was ever going to have today. If it weren't for the potluck I'd be sitting home alone eating a frozen pot pie." My heart gripped within me when I thought about how I'd almost denied them this.

When we walked away, I whispered to Agnes, "Where did all the catered food come from? There's a whole pan of turkey on the table."

She shrugged. "I thought it was you. It showed up right after Don got here to help me put the tablecloths down."

I caught a glimpse of Dad across the room. He was glowing.

With Benny on his left and Marguerite and Old Lady Henson fighting over who was on his right, he was having the time of his life.

Whimsy St. James entered the trailer and hugged the wall around the back to get into line. She filled her plate of food and left as quickly as she'd come without saying a word to anyone.

Myrtle Jean sidled up next to me in line and put a spoonful of mashed potatoes on her plate. "Don't mind her. She's been a mess since her momma died of Covid while she was in rehab. She just needs time."

Robin wheeled over to the table and beamed a smile. She had a good-looking blond man with her. His eyes darted mistrustfully around the room as he grabbed a plate. "Glenn, this is Layla Virtue. She owns the whole park. She's *Don's* daughter."

Glenn's eyes popped a little as he gave me a once-over. He put his fork down and his hand out. "It's nice to meet you, Layla. Wonderful dinner you've put on today. You're so generous. I'd love to take you to coffee sometime to say thank you."

Bile rose up in my throat, but I put on my cop face to protect the investigation. If these two were con artists, they'd be quick to notice a change in tone or body language. And who knew if they could burn the evidence remotely? I flashed a smile. "It's nice to meet you too, Glenn. I hope you're settling into the community well."

"Absolutely. Everyone has been very open." He jumped like someone had pinched him.

I was saved from small talk when Donna grabbed a plate and gave me a nudge. "I need to talk to you."

"Right now?"

She slid her eyes to the side. "Ah, no. Let me get some candied sweet potatoes first. I can't talk without a pile of melty marshmallows."

She filled her plate and snapped at Kelvin, "Don't you fill up on bread."

Kelvin cut his eyes to mine and stuffed a roll in his shorts pocket. "Yes, ma'am."

Donna and I took our plates and headed for two empty chairs in the back. I checked my immediate vicinity for eavesdroppers and lowered my voice. "Donna, I'm sorry I accused you of blackmailing my father. I know that you aren't behind the threats we've received."

Donna chewed thoughtfully, considering my words. "No, it's my fault. I overreacted when you wouldn't ask your dad to do the fundraiser for Kelvin's school. I get a little hyped when it's for my grandson. I didn't know about his dementia. I'm the one who's sorry."

"Thank you. I just want my dad to be safe for his final—"

My words were cut off when the trailer door swung open, and Dayton Castinetto walked in carrying a covered dish. He looked around the room until he spotted me.

Donna whistled under her breath. "Sweet baby Jesus, Superman just arrived."

"I'm sorry, Donna. Can you excuse me for a minute." I crossed the room until I stood in front of the detective. "What are you doing here, Castinetto?"

He lifted the dish. "I'm here for dinner. I was invited."

"By who?"

"You don't have to sound so disappointed."

"I'm sorry. I'm not. I just mean . . . why didn't you say anything this morning?"

"Relax. Your dad invited me a couple days ago."

Dad ambled over and put his hand on my back. "Hey, baby girl. Who's this?"

Castinetto paled. "It's Dayton, sir. Castinetto. You invited me. I work with your daughter."

Dad spread his legs and crossed his arms in front of his chest. "Righteous! What instrument do you play?"

Castinetto shifted his eyes to mine. "Uh . . ."

I was full of holiday joy and gravy, so I decided to take it easy on the officer even though he was one accusation away from being my full-on nemesis. "He's a cop, Dad. He was at the trailer when it was vandalized."

Dad nodded, but his eyes were as blank as his memory. "Of course. Well, come in, dude. We have plenty."

Dayton handed me the casserole dish. "The superintense woman in spandex said I had to bring something. This is my mother's corn pudding."

Agnes appeared out of nowhere and grabbed the dish. "I'll take that."

Nick made eyes at me across the room. I could tell he wanted to come over here and be all up in Castinetto's business, but Robin and her brother had him captive and he was making nice to stall them from leaving early.

Old Lady Henson sashayed across the room with that new husband look in her eyes. I gave her a hard look. "Nope."

She gave me some stink eye and shook her fist at me before making a pivot for the dessert table.

Myrtle Jean called Dad and waved him over. "Don, come play something for us."

When he walked away I made an apology to Dayton. Apparently 'tis the season to apologize. "My dad is having memory issues. Don't take it personally."

Dayton watched Dad pick up his guitar. "It's fine. Wow. I haven't heard him play live since Madison Square Garden in 2008."

I froze with all my senses screaming danger. "So you do know who he is?"

Dayton's lips flattened. "I've known you since high school, Virtue. Of course I know who your father is."

"Why didn't you say anything when I was on the force?"

Our eyes met. "You're your own person. Besides, it's no one's business but yours, and you never mentioned it."

I didn't know what to say to that, and it created an awkward vibe between us. Castinetto cleared his throat and pulled out his cell phone. "I've got that footage from the convenience store across from the church that you requested. Want to see it?"

"Yeah. Absolutely."

He pulled up a video and fast-forwarded through about twenty minutes of people coming and going before the church went quiet. Suddenly, a lone figure appeared in the dark—time-stamped 8:03. The video was too far away and grainy to know who it was, but they were very thin. And they either arrived on foot or parked really far away. They paused at the front door. It opened for them, and they went in. A while later they came back out and rushed off on foot—time-stamped 8:19. The video ended at eleven P.M. when the convenience store clerk changed tapes. No one else went in or out in that time.

"Well, that was fascinating and all, but where is Archie Wilkins in all that?"

"He must have arrived earlier in the evening for confession."

I shook my head. "I don't think so. That doesn't back up anyone's testimony."

"Then what do *you* think?"

I rolled through our visit to the church in my mind. "He must have entered from the side door by the graveyard. The security camera's angle doesn't pick that up."

"That would mean that he'd been there before."

"It would also mean someone let him in. It isn't exactly a main entrance the average person would use unless they were regulars, but the priest and the parish secretary both said they didn't know Archie."

"You think they're lying?"

"I always think everyone's lying, Castinetto." Except little kids. I told Castinetto about the journals and some of the more murder-worthy motives that were detailed within them. "Archie was living well above his means. He was making his money somewhere that didn't come with a W-2 for taxes. What if he was blackmailing the parents who had secrets they were willing to kill to keep hidden?"

Dayton reached for his cell phone. "Give me a list and I'll subpoena their bank and cell phone records."

"That will take too long."

"What are you going to do?"

I glanced at Nick. "I don't know yet. But I know where to get help."

Dad started to play around and freestyle a bit. Then Kelvin tapped him on the knee. "Can you play the Minions song?"

Dad's eyes rolled back in his head. "Little dude, I have no idea what that is."

Donna walked up to Dad with her cell phone out. "He means this."

Dad watched it for a second, the light flickered in his eyes, and he grinned. "Oh yeah." He stood to his feet and launched into a perfect rendition of one of the greatest guitar solos of all time, Eddie Van Halen's "Eruption."

Kelvin's mouth dropped open and he stood mesmerized. Donna caught my eye and threw me a wink.

When Dad wrapped up the solo he fell back in his chair out of breath to the room's applause. Agnes handed him a soda, which he downed. He held up a hand and tried to catch his breath. "Thank you. I'm so excited to be here in . . ." He looked at me.

"Virginia."

"Virginia. You've been a great audience for such a small stage. I always wanted a big family, and I thought rock and roll was it. But most of those people moved on without me when I got sick. So now I have a new family. And my best family." He put his hand out to me. "My wonderful baby girl. Come sing our new song with me."

All eyes were on me, and I could have just crawled out of my skin. But I took Dad's hand and let him lead me to the empty chair next to him. I took the acoustic guitar and played backup to Dad's lead on the song we'd been writing together. I knew it was beautiful, but I didn't realize how moving it was until I saw the tears flowing.

How many more times would I get to play music with Dad? When I was a teenager, I thought he was so cringy and embarrassing. Guys would sing the more salacious lyrics to his songs and tell me, "That's from your dad," just to creep me out. And his stage outfits left very little to the imagination as was mentioned to me in graphic detail many many times by the few girls I called friends. Now I just wish I'd spent more time with him. I had no idea that one day it would be too late.

I caught Robin recording us with her cell phone. I gave a look to Nick, and he followed my eyes. When our song was over, Robin and Glenn gave us a rousing round of applause with everyone else then said they needed to get home.

Nick said he'd get the door for Robin, but he tripped on her wheelchair and fell over her legs. He apologized profusely and she told him it was okay through gritted teeth. After Agnes closed the door behind them, Nick flashed me Robin's cell.

I texted Ronnie Voa that we had Robin's phone to add to the evidence. After we deleted a certain bootleg video, that is.

Chapter 44

I BALLED UP THE LAST PAPER TABLECLOTH AND STUFFED IT IN THE trash bag Nick was holding open. "If Archie was blackmailing the parents of his students, that would explain his high living." Everyone had gone except for Nick and the girls and Bree's parents who were currently in the community room kitchen washing dishes even though we told them they didn't have to.

Bree handed me the box of unused plastic cutlery. "I tried to make them go home, but they're so excited to be here. My mom said this was her favorite Thanksgiving ever."

I snickered. "I saw her swapping recipes with Clifford earlier. I hope you like pickled beets."

"Eww." Bree grabbed the foil and headed for the kitchen to put it away.

Nick dumped the rhubarb pie and tied the trash bag shut. "If you can get me Archie's social security number I can access his bank accounts, but this would have to be just between us."

Charisse placed a covered dish on the bare table in front of me. "I can get you the social security number. We don't have to have you home soon, do we, Scarlett?"

The sophisticated Asian was sitting cross-legged on the counter eating directly out of a nine-by-thirteen sweet potato casserole. "Nope. I got all the time in the world. I just love marshmallows. Graham's mother doesn't know what she's talking about."

We finished cleaning, turned out the lights, and made our way through the crunchy leaves on the lawn to my house with a procession of leftovers. I stopped at the security van and handed over plates of food to the very excited surveillance team. With another hug from Bree's mother, we sent them on their way and went inside to do what might be considered illegal research—if you're caught.

Dad was on the couch in front of a football game—with Ringo, who was curled into a tight ball at his side, and the cat, who was curled into a tight ball in his lap. All three of them were sound asleep.

Nick grabbed a pumpkin pie and headed up the spiral stairs with the rest of us right behind him with forks, plates, and whipped cream.

His room was a little messier than it had been when he first got here, and I took that as a good sign that he was getting comfortable. He slid my new laptop to Charisse so she could do her thing, and he fired up his computer and several monitors.

Bree, Scarlett, and I sat on the edge of his bed, totally clueless as to what they were doing, but at least we had the pie.

Charisse was silent for a few minutes, the only sound her clacking the keys on the keyboard. She read off some numbers for Nick. "If anyone finds out I gave you Archie's personal information from our investment firm I could go to jail."

Nick responded, "Don't worry. I'm hopping around cloaked servers to mask our IP address."

I squirted enough whipped cream for three pies onto my little slice. "They won't find out, and Castinetto can get a search warrant to collect the information if we find anything useful."

Nick's monitors were displaying a bunch of gibberish that seemed to make him really happy. "I got something. Hey, save me some of that pie."

"First tell me what you found, and then we'll see if you deserve pie."

"Archie Wilkins is tied to four bank accounts. The one his

wife showed us. The one he uses with Charisse's investment group. One in the Cayman Islands. And one for a charity called Compassion Foundation Worldwide. The one in the Caymans has a few hundred thousand in it."

I took him a piece of pie slathered in whipped cream. "Alright. You earned this. Can you show me the charity one?"

Nick tapped the keys for a minute. "What do you want to know?"

"What kind of money are we talking about?"

Nick scrolled through the page. "Some medium-sized donations, some small. Nothing big enough to seem suspicious on the surface. A lot of the small ones came from deposited checks."

"How about after Archie died?"

"Not a single deposit."

"Where is the money coming from?"

The girls crowded around me.

Nick clicked on a recent check deposit for a thousand dollars. "This one's from Carol Hodge."

I squirted some whipped cream into my mouth and felt the excitement flowing in my veins. We were close. I could feel it.

Charisse was typing furiously on her laptop, while Bree ran downstairs and grabbed the notebooks. Scarlett took a stack of Post-it notes off Nick's desk. We laid the books out across his bed and put sticky notes with each child's name on them, then added the corresponding donations from their parents.

Nick clicked on some more of the recent checks. "Here's two thousand from Anna Green. Another from Janice Pearson. This one is an electric funds transfer through Venmo. Twenty-five hundred dollars from Nigel Whitcomb, marked as '*donation to feed orphans.*'"

Charisse snorted. "That tracks with the Compassion Foundation Worldwide website. Feeding orphans, giving medicine to the sick, jobs to the homeless. Talk about your Mother Teresa."

Nick read off a few more deposits. "It looks like these five were making the most recent monthly donations. The others are one-offs."

We were able to match most of the donations to a few of the children's diaries. Scarlett and Bree wrote the numbers and dates on the sticky notes and there was a definite pattern.

"Do that one for five grand. There were a few of those recently."

Nick clicked on the deposit. "That one isn't a check. It's an ACH. No name. Give me a minute to trace it."

Charisse put her hand out. "Bring me some of that pie. I just found the 501c3 registry for Compassion Foundation Worldwide. Guess whose name is on the tax return as their chairman."

Bree bounced on her toes. "Ooh, I know. Archie Wilkins."

Charisse snapped her fingers and pointed at Bree. "You got it. Now guess who signed the tax return as their treasurer."

"Surely not Marion Wilkins." I only had a thin thread of respect left for humanity and that might snap it for good.

Charisse bit her bottom lip and shook her head, her eyes wide. "No, but you're close. Sophie Wilkins, the oldest daughter."

I picked up the can of whipped cream and gave it a shake. "That entitled little—" I squeezed the cream into my mouth making a loud *shhkkkkk*.

Nick held his hand up. "I got it. The ACH bounced around a bit, but it originated from a personal account registered to Roger Hart."

I passed the whipped cream to Nick. "Wow. The congresswoman really doesn't want her secrets to get out. Where does the money go after he deposits it?"

"It's transferred to the Caymans on a monthly basis. Marked as administrative expenses."

Scarlett snorted. "That is one well-paid admin."

When we'd gone through the past two years of *donations*, eight journals had sticky notes covering them, the most recent donations coming from the parents of Benjamin Whitcomb, Ava Green, Elijah Hart, Noah Pearson, and Clara Stableman. "The other donations are from names I don't have journals for, but I bet we'll find them locked away in Archie's closet. And for the rest of his current class, either their family secrets aren't worth blackmailing for, or their bank accounts weren't up to it."

Nick surveyed the notebooks. "So, what do we do now?"

"I'm calling Castinetto. And tomorrow, we're going to give Marion Wilkins another little visit."

Chapter 45

After my friends went home, Nick and I sat up for a while enjoying the quiet. We only had a few more hours together before he went back to his trailer. That was good. You know, good for him. He was doing much better. It made sense for him to leave.

We said good night and retreated to our own rooms. I had a fitful night, full of anxiety dreams. The one where I'm on top of a high-rise hotel and a tidal wave is coming at me is a personal favorite. Ringo wouldn't leave me to get in his own bed—which would have been preferred since he's a bit of a moose. So, I woke up with him lying across my legs again. He only jumped out of bed because he heard the knock on the front door.

I pulled on jeans and a sweater and tried to get out there before Dad. Dad being awake before two P.M. was still something I was getting used to. That was pointless. He was standing in the foyer with the cat, the door already open to Foster and Pippi in matching light-up Christmas sweaters. The security guard who had accompanied them to the front door gave a wary look to the fancy black pig. Dad was completely unfazed by all of it.

"Layla. Layla's dad. How you?"

"We're good. How are you, Foster?"

"Pippi and I enjoyed the potluck yesterday. She especially enjoyed the marshmallows."

"That's good. What brings you over?"

"You said you'd start on Pippi's playground after Thanksgiving."

Dad snickered. "All yours, baby girl." He left me to deal with this by myself.

"I did say that, Foster. And I meant it. But maybe after I wake up. Okay?"

Foster's face slid into a frown. "It's after Thanksgiving. Pippi is excited."

Dad laughed in the kitchen. "He's got you there."

Pippi, whose wagon was covered in pine garland for the season, had a lot to say about my delinquency that Ringo interpreted as *Prance around and bark for me.*

"I'll tell you what, Foster. I have to work on Saturday morning, but why don't we get together and make some decisions when I get home? In the meantime, I need you to do something very important."

Foster's shoulders rolled back, and he stood a little taller. "Okay, I'll do it."

"I need you to go over your blueprint and pick your top three things."

The worry was already showing across his face. "Only three."

"Your *top* three. We'll start there and see what we can do."

He gave me a nod. "Pippi, we have work to do."

Pippi ran to Foster and made a leap into her wagon. They disappeared down the sidewalk. Ringo wouldn't come inside until they'd gone around the bend.

Dad came around the corner eating a turkey leg. He smirked at me. "What are you gonna do about that playground?"

I gave him a frown. "Who ordered all that extra food for the community dinner?"

Dad's eyes widened and he backed into the kitchen. "I gotta take my meds."

"Yeah, you do."

I texted the ladies that I'd meet them over at Marion's in one hour. After I cleaned myself up and had a piece of breakfast pie and a kiss from my baby, I hit the remote start and went out to the Jeep.

* * *

Marion must have had a team of men working on the outside of her house all morning. Every window and door were draped with garlands, wreaths, and bows. Lights were wound around all her trees and the edges of her house. I hadn't even thrown away the turkey carcass yet.

Scarlett's Porsche came down the road. She parked across the street, one house over from me. The ladies got out of the car, and we met in the driveway. The curtain in the front window fluttered and closed.

Charisse snapped her fingers and pointed. "Did you see that?"

"Yep. They know we're here."

After a quick knock and a bunch of scuffling inside the house, the younger daughter, Grace, opened the door. "Mother's in the kitchen. She's expecting you."

We passed three exquisitely decorated Christmas trees on the way through the house. Marion was sitting at the table drinking from a fancy bone china teacup; a faint whiff of cloves and cinnamon clung to the air. Sophie was at her side, a crystal ornament lying on the table in front of her as if she'd been decorating a tree.

I pulled out the chair across from Marion. The girls took seats around me and waited in silence. "Thank you for agreeing to see me again."

Marion's eyes were ringed in dark shadows. The lines around her mouth were more pronounced than the last time we'd met. "Do you know when my husband's body will be released for burial?"

"The coroner often waits until the investigation is closed before they release the body."

Her bottom lip quivered. "Why?"

"In case they find something that requires another sweep for evidence."

Sophie moved behind her mother and glared at me. "Haven't you people asked enough questions? It makes me think the police in this town don't know what they're doing."

Marion put her hand over her daughter's on her shoulder. "Is there anything we can do to move things along?"

"There is actually. You can answer my questions truthfully this time." I looked directly at Sophie. "All of you."

Sophie swallowed hard and her eyes darted around the room. "Why are you looking at me?"

Charisse casually crossed one leg over the other. "Let's start with Compassion Foundation Worldwide. I believe you're the treasurer, Sophie, are you not?"

Marion sputtered, "Well, of course she is. It's clearly documented on the tax forms. Archie wanted to keep overhead low so he could see that most of every donation went to people who needed them."

"And who exactly do these donations go to?" Scarlett asked.

Sophie's face drained of color, and she reached for the empty chair by her mother.

Marion's neck resembled a ripening peach as a blush began to climb up from her chest. She spoke to me like I was one of Archie's students. "People in need. Archie was very civic-minded. He cared about the intimate details of people's lives and looked for ways to make them better."

Grace looked at her sister, a worrying frown creased her forehead. "Isn't that right, Soph? Soph?"

Sophie's voice trembled. "I don't know where the donations go. I only made the website and filled out some forms. Dad wouldn't tell me anything about the money."

Bree's eyes softened with compassion for the girl who was only a little older than herself. "Did you ever ask him?"

Sophie nodded. "He said it was better not to know the details because it would change the way I saw people in the community. But he assured me the money always went to good people who deserved it."

Scarlett chuckled under her breath. "That was not a long list."

"Then why do you look guilty, Soph?" Grace prodded.

Sophie dropped her chin. "We had a donation bounce a few weeks before my father died, and when I worked with the bank to fix it, I found out they didn't see any of the disbursements Dad has written on the books. They only showed transfers to an offshore account."

I pulled out a few sheets of paper from my purse that had the printout of the last year of activity in the charity bank account. Marion and her daughters leaned in to read it together.

"In fact the only disbursements ever made from this account went back to Archie and were marked as administrative fees. About twenty thousand dollars a month."

Marion was looking less sure of herself by the minute. Her gaze jumped from the printout and settled in her teacup.

Sophie dropped her face into her hands.

Grace's eyes filled with tears. "Are we in trouble?"

I collected the printout and put it back in my bag. "Not with me. I'm not investigating the fraudulent charity. I'm trying to find your father's murderer. And I'm pretty sure it's linked to how he was getting these donations."

All three Wilkins women wore the same pitiful look of despair. I'd just changed their view of the most important man in their lives forever. And it would only get worse in the coming days once the investigation into the charity and blackmail began. The least I could do was find his killer and let them bury their loved one. "Alright, ladies. It's time to toughen up. We need to catch a killer. I need your help. Did Archie have a laptop, computer, or cell phone that you didn't give the police?"

Bree added, "Or an iPad."

I tried not to smile. "Or an iPad."

Sophie and Grace shook their heads and vehemently denied any knowledge of such items. Marion meekly stood to her feet. "Yes. A cell phone."

Their solidarity briefly shattered, the girls both appeared horrified. "Mo-om!"

Marion pushed away from the table and left the kitchen, her daughters discussing amongst themselves their mother's treacherous secrecy.

"Are you kidding me? He had another cell phone."

"How could she keep that from us?"

"And the police. Now we all look guilty."

Charisse and Scarlett, the other mothers in the room, caught each other's eyes and shook their heads as if to say, *Kids.*

I added, "Technically, you *are* all guilty—of obstructing the investigation."

Silence fell on the room once again.

Marion returned and placed a metal lock box in the middle of the table next to the bone china teapot. It was secured with a tiny padlock. "I don't have the key."

"Not necessary." Charisse reached for the padlock, stuck the tine of a fork in the hole, and twisted it until it popped open. She saw the looks we were giving her and said, "My daughter had a similar lock on her diary. Don't judge me."

The box was full of bundled stacks of cash and three burner phones. I gave Bree and Charisse each a phone and we turned them on.

Bree held hers up. "Mine is password protected."

Marion crossed the kitchen to a cabinet by the refrigerator and took down a bottle of Blanton's single malt whiskey. She returned to the table and poured a hefty shot into her teacup. She placed the bottle on the table in front of her, oblivious that the four visitors had become frozen with their eyes locked on the amber liquid. "Archie wasn't very original. He used the same password for everything. Our anniversary." She chugged her "tea." "Eight one eighty-one."

None of us moved at first.

Scarlett took the phone from my hand. "You heard her. Eight one eighty-one. We're looking for text messages, emails, social media."

After a minute, Charisse gasped. "I've got what we're looking for. We can go."

I pushed back my chair and picked up the lockbox.

Sophie asked, "Where are you going with that?"

"It's evidence. I have to turn it in with the phones."

Grace's lip quivered. "Will we get it back?"

"That will depend on the outcome of the investigation and how the money was obtained."

Sophie sunk into her chair. “Great. We’ll never see it again.”

We excused ourselves and gathered in the driveway around Charisse. “What did you find?”

She held up the phone displaying a message. “This is the last message old Archie received the night he was murdered. No name. Just a number.”

Meet me at Our Lady of Mercy at 8 PM.

“Sweet. Now we need to find out who that text came from, and I think Castinetto can make his arrest.” I pulled out my cell phone and dialed Nick. “Hey. You still at my house?”

“Yeah. We’re having a bit of a hard time today. We received another threat from the blackmailer that the price has doubled because payment wasn’t made—along with several pictures of your dad at the community potluck.”

“How? We took her phone.”

“We didn’t take his.”

“Frickin’ Robin. I’ll check with Ronnie to see if they got what they needed from her trailer. I want this over.”

“Your dad’s just worried that you’ll be upset. I’ve got him watching *Spinal Tap*. He thinks it’s hilarious.”

Scarlett smacked my arm and spun her finger in a corkscrew for me to hurry up.

“Hey, Nick. Can you do me a favor?”

“Yeah. Anything.”

“I’m sending you a number. Can you tell me who it belongs to?”

I heard the sound of him running up the spiral stairs. “Send it.”

I sent the number in a text. “Thanks. Let me know as soon as you find something. Also . . .” I pointed my key fob at the Jeep to start it up. A thunderous boom knocked the four of us off our feet as my Jeep exploded.

Chapter 46

My ears were ringing as ash fell to the ground all around me. My vision filled with the image of Melissa bleeding out on the asphalt at Stratton Park, as it always did. This time the image was sharper than usual. I could hear Melissa's voice as she yelled, "Hurtado isn't here! It's Jacob! He killed Oscar and Eddie!" I started to crawl across the glass to get to her, but someone pulled me back.

"Layla. Layla, come back to us." Hands gripped my shoulders, and someone was rubbing my back. "You're okay. We're still at Marion's house. Your Jeep exploded, but we're all safe." The voice was Bree's. She was probably also the one who was rubbing my back.

My voice came out haggard and breathless. "Okay. I'm okay."

Charisse's grip loosened and I was able to sit back on the curb by Scarlett's car. Somewhere in the distance, sirens were going off. People ran out of their houses to see the carnage up close and personal as ash floated gently around us. It was a white Christmas, but not the kind they wanted.

The street filled with emergency responders while the four of us sat on the curb and watched the angry neighbor whose house my Jeep exploded in front of argue with the cop that someone had to pay for his property.

Scarlett snickered. "Wow, he's pretty pissed."

Bree opened her purse and took out a pack of gum. "Well,

the bomb took out his reindeer mailbox." She took a piece and offered it to the rest of us. "He probably just put that up this morning."

Charisse pulled out a stick and unwrapped it. "The neighborhood owes you a thank-you for taking out his giant inflatable Santa. That thing was hideous."

As I watched the firefighters hose down my Jeep, behind me I heard a police officer arguing with someone. "You need to get back, sir."

"That's my best friend and she might be hurt. Just try and stop me."

Nick appeared before me, his face ashen and filled with fear. He dropped to the ground and pulled me into his arms. "Layla, I heard the explosion. Are you okay?"

"Someone blew up my Jeep."

I tried to look brave, but my lip trembled, giving me away. "I have fifty-eight more payments to make."

He chuckled and stroked my hair. "It's going to be okay. What happened?"

"I don't know, but one thing's for sure. I will never have another car without remote start."

"We'll give the manufacturer a five-star review."

Scarlett moved over to let Nick sit between us. "Did you do your fancy voodoo to find out who was texting Archie?"

He settled onto the curb with us as a Channel Five News crew ran through the yard to set up their camera. "I didn't have to. The number is registered to Roger Hart."

Charisse clucked her tongue. "The congresswoman's husband used his own phone?"

Scarlett shook her head. "He's obviously not a drug addict. Covering your tracks is one of the first things you figure out."

Charisse agreed. "Or having an affair. Michael could give him tips."

The rumble of a sports car growled up the road behind us and one door slam later Castinetto was at my feet. "Thank God you're okay, Virtue. What happened?"

I stared at Dayton for a long couple of moments. Did he just try to kill me? His concern *seemed* genuine.

"Well, I'm pretty sure I know who killed Archie Wilkins." I passed him the lockbox with the cash and burner phones. "It would be best if we question Roger Hart at Our Lady of Mercy. Call the church and let them know we're coming."

Castinetto's eyebrow shot up. "Who is this 'we'? You were almost just blown up. You need to go home and rest."

I jumped to my feet. "I don't want to go home. I've been threatened, shot at, and a bomb just destroyed my Jeep. I want to end this."

Castinetto looked at the row of faces staring back at him from the curb. "Virtue, I can't take all these civilians to make an arrest."

Bree popped her gum. "Just take Layla. We'll be fine. She can tell us everything later when we go for dinner."

Charisse and Scarlett agreed and started floating restaurant ideas.

I searched Nick's face to see how he felt about me leaving him to go into more danger.

He grinned, a spark of amusement joining the concern in his eyes. "I get it. It's your job. One of them anyway. I'll be there when you come home tonight. Besides, someone has to keep Don from feeding that cat the rest of my turkey."

Castinetto sent a black-and-white to pick up Roger Hart and take him to Our Lady of Mercy. The beat cop argued for only a moment because it was unusual to interrogate a murder suspect outside of the station, but Castinetto had rank. He was instructed to encourage Roger that he was not under arrest but helping us with our inquiries by meeting us on-site. I called ahead and asked Gladys if we could meet with Father Matthews while we questioned Mr. Hart, saying the priest's presence might make the congresswoman's husband more apt to be honest.

Friday evening Mass didn't start for another hour, so Father Matthews met us in his office. I placed my coat and purse on the love seat next to Castinetto who looked like he'd been summoned for chastisement. The priest was nervous, which came out as chatty.

He fiddled with his collar, pulling it and stretching his neck. "Well, I don't rightly know how much help I can be to ya. I'll do my best, but you know I can't make anyone confess anything they don't want to. Not even in the booth."

"Don't worry." I tried to calm him. "Why don't you ask Gladys to make some tea? We'll keep this informal."

He wrung his hands. "Okay, I can do that." He called over his shoulder, "Mrs. Beacon?"

Gladys appeared in the doorway instantly. "Yes, Father?"

"Some tea please? And use the cart this time."

She disappeared in silence, her sensible shoes not making a sound down the hallway.

Father Matthews breathed through a chuckle, "Silly woman." He turned his face to me again. "Now who did you say this was?"

"Dayton Castinetto. He's a homicide detective with the Potomac County Homicide Division. He's here to make an arrest in the Archie Wilkins murder."

Dayton stood and grasped the priest's hand, staring him in the eye until Father Matthews let go. "Thank you for seeing us."

Father Matthews dropped into the armchair, flustered. "Fine. Fine."

A crackle of police radio echoed in the hall and Roger Hart was led into the office by the beat cop who'd picked him up. Roger was of medium height, with expertly styled chestnut hair, and very thin. He looked like a man used to spa treatments, and smelled of expensive aftershave, but there was a haunted, fearful look behind his eyes.

Castinetto indicated that Roger was to sit on the love seat while he stood next to me in front of the priest's desk—Intimidation 101.

I made small talk until Mrs. Beacon returned with the tea cart. She cut her eyes to Father Matthews and he gave her a quick glance and immediately went to examinine his hands. "So, Roger,

I had the pleasure of meeting Elijah in school the other day. Did he tell you?"

Roger's well-moisturized face paled. "He did mention that a lady cop asked them questions about their teacher."

"Mmm. They were a great class. Very open and honest. But I guess that's a trait that Mr. Wilkins cultivated in them by having them journal their thoughts and feelings every day."

Roger wrung his hands and cleared his throat.

"Have you ever read Elijah's journal, Roger?"

"He wasn't allowed to bring his journal home. Archie didn't want the parents influencing what went on the page. Better for him to gather the dirty little secrets if they stayed firmly in his grasp."

Gladys tried to pass Father Matthews a cup of tea and he waved it away.

"We've also seen the bank account for Compassion Foundation Worldwide. You made some pretty hefty donations."

Roger seemed to shrink into himself.

"You really wanted to stay anonymous. Your money bounced all over the Internet before hitting Archie's account. How'd you accomplish that?"

He flicked his eyes to mine. "My accountant did it for me. He said it was untraceable."

I nodded. "It was pretty close. You obviously know why you're here. But I should tell you that we have you on security footage entering the church the night Archie Wilkins was murdered. Then we have you leaving a few minutes later."

His eyes were glassy, and the whites were turning red. Roger shrugged, the smell of despair overpowering his expensive aftershave.

I sat on the chair next to him and softened my voice. "Tell me what happened."

After a moment of gathering himself, he said, "Archie Wilkins encouraged his students to write down things that happened at home. Things that upset them, things they didn't understand, things they couldn't ask their parents about. And he would give comforting advice and encouragement to them. Then the bastard—pardon me, Father—would set up a one-on-one session with the parents in guise of a student progress meeting.

"My wife is a busy woman, so most of the family obligations fall to me. Archie knew she was up for reelection." He breathed a bitter chuckle and clenched his fist. "He said he'd leak Elijah's journal to the news if we didn't pay for his silence."

Father Matthews shook his head and gave me a look of compassion for Roger. The teacup rattled in Gladys's hand, and she placed it on the cart to still it.

I pulled the bank register printout from my bag. "Five thousand dollars every three months. That's expensive silence."

Roger pulled himself up a little taller. "My wife does a lot of good for the people. Trying to keep drugs out of our state. She has a job that really matters—it's stressful for her. She doesn't always handle it well." He swallowed hard. "She has some problems."

"Problems, as in she's abusive to you."

His words came out rushed like he was afraid he'd lose his chance to say them. "We're working on it—she's always . . . sorry." He cast his eyes to his lap, his momentary bravado slipping away as his memory caught up. "She says she's sorry."

"So, you texted Archie to meet you here after Mass. Why?"

"He was delusional about how much money a congresswoman gets paid. I'd been dipping into our retirement account to make his demands and I wasn't willing to do it again. I met with him by the confessionals and told him we were done. If he went to the news I'd call the police and tell them he was blackmailing us.

"Archie laughed in my face. He said he was one of the most upstanding members of society and no one would believe the accusation came from him."

Roger's eyes filled with tears. "I lost my composure. All I could see was this little weaselly man in a bow tie and sweater vest, manipulating my child and capitalizing on my family's difficult circumstances for his own selfish gain. I grabbed the nearest thing, and I swung it at him as hard as I could. I didn't mean to *kill* him. I just wanted to shut him up. But I didn't know . . . I'd never hit anyone before. I ran away like a coward, and I just left him there. And now I've done the very thing I was trying to prevent. I've ruined my family."

Roger put a fist in his mouth and sobbed. "What have I done? My wife has very good lawyers. She might have lost her seat in congress, but she wouldn't have seen jail time. I should have just turned him in. Blackmail is a felony."

I glanced at Castinetto. He gave me a grin and a nod. "You're right. Blackmail's a felony. But it's not as bad as murder. Right, Gladys?"

The church secretary's eyes darted to Castinetto; she threw a look over her shoulder at the exit but the officer who brought Roger in was stationed at the door and he moved his hand to the butt of his gun. Gladys lowered herself primly into the remaining chair.

Roger sat up a little straighter. His tears had stopped, and his eyes snapped curiously to Gladys.

Gladys glared at me.

"Roger, who let you in when you came to question Archie?"

Roger's voice sparked a hopeful tone. "Mrs. Beacon let me in. The door was already locked, and I had to wait for someone to open it."

"Was Archie waiting for you in the sanctuary?"

"He was in Father Matthews's office. Mrs. Beacon went to fetch him."

"And then where did Mrs. Beacon go?"

Roger shrugged. "I don't know. She disappeared."

"You didn't go far though, did you, Gladys? Everyone is so used to seeing you that no one really pays attention to you anymore. But you're always there. Watching and listening. You know whose wife left him for a dancer and who's about to lose their house. Everyone's dirty little secret shared in confession. And I'm willing to bet you know what Charlotte said about you in her journal."

Gladys shrugged. "So, what if I steal a couple berries now and then? My granddaughter exaggerates. That's hardly a crime. What are you going to charge me for? Grand theft fruiting? I'm our sole provider, and we live on a fixed income. What's criminal is the price of eggs and the amount of Social Security I collect."

"Then why were you giving donations to Archie's phony charity?"

Father Matthews groaned and crossed himself.

Roger was really getting into the questioning now. "Yeah. Why, Mrs. Beacon?"

Gladys calmly clasped her hands and tucked her feet under the chair. "I thought it was a real charity. It's easy to fool an old lady."

I leaned forward with my elbows on my knees. "Do you know how Archie Wilkins died, Mrs. Beacon?"

She shook her head. "He was bludgeoned by Roger."

"That didn't kill him. He could have lived if given medical attention. It was the overdose of fentanyl-laced heroin that was administered after he was hit on the head that stopped his heart."

Gladys patted her chest. "Oh my. I wouldn't know the first thing about that."

I clocked Father Matthews's eye roll before he stopped himself.

Castinetto was not one to suffer fools gladly. He definitely didn't like Gladys's cool attitude. "I find that very interesting, Mrs. Beacon. Because your daughter is currently doing fifteen years in the Virginia Correctional Center for Women for drug trafficking. Addicts always leave hiding places that they can go to later."

I nodded. "So, Gladys, we figure you found some of your daughter's stash, and you planned to use it on Archie after he met with Roger. And to your surprise, you didn't even have to incapacitate him. Roger had done that for you."

Roger's hands flew up in surrender. "But that was unintentional. I'm not an accomplice."

Gladys's eyes narrowed and I could see her wheels turning.

"That's a good theory, but I had already left the building before Archie was killed."

I sucked in a breath through my teeth. "I don't know, Gladys. Why does the security camera across the street see you enter the church in the morning, but it doesn't see you leave later the night Archie was killed?"

Her eyebrows dipped and she gave her head a little shake. "I must have gone out the back door right after I let Roger in. I'm sure I told the gentlemen they only had to leave when they were done. The door locks by itself."

Castinetto dropped to the love seat next to me. "Problem is . . . the traffic camera around the corner clocked you leaving twenty minutes after Roger left the building. And officers are at your house right now with a search warrant looking for any evidence your daughter left behind when she went to prison. What do you think they'll find?"

Her eyes flashed fear for the first time.

I pointed to her neck. "If we test those pearls you wear every day, I'm pretty confident we'll find traces of Archie's blood on them too, won't we?"

Roger's eyes gleamed with hope.

Gladys picked at the hem of her cardigan. "Archie Wilkins was hurting a lot of people with extortion. They'd come in here month after month, crying in confession about what he was doing to them. He had to be dealt with. Can't you see that I was doing the Lord's work?"

Dayton breathed a near-silent snort of awe.

Father Matthews winced. "Oh, Mrs. Beacon. And why do you know what is shared in confession?"

"I bet during confession is when she does some of her best recon." I raised an eyebrow at the church secretary, almost impressed by her espionage.

Gladys held my look. "I hold a very prominent position in the church leadership. Do you want to ruin that? Is that fair to Charlotte? I only wanted to convince him not to tell Social Services what she'd written in her journal. Hasn't she been through enough with an absent father and a mother in prison? Hasn't Archie Wilkins done enough to our family? To our community?"

She held her palms up. "Maybe he took the drugs himself. He was a terrible human being. When I found him, he was already lying on the floor. I thanked God for divine providence. I never laid a hand on him."

"Mmm-hmm. How did he drag himself into the confessional?" I asked.

Gladys shrugged again. "It must be a miracle."

Castinetto stood and motioned for the beat cop to cuff the church secretary. "Gladys Beacon. You're under arrest for the murder of Archie Wilkins."

Gladys rolled her shoulders and lifted her chin. "He had it coming."

Chapter 47

"PAULA, WE NEED TO TALK ABOUT THESE OUTFITS YOU KEEP STICKing me with. I get that your former client was a birthday party clown and all, but I'm losing all my rock star cred here." I stood in the Neiman Marcus Café at the Tyson's Galleria dressed as a Christmas elf in pointy shoes with bells on the toes. This was my second cell phone break, and I decided complaining to my manager was the best use of my time.

"Layla, honey, you don't have rock star cred. You barely have food court cred."

"I've been asked 'Which way to find Santa?' twenty-six times and gotten three donations for the Salvation Army. You've got to get me some better gigs."

"Why aren't you with Santa now? You're supposed to be playing backup while the children sit on his lap."

"He said my 'Christmas Eve in Sarajevo' was disturbing the kids."

The store manager spotted me on my phone all the way from the makeup counter and sent a very unfestive hand gesture my way.

"I gotta go." I clicked off and shoved the phone into the waistband of my green tights since this ridiculous red sparkly miniskirt didn't come with pockets. I kicked on my loop station and started "Oh Come All Ye Faithful"—the Twisted Sister rendition. That was apparently not good enough for Mr. Plaid Pants, because he marched across the shiny floor to register his third complaint in two hours.

"Miss, I hired you to play Christmas classics. Not this noise that keeps coming out of that speaker of yours. Do you understand me?"

"Absolutely."

He sniffed and pushed his square glasses up the bridge of his nose. When he started to stomp away, I began a funky rendition of "You're a Mean One, Mr. Grinch."

"And that was when you got fired?" Scarlett passed me the thermos of warm cocoa.

I poured a little into the paper cup that Bree gave me. "I think my refusal to play that hippopotamus song early in the gig really got the discharge ball rolling."

Charisse downed her cocoa like a shot. "I get that you didn't have time to change because mall security escorted you to the exit, but why couldn't you answer my text asking if you needed a ride?"

"My cell phone slid down my tights and I haven't fished it out yet." My ankle glowed and dimmed like a lighthouse with unanswered messages. "The green bodysuit over my tights has crotch snaps and . . . bah. It's a whole thing."

Bree collected our empty paper cups. "Well, don't worry about that now. You can change at the restaurant when we leave here. We'll cut you out of those tights if we have to. Are you ready to do this?"

I faced the Gibson with the new knowledge that Ricky Hurtado owned it. Scarlett had made us a reservation for the VIP room on her husband's credit card so we could get in there and see if the visit brought any more clarity to my memory. "I'm ready. But if I have to pee, you might need to extract me from these tights sooner rather than later."

Scarlett headed for the door. "Let's do this."

The Gibson was decked out for the Christmas holidays with lights strung around the perimeter of the room and a mini decorated tree at the end of the bar. Four red stockings were hung on the mirror behind the bar with the names Gwennifer, Tina, Roxy, and Nancy. The sandwich board listed a white chocolate peppermint martini as the Instagram special of the month.

Jorge was working the bar. A well-dressed man entered after us and approached him. "I'm here for my takeout. Name's Stanley Kowalski."

Jorge wiped the counter at the end and patted the bar. "Take a seat." He disappeared into the back and returned with Nancy on his heels. She carried a large paper takeout bag and held it out to the man at the counter. Catching us in her sight, her expression changed to irritation for a brief moment before she caught herself. "Here's your wings," she said as she passed the man his order.

Scarlett took a step forward. "Party of four for the VIP room reserved under Mrs. Graham Weatherspoon."

Nancy threw her hands to her hips and stared us down. "What do you want to do in there?"

Charisse replied breezily, "Same thing everyone else does in there."

Nancy shook her head. "No. That's not for you gals. Why don't I get you a nice booth in the back? Come on. First drink's on me."

Bree twisted her hair around her fingers. "Eww. No. Why can't we have the VIP room, Nancy? We booked it."

Nancy huffed and looked from one face to another through narrowed eyes. She sucked in her cheek. She nodded to me. "You're the gal who still can't remember anything."

"That's right."

"You think this is gonna help or something?"

Scarlett threw her hands to her hips. "How about you just lead us back there and leave us to our own business, okay, Nancy?"

Jorge was frozen in place at the bar watching, the shammy cloth dangling from his pointer finger. The look on his face was a warning that we didn't want to push any farther.

Nancy's features hardened. "Okay, fine. I hope you ladies

know what you're doing." She reached for a tray and filled it with four shot glasses and a bottle of Mandala Día de Los Muertos tequila. "Follow me."

With quick determined steps she passed the bar and turned down the long hallway. A heavy wooden door sat under an emergency exit sign at the end of the hallway right before the VIP room. She pushed her hip into the door, swinging it open.

A memory flashed in my mind that I had followed her down this hallway before.

"Have a seat, hon. He's been waiting for you."

The girls and I entered a dark wood paneled room with a glossy mahogany table and eight green leather armchairs. The air hung heavy with cigar smoke and debauchery. My mind flooded with memories of a big man sitting in the leather chair on one side of the table while Jacob stood just off to his side.

Chapter 48

"Layla Virtue. Glad you could finally join us. Sorry to ruin your little sting over at my warehouse."

Ricky Hurtado. I'd only looked into his dark eyes one other time and had to walk away to protect my cover. A goon with an AK-47 stood to his right.

Jacob had set up this eleventh-hour meeting and said it was crucial to the operation. I hadn't realized he would be here. He was dressed in his riot gear, ready for the warehouse raid. I gave him a look that asked what was going on. We had two dozen officers waiting for my command to move in. He moved his hand down to his thigh and crossed his fingers. It was a silent code we used to mean you and me are a team. No one gets between us.

Nancy placed the tray in the middle of the table. "I brought your favorite."

"Thanks, Ma. You ready to get started?"

The goon patted me down and ran a device up one side of me and down the other looking for a transmitter. He nodded at Ricky.

Nancy took the seat at the head of the table while Jacob moved behind me and gently pressed my shoulders, guiding me into the empty chair. I would have looked to see how many perps were at my six, but I dared not take my eyes off the gun.

Hurtado laughed at the look on my face. "I know you're in awe, Officer Virtue. It's okay. Not many people have the honor of sitting face-to-face with the Scorpion and live to tell about it."

Nancy poured a shot and gave me a lazy grin. "You've been after me for months. Trying to get a look inside my operation. Now's your chance." Nancy slid the shot of tequila across the table. It hit my glass of ginger ale. "Go on, chickie."

"I'm on duty."

"If you want answers, you'll need to take that shot."

I felt Jacob's hand rest on my shoulder, his voice low in my ear. "Come on, baby, it's one shot. I've got your back."

Yeah, but got my back for what? I thought about resisting, but I told myself I didn't want to stand in the way of getting the Scorpion to talk since no one had ever gotten this close before.

Even now I knew that was a lie.

I reached for the golden liquid and downed it. It was soft and sweet and forbidden. Warmth and shame mingled on my tongue.

Nancy smiled. Pleased that she'd gotten me to do something I knew I shouldn't. "Wonderful. See, that wasn't so hard. I'm a generous woman."

She poured another shot and sent it to me.

I had less resolve this time and knocked the shot back immediately. "Talk."

She grinned and I felt like a mouse cornered by a venomous snake. "I'm expanding my territory, and I need someone to manage a new location. We'll distribute through the bar just like we do here. Just come in once a week and get your takeout. I'll put everything you need in the bag. All you have to do is pick it up and deliver it to your contact. And you let me know about anything you hear coming from the Boy Scouts. Every once in a while I'll call on you for a favor. You'll do what I ask without question and you'll get ten grand a week. Easy peasy lemon squeezy."

I looked at Ricky. "You're a scumbag. The drugs you bring into my county have destroyed families. How many children have died from overdose because of you? Why in the world do you think I would do this, Hurtado?"

The goon with the gun flinched and Nancy put her hand up.

Ricky held a burner phone. "Because right now your team is in my warehouse, and it's wired to blow as soon as I hit send. Join us and they live. But if you refuse my mother's generous offer, there will be nothing you can do to save them and you won't even remember that you were here."

Nancy ran her finger lazily around the rim of a glass. "Not to mention I'll make you deliriously rich. Half of your guys already work for me. You have no idea how far my reach is."

Ricky snorted. "Poor Layla. You've been so focused on taking me down and the whole time your own team was working against you. Just stop fighting it."

That tequila was hitting me a lot harder than it normally did. I was feeling a little fuzzy around the edges. "I've been rich. It didn't make me happy. And I would rather die than help you kill one more child, you piece of filth!"

The goon fired off a shot and I hit the floor. It missed me by a mile. Nancy sprang from her chair and ran for the door. "You fool! We're open for business."

Hurtado shouted, "You should have groomed her better, Jacob. Now she gotta die!"

An invisible knife carved out my heart. Groomed me better. Just who is Jacob working for? I shouted back, "I think you're lying through your yellow teeth, Ricky. There are good cops in my division. You don't have everyone! I know for a fact that you don't have Castinetto!"

Jacob's laugh behind me sent a chill through my riot gear. "Castinetto doesn't have the balls for this."

Nancy returned and slapped the table in front of me. "Enough!" She told someone behind me, "Do it now." Heavy hands pushed down on my shoulders, a pinch—sharp on my neck.

Everything went dark.

Chapter 49

THE GIRLS WERE WATCHING ME RAPTLY. THEY COULD TELL SOMEthing was happening in my mind. I faced Nancy, rage rising in me like a tidal wave. "You drugged me. And you killed my friends."

Her expression went from curious to resigned. She reached into her apron and pulled out a Sig Sauer pocket pistol. "Well, this is unfortunate. You were supposed to die at that warehouse, but Jacob screwed up and dropped you too far away. You made a good scapegoat for a while, but it's too bad you got your memory back, chickie. That was the only thing keeping you alive."

The girls reacted very differently than I expected. Bree threw herself in front of me with a powerful scream while Scarlett hurled herself across the table at Nancy, Dukes of Hazzard-style. Charisse swung her Fendi bag in an arc at the crime boss's head, hitting her on the temple.

Nancy pointed her gun at Scarlett and then at Charisse and back to me. "Stay where you are!"

I couldn't take the chance that she'd fire off a shot and hit one of them. They meant too much to me now. I reached for my gun out of habit and came up with a candy cane and disgust. So, I grabbed the drinks tray, flipping the tequila and shot glasses in the air. "Get down!" The girls flattened and I winged the tray at Nancy, hitting her square on the windpipe.

She clutched at her neck, reeling on her feet and went over

backward, hitting her head on the stone floor. A trickle of blood pooled under her ear. She was out cold.

"Someone call 911."

Scarlett rose up to her knees and one eyebrow raised. "You want to get her an ambulance?"

"I want to have her arrested. Mention Castinetto when you call. Apparently, he's one of the good guys."

Chapter 50

DAYTON CASTINETTO STOOD OVER NANCY, WHO WAS ALIVE BUT unconscious, as the paramedics worked on her. "And you did that with a drinks tray?"

"I don't have a gun anymore."

"Well, thank God for that."

Tequila ran down the table and pooled onto the floor at my feet. The room was filled with the smell of alcohol mixed with the sharp scent of blood.

Charisse gave Dayton a charming smile. "Detective, do you think we could take this to the other room?"

"Actually, you don't have to hang out here. Why don't you all go home, and I'll send officers to get your statements later?"

A team of cops swarmed the Gibson and locked the bar down. Everyone who worked there was being taken to the station for questioning. The drug-sniffing dogs were going crazy. As Jorge was being put into a car, he called over his shoulder, "I didn't know what she was doing. I only knew it was sus because the takeout bags never came from the kitchen. You have to believe me."

Bree twirled her hair around her finger. "Why does everyone always say that? You don't have to believe anything."

The officer shut the cruiser door and Scarlett said, "I think he's lying."

I chuckled. "With your natural mistrust of people and assumption that everyone is lying, you sound like a cop, Scarlett."

She raised an eyebrow. "Hmm. Before I met you I would have called that an insult. Now I'm not sure anymore."

Charisse struck a pose like a Charlie's Angel. "What about me?"

I thought over the last few days. "You'd make a good analyst. Most people don't realize that a lot of cop work is paperwork and research."

Charisse put her imaginary gun away. "I could see that. Crunching that data and all. I'd kill at that."

Bree smiled broadly and pulled at her hair. She looked at me with big questioning eyes waiting for her imaginary assignment.

"You, I see as the family liaison."

Her smile dropped. "What's that mean?"

Scarlett put her hand on Bree's shoulder. "Cupcake, that means you'd hold their hands and tell them it will be okay."

Her nose curled as she looked at me again. "I don't wanna do that. I want to do something fierce. Like bomb squad."

"I don't want you doing anything dangerous. How about taking care of the police dogs when they're puppies?"

Her eyes grew and I could practically see them swirling. "Yaaas. The police puppies. And the bomb squad 'cause I'm fierce."

Charisse laughed as we walked toward Scarlett's Porsche. "Sure, honey."

I grinned in spite of myself. "Oh yeah, I saw the way you threw yourself in front of me."

Scarlett snorted and shook her head in amusement. "You are definitely fierce, Bree."

Nick had a few boxes packed by my front door when I arrived home from my Sunday brunch gig in Dad's Aston Martin. He met me at the door with Ringo, who had to perform an extra thorough security sweep since I'd been around onion rings.

I pointed to the boxes. "What's all this?"

"Just a bunch of stuff I brought over. I've packed up to go home. I'll be out of your hair today."

That was a gut punch I did not need. "That's still happening today?"

He nodded. "I need to see your phone. Also, Bree's mom is here."

I raised my eyebrows, and he nodded toward the greenhouse patio. I handed him my cell phone and headed for the French doors. Halfway through the living room Dad caught me.

He was sitting on the couch in red satin pants that looked painted on and a black ruffly shirt open halfway to the waist. I'm pretty sure he'd worn that getup to the MTV Music Awards when I was in high school. The cat was curled in his lap. "Guess what, baby girl?"

"What?"

"We're on . . ."

Dad's face scrunched up and he looked across the room to Nick who supplied, "TikTok."

"We're on TikTok and we're trending."

"What in the world are you talking about?"

Dad handed Nick his cell phone. "Show her, dude."

Nick brought up a video of me and Dad playing the song we'd been working on at the Thanksgiving potluck. "Who posted that?"

Nick shrugged. "The account name is Hot Momma, but it doesn't give any details. They didn't say anything about where you are, or how Don is doing. Just Happy Thanksgiving and the song."

The number of views was close to a million. The comments were mostly praise with a lot of *Who is that with him?*

Dad gave me a cheesy grin and stroked the cat behind the ears. "I still got it, don't I, Zappa? Even if I can't remember where I left it."

I handed him the phone. "You'll always have it, Dad. Don't worry."

I made it into the glass-enclosed patio where Bree's mom was admiring the potted miniature weeping cherry. She turned her face and smiled at me.

"Hi, Susan. What can I do for you?"

She reached into her tote bag and pulled out a foil-wrapped block. Her eyes filled with tears as she handed it to me. "Butterscotch fudge. To say thank you."

"You've already thanked me."

"I know. But it's a bigger deal than you know. Bree has tried to end her life two other times. We barely made it to her in time the last time."

She reached into her bag again and pulled out a folded piece of paper and handed it to me. "I found this the night you all came over. I think it's only because of you and the other women that she didn't go through with it."

I read the tight scribbles across the page, my eyes streaked with tears and my heart clutched in my chest. "She was leaving a note."

Susan nodded; a tear escaped and ran down her nose. "She promised me she would never do anything like this again. Something you said really got to her."

Something I said? I felt a quiver of fear in my heart. How many times had I thought to do the same thing? If I ever had that temptation again, what would it do to Bree? Or Nick? We were all just hanging on by a thread.

I let Susan hug me for the umpteenth time. "Promise me you'll keep an eye on her."

"I'll do my best."

She let herself out and I sat on the pink couch for a while and stared at the tear-stained paper in my hand. *I'll do my very best.*

Nick found me a while later. "Castinetto's here to see you. And apparently the cat is going by Zappa now. What's wrong?"

I showed him the letter. "She was gonna do it, but she called me instead."

Nick squatted next to me and put his hand on my knee. "Thank God you were there for her. And for me."

"Who will be here for me if you or Bree go through with it, Nick?" My lip trembled and I left the room before I fell apart completely.

Castinetto stood in my foyer facing Ringo who hadn't forgiven him for making me upset the last time.

Ringo gave me a tail wag asking if it was okay that he was here. I put my hand on his head. "Good boy."

"He sounds like he wants to kill whoever is at the door, but his tail is wagging like he thinks I'm his best friend."

"Yeah, we're working on that. Are you here for my statement?"

"Not exactly. I want you to come with me."

"I have to go down to the station?"

He frowned and his eyes blazed with irritation. "No. Will you just trust me?"

"Okay, don't get touchy."

I got in his Charger, and he tore out of my driveway in a shot. "There's something you'll want to see if we're not too late."

"Oh-kay. My curiosity is piqued, but also, this better not be an arrest for whacking Nancy with that tray or I'll be super pissed."

"Relax. And I thought you'd want to know that Nancy is in the ICU. Apparently, there have been complications with bleeding on the brain. She's in a coma but doctors are optimistic."

"Great."

He started doing the loop around the lake. "So that Nick guy, he's your boyfriend?"

"What? No. We're just friends. Quit worrying about him. He's not involved in any of this. He's a good guy."

"Okay." He turned onto Fontainebleau. There were two squad cars, a police van, and a couple of unmarked Feds all in front of Robin's house with Ronnie Voa. Her trailer door was open. A woman with strawberry blond hair and an FBI windbreaker led Robin's brother, Glenn, out to the van in handcuffs.

Castinetto put the Charger in park. "So that's Sloane Harlow. She's with the FBI major crimes division. Your security guy called her in."

"Ronnie mentioned he had someone."

Adam Beasley and an officer I knew as Daniels carried Robin

out in her wheelchair. She was screaming profanity and slapping them. "Put me down! I'm suing this whole department for infringing on my rights. This is ableism."

Beasley saw me sitting in the car and gave me a wave and a thumbs-up. He dropped his side of the wheelchair but recovered it on the bounce.

"Oof. That's gonna be a mess."

Castinetto let out a long breath. "She barricaded herself in the bathroom. What could they do?"

"So, I take it you got what you needed yesterday?"

"Sloane said they got enough evidence from the trailer, the computer, and the cell phones to put those two away for a long time. In addition to blackmailing your father, the brother had checks from three of the park residents to do home improvements he was never gonna do, and they were catfishing one Myrtle Jean Maud. Feds were able to step in right before she wired money to bring *Claude LeBlanc* over from Paris."

I groaned.

"First-class."

"Poor Myrtle Jean. Hopefully, Clifford can help her get over Claude."

"And that's all in addition to their usual phishing scams that prey on the elderly."

We watched as two more officers carried out a small, weathered rowboat. Then they secured the trailer and put crime scene tape across the front door.

Castinetto turned the Charger off. "I thought you'd also like to know that Gladys Beacon has been charged with first-degree murder. We found heroin and needles that her daughter had left behind in her sewing kit."

"What about the pearls?"

He snickered. "You were right. There was blood evidence on the pearls."

"Killers never think about the jewelry."

"I interviewed Gladys's daughter in prison this morning. She told me Archie Wilkins had tried to blackmail them, but they didn't have the hundred Gs to pay him. He's the one who turned her in for drug trafficking."

"Poor Charlotte. What will happen to her now?"

"Social Services has reached out to her other grandmother. They're flying in from Albuquerque tomorrow."

"That's good."

Castinetto was quiet. We watched one of the police cars and the van drive off, lights flashing, sirens silenced. "I wanted to tell you that you did a good job on the Wilkins case. I fought hard to keep you out of it, but I was overruled. You surprised me."

Way to make it awkward. I did not like awkward. "Gee, thanks."

We got out of the Charger and Dayton spoke with Ronnie and Sloane for a minute. She turned to look at me, then came over with her hand out and a smile on her face. "Layla Virtue. Sloane Harlow. It's nice to put a face to the name."

I gripped her hand. "Likewise." She had a smattering of freckles across her cheeks that were mocked by the crow's feet at her eyes. The skin on her hands was lightly crepey. She was older than she looked, which gave me a good feeling that she knew what she was doing and would be confident enough not to let anyone tell her how to do it.

"I hear your father was being blackmailed by these two. He should have nothing more to worry about, but pictures have a way of staying in the cloud forever, just so you know."

"Thank you."

"And Officer Castinetto has filled me in about your ex-partner. Let me put out some feelers in the bureau and see what I can find out."

"That would be great. Thanks."

"Detective Castinetto thinks very highly of you."

I cut my eyes over to where he was talking to Ronnie. "Since when?"

Sloane hooked a smile. "No, really. We heard all about how you discovered the schoolteacher was blackmailing his kids' parents. He was very impressed."

I chuckled. "He doesn't show it. He tried to keep me off the case."

She cocked her head and studied Dayton. "Hmm. He's been concerned for your safety."

We made small talk for a couple of minutes; then she left me to rejoin her team and Ronnie.

Adam Beasley wandered over behind Castinetto. "Officer Virtue, I'm so glad you're okay."

Castinetto felt the need to correct him. "It's just Layla now, Beasley."

Adam ducked his chin. "Sorry. Did Detective Castinetto tell you we know who set the bomb in your Jeep?"

I gave an exasperated look at Dayton. "No. He did not."

"I was getting to it."

I spun my finger in a motion that meant *Well, hurry it up.*

"All the neighbors have doorbell cameras in that neighborhood. They picked up a man by your Jeep when you were inside the Wilkins residence. He was identified as Chaz Lopez, one of Hurtado's men. From the different angles we can tell he planted something underneath the Jeep in the chassis." He put his hand up to quiet me when he could tell I was about to launch into a barrage of questions. "He's been arrested. You're safe."

"I don't know that I am, Castinetto. How did he always know where I'd be?"

Dayton chuckled. "Well, for one, that Jeep was ridiculous. It wasn't hard to track. It was the color of Velveeta."

Beasley took a step backward. "Uh-oh, you made her mad."

Castinetto hung his head and groaned. "Okay. I suspect he had help from someone familiar with the case file to know the places you'd be investigating. Then he just had to watch for you."

Beasley blew out a breath. "Whoa."

"Why not try to kill me at the Gibson or Muddled—the bars Hurtado owns? If they were following me, they would have known when I was there too."

Dayton shrugged. "I don't know exactly."

Beasley's radio went off and he groaned before responding

that he was en route to a traffic accident in a shopping center. He got in his car and smacked the dash. He yelled out the window to Castinetto, "I accidentally turned the dash cam off again, Detective."

Castinetto let out a sigh of a thousand unsaid words.

The Feds got in their cars and drove off behind Beasley. The minute they were gone, the neighbors began leaking from their homes to convene in Robin's yard and discuss everything they knew about the situation—which was nothing.

I reached for the door handle. "Let's get out of here before they start asking me for things."

Castinetto started the engine and pulled onto the road for my house.

"There's something you need to know, Castinetto."

He glanced at me briefly.

"What?"

"I got my memories back at the Gibson. I was gonna wait for my official statement, but since you brought up your theory about someone on the force feeding Hurtado information, I figure now is probably better since I can confirm that."

"What have you got?"

I filled him in on everything I saw. "Thing is . . . I remember Jacob breaking up with me before we left my condo to run the op."

"Why would he do that?"

"He said he wanted us to live together. I wasn't ready."

Dayton pulled into my driveway. "He's an idiot."

"Anyway. When I was at the Gibson, he was definitely working for Nancy, aka the Scorpion, and now I'm wondering how long that had been going on. Hurtado has several fake businesses he uses as fronts for distributing drugs. Muddled and the Gibson are only the latest. When I ran the narcotics unit, we watched Hurtado's operation for months. I had men on the inside who I know were loyal to me. But every time we got close to taking him down, someone tipped him off and we lost all the evidence.

"Jacob set up that meeting with the Scorpion. We didn't know for sure that the Scorpion was real, let alone her identity. So how did Jacob get in her inner circle without me knowing about it? I didn't set up that op. He told me the other day he was undercover with the Feds trying to take down Hurtado's supplier. So I'm thinking he's gone rogue before when he worked for the narcotics team. What's to say he hasn't gone rogue on the FBI?"

Dayton was thoughtful for a minute. "Don't freak out, but I'm working on it."

"What do you mean you're working on it? You mean with Sloane?"

"I can't tell you."

Anger seared through me. "You can't tell me? I just gave you everything you've been on my case about for months and you can't tell me!" I got out of the Charger and slammed the door.

Dayton sucked in a breath but he followed me. "Will you just trust me, Virtue!"

I marched to the front of his car, waving my arms wildly. "Trust is supposed to go both ways. From where I'm standing, it seems you think I'm the only one that applies to."

"That isn't true."

"It's obvious that you think I'm a screwup. I admitted that I took those shots because I thought you'd be able to get past it. But you're still stuck on me being drunk at Stratton Park, aren't you? Two shots doesn't make one blackout drunk, Castinetto. Nancy clearly drugged me with more than just GHB. And have you forgotten how we met? You selling me pot behind the gym at my high school!"

Dayton's neck turned red. "Everything I've done has been to protect you. I know someone set you up that day. I know two shots won't get you totally wasted! Why do you think I've wanted you to have nothing to do with this case? Why I've tried to keep the other cops away from you. I don't know who we can trust. I've threatened to fire anyone who comes near you. It sounds like you're the one who can't let go of the past, Virtue. What do I have to do to get you to trust me? Can't you tell how I feel?"

My stomach was doing that really weird flip-flop. I stammered, "I—I have no idea what you're talking about, Castinetto."

"Really?!" Castinetto grabbed my wrist and pulled me to him. His eyes flashed a mixture of anger and something else. Something I hadn't been able to pin down before. Something that made me feel weird and maybe just a little giddy. There was another flip.

"What are you doing?"

"Shut up. I'm gonna kiss you."

My heart pounded in my chest while my mind raced with confusion and elation. He made me so mad. But now all I could focus on was his mouth.

He pulled me closer until I felt his breath on my face. His hands caressed my back, his lips covered mine. And whoa. Did he kiss me.

Chapter 51

WELL, I DEFINITELY DID NOT SEE THAT COMING. I MEAN I'D thought about it before. Way before. Before Dayton became such a tool. But I never expected . . .

I walked into my house in a daze.

Nick was setting another box on the pile by the door. "Hey."

"What?"

"What?"

"*What?*"

He chuckled. "Are you okay?"

Ringo watched the conversation like a Ping-Pong match.

"Why wouldn't I be?"

"I don't know. You're acting weird."

"No, I'm not. You're weird." I tried to concentrate but my head was a swirl of confusion. *What just happened?*

Nick pointed over his shoulder. "Okay, well, I have one more box to go get."

"Fine."

Ringo grumbled and dropped to his belly.

I couldn't sit here and watch Nick leave; he was tearing my heart out.

I went out to the porch and flopped into the chair. Pulling the demand box onto my lap, I lifted the cover. The first one was a request to build a screened porch. That one I could approve as long as they meant in their own yard. You never knew with these people.

The next one was more a criticism of me than a request. *It's obvious you have no idea what you're doing, Layla. You're going to destroy the park. Signed, Whimsy St. James.*

Okay. Ouch. Jeez, give me a chance.

There were several more in the box with pretty much the same theme. I suck and I ruin everything. The final one was pretty vitriolic—that I only bought the park to push Agnes out. I suspected this one was from Marguerite. I mean . . . had I known that would happen, I might have tried it. But that was before she became such a good friend to Dad.

I stared at the pile of complaints in my lap. I didn't sign up for this. I didn't even want this job. I was barely holding it together with playing low-budget gigs—the one job I had before Dad came to visit me.

I scooped all the notes back into the box and marched over to Agnes's double wide and banged on the door.

She appeared in the doorway in shiny gold liquid leggings and a giraffe-patterned sweater, and what I thought was a thin black paintbrush in her mouth. "Good heavens, Layla. Don't dent the frame. What do you want?"

"What is that thing in your mouth? Is that like a Morticia Addams cigarette holder or something?"

Agnes rolled her eyes. "It's an opera-length cigarette extension, for your information, and they're very chic."

"Maybe during the Great Gatsby . . ."

She tapped her foot. "Is that why you came over here today?"

"No." I shoved the box of demands at her. "I don't want to do this anymore. Okay."

For some ungodly reason, tears welled in my eyes. My lip started to quiver—and before I could stop myself, I was crying. "Everybody hates me. And I don't have time to handle all their demands with my dad being sick, and Nick's leaving, and someone's trying to kill me. Okay. I just don't have time to measure the secret laundry room to put in another dryer because I have to break ground on Pippi's playground or Foster will pester me until I start drinking again."

Agnes stared at me bewildered. An inch of ash hanging from her forgotten cigarette stick. She moved over and held the door open. "Come inside."

I don't know what I expected when I entered her double wide, but this was not it. Her living room was stark white with whitewashed plank flooring. And her furniture was black leather with one blood-red pillow. I realized one moment too late that the full-body nude portrait over her propane fireplace was Agnes herself. "Oh God, Agnes!" I slammed my eyes shut. "You gotta warn someone of that before you bring them in here."

The creak of leather let me know she'd taken a seat on the couch. "Why? I look amazing. You're standing on that same white fur rug now."

I sighed. "I did not need to know that."

"Sit down and tell me what's wrong."

I told myself to keep quiet. What I was going through was none of Agnes's business. But the words tumbled out of my mouth like dice from a Yahtzee shaker.

I told her about Robin and Glenn and how they'd been the ones who were threatening Dad. And about Jacob and Ricky Hurtado, and how my Jeep had blown up. And Nick was going home because he was ready, but I wasn't ready. And about the suicide note Bree's mom brought me—without telling Agnes it was Bree, because Agnes was nosy enough as it is.

Agnes tapped her cigarette holder on a crystal ashtray and set it down. "I don't really think you're upset about a few silly complaints. And just so you know, they all complained about me all the time too. I just wasn't foolish enough to put a box on my front porch, inviting them to voice their opinions on a daily basis. But I got nothing but flack at every meeting. Foster's been on my case to build that playground since his gran died. You know what I think? I think you're really scared of losing your father, and the recent trauma with your ex and your friend and the trailer park nut jobs are spilling over, pushing you to the edge."

I sat with that thought for a minute. There was a lot of truth in what she was saying. I was still reeling with the betrayal from Jacob, a man I had trusted more than anyone else, and trying to come to terms with Dad's disease and eventual death. I was afraid of losing all the people I'd let into my life. Nick, Bree, the girls. Even the nut jobs in the trailer park. They irritated me half to death, but they were the closest thing to a community I'd ever known.

"Agnes, this job is a lot harder than I thought it would be."

Agnes grinned and nodded.

"And there is literally no money to pay all the bills that are due."

Agnes clucked her tongue. "Nope."

"And no one seems to appreciate all that I have done to make things nice for them."

"Welcome to my world."

"Would you consider staying on? You can keep your trailer in exchange for managing the property."

Agnes put her hand out. "On one condition."

"What's that?"

"You have to deal with that pig's playground."

"How am I gonna pay for that, Agnes?"

She cocked her head. "You know exactly how. Your father is longing for you to ask for his help. My advice? Make it something that improves the value of the property so it's money well spent."

That was shockingly good advice. Where was that business sense when she suggested a flock of sheep to keep the grass cutting down? "Thank you, Agnes. I'll ask Nick to set you up with an email account, so you won't have to go door to door anymore."

She frowned. "How am I supposed to check on everyone and see how they're doing if I don't visit them in person?"

"I'll leave the details up to you." I accidentally cut my eyes to that nude portrait one more time and groped for the door.

I crossed the yard with determination to tell Nick the truth. He was waiting for me in the kitchen with two mugs of cider. "What took you so long?"

"I've asked Agnes to take over managing the property again."

"Does that mean we're getting the sheep?"

"I hope not. I'll wait till the new year to tell her I have veto power. You know . . . if she'll let me have it."

Nick snickered. He slid my cell phone to me. "I have something to tell you."

"I have something to tell you too."

He dipped his chin. "Okay, you first."

"I don't want you to leave. I know you have to. You have to live your own life. I would never want to stand in your way of that. But if I'm being honest, I love you being here. Not just because you're amazing with my dad and without you we'd live on crackers and Cheez Whiz. But also because you're my best friend. You center me. This"—I circled my hand over my head—"feels more like a family with you here. Even though you're only on the other side of the lake, I'll miss you. That's all. I just wanted you to know."

Nick's hand was folded over his mouth, but his eyes were glassy. "I was hoping you'd ask me to stay. I don't want to go. I realized that I miss having a platoon. I'm lonely. It's why I train service dogs. But every time one leaves me for a new assignment, I'm crushed a little more. My heart feels fuller when you're around."

My lip quivered and I reached for Nick to hug him. "So, you'll stay?"

Ringo shoved his entire head between us. The breeze from his tail flipped my hair back and forth.

Nick nodded against my neck. "As long as you want me to. Or you know, until I meet someone. I hear they're starting a senior yoga class at the community center."

I pulled back to look at his face. "Myrtle Jean is available. Her French boyfriend was really Robin and her brother."

His eyes widened. "I don't know if my style coordinates with her squirrel-themed sweaters."

"Don't be so modest. Your nerdy style could win over all the old ladies."

Nick laughed.

"What did you have to tell me?"

He looked me in the eye. "I was thinking about how you were targeted every time you went somewhere for the Archie Wilkins case. I found a tracking app hidden on your phone. Someone's been following your movements."

"Can you tell who it is?"

"No. But I didn't remove it. I didn't want to do anything that could jeopardize your investigation. Knowing someone is tracking you could come in handy." He reached into a bag and produced a new cell phone. "Instead, I helped your dad buy you an iPhone for Christmas. I've already set it up for you, and the only people who have your number are your AA ladies, me, and your dad. I didn't know who else you could trust."

"I don't know either. Jacob is either a special agent or a liar working for Hurtado. We have no way of telling which one is true yet. And someone high ranking on the force is on the drug lord's payroll. I know Castinetto is on my side, but who knows if he's being tracked. Now that I know the identity of the Scorpion, they'll really be coming for me. Whether Nancy lives or dies, Hurtado will want retribution. I feel the storm building. Like there's a war right on the horizon. And no one around me is safe."

"What are you going to do?"

"I'm gonna take the fight to them. If it's war they want, war they're gonna get."

Nick took my hand in his. "Then we'd better get ready."